Token Tales

and

Fragments

Recalling a Time of Heroes and Sages

by Billy Ironcrane

Doug
Thanks for your
friendship and
your help with
This .

B—

For permissions contact:
www.ironcrane.com/html/contactus.html

Published by:
Mc Cabe and Associates
Tacoma, WA.

Illustrated by Renee Knarreborg
Cover design Mc Cabe and Associates
Cover image and author photo by Doug Goodman

ISBN-13: 978-1-7324154-4-7
Library of Congress Control Number: 2020917265

To Thongbai

Always persevering, always smiling

Contents

Illustrations

Token Tales
and
Fragments

Introduction

Seeming at first a collection of loosely related short stories, this gathering of tales shares as common setting a particularly bleak period in Chinese history.

Somehow, the accounts have seated themselves in my subconscious and taken over. Writer's malaise? Well, not exactly. Perhaps it's best I come clean. It all started with a mysterious stranger I once met.

A lifelong martial artist, I've long made it a point to practice intently each day, even now in my advanced years. Long ago, while living in south Jersey, I got into the habit of practicing fighting forms on the sand flats. Right there in the broad expanse where the Delaware Bay joins with the Atlantic Ocean. At low tide, one can journey far off from the distractions of shore. Sometimes getting nearly a mile out, empty space. Privacy. Perfect for practice and concentration. Timing the shifting tides carefully, one might find several hours of absolute quiet and peace.

Hard to believe now, but that's where I first encountered him. Decades have passed, but the memory clings like an appendage, always with me. Did he spring from my shadow? Or perhaps from some other hole in the fabric of reality? I never saw his approach.

"Call me Sonny," he said. He pointed off somewhere then added, "I've been watching you for some time. I've never seen anyone come out here before. Not like you anyway. And doing what you're doing. You make me think of people from the old days. You're quite good. Forgive my curiosity. Sometimes it just gets the best of me."

At first, I was guarded. His demeanor intimidated. I expected, perhaps hoped he would politely leave. Without invitation, he began critiquing my practice. Friends know that is not the best way to get on my good side. In short order, I found he had noted everything, every detail. He recalled every hitch, flaw, or imperfection in my flow. Could anyone's eye be so true? How long had he watched? How many times?

Then, without overture, he began instructing, making sure I got it right. His confidence absolute, his suggestions sure and certain. He stood there like a great rock, solid throughout, no discernible faults. Dangerous. And then his eyes, my own perhaps tricked by the blazing Jersey sun. His ignited and seemed to spark when he spoke and stared my way.

Over time, we met often. Mostly by his choice, no specific plans, no luxury of schedules. I was there, he showed up. We both knew the tides, and nature's inclinations. Sometimes he appeared as a biker, looking like he just popped off his hog, sporting leather and chaps, helmet dangling by its chinstrap from his hand. Sometimes he wore army fatigues, or even a blanket over some vastly undersized pajamas, or were they clam diggers. Once he came in a saffron robe. Funny in his ways, he had his quirks, and I went with it. Dare I say, we eventually became friends.

It was he who told the stories I share. He confessed he had seen my writings in various publications, and knew I would understand their significance. He also assured I was the one fit to transmit them. He was simply too busy with other more demanding affairs.

When the tides turned, we returned to shore. We would frequently end our visits conversing for several hours on the beach. Mostly, I looked forward to his concoctions and secret elixirs. These he pulled like rabbits and pigeons from hidden pockets and pouches on his person. Each had its purpose he assured. Some stimulated clarity of thought, others gave wisdom. One, he promised, would promote longevity. He gifted it to me, saying he didn't need it. He cautioned I should not take it until I knew for sure I could handle it. Who knows? In those moments, they gave great highs, and opened the chambers of my mind to assimilate the many tales he related from what he called his very remote past.

From the start, he made one thing clear. I owed him payment for the lessons received. At first, I balked. I was living hand to mouth back then. Did I ask him for his lessons in the first place? Ignoring my objection, he assured there would be no problem. Over time it became clear. He insisted payment could take only one form, and it had nothing to do with money. I was to preserve his many stories, and write them as if they were my own. He told me to keep the royalties as his thanks. "Don't worry about remembering all the details," he said. "At first, they'll bubble back up in pieces and fragments. They may not even make sense. Just random spurts. You are to keep writing. Don't fret if at times it makes no sense. Just play with the pieces and fragments. They'll start to come together. You'll see for yourself. It's an important message from the past which must make it to the future."

What he said then shocked me. "Only you can do this. Treat it as though your life depended on it. For it does."

I asked, now almost defensive at such words coming from a friend, "You're threatening me over this?"

"I threaten no one. We all have what we must do. Try to remember that. Everything else will fall into place."

Then he was gone.

At first, they were written independently, each account standing apart from the others. Sitting here today, I can remember writing and typing furiously for several years, trying to get each story down as it raced through my mind. Some days the threads disappeared, and I would break into a panicked sweat. When they returned, my relief was palpable. Like someone who pulled the ripcord and felt the tug of an opening chute. Now you can see what I mean. They have indeed seated themselves in my subconscious and taken over. Why was this happening?

For that, I have no answer, except I surely do hope he and I will meet again. I'll make it a point to ask him.

The day we parted, he begged I swear an oath as to the writing. I told him it wouldn't be necessary. I pay my debts. He had my word on it. He smiled broadly, nodding his head as he took full measure of my promise. A second sun seemed to light the beach. "Better than any oath," he said.

As he began to fade from view, I called out, "What do we call it when it's written?"

His answer, "Start out with *Token Tales and Fragments*. You decide what comes after that."

Background

The happenings depicted herein follow the collapse of
the Han dynasty (206 BCE - 220 CE). Considered by many
the golden era of Chinese history, it spanned nearly four
centuries. Regrettably, what started and flourished under
exemplary rule became corrupted. Expectations and hopes
aside, it disintegrated upon itself from within. Three great
leaders emerged to contend for power and the divine right
to revive the once empire. At first, each sought to preserve
the Mandate of Heaven — establish legitimacy, and with
that some semblance of continuity. There, they failed, and
had no choice but to make do without.

Stories from those times abound and have wound their
way into the vaults of collective mythology. Like carefully
preserved trails, the heroic portrayals of sacrifice, loss,
struggle, hope and achievement define our essential natures.
Well worn guideposts, they hint to where we head, and
where we might end.

Though precise details may at times be elusive, we have
the best efforts and records of historians to light our path.
The doings and achievements of the many heroes, along
with the misdeeds of their villainous counterparts, have

been elegantly preserved. We find their reflections in the carefully woven tapestries of artists, poets and writers. Who better to reveal reality, and what we should make of it?

Foremost among their works is *Romance of the Three Kingdoms*[1] by the 14th century playwright Luo Guanzhong. His account addresses the period immediately post Han. Lasting approximately five generations, bedlam reigned. The once glorious empire had fractured into three unendingly contentious warring kingdoms.

Culminating that tumultuous period, we know the empire came briefly under one rule. Then in a quick moment, like a precious vase carelessly mishandled, it shattered completely. From there, it reeled fragmented and hopeless for hundreds of years. A new blight of warlords re-delivered the population to disunity, carnage, starvation, disease, indenture and destitution.

Our current stories begin then to take their root. Walk with us as we scan remnants strewn about the landscape of time and events. Might they ever meld into a coherent whole? A vessel perhaps? One capable of lifting us from the failures of our predecessors and delivering a working portion of hope for the future. Our future.

---

[1] There are a number of commendable translations available. Among my favorites is: Luo, Guanzhong, and Moss Roberts. *Three Kingdoms: a Historical Novel; Complete and Unabridged*. Berkeley: Univ. of California Press, 2005. Print.

There's a reason for these stories. They never happen on their own, or for no purpose. As well you know, legends and myths survive to serve our needs, to help and guide us, and perhaps to best explain the otherwise unknowable.

I may be a recluse, but I am not a poor man. I place my stock in truth, and my belief it will shed light wherever it leads. In time, these token tales and fragments may well become your maps as they have been for me. Hopefully they will one day loose and guide your thoughts away from uncertainty and chaos, and head you toward life and freedom.

Spoken by Sonny (1967)

Middle Kingdom

Empire Adrift

Part 1

Apprenticeship

Fire and Water

During our final months together, father took great care to tell me all he could regarding his time with Sying Hao. He met this mysterious stranger[2] while a young man, falsely branded an outlaw and constantly on the run. His days would have been numbered had he not come upon this special friend. To survive the perilous times, he accepted Sying Hao's invitation to return with him to Southern Mountain, a remote western sanctuary previously unknown to my people. Sying Hao became his teacher, and guide. In father's words, "Each day would be as a month somewhere else." He said there were no ends to the lessons, the challenges, and the experiences. All capped by his adventures in the west, and the long tortuous road which brought him home. I've no doubt now he wanted me to know of his story, and in that I would come to fully know myself. But here, allow me to step aside and relate for you those bits and pieces of his accounts I am able to recall.

We journeyed together to Southern Mountain, and spent the season in its pristine embrace. More than I, Sying Hao was completely at home in the vast wilderness surround. He had grown accustomed to deep solitude. For me it was a

---

[2] The fateful meeting between Bao Ling and Sying Hao is fully detailed in our previous work, *Seed of Dragons*.

harder path. I missed life as I knew it. Homesick, my thoughts remained with my village and people.

Funny how we come to our views of the world. Some can never shake the dust from their shoes. Others stay put. I can stay put just fine. It's just that fate deemed otherwise. I've observed how warlords amass collections of villages, then cities, then provinces. Still, they have no place they can call home. A simple spot will not simply do. For them, life comes with an eternal itch, demanding they scratch incessantly, but finding no relief. Lots of dust beneath their shoes. Ever alone, trusting no one, always posturing to fight, conquer or flee. For companionship, they sate their gnawing despair using hand picked maidens from the pool of unwilling subjects. Flushed from where secreted by terrified parents in abandoned wells, trap doored cellars, outlying hills, or simply buried beneath straw in stables. No place certain in its assurance. Long experienced in seeing through these ploys, warlord lackeys always knew where first to look.

Victims, once used, are sometimes tossed a few coppers, or if performance exceeded expectations, a token or two of gold. Then they find themselves quickly discarded. Can pleasure be so fickle?

Occasionally, against all likelihood, one maiden ascends high above the rest, and remains. Perhaps blessed with a fetching combination of curve or twist. Or a flick of hair, tint of eye, or simple smarts woven into a spell of mesmerizing beauty and irresistible allure. Punctuated with charm and uncanny instincts for survival, she knows from study of her oppressors to carefully peruse the landscape. Only then, hitch her cart to the right steed. Even better she be blessed with an empathetic ear. Cap this with wisdom suited to the role of warlord's tear pillow. To his followers the warlord must evoke strength, character and determination. But, is he not also human, a man like any other? Does he not bleed when cut? Suffer pain? Weep in sorrow? Agonize in frustration, hurt and anger? Who is there for him to confide in? Warlords are people too! So I've heard.

Buy into that at your peril! Better that you emulate them. Exploit them as they do you, their very weakness becomes your salvation! With the mysterious ways of the world, more than one slave girl has become an empress.

Ah yes, an empathetic ear. With one of those things attached to a winsome young maiden's head a next meal is assured. With luck, the largess may extend to parents and family. Should she be so skilled as to develop other gifts, she might stretch her run of favor so the entire clan reaps the warlord's protection. It's about gleaning honey from thin surrounds. With luck, time, and careful dealing, they'll grow their own influence. Once there, they can harness destiny. More promising benefactors arise as new possibilities for advantage. One can't be too careful! A bad toss of yarrow stalks might just have family fortunes crashing down. Always have a fall back, or a back door. Questions of precarious balance resolve best when finely tuned.

The intricacies of these and other machinations have been carefully mapped for all time in the writings of the sages. The Yi Ching[3] speaks carefully to the unending changes and their rippling influences. A singular classic, delineating strategies and ploys for those immersed in the play. Among the skilled, for every turn, a counter exists. Not many know this, or how to do it! Those who do can be lethal. Sometimes a hero, or better yet, a heroine emerges from among them.

Me, at day's end, I'm satisfied to sit on a hilltop. Passersby can listen to notes spilling from my flute as I celebrate the wind and birds gracefully gliding in the distance. All accompanied by the gentle murmur of insects sounding in meter.

Yet sometimes on returning to our mountain haunts, I pondered what a strange fellow I had become. Flawed? Perhaps. Who's to judge? I don't have the answer for myself. Once my full story is told, you may be so kind as to share your own thoughts on this.

Is it any wonder I became a pariah to the usurpers and their thugs? Dealing with the thought of nobodies like me — a waste of their precious time. With no interest in their manipulations, no commitment to their endless ends bound

---

[3] The Book of Changes. A book of divination and insight into decision making amidst uncertainty. The oldest of the Chinese Classics, with history reaching back more than two and a half millennium during which it has been carefully studied, analyzed and commented upon. As a tool for self assessment and managing one's goals within a universe of uncertainty, it remains unparalleled in rooting one's own character, wants and motives to varying potentials for success and achievement.

me to them. Worse yet, at least from where they stood. I didn't fear them.

Looking back, I'm sure they figured tolerating my continued existence would spell their own demise. I don't doubt it's true. I see now one can only ignore these things for so long. Back then, I only wanted to be left alone. Fire and water. Two opposites unable to co-exist. Big fire, small water. Small water, that's me! Just a little trickle alongside an inferno. Negligible, but still a threat. When you must dominate everything, the smallest hint of resistance demands your complete attention. It's that old itch again!

Anyone leaning my way would see the game for what it was. Label the power brokers as bores and ignore them from existence. Regrettably, that rarely works. Those who try may pay with their lives, or their children's for the effort. And don't think it's over! The game still plays today, in all places, with all people. Only time will tell its finish.

Meanwhile, the brokers continue their relentless push toward the inevitable moment of grand consequence, which even they can't fathom or figure with confidence. Is it any wonder they see no better option than to rid themselves of me and anyone like me. Impediments! Collecting all they can to their sides as grist for extravagant designs. They align their forces only to stare across fields of reckoning to their own folly and unlikely reflections. Everywhere you look, history dots the landscape with their remains.

A Lesson in Quirks

It didn't surprise me. Sying Hao proved a sophisticated man. Broadly learned and experienced, he immersed me in the classics. Taking words and lessons from the sages, he showed how they might unlock the secrets of life and understanding.

I stumbled through these lessons at first. As we grew inseparable, I felt always to be the student and he the teacher. He took care to protect me and how I felt about myself, my past, and the good people I left behind. Over time, perhaps to bolster my confidence, he assured the current between us flowed both ways. He made a frequent point of interrupting our doings to thank me for something I did, spoke of, or shared which he acknowledged had brought change within himself. More than once he voiced, "Never sell yourself short Bao Ling. There is more to you than meets the eye. You have brought much in the way of fresh insight into my life, and for that, I am in your debt."

As you can see, he had a considerate way. It lightened my heavy spirits. Yin and Yang, Yang and Yin, we were different but still a kindred match. Think of it as you will. I calculate to have gotten the better from our time together. I wonder what he would have said?

I can't deny it. Driven there by fate and circumstance, Southern Mountain seemed a paradise to a midlander like myself. Waters sparkled pure, and ran clean. Meals easily foraged. Game readily caught. At first I marveled at the abundance, and ate heartily. Sying Hao favored the wild edibles. He supplemented with pickings from what I called his "gardens." Patches and stashes seemingly everywhere, which he had planned and planted to suit his likes and needs. He took field game only as a last resort, usually when the fishing had slowed.

"Tell me older brother, with game so readily available, why not revel in its abundance? Partake of the full bounty to your health and contentment?"

He answered simple and straight. "I'm healthy enough. Truth told, when I eat the flesh of sentient creatures, my mind plays sinister tricks with me. Surely, the fault lies in my own imperfections, or weaknesses. Still, I've grown accustomed to them and am not inclined to give them up. It's the warm blooded creatures which trouble most. You see, no sooner do I look at prey as nourishment when I feel to be invading their contentment and joy with life here on Southern Mountain. In a sense they're no different than us Bao Ling! It's then I know their tragic sense of loss. Their unsolicited sacrifice on succumbing to the demands of my palate. Why, to them, facing their end, I'm no different than your warlords. Just take what I will to suit my needs. Worse yet, there's that certain wave of fear and anxiety which once they're smitten, doubtless poisons the spirit of their remains. I tell you Bao Ling. I feel it hard and deep within myself. So relentless and unforgiving can be my own twisted mind, and its tendency toward guilt. I don't blame you or anybody else. It's me. It's who I am, or what I've become."

He would force a laugh, then stare directly into my eyes. A smile would light his resignation as he said this. "I don't control these things. Maybe I've succumbed to compassion. Can that be wrong? They fall and as their life energy drips from pierced bodies, their eyelids close slowly over the windows of their existence. Perhaps a lingering thought of their mountain paradise dims, leaving only the sounds of wind and songbird to echo from their fading awareness. Many times I have walked about. Thinking perhaps to shoot a crested pheasant for my dinner. Delicious, one would think. Then with my arrow drawn, and the shot clear certain in my mind, I can not release the string."

Laughing at his foibles, he explained, "It's like shooting myself! My sensibility suddenly goes to the bird. With borrowed eyes, I see my own stalking presence. There, in the distance, about to release, then hesitating. Why, for a moment I don't recognize it's me I'm staring at. Repulsed by my own hunter's disfiguring glare of hoggish certitude honing in on a creature soon expected dead.

"Good man, I think to myself as I watch the shooter ease off the bow's tension. Then again I am he. A good chuckle over my quirks before I strategize what best to forage in lieu of pheasant reprieved.

"Please understand. Just like you or anyone, if it comes to survival, I will eat what I must; and do what I have to do. No one would expect otherwise, not even the beasts. But to do so as a habit, or indiscriminately, or without compassion? Never!"

Truthfully, I thought he was joking! I waited expectantly for him to say more, looking for the final twist which would have us both sharing a hearty laugh. In the silence, I saw his words had not been in jest. Nothing further came.

He meant it as a lesson. Compassion represents the greatest challenge. Some argue it's impossible with the world as it is. There are at least as many justifications to kill or destroy as there are reasons to show compassion. An alarming game of numbers, justifying a singular self-serving end: to take the easy path. He wanted me to look hard into the heart of one to find the other. Compassion must reach in all directions, to all things, and requires constant cultivation within. Touched by his example, in time, I too gradually lost my appetite for creatures of the wild. I didn't know it until long later; the change within opened new doors and new awarenesses. I'm sure it had been the same for him.

Fenghua Yan

Among my recollections, what followed no longer seems accidental or fortuitous. Enchanted — surely. Living there, adapting to its ways, expanding awareness. One couldn't help but change.

Elsewhere, in the contentious world, others sought to imprint their thumbs onto your spirit. Pinning it down so they knew with certainty where you were. Your predicament became their license. Among their tools, greed, fear, hatred. Would you believe it? Righteousness too, transformed into indignation. All twisted inside and around to where you couldn't even recognize where you had left the road or how to get back. Manipulations, mostly subtle, rarely seen. They sowed, then harvested what you deemed your very own ripened thoughts. All while convincing you they originated from within your own reason, and reflected your own sound judgment. A journey to the east that always had you trekking west!

I ventured west and found freedom from those influences. Shedding an old and tattered skin. From weary, wounded and sad, I had changed into something new.

Sying Hao had been there a long while. He would never say how long. His intimate acquaintance with the mountain and all its wildlife and subtleties gave its own answer. In one way or another, his hand could be seen in everything.

I learned there were others too. Among them mystics, drop outs, monks, wanderers, poets, cave dwellers, foragers. And of course treasure hunters, ever scouring for gems or precious metals. Fanatically guarding the secrets of their hidden camps or their stashes. Close on their scent, the scoundrels, the outlaws. All convinced the wilderness and isolation would secure their pickings, and their futures.

The mountain's limitless expanse welcomed all on equal terms. At first, anyway. Only the hardiest few survived once their initial purpose had been whittled down. The wild could be counted on to deal its harsh measure, winnowing out what didn't belong or deserve its kindly but demanding benevolence.

We lived well. Sying Hao had many shelters scattered about the back country. Some, well equipped cabins. Others, little more than leaning covers alongside boulders or ancient trees. Mostly hidden. All were comfortable and warming. Rarely would we be so far from one of his nests we'd have to sleep exposed in the elements. Not that we couldn't if necessary. Some of his hideaways, albeit primitive, compared favorably to my own family home in the midlands. Some had scrolls, even entire libraries. Was he preserving them for the future? I never asked. Others stored tools, weapons and implements. Each served its purpose, which only he knew. Somewhere within it all, Sying Hao had a scheme. One which he never voiced.

"How had he become so tied to this place?" was a riddle I often pondered. He could have done, or been anything he chose on the outside. But then again, Southern Mountain did have its charms, greatest being its fullness and completeness. To my simple take on things, nothing seemed to be lacking. Although admittedly, my inner thoughts never left home. I often wondered what inner thoughts he harbored.

On the foot trails, I did at times encounter others. Some said they knew of Sying Hao. Those who truly did paid him quick respect, albeit with cautious deference. Once, some hunters confided how they envied my being his companion. They did not know him to keep the company of others. Learning of me surprised them. They referred to him deferentially as "Fenghua Yan (weathered rock), the man of Southern Mountain."

They too registered what I felt to be his mystical link to the location. A mystery only time has been fully able to unravel to my full understanding.

Months passed. We delved more deeply into the thoughts and writings of the ancient masters. Together, we passed rain soaked days doing calligraphy. At first I resisted. A waste of energy. Misspent attention. Now I see more clearly. I resisted because it proved difficult for me. Before then, I had never wielded an ink brush. My first efforts pained me to view. He insisted it would still my mind: "More so than post standing! Besides Bao Ling, you have a steady hand. Your efforts will improve with practice. See it as an adventure, don't make it a burden!"

More to my liking, we would compose poetry under the stars. Or while trekking on moonlit snowy evenings. He drilled me in the readings and interpretations of the Yi Ching, which he called the Oracle. He shared how movement in the heavens imperceptibly drove the hearts of men, and their doings. Even the drift of an arrow in flight submitted to their influence. He explained how the stars and constellations were akin to the Oracle. "They too have the capacity to echo directly the great mysteries. But their secrets are forever safeguarded by Dharma." I asked he explain, to which he added, "Stars and planets will speak, but only to an unclouded mind. With overlays of greed, desire, fear or subjugation, the message becomes lost or muddled. They will trick you. Telling you only what your selfish ears want to hear, and in that, bring about your ruin. They are meant to be tools benefiting all. They have their own ways of seeing to that."

Elaborating how indulgent thinking gets in the way, he told me he once witnessed a great sage come before the court. His intent: to deliver wise counsel to the ruler. The sage spoke only truth and wisdom. His charts were clear. His words impeccable. Like jewels filling the room to its very brim. "Exquisite!" recalled Sying Hao. Hearing the sage, and somehow resonating with the vastness of his perception, Sying Hao felt as though lifted to the clouds above. He opened to freeness then found himself playing staff alongside the enlightened spirit of Lord Monkey. Their movements, a reflection of what unfolded below. Pausing in their frolics, the two looked down to the imperial hall. Monkey observed: "The turds will get it all wrong!" And of course, they did. The King patiently heard out the sage. He then looked to his advisers for their take on the message. Indeed, his own royal thoughts were already racing to the bed chambers. A nest of concubines feigned impatience in the distance. The counselors mulled, then fidgeted. Finally, they spoke. Taking no chances, some agreed verbatim. Others, wanting to flash their own smarts, tendered counterpoint and objection. Some then cautiously weighed the merits of potentials versus risks and alternate possibilities. They counseled only patience. At least one proclaimed the Sage an enemy agent who could not be trusted and should be boiled alive."

"Don't tell me …?" I asked.

"Without being blatant, they contemplated how to marginalize the Sage. '*To hell with competition*,' they thought. He, not inclined to be anyone's prey, sensed the predicament. 'I must pee,' he said, and stole discretely from the palace only to subsequently vanish. Trust me, they searched every corner and nook. Not a trace! Truly enlightened beings are like that. Slippery as eels, their tolerance for fools nil. They will speak true. Sometimes their words will find welcoming ground. Most times they'll descend upon baked rock. It took less than a generation from that moment. The Han were finished. Their line extinguished, and the empire delivered again into chaos. You'd think we'd learn something from the episode. Not surprisingly, historians recalling that day lay barred from recording it under threat of castration. Who needs to hear all would have been well, when it hasn't? If only the Sage's words had been understood and heeded. Dastards you see, must bury their tricks and tracks. So, we are left with what they want for us to know. Though you won't find this incident in any record. It's true nonetheless."

As you know, among archers, Sying Hao had no equal I could name. That's not to make light of his other accomplishments. I reckon he was beyond measure at most everything. I puzzled where he found the time to become so proficient at so many things. He would say, "When you find things you have natural talent for, develop them like your life depended on it. Remember, time is of the essence, you can only take things so far as your allotted breaths permit. You won't have longer. A moment wasted is forever lost to your opportunity for discovery." Of course, there were things he could not do, or for which he had no interest. He would not cater to the whims of aristocracy. Nor would he become their agent or strategist, though in that capacity he would have been lethal.

"Been there, done that," he would respond summarily, then mumble something about lost time squandered from his life's true purpose.

I had planned to take only a brief sojourn on the mountain. Just long enough for my pursuers to lose interest. I trusted they would tire of chasing their absent phantom. Whatever my thoughts, or intentions, the stay grew as the lessons continued and more seasons passed. My need for deeper understanding and insight dictated what I had to do.

"Don't fret little brother. They will not lose interest so quickly. Perhaps at first, frustration over your disappearance will have some returning to their barracks. They'll vet other threats. Their leaders won't forget you though. They'll want proof. Rumor of likely demise won't suffice. It will gnaw at them. New bounties will be proclaimed. They'll want to see your corpse. They'll post generous rewards for anyone who can lead them to it. Of course, they won't find it. You're here. They're there! Then, starting anew to doubt your end, they'll up the bounty for any information regarding your whereabouts. Better yet, anything leading to your capture or death. The payout, and the temptations will grow with each passing season. Temptation will push beyond the most resistant loyalties among your comrades. Reward beyond their wildest imaginings. At that point, your neighbors, friends, perhaps your own kin, will look hard and long at handing you over."

The thought of it saddened me. In part because what he said was true. In part because I had no choice. "You have truly been an older brother to me. But my future is in the midlands, upholding all I hold precious and what makes me who I am. Please don't find me foolish."

"Or course not little brother. We're all marked and calibrated by our births. And molded by our life's purpose. Few can stay true to one or the other, let alone both. Hence, the constant turmoil within. On that matter, you are indeed like the dragon. For a moment, here in repose. Let us just say that for now, this dragon lies patiently within the confines of his watery lair. There he waits in the shadowy depths for when pursuers accept his disappearance as demise. Hearing no more, they'll simply write his memory off. 'Did he even exist in the first place?'

"Your return will be doubly appreciated, and your presence doubly felt. Who knows, perhaps your people will be ready to act with you. To join you!"

I agreed, but only with grave reservation. You see, I knew what was happening in my absence. I felt every effort to resist mattered, no matter how token. My not being there meant someone suffered needlessly, or because they protected me. The thought I might have made a difference riddled me with guilt.

Sying Hao

Growing Skills

Sying Hao worked tirelessly honing my skills over the passing months. At first, tracking and following. I learned the signs of movement and its impact on the surrounds. Shifts in leaves and grass, soil and dust. Changes in shadows. Fur, hair, fabric and waste, always dropping or catching as one moves about. Abandoned campsites whispering how many had passed, what they carried, what they ate. There's more, though I can't readily explain it. Sometimes we might sense their thoughts and intentions — traces of spirit held captive by the surrounds.

He had also mastered concealment. Some aspects of this I already knew. Finding cover and changing appearance had served me well in past brushes with prying intruders. I learned to always pack a spare cap or two. Outer garments as well. No telling when a quick change might be in order. Add to this a bit of pretense. A faux limp, lost hearing or eyesight, diminished capacity. Perhaps the opposite, blatant arrogance right in their faces. All proved effective in vanishing Bao Ling from those who would cut him down.

But Sying Hao affected no overt ruse. His artistry bordered on wizardry, far exceeding my pale efforts.

Once, a band of brigands crossed into our domain. When we learned of them, Sying Hao looked to me, "Let's go."

"Trouble?" I asked.

"Trouble? Uncertain. Opportunity to learn something? For sure."

We watched from high ground. The highwaymen set camp, then posted their guard.

"Stay here and observe."

He wanted me to keep distance and be ready to assist if beckoned.

Darkness fell. I studied carefully as Sying Hao walked easily up to the perimeter guard, looked him squarely in the eye, said nothing, then proceeded into the camp. The guard merely turned from this momentary distraction back to his duties. From my vantage, I could see Sying Hao went straight to its heart. There, he paused, then sat with the grouped brigands by their warming fire. He remained studied, intent and silent, while they grew loud and boisterous. For some time, they talked and moved about him, paying his presence little heed. I hungered and grew cold, jealously watching while he heartily shared their victuals. Should I go down and join them? It seemed safe enough.

No, there had been no signal. I had my orders. Stay put and watch.

Though Sying Hao didn't partake, he monitored with interest as his road worn companions began knocking down flasks of rice wine. Did you know? At night, sound travels far and distinctly on the mountain. Before long, I could hear song, emotion, sudden outbursts between moments of reflection. Finally, a wash of silence as they drifted toward slumber. Stars turned full bloom at this point. A subtle crystalline glow lit the woodland. Sying Hao stood, then glided like a shadow from one to the next. Several already slumbered, while those still awake stared misty eyed at his dream shadowy figure. He headed to the leader's cover, an impromptu shelter set mid-camp. He entered and then removed what appeared to be a bulky pack from the otherwise vacant interior. From the perimeter, the leader approached, studying Sying Hao warily as he sat there sifting the contents, assessing carefully. It almost looked as though Sying Hao were perusing wares for purchase. A transaction underway perhaps. Could that be what this was all about?

By then, the fire had dimmed. Barely visible, the leader and Sying Hao relinquished their focus on the pack and concluded whatever they intended. Sying Hao started toward the exit, parcel now slung cross body. Perhaps forgetting something, he paused to reflect, then returned again to the fading fire. Picking morsels from what remained of the evening's feast, he looked toward me, still concealed in the distance. Pointing to the food then to me, he signaled I would have my dinner after all. Loaded and ready, he drifted lazily toward the perimeter and in seconds was with the guard, briefly following behind, stepping in cadence along with the guard's measured pace. Then, traversing a clearing, Sying Hao edged left, and exited, while the guard remained ever vigilant and continued forward.

I knew it would be some time before he returned to our perch on the hillside. I lay back and enjoyed what lingered of the night sky spectacle. In the east, a hint of glow, and promise of new dawn.

Sying Hao arrived just as the tiring moon aligned alongside the war star rising on the new day's horizon.

"Here, some food from our guests," he smiled, handing over some baked roots and venison.

"Thank them for me," I smiled back, anticipating relief to my hunger.

"No need for that. I stole it. They're one of the advance infiltration teams here to measure and scope the sector. No fools, their overlords know hungry and uncompensated armies grow discontented. Can't have that and last for long — so they send scouts and patrols to scour for new targets. Lead patrols travel light and go only where they can skim what can be had. Units like these cater to the constant need for more. Sniff out potentials. Mark targets for those who follow. As reward, they are free to pick and glean what they find of value and can carry on their steeds. They miss no opportunity to satisfy needs, wants and ends. For them, survival churns its own rules. They hold coveted positions, tasked with setting the tone for their comrades sure to follow."

"Your friends, not mine," I replied, reflecting on his apparent acquaintance with the band.

"Not my friends, I've never met them."

Shadow Visitor

Skeptical, I interjected, "Need I remind, you just spent an entire evening fraternizing in their midst?"

Puzzled, Sying Hao looked at me, then laughed. "Oh, that. I assure you, they never knew I was there. A demonstration, nothing more. I thought you'd appreciate my efforts at subterfuge and concealment."

"What? You're telling me they never knew you were there? Are you forgetting I saw you mingling with them most of the night?"

"Did you see me speak with them? Did I interact with them?"

He had me there, I had to think it through for a moment. What exactly was it I thought I saw?

"You stopped before the guard, and walked with him afterwards. You shared food with them. You rummaged the leader's pack as he stared intently at you. Did you not notice him scrutinizing your every move?"

"Bao Ling, you saw because I told you to watch me. They did not see because I told them not to watch me. When they awaken this morning, they will have no awareness I was ever there. Except on rising they will find their booty gone."

"Their booty?"

Throwing the bandit leader's pack to my feet, he said, "Yes, this bag, a collection of priceless tokens plucked from the weak. In due time, we'll deliver this to Crystal Springs Temple. The abbot is a friend, a man of faultless character. He will talk among the locals, learn what took place, and return what he can to what's left of the rightful owners."

I opened the bag. Jade, rubies, gold, sapphires, and more. Some shaped as jewelry or coins, some simply there in their native forms. I had no doubt what it meant when I saw it. These trinkets were how peasants stored the little wealth they had. Peasants were peasants, yet among the poorest were those with sense enough to keep some measure of reserve for an emergency or time of need. Often, this took the form of jewelry. Perhaps a fine gift to a spouse or daughter. Or it might be a golden nugget painstakingly secured, then hidden away. The brigands knew it would be there. And they knew how to get it from you, securing the whereabouts digit by digit if necessary. You see, there exist some emergencies for which no degree of preparation, or perseverance suffices.

"Back up" I said. "You mean to tell me you spent the night in their midst, shared their food, then fleeced them clean, and they never knew you were there?"

"Neat trick, huh?"

"With respect. I don't think I believe you. I'm not sure such a stunt is doable, certainly not by me."

"Depends on who you are little brother. If me, for certain."

What can I say? I had already learned much from our stay in the wilderness. But after this display, nothing ever again surprised me. I tell you, we swim about in a sea of magic. Like fish in water, most never sensing it's there! Until someone who knows better hits us on the head with it! I've since learned how much better he knew. My head still aches, but in fond recollection.

After that, my studies with Sying Hao continued, only more intently. The stakes had risen. His performance left little doubt how much more I had to learn. For example, we would sometimes spend days studying particular animals. Memorizing their movement, noting their practical guile, and analyzing their respective instincts for survival.

He taught me how to shift consciousness and to place my self into the mind of another creature, then learn what the beast might do with my awareness. At first, I thought it to be a time-killing game. A gesture countering boredom. Once I felt the same of grandfather's "standing like a post" before I learned its true value.

Sying Hao tutored, "The way to gain an unteachable skill is to first pretend you already have the skill. Then bring it alive within yourself. While you are acting as if you have it, execute it for real. Note its first true manifestations. Lock them in, make their presence a familiar place where you can return at will. Let that take you to the ultimate full awareness."

This insight has proven true time and again. Never forget it! An alchemy governing all other things. A foothold through the door to ultimate learning, and insight into the not otherwise knowable!

For clarity on this, Sying Hao once shared the legend of Erge Lafah from the Southern Kingdom. "Like Ah Ju Na, Erge Lafah aspired to be the greatest archer. Undaunted by his lowly status, he went uninvited before Da Rou Na, the supreme teacher. Though duly impressed with the audacious young man, Da Rou Na rejected his petition outright. You see, Da Rou Na had already committed himself to Ah Ju Na, and wanted no distractions. Rightfully, he refused to split his focus. By way of excuse, he explained they were of different castes. Da Rou Na was prohibited from teaching below his own royal caste.

"Erge Lafah understood, but wouldn't give up. He left the world and became a hermit. In the remote wilderness, he built an image of Da Rou Na from sticks, mud and straw. This image of the master became his teacher in the wild. There it stared unflinchingly over Erge Lafah's slow but steady progress in archery over the weeks, the months, and then the years. In time he became supreme. Eventually, Da Rou Na learned of this and extracted a high price for his unvolunteered contribution to Erge Lafah's mastery. But that is another story. Using the mind to create the impossible from nothing is the lesson. The point is in the possibility. It is the way of the true immortals. For them, all thoughts can be steered to substance. It just takes patience!

"In your case Bao Ling, I am not qualified to be Da Rou Na. That would require better men than me. But I can be his presence in the form of your own mud dummy."

Born Anew

No less important than the physical skills, we immersed ourselves in the classics. Seasons drifted by, barely noticed. Always, he chose, and selected. Guiding each step of understanding, then standing back. Timid at first, eventually I grew more confident. One day, I challenged why he gave so much attention to them. "They have so little bearing on our existence here. Why waste the time? Where do they fit into what we need to be doing?"

He answered sharply, "They've done the work, Bao Ling. Everyone has opinions. Thoughts on how things should be. Few do the work. Opinions and beliefs are everywhere. At times, shared recklessly, at times imposed. We end up bumping into the same walls over and over. Or trapped in conceptual boxes from which we have no escape. For every true solution, one steers through fields of possibilities. Sometimes endlessly, as though stuck in a maze. Solutions? Most, when tried, will make things worse. Why is that? We're like peasants, looking for gold coins in a latrine. Few will ever choose to soil their hands. That leaves you and me. We can ponder whether others are out there. But right now, I see only us. If not us, then who?

"Honestly, I don't agree with all the sages. I too have opinions. And my own ways of seeing things. Though I might sometimes disagree, I give them their due. They've done the work. They, not us, have invested their lives in sounding their thoughts and recording their philosophies. Should their steering be off, they are nonetheless far closer to truth and righteousness than most could ever pretend to be.

"Study closely what they say. Emulate their peerless example. Just as you emulate your parents, and your teachers from the past. Never sell their efforts short. Many have paid with their lives. Or worse.

"Long after the sages are gone, those who crave and misuse power still cower beneath the judgment inherent in their words and example. Does it surprise anyone so few of the manuscripts have survived. So many wantonly destroyed by tyrants who rue the possibility their subjects may learn from sagely example how to think for themselves."

I thought of Sying Hao's vast collection of scrolls and tablets. Preserved ever so carefully in his mountain retreats. I would never again doubt their importance.

Regarding my learning, we never lost a moment. We knew time to be short and paced ourselves accordingly. As my mentor, he possessed intimate knowledge of the great thinkers. He articulated their thoughts and underlying motives so well I felt he had known them. Perhaps he had crossed their paths? His nimble mind navigated the core and value of the most contradictory philosophies. Seeing deep within them, he reconciled differences in a seeming instant. Emphasizing perspective, he cited Yin and Yang. Seeming opposites, each always becoming the other. Like shooting his arrows, he never missed the mark. Somehow, he melded them all into his own convincing view of what should be practical reality.

"I celebrate the differences! What's to fear in disagreement?" he would crow. "Truth exists everywhere. Often it's found in opposing thoughts and apparent contradictions."

Then he'd argue with me endlessly over philosophical nuances. Bouts which ran unrelenting until we reached a workable coherence, sometimes just short of outright confrontation. In that sense, he gave no respite. I had no choice but to see the front, back, up and down of all things, more clearly than I ever had before. He agonized over Confucius, marveled over Laozi, scrutinized Sunzi, admired Mozi, idolized Zhuge Liang, and simply loved Zhuangzi[4].

"Zhuangzi, now there's a guy whose philosophy had teeth." By this he meant the practical impact of the teachings. Having teeth presumed capability of drawing nourishment into the spirit body, without which the whole being could not energize into outward radiance.

Anyhow, that's how he explained it!

"Zhuangzi was no dupe for temptation or self aggrandizement. Rather than succumb to the allures of

---

[4] Taoist sage; disciple to Laozi. Often referred to by Sying Hao as one to be emulated.

courtly influence, he once put even great King Wei into his place. His litany of words sharper and more penetrating than the edge of any sword. And you know what? King Wei became the better for it.

"And never forget, Zhuangzi was a family man. He raised children and lived life as a regular person. Just like us, humbly. And like us, he struggled to make ends barely but adequately meet. You would have liked him Bao Ling. Think of it. A person just like you. Now become a beacon. Shining bright as sunlight into the deepest and most arcane reality, illuminating for all to behold. All the philosophies of his era tied into useless knots, using nothing but his iron grip on absolute truth. Not to downplay the others. They all remain special of course. Valid on their own merits. But Zhuangzi. He is the real dragon. Why? I say again, because his words had teeth, and the bite of his understanding chewed effortlessly through any foolishness in its path."

Of course we studied others too. That included what came to us from the fabled kingdoms beyond the great mountains. The steadfast pursuit demanded I be born anew, digging deeper and discovering new roots in different places. Changes within me could no longer be ignored. I saw and understood things I never before imagined. Until experienced first hand, I hadn't known of my thirst for knowledge and heightened awareness, nor of my deprivation. A blessing indeed, but not easy coming to terms with. These changes came with their price, usually leaving me with a poignant sense of loss. Honestly, I was becoming too complicated. While I valued new awareness, I missed the elegant simplicity of my prior take on things. For the first time, I had to surrender bits of my past. Some aspects seemed now to be impediments to further growth. I feared I might not ever fully recover who I had been, and had no idea what, if anything, would or could take its place. This came from my heart. The sense of loss at times overwhelmed. Realizing these changes within, one day I cursed Sying Hao for bringing it all upon me! That was a very dark day!

When not engaged in intellectual grappling, we worked on real fighting. As you know, I came from a line of skilled martial artists. Sying Hao saw this in me, and attested to my having proper grounding in the classical fighting ways.

He possessed extraordinary skills in all respects. Among his varied hinterland acquaintances were the noble warrior monks of Small Pines Wilderness. They appeared each season with their disciples, petitioning he share his understanding and skills by testing against their own perceptions of movement and strategy. Friendly contests for sure but true challenges nonetheless. They were a marvel to behold. Eventually, I partook. A simple matter of showing friendship and proper respect.

These monks wandered about as traveling mystics, beggars striving only to be sufficient onto themselves. Their steering clear of foolishness seemed only to draw it all the more upon them. They were who they were, seeming magnets for trouble and challenge. The constant trials never lessened their quest for self awareness and actualization of inner potential. Nor were their efforts diverted for long. Rather, they accepted persecution as part of the path. I liked them. Whenever they left, Sying Hao would inevitably shake his head and say something to the effect, "Now those guys walk a hard road!"

I considered them heroes. Each and every one. Gold coins, shining from within the muck!

The Southlanders

Sying Hao's archery stood supreme. There lay our strongest bond. Because of my past, and my inclinations, our time together invariably reverted to archery.

He marveled at my primitive skills in improvising a bow and conjuring crude but effective arrows from wild woods and bamboo. He acknowledged my preference for gas bladders of fish for the binding glues. He agreed to its superiority over other choices, if one sought longevity and durability. Excepting for fumes of course. Sying Hao had quite a nose for scents. He could sniff intruders two days out. Understandably, fish bladders were not especially to his liking.

He showed me some of his tricks for rolling sinew with fibrous weed. Fireweed for one. This created a longer lasting string. He didn't fully trust sinew on its own, particularly when it became wet and its tension changed. He was careful to cut it and blend with hemp or other fibers, sometimes fragments of linen. New to me, another thing he taught was the importance of removing mass from the string's center. My people would make a string of uniform consistency. Density and thickness constant over its length.

Perhaps a bit thicker in the mid. Our way suited my purposes, which were generally close in. Shooting from great distance, Sying Hao's specialty, raised the significance of every quirk and nuance of the weapon. The added mass of a string woven thicker in the middle would slow the release. In a given situation, this difference might be critical. Timing could change, as would ability to strike from afar, or to pierce armor.

Sying Hao preferred silk, when available. The combination of light weight and strength was superior among all possible choices. In fact, he always kept on his person an array of silk strings he had developed over time. Like children, he would say. Each had its purpose: distance, power, silence, resilience, or longevity. He would select and use as needed. Amazingly, he could change from one to the next in less time than most would take to set and release a shaft.

Should he find himself without strings, he could fabricate workable alternatives from almost anything. I've seen him do it with grass, thistle, nettle, hemp and cattail. Within the time most would take to brew tea, he would forage, then sit, roll and weave, twist and loop. Soon enough a string would emerge. He finished with a bonding agent, usually some type of sap or resin. The end result? A string that would typically match my own best efforts. All in a fraction of what it would take me. Eventually, he shared his methods. But not until after enjoying my long frustration in trying to match his efforts. I learned his ties, the reverse twists, the weaves, and how to thin the middle and weight the ends to ensure maximum energy to the arrow. Finally, to tip the ends of the bow with smooth polished horn, giving the string clean bite into the bow's natural, but sometimes undisciplined leverage.

A time did come when we descended the remote southern slopes to the torrid wetlands of the distant south. The people there lived in villages much like ours in the north. They appeared different from us with skins darker complected. They tended toward colorful dress and inclined to wearing gold for all to see. Clearly, the sticky fingers of empire had not yet reached into their isolated domain. No one in the north, excepting perhaps the nobles, or those attached to the court, would be so bold or foolish as to openly wear their wealth. Fact is, gold could not be found anywhere in my native village. We had been picked clean generations earlier. If not hidden carefully, even the metal for utensils and tools would be confiscated, melted down and reformed into implements of warfare and death.

Situated where they were, they had been spared.

And it showed in their natures. The Southlanders appeared to be a joyful lot, content with their existence, and … well, happy.

It bothered me. It shouldn't have, but it did. I was jealous of what I saw. At our best my people could be content in the moment. But happy and carefree like what I saw with them, I don't ever recall that. Turns of events had forever darkened my perceptions. No matter what I saw in front of me, I always suspected a great missile would any moment drop from the sky and fragment before me, spreading fire, destruction and misery.

On first meeting, the Southlanders jokingly referred to me as "stone face." Never to my stone face of course. Appropriate, I must admit. I recognized how I remained stuck in my own skin. Unable to reflect or partake in their joyful radiance because it threatened to inundate me. I kept my distance.

What a terrible place to be stranded!

Sying Hao? Well, him they clearly knew and loved. He was recognized everywhere, and always welcomed their smiles. He smiled warmly in return, taking care to explain my dour countenance as somehow related to a long bout of the runs from tainted water. The only fib I ever heard cross his lips. As good an explanation as any I suppose. They typically nodded in polite and empathetic understanding while patting my back and assuring they understood.

I wonder if they truly did, or what in fact it was they understood.

Something from Nothing

The Southlanders had many remarkable talents and skills. Their domain teemed with mulberry trees, and they had perfected the cultivation of silk worms. That of course is what drew us there. They knew Sying Hao would come. They had safeguarded the purest and highest quality green unprocessed fiber for his dedicated use. There, with the elders watching and studying his technique, he wove a number of strings. When finished, he passed each to the elders. They accepted respectfully extending both hands, as if receiving gemstones. Rightfully so. No gemstone could lay down a wild dog, or a stalker on the hungry prowl.

In time, I too learned the worth of these strings. Sying Hao first let me gauge their potential using his bow, then on one of my own. They were light. As far as I could tell, impervious to temperature change, or the elements. The outstroke proved clean and quick. Arrows exploded from the bow. Only then could I see there was a problem with the stiffness of my own arrows. It seemed they struggled against this superior string.

Contrary to what you might expect, the arrow does not shoot straight when released by the archer. The force of acceleration stresses the shaft considerably. Frequently, the shaft distorts as it begins its flight. You can't see it. It's too quick for the eye. But it's there nonetheless. Why in some instances, the arrow will flex between the string and bow handle, snake its way around the bow, then rebound into its intended flight. You can understand, there are endless variables to consider. The archer carefully selects arrows for particular purposes because of this very effect.

Some bows call for stiffer arrows, some for more flexible. The archer develops intuitive feel for his preferred bow, and soon comes to terms with this mystery. A paradox[5] of how to shoot straight when everything is moving, and deforming. The most skilled archer will, in time, come to know what degree of shaft stiffness each bow requires. His arrow building will reflect that awareness. Eventually each bow will have its own cache of arrows all within a narrow range of give and flex, suited to the needs of the respective bow and its intended use. That being said, a great archer is a great archer. Nothing reconciles the variables better than consummate skill.

Sying Hao knew this science intimately. The subtleties I learned went beyond all I first reckoned possible, and in time he entrusted what he knew to me. Initially dumbstruck, I asked how he had ever managed to acquire the skill. How does one come to understand, and to master something which he can't see, or know for certain exists? In earnestness, he answered, "It's an art shrouded in mystery.

---

[5] The Archer's Paradox. The expertly designed arrow will flex its way around the bow and return to its aimed path once free of release.

Yet, for one who watches carefully, there nonetheless to eventually unravel and understand. So much of life is like that. Most don't have a clue. That's one of the reasons we study the sages. We learn to see what others can not! Think of it. All the things right under our noses, to which we are blind!"

In the end, he confided he had been gifted the skill by another. "An ageless being, Bao Ling. Someone who had an eternity to mull over things such as this, and to unscramble their secrets." For me, these insights opened the doors to what would once have been impossible. As to the ageless being, I figured Sying Hao to be toying with me. Clearly his humility would not allow him to selfishly claim what I suspected to be his own exclusive discovery.

As to bows, my skills though honed when we first met, had their limits. I specialized in self bows, those made from a single piece of wood. Time and circumstances permitting, I would sometimes build up handles. Occasionally I would reinforce tips should the luxury of horn allow quality nocks for the ends. In the outlands near my home, a wide variety of materials were available and it was possible to construct a workable bow even with limited tools. One learns to improvise from necessity. For sure, in dire circumstances a bow can be fabricated quickly. I've had to do it. More than once, bounty scouts surprised me. They nearly had me, careful in their ambush to capture my weapons and supplies. They figured me helpless, and counted me soon dead.

I remember one frantic dawn, I barely dodged their murderous chase. My oft fickle friend, darkness, had lifted all too quickly. I managed to scavenge a clean shoot of young ash which I trimmed as best I could into a bow. I barely had time to fabricate two shafts crowned with hastily shaved stone tips. Though not an archer's finely tuned weapon, at ten paces the shafts did their job, catching the frontmost two off their guard. They never expected I would attack, so that's what I did! When they knew what I was about, it was already too late for them. Seizing their weapons, in turnabout I pressed to their rear, then neutralized the stunned others to secure my escape.

Sying Hao said he admired my ability to do this. He praised the efficiency of technique, allowing that in a pinch, there might be none better than I when it came to fashioning a weapon from nothing.

Then, as politely as one could say it, he added, "Perhaps that's because I've never had to."

For me, his meaning was quite clear.

Sying Hao, Teacher

You must understand. No cache of gold or gems could
mean so much to me as recognition from Sying Hao.
Hearing him say "None better," I knew how a rich man felt.
My true treasures had always been skills, and the growth I
achieved from what I had sacrificed to perfect them. Sying
Hao knew the measure of sacrifice, and of skill. He had
been there. His words counted.

Even his polite admonitions. What he saw so easily and
well remained invisible to others. Subtle words mostly
unnoticed, except for those on the receiving end of their bite.
His acknowledgment of my efforts assured I existed in fact:
what I represented mattered, at least to him. And that
counted for me!

He asked what I knew about the composite form. These
were the bows favored by the nomad tribes of the far north.
I had only heard of them, a fierce and independent people. I
responded I knew little in regard to composites. In shape
and form they appeared to be very complicated and
required materials and techniques beyond my personal
experience and ability to access. Plus, they demanded time
and attention I could not spare.

He told how composite bows had elevated the art of bow craft to its highest level. Artisans perpetually pushed to achieve perfection, always putting their theories to practical tests. The typical objectives were distance, reliability, portability, durability, and knock down power.

Sying Hao explained how their art had evolved over centuries of constant experimentation. A never ending process of application, feedback, study and modification. "You'll find little is not already known about the materials, the fabrication, and the application. Still, each one is different, like a fine musical instrument. Each master imparts a bit of himself into the weapon. Its character is permanently cast under his mold and influence. Bao Ling, your bows are fine for what you use them for. Your skills however, have reached the limit of where they can take you. You can grow no further from where you are. As your brother, it falls to me to ensure you can create bows worthy of your yet unrealized potential."

With that, our energies turned to making composite bows. We amassed collections of hard maples, ash, bamboo, mulberry, spruce, bone, horn, hoof, and sinew. We soaked, heat treated, shaved, cut, scraped, rubbed and polished. We scoured the high country for the horn of antelope or goats, which Sying Hao preferred over the horn of water buffalo. He also explained how heaven or perhaps fate would occasionally deliver the remains of ancient beasts from beneath snow fields. "They are unlike anything you have ever seen. The beasts were true mammoths. Nothing living today compares. With some luck, one might find remnants of giant tusks, icebound among their remnants and bones."

This ivory, he said, was better than jade, which he also liked but said took too long to work. He had amassed an enviable collection from those relics. He stored them carefully throughout his network. I found it a remarkable material. "Ivory," he called it. Was it stone? Was it horn? Who could say? As to how it performed? That I can answer. Unrivaled!

He taught me much about glues beyond my preference for fish bladders such as sinew from the legs and backs of wild deer. He would pound the sinew into workable fibers, then weave or roll into cord. He taught to always keep some dry and handy. In emergencies, it could be activated by saliva and used to make quick bindings. He assured they would hold true once formed and dried. The same with hides, which we slow boiled in layers. We drained and collected the syrupy residue in what seemed a never ending process. When done, he patiently allowed months for complete drying before storing for future use as bonding agent.

We built special lodges where our collected materials could be protected from the elements. Or thieves, should any be so foolish. We kept the environment moderated through combinations of heat, ventilation, misting, and airing. The required oversight was never-ending, and always with a purpose. Sometimes we wouldn't sleep for days, trying our best to stay ahead of threatening weather, and seasonal shifts.

When I questioned the effort versus the anticipated return, Sying Hao admonished, "Bao Ling, if we can produce one great bow, capable of matching your potential, our sacrifice will not be in vain."

At times, my spirit dulled. I thought of home, and what I felt to be friends abandoned. Despite the good company of Sying Hao my darkness sometimes overwhelmed me. Questions arose as to my judgment and choices I had made. What was I doing there? While our lives at Southern Mountain were humble and sometimes difficult, I was far better off than any of my relations or other contemporaries.

To lighten my mood, Sying Hao would offer, "Bao Ling, cheer up. Nothing is so without purpose as you seem to think. We've found each other for a reason. True, only the eyes of immortals can see all sides and views. But this I know. Had you not come to Southern Mountain, your people would have had to bear the hopelessness and weight of your death. It is they who would have been riddled with guilt, not you. How could they live with their inaction as you were hunted down and humiliated like a vile beast. Your job now is to keep your focus. Make every moment count. Perfect all you learn. Make ready for your eventual return."

Under Sying Hao's guidance, my first composite bow took final shape as leaves turned from green to yellow to brown. He carefully tutored me in his techniques: laminating the wood and sinew on the outside, over meticulously integrated horn, all delicately compressed within. The tips of the bow curved away, re-curving in the traditional style. This of course required the tips be enhanced to handle the enormous stress.

To that end, we trimmed and fashioned bone or ivory from the ancient relics to reinforce the endpoints.

Remarkably, once aligning to his principles and specifications, the entire bow and its components worked effortlessly in harmony. The energy of the draw a much higher level than I had ever encountered. To be sure, my wood bows and my strings would have failed under the stresses of these enhanced tensions. The same could be said of my stamina. Though hardened to current toughness by my sojourn in the wilderness, it faltered against the seemingly endless cycle of testing then modifying. I could see how one might become prisoner to this process, if one sought to do it right. I marveled at how Sying Hao kept his focus true. No wonder he could shoot invisible locusts from the air![6]

---

[6] A reference to their first meeting, detailed in *Seed of Dragons*. Sying Hao was able to shoot a locust so far in the distance, Bao Ling could not see it.

Part 2

A Celestial Bow

Seal Tightly the Bridge

We made other composites, mostly as gifts and specimens for leaders in the south. Until now, they had been spared the turmoil in the north. No one doubted, their time of trials would come. News from afar had been clear. Carefully, their leaders watched and listened. What had unfolded elsewhere now crept their way.

Sightings of well armed military units became common. Spies told how they probed and scoped the mountain surrounds, and the western wilderness. Soon enough, eyes would turn southward. The mountain, its unforgiving terrain and ferocious turns of weather, had until then insulated the south from mayhem. Fate and circumstance had blessed their ancestors. Soon that would end.

Perhaps the focus on my personal bow buoyed my spirits as the seasons turned yet again. We were well along in the process when Sying Hao declared the quickest path to mastering bow making was having a sample of perfection. He told how most artisans forge reality around their own expectations of what it should be. Almost as though conjuring. "Doing so is fine," he allowed, "but leads to many false starts and blind ends. Better to have seen perfection first, then shape one's thinking from that. Knowing what is truly possible helps one avoid paths which lead to lesser outcomes."

Jokingly, I gibed, "Yes elder brother, if only we had one of the celestial bows to feast our eyes upon. We'd have a clearer view to this perfection of which you speak."

Saying nothing, he smiled politely and nodded his agreement.

Not long after, Sying Hao arrived at our hideaway with a parcel wrapped in lightly oiled lambskin. It appeared well weathered. Seasoned as if it had been sitting in some protected enclave, hidden from prying eyes.

"This, my friend, is 'Dragon' the celestial bow you hoped to feast your eyes upon. It was passed to me by a warrior sage, as a token of friendship and gratitude for my having saved his life. Or at least that was his rationale for justifying the gift. I figured he just wanted me to have it. As to saving his life, who can say? Among warriors, he stood supreme. As to equals, he had only one. In battle, it's true I filled a place by his side. Arguably, I held my own. As I remember it, I survived in the end only because his brilliance sheltered me. From the earliest, I went with him by choice. Others too timid wanted no part of the daunting challenges ever rolling his way. There, I proved unique. In that sense, we stood our ground as brothers, or should I say father and son, for in time he became father to me in all respects. I remember once, it fell for us to guard the bridge over Red River. The steep cliffs and the raging torrent below made the bridge the only gate to the west for over 200 li. Liu Bei's ravaged troops had only just crossed over. The advancing enemy closed from the other side, then slowed cautiously, checking for traps and ambush. Liu's only hope lay in his plan to stall the enemy advance at the bridge and thus buy precious time for full evacuation.

"You see, Liu was burdened with the population he had once administered in Jing. Those poor folk had their fill of despots, warlords, brigands, kings and would be emperors. Others who came before had kept them in misery until Liu Bei gained control of their province. For once, they prospered, and for a short while grew content. Now, insurmountable forces and treachery[7] fell upon Lord Liu's still fledgling band. They were fighting for their very existence. His only hope lay in the westward trek. Unexpectedly, the people he administered abandoned their homes and possessions and elected to follow Liu joining his army in retreat. He and his commanders wanted no part of this. Provisions were short, but not so short as time. The mass of stragglers all swore allegiance to Liu Bei and his goal of restoring Han. They pledged to seed the western

---

[7] Liu Cong, second son of Liu Biao, seized political control of Jing just at the time of his father's untimely passing. A weak successor, he eventually accommodated with Cao Cao and Wei, abandoning the loyal Liu Bei, whose forces had been protecting the northern line. As he began his forced retreat, Liu Bei passed Xiangyang and called out to Liu Cong, who could only hide his face from one he once called "uncle." Embarrassed by the treachery, many officials and citizens elected to leave with Liu Bei rather than serve a coward who had turned from a loyal friend, and sold out their homeland.

land with their determination and talent, and to actualize the base of support his forces and dreams so desperately needed. Zhang Fei and Guan Yu deemed it daft folly. Zhuge Liang had doubts too, as evidenced by his silence, demurring entirely to Lord Liu. Liu decided for everyone. They would come. Many would perish. Those who survived would form the nucleus of a new homeland in the west. It was agreed by all.

"He already knew. Had he sent them back, they would have been slaughtered and fleeced clean. He could not abide with that. And on this matter, time proved his decision correct.

"With few men to spare, General Liu ordered my Master to hold the bridge while his army evacuated. He made sure to push the unarmed and helpless far forward to the front, hopefully kept from harm's way. Enough forward to where they would not impede the defense in the rear. It seemed an impossible task. Guan Yu and Zhang Fei both volunteered to remain with my Master. General Liu ruled against it. The retreat would fail without their securing his immediate rear and preventing the column from stalling under the weight of the weary population. I begged permission to remain at the bridge. Master staunchly refused, directing me to the side of Zhuge Liang. But then Lord Liu intervened, saying only, 'The young squire stays.' He rode to where Master stood and declared, 'None better than the son to guard the father's rear.'

"That quickly everything stood decided. Say what you will of Liu Bei, the man knew how to make decisions.

Master walked to me and said, 'This may be our last adventure together. Prospects look grim.'

"Then he blinked his green golden eyes, adding, 'But ... I have a plan.'"

Liu Bei
"The Commoner's Hero"

Working the Moment

"He handed me the One-Li bow. That's how he called it. 'Sying Hao, the time has come for you to wake Dragon from his slumber. Let the bridge fill with the vanguard, then cut them off from the main body with One-Li. Take down those who follow as they enter from the far side. I will deal with the lead.'

"Then Master walked slowly forward, taking position on the span.

"The vanguard consisted of a phalanx of fifty mounted and battle hardened knights, now emerging from the far end. They represented the cream of warriors from our foe's army, already coalescing behind in the thousands. They intended to sweep the bridge clean of all resistance, clearing path for their comrades to follow. We had already witnessed their brutal savagery sawing through our staged infantry in the days prior. Our fellows decimated by the hundreds. Once confirming only me to be in the rear, there would be no reticence or hesitation on their part.

As instructed, I allowed them to enter. As they neared center, my teacher took his ground one third forward from my end. Meticulously, he set his weapons about, all within easy reach. As you know Bao Ling, a great General can single handedly guard a pass. Or in this case a bridge barely wide enough for ten men standing abreast. The vanguard attacked ferociously, expecting to annihilate our feeble resistance. Spurred by the fearless vanguard, the main body massed on the far end, then began to accelerate forward. I raised the One-Li Bow for the very first time, feeling my tight grip on its waist to be the only thing preventing me from washing away into the abyss below, flushed to insignificance by the advancing storm. Having only my focus to counter my urge to run, I set my first shaft and drew. The pulling effort far exceeded my expectations. I took aim as best I could, still fighting to steady the weapon, then released. My first arrow sailed pointlessly. I stared desperately as it angled over the midsection of the bridge, consumed by the raging torrent far below.

"A terrible miscue. In the distance, some pointed toward me and laughed aloud. Mocking! A few brazenly spun about and exposed their asses at me. Master saw them, then turned toward me and laughed, 'Sying Hao, you think perhaps we should switch places?' He winked his left eye, which glimmered like jade in his crimson warrior's helmeted mien. Saying nothing, I breathed deeply, then relaxed as he had often taught. Sink my spirit to ground. I drew a second shaft and looked to the far side thinking only how the distance easily exceeded the namesake one li. I had never before shot an arrow that far. Believe me, I had tried but to no avail. Now, in the moment, everything seemed possible. Or so I hoped! I relaxed the bow and for the first time, studied its form, also noting teacher's carefully honed arrow. Its precisely shaped feathers carefully set to guide the extended striated shaft straight to where the eye of the archer had placed his intent. Their commander took his position adjacent to the far port, then organized his main troops for a quick crossing. He turned toward me and I could see the onyx black glimmer of his eyes.

"As I held One-Li, I could palpably feel my summons to its dragon avatar. But I had no idea how I was doing it! In obedient response, its bodiless spirit-form moved from ground to bow and then to my limbs. Entering like a snake through my naval then coursing up my spine tracing the great governor down frontally to my mid section. There kan and li mixed, igniting the cauldron of awareness which culminated at the base of my skull. My eyes lit with this fire, and I looked to the enemy commander. All I could see were two fields of immense darkness, separated by emptiness. They were so vast, and near. It was as though I could reach forward and touch them.

"Trusting the moment, I lifted One-Li, drew full, and released the shaft. I felt the fast approaching heat and clamor of battle on my cheeks, then looked to my Master. Four magnificent warriors now threatened to his front. The others looked to somehow break angle along side and gain advantage to entry. In the distance, at the far side of the bridge, a tangible silence emerged. Like an ominous shadow, it flowed forward across the bridge, pulling everyone's attention to the rear. Their horse mounted commander sat motionless on his steed, my arrow through his left eye. Its tip exited the rear of his skull, emerging from the back of his helmet. Again, they all pointed my direction, staring in disbelief. No taunts or jeers now. No asses flashing. Last thing they wanted was a second arrow headed you know where. I felt pretty good just then! I drew a second and fired toward the four advancing on Master. The arrow could be seen flying through the far right cable rail and over the side of the bridge. A miss! I stared in disbelief, wondering how I could have missed the sure shot. Had my new found confidence gotten the best of me?

"Only then did I see the gaping hole in number two's armor breastplate, and pieces of lung and kidney dripping from his rear as his body folded down.

"One-Li was no earthly bow. Its shafts were bolts of lightning. Master quickly gained control of the remaining three, then advanced on the balance of the vanguard. No mortal could match Master in single combat under these close conditions. I suppose it would be possible to overwhelm his skills with a cluster attack, or with projectiles from afar, but his ability to position and strategize in the moment matched his combat skills. I made sure nothing came from the far side.

"With his sides secured by the geometry of the bridge, he knew to systematically work the angles and the energies. Like a cloud hopping wizard, he always found superior position, gaming the metrics to where he faced one isolated and unlucky opponent at a time. Blocked by the one, the accomplices found themselves neutralized. Forced by clever maneuver to just outside the perimeter of direct threat. His quick glance to me, then to the other side of the bridge corrected my focus to the relegated task. My gaze zoomed to the far end as I launched arrow after arrow into soldiers looking for a track forward. Those standing fell to my fury. The momentum of some shafts evident as they passed through officers, then through those following close behind, some taking down horses almost as an afterthought. I watched four bodies drop from a single well placed shot. I looked back to Master and found him standing atop a pile of dead. From this grim podium he screamed invitations to the far side to all who might wish to taste his steel as they departed to join the banquet of their ancestors.

"He sure knew how to work the moment!"

Father, Son, Bow

"Reinforcements no longer surged forward. Made timid from fear and in awe of the unprecedented demonstration of Master's martial skill. And, might I humbly add, of the archery just witnessed. While we defended, and purchased needed delay, General Liu had workers bring oil and fire forward. He ordered the bridge burnt and downed from our end. But only after we had finished and safely evacuated. With the bridge down, the enemy would need days before crossing the waters below and continuing the pursuit. In the art of warfare, that meant a door now slammed shut. Liu gave this order with great reticence. An edifice of such magnificence would take at least a year to rebuild. Many lives would change for the worse from the absence of access, and escape. But the decision was right, and guaranteed the safe retreat of Liu's battered army along with the herded populace.

"Master approached me in the aftermath, suggesting we celebrate with a quiet meal and give thanks for our survival. As time marched on, we shared many like experiences and meals. Our love as father and son reached deeper than blood into our very spirits. I had been a war orphan. Left hopeless and abandoned on a bloodied field. Somehow, I found him. And from that day, I always felt loved and appreciated, and never again alone. Likewise, as I glowed in achievement, he might have honored me with words, but didn't. He only looked my way, eating quietly, and solemnly. Many had died after all. He would never dishonor their sacrifice, or gloat over it. He often found words inadequate, particularly when the weight of message required more. It was not so much what I had done as the magnanimity of his appreciation for this humble squire, now proxy son. For him, it could only be memorialized by the greatest gift he could bestow. That would in time be the Dragon Bow. For the moment, we ate quietly, grateful for the day and our survival.

"I knew him as Colonel Sun. After rescue from the field, I became his squire. He, above all others, guided my nascent skills. When he finally passed the gift, he whispered, 'For my shadow of these many years. Since we first crossed paths, Sying Hao, my flanks and rear have been sealed tightly, and all adversaries kept to my front. For an old warrior like me, that stands greatest among luxuries. I tell you, we are of the same stone Sying Hao. You could have been the one at the bridge. Never forget that. Only you are worthy to mind the Dragon Bow for me. Remember, wherever you find One-Li, the spirit of Colonel Sun will be close by.'

"And here, Bao Ling, is the One-Li Bow to guide the balance of your apprenticeship."

I reached for it timidly. The bow was a work of art worthy of an emperor. Not because it was gilded, or crested with gems, or trimmed in precious jade or metal. Just the opposite, I found it unpretentious. A portrait of consummate elegance. Steeped in utter simplicity.

Balance was perfect. The substance within was evident at first grasp. But holding it, one barely noticed it was there. Somehow, it always seemed to center on the one point[8]. Elements of bone were carefully set at the tips, and lined the center, some also visible in the laminations at the handle. It felt cool to the touch, and like jade, would not warm if one held an ember to it. Sying Hao explained it had bone and horn from animals who once roamed the out lands. He believed the materials pre-dated the reign of the fabled Yellow Emperor. And as you know, that goes back to our very beginning as a people. Per Sying Hao, those creatures would be like gods to the animals of our day. When I asked for explanation, he described some were as tall as town gates were high. Massive enough to circumvent or walk through any barricade, adding, "They lived free, and unbounded."

Who could say? What I knew from my inspection was the elements of this bow looked like nothing I had ever seen before.

Then I laughed, believing of course he was testing my gullibility. Still, the material was superior to anything I had ever encountered. Issues of gullibility aside, its capacity to store energy on the draw far outweighed any skepticism or doubt.

---

[8] Our metaphysical center usually placed three finger widths below the navel and two thirds in from the frontal abdomen.

Colonel Sun

I Heard the Voice

For several weeks he had me sit and stare at One-Li. He explained, "Bao Ling, as I've said, this bow has origins in the deepest past. It may be singular. I've never seen another like it. I have served at court where something like this would have captured great interest and scrutiny. By its perfection, one might speculate the hand of the Yellow Emperor. Or perhaps the bow was always there, serving the likes of others like Colonel Sun and their chosen successors.

"I should add, it has a mind of its own. Its magic avails only to those deemed deserving. Colonel Sun joked he had put a spell on it. Who knows? Nothing from him would surprise me. Some have tried to draw the string, only to find it stiff and unmovable. Others have found it too heavy to lift with only one arm. Unwieldy, impossible to transport on horseback without the animal buckling in discomfort. I can't explain it, that's just how it is. Sun would joke how others had tried to steal it. He never chased after them. Inevitably, they soon tired of its rebellious nature and decided returning it would be best for their health."

Hearing that, it surprised me I could lift it first try without issue. I wondered how that could be. I admired its majestic taper, and the careful splicing and dovetailing of wood, sinew, horn and bone into an integrated single piece. Defying conceptions, its color changed with the angle of light. Sometimes blood red. Sometimes yellow like the summer grass. Sometimes dark and ominous, like the visage of Ka Li[9].

"But brother, it's light as a feather. I can barely tell it's in my hand. May I try it out?"

He smiled knowingly, probably recalling his own once excitement now replaying in another. "Certainly. You can take one shot, Bao Ling. No need to stir the dragon from its rest. Come, let's find a clearing. There you can personally witness your arrow becoming a phoenix."

Uncertain what he meant, I accompanied him to a nearby meadow. I started to set a target. He said not to waste the time. "Just pick a spot in the far distance, and let the shaft sail."

"But how will I know its character by simply shooting an arrow into the air?"

He laughed at that. "This will be different Bao Ling. If the bow likes you, it will dance its magic before your delighted eyes."

Deferring to the wishes of older brother, I stood, set a shaft, and drew. It felt like running my hand over silk. I

---

[9] Ka Li - Vernacular reference to Kali, Hindu goddess of death.

imagined wheels aligned within, somehow facilitating the flow of energy. What should have been a rigorous draw became a casual movement. I relaxed my grip and studied the bow carefully. Nothing I saw explained why. I looked to Sying Hao. He sensed my puzzlement, "It seems to have an inclination to you Bao Ling. I would venture you have aroused its curiosity. Savor the moment."

I drew again. More so than at first. There looked to be no end to how far I could draw. Suddenly my arrow slipped and dropped unexpectedly from the bony guide. I clumsily tried to recover.

"Here Bao Ling, I have my own arrows, more worthy of One-Li."

He handed over a shaft, nearly half again as long as my own. It too was a work of art. No surprise for me. I was already well aware of Sying Hao's skills and forethought in everything he did.

"I feel I should aim at something."

Sying Hao replied, "Pick a place in the distance. See if you can hit it."

There were trees on the far side of the meadow, framing a tall pine at their center. I said, "The pine it is."

As I drew, I had no gauge or sense of what effort would be required to carry my shaft to the pine. The draw on One-Li felt meek, almost timid, and light to my touch. I kept pulling further back, still not sure my arrow would cover the distance. I estimated 400 paces, a commendable shot for any bow. Certainly further than any I had ever taken, or seen.

Sying Hao playfully prodded, "Bao Ling, we don't have eternity, take your shot while we still have daylight!"

I looked disapprovingly to him. Turning back to front, something caught my attention and made me freeze.

It was then I first heard the voice. Not words, not thoughts. Something deep and profound. Subtle at first, little more than a hint of whisper. Rolling my way from afar, buoyed atop the dust of history. Recalling epic deeds in the hands of now immortals. Proclaiming, "This, I am!"

I understood the the images. The words I could not say, or repeat. Nor could I conjure thoughts to match their import. I stood merely an empty cup. A flood washed over my opening, saturating my spirit to overflow, giving new substance to whatever emptiness lay within. I seized all I could hold.

Losing my grip, I let the arrow slip. I began to curse my lapse of focus. That is, until I saw the shaft race forward, having its own mind, barely visible for its speed, ascending in a direct arc over the meadow, and then the stream. Though I could see a modest drift from the wind, it was still ascending as it passed over the target pine and disappeared from my view.

Sying Hao nodded his head, then looked to me, "Little brother, this bow has taken a fancy to you. You have nudged the dragon from its sleep. Very few can ever say that of themselves. Tell me, did it speak to you?"

One-Li

I didn't know how to answer. What had I felt, or thought I heard? Imagined? Questions ... misgivings? Something had passed, but what? While I stood dumb, lingering echoes rebounded within my skull. Dazed, I could unravel none of it. At least not then. I had glimpsed mystery, but could not articulate it. Nor could I define it. But now, through the bow, I had become part of it. Initiated through intimacy. I turned to Sying Hao. Uncertain why, I said only this, "I have heard the name Liu Bei mentioned among my people, but know little of him. And your teacher, Colonel Sun, the one you call father. You must be sure to tell me more of him, and how the two of you became tied to Liu Bei."

"Yes indeed Bao Ling, it did speak to you!"

The bow became our third companion. Weeks passed as we attempted to fashion our own distillations of its qualities. Sying Hao repeatedly interrupted my work, insisting I yet again scrutinize the craftsmanship of One-Li. Always, I found something missing in my effort, or discovered something new. This had become a deep exploration, and I felt to be plucking needles from the bottom of a deep sea. Insights hidden from normal view. Secrets of genius from ages past. One had to look very hard, and study intently. Hours became days, days grew into weeks. Often, nothing. Then, deep within, what was that glimmer?

He stressed, "You have a masterpiece before you. Use your mind. Deconstruct everything you find. Let others cling to their opinions and their schools of thought. Their philosophies and methods. Your method will be emptiness. A clear and unclouded mind, fully open to what it sees. When it comes to survival, reverse engineering, experimentation, revision, and an impeccable quest for perfection will leave all others in the dust."

Our efforts may have been valiant, but inevitably fell short. The secrets were there. In plain sight, but blended seamlessly into the core of the final construct. There, but not there! An agonizing paradox! To unlock them, one would have to destroy the bow. No sane person would consider such risk as prudent when weighted against the uncertainty of outcome. Sying Hao proved correct on one important point. Over time our study of One-Li improved at least my own skills, to where they approached those of Sying Hao. Though not dragons, my newly finished bows began to take on their own notable character. Progress rewards diligence. I vowed to keep at it, so long as I lived. Who knows? Perhaps the voice within would one day unveil the way.

Typically, once constructed, we would take our prototypes to the wild. We tested them rigorously. For sure there were failures. Some, I would just as soon forget. But Sying Hao quickly reminded, "Nothing gives a better lesson than utter failure." Likewise, nothing quite matches the satisfaction one feels when a bow is constructed to mindful purpose, and the archer confirms the goal achieved. You see, archery is like that. You have a clear purpose. You focus intently. You put your best effort forward, weigh the outcome, then accept or adjust. The discipline demands you remain in the moment. You are only as good as your last effort.

After enough play in the woods, some managed to pass final muster. Those we befriended and kept. They became as equals in our growing fraternity. Each had its name. Lightning, Sting, Dragon Fly, Strong Boy, Feather, Puff, and many others. We chose their titles carefully. Each signifying their measure as we gauged their mettle in our tests.

By combat reckoning, all would have surpassed my best prior work. By practical measure, in the hands of a competent archer, each might deal a lethal strike at 300 paces. Our progress could not be denied. Still, all merely echoed the Dragon Bow.

"Why did he call it One-Li," I asked Sying Hao.

"Well, little brother, it really has no name. One may refer to it as one wishes. Well, actually it does. It whispered its name to me once when I stood alongside Colonel Sun. I thought I was hearing things, but he heard it too! We looked to each other wanting to shout it out. Though we shared a revelation, neither of us could form it into words. At least not in any such way that the name would still have been a name.

"We left it at that. Before entrusting it to me, Colonel Sun was long in the habit of calling it 'One-Li.' No stranger to the workings of the mind, he knew the thought of being downed from a distance of one li would cause any foe to think twice before closing. Whenever possible, he preferred to intimidate and subdue his enemies from a distance. He disdained violence, particularly when it served avarice and favored the few over the many. He wanted for nothing, and had no inclination to impose. He would never strike to harm if it could be avoided. He always opted for resolution over bloodshed. Sadly, like you, we were captives of our self-possessed age. His good efforts in that regard rarely succeeded.

"As an example, he might issue courtesy warning to an approaching enemy. Folks knew of him, just as they knew of Guan Yu or Zhang Fei. The three noble warriors cast long shadows over their times. Their presence had to be taken seriously. Before engaging hostiles, Sun often voiced his preference for compromise and a negotiated equity. He always took care to offer clear paths to that end.

"The alternative should they reject? The promise of his unbridled wrath! Most would read into these offers their own misguided perceptions of weakness. Their thinking? 'Why would anyone offer to negotiate, if they could truly win and take all?' Typical responses would be laughter and mockery. On the battlefield, you could hear them bellowing in the distance. More than once our envoys returned bearing the scent of excrement, showered upon them on their departure.

"Sun would see their return and wordlessly nod, grimly acknowledging his course had been determined by the arrogance and stupidity of others. But still, he persisted.

His final effort to avert needless carnage would typically be One-Li. On his own, he would circle about their encampments. From safe vantage, he randomly showered arrows at the feet of the leaders. Sometimes just as they emerged from their daily duties. These, of course, were warnings. But lest the message be lost, he would scribe characters on the shafts reading 'This is Sun's mercy, take note' or 'Sun gifts your life.' For effect, he might add, 'This shaft found its intended target. Its brother hungers for your blood and will soon follow.' No enemy could doubt his patience grew thin should he say 'Sun never gifts life twice to an offer of mercy foolishly rejected.'"

Dragons Are for Real

"His intent of course to instill fear and uncertainty in the enemy. But it wasn't bluster or bluff. He meant what he said. More so, it underscored his abhorrence of violence, and his desire to avoid purposeless death.

"Ever notice what happens when you pour folks into uniforms. Teach them a few moves. Equip them with implements of sure death. Then label them heroes or saviors. Suddenly, they find themselves with purpose. Something which eluded them in the past. Identity, a new and heady sensation quite unlike the uncertain void which had been their prior existence. An intoxicating brew, one even alchemists would envy. Endowed with justifications of new purpose they can conjure up rationalizations for just about anything. They feel pretty good about it, and themselves too.

"Great generals, all the way back to Sun Tzu[10] knew this well and tapped it to advantage. Provide them proper raw material. They will deliver you a killing machine for the

---

[10] Sun Tzu - Sunzi 544–496 BCE. A military sage. Authored the "Art of War." A classic work oft cited by modern military and business strategists.

small price of a daily meal, a few dangling baubles and an occasional piece of silver. Those transformed will sing your praises till the end of time. They'll study your every word, hail your genius, your diligence, your benevolence, and your power. They will cling to you like suckling piglets, counting on your largess. On your order, they will perform unspeakable acts without question or reservation. At least none which they'll voice. In commitment to cause, they'll trust all will be for the best.

"Sun was different. He was no Emperor's fool. He picked friends very carefully. His mind was clear, like water. Or a mirror free from dust and distraction. In time, word of his skills spread. Enemies knew. Give this guy wide berth. In part, because of that, Sun took it upon himself to extend the courtesy of warnings delivered personally at the feet of his enemies. Some would wisely register the notice. Accept the courtesy with whatever dignity they could muster. It seldom took long to prudently reflect. Before the next day's sunrise, their emissaries would arrive to revisit the possibility of a resolution. One where 'all might save face.'

"Saving face meant the idea would have to come from them. Sun understood this well enough. But he was no one's fool. As a gesture of honest intent over reciprocation, he might well test their change of heart. These emissaries could be invited to prove their good will by cleaning the excrement still caked on the clothing and furnishings of his own messengers. Then they would be asked to remove it from his sight and return it wrapped as gift to the enemy camp from whence it originated. He would then graciously await confirmation of its good faith acceptance. Saving face you see, is a two way street. Whatever happened, the recipient would soon come to intimately know Sun's well honed sense of propriety.

"When efforts proved fruitful, word would spread of Sun's magnanimity. And of course, his legendary bow, memorialized as the reverently whispered 'One-Li.' Enemies marveled at Sun's ability to send clusters of last moment, potentially lethal messages from distances twice beyond what had been previously deemed humanly possible.

"Colonel Sun would say, 'There is much more to this than meets the eye Sying Hao. I have only touched the surface of One-Li's essence. When I hear its whisper, I know there is more waiting to be said. I don't know what all there is to know. Not yet. I don't question, nor do I hope or reach for more. That would be greedy, and I am not a greedy Sun. Dragon Bow and I are companions, just like you and I Sying Hao. We will share all we are meant to share, all given freely and without reservation. Never demanded or simply taken. I will accept what Dragon gives me, and be just as grateful for what it does not.'

"For that reason, Colonel Sun always thought of One-Li as 'a dragon asleep.' Always there, but never fully revealed. He would say that at times One-Li was little more than another piece of outer clothing. Slung casually from his shoulder to waist. Barely noticed, silent and passive.

"Inevitably, there would be moments when in the furnace of hopeless engagement, Colonel Sun and One-Li would stand alone. Abandoned by terrified companions in the middle of a raging battlefield. He told how in those instances, Dragon would spring to awareness. 'Sying Hao, it's as though I'm transformed into Ah Ju Na. The spirit of creation and life itself is beside me guiding my hand and my thoughts as time stops in its tracks. The awakened bow becomes my dragon. Before I know it, I am steeped in its essence, it ... now part of me but apart from me, and yet we, flowing as one. I see the arrows fly. I stand there, dubious yet marveling at the feat. I recognize I am intimate with, and part of what is making it happen. It is me, and I am it. Could it have been any different for Ah Ju Na?'

"I bore witness to those spectacles. Sun, at first impression, vulnerable, surrounded, and certain to be defeated by the overwhelming numbers. Taking root and standing firm, he reaches patiently behind. Reverently, he removes the bow and sets his arrows to front waiting stoically for the onslaught. Listening to the profanities and intimidation amidst the frontal cacophony, Sun marks those who sing most audaciously. He will remember them.

"Their leaders would not dare be so audacious or apparent. Many generals disguise themselves as peasants, or foot soldiers. It's how they survive. But Sun knows to read the words of command on the faces of those advancing. He sees who is who on the threads of weaving movement and changes in their approach. At a distance of one thousand paces, Sun and One-Li spring into action. Arrows flying, propelled by thought and intent to the vitals of their targets. Long before the frontal line primes its charge to overwhelm, dropping bodies clog the path. Gallant but bewildered steeds slip and slide on the bloodied soil. Finally, the death charge begins. With leaders now downed and carnage clogging the works, their efforts become clumsy, chaotic and sluggish. With his exaggerated smile, Sun greets the frontmost foot soldiers. None can match his wind roiling sword. Our own troops, shamed into action by Sun's fearless example, finally charge frontward, and soon envelop Sun in their protective phalanx.

"For those who witness, none can dispute the existence of dragons once awakened from their repose."

Part 3

Favors Extended

Weight of Temptation

"Bao Ling, I must return to the Southlanders for awhile. I owe them for their fine silk cord. The account will only be cleared when I deliver the bows we've promised them.

"You and I already know. The time will come when they'll need many more. With our good efforts as their guide, they'll be able to elevate their own craft to produce weapons of comparable merit. Of course, it's necessary I spend time with them to polish and refine their skills. I'll return once they've taken their first steps and have the basics in place.

"There's something else. I'll have to go alone. You'll be headed north for I have an important task to ask of you. There remains the matter of the bandits' spoils, which we have a solemn duty to return to the rightful owners. I can't be in two places at once, and we can't let more time slip by. You'll have to do it for me. There will be risks. While not wanting to encumber you with more troubles, I must ask you undertake this responsibility on my behalf."

He paused, then added, "Though small by a prince's measure, the brigands' pouch would certainly enrich whoever came upon it. Those who know it's missing will come looking. Keep it from them. Its contents could mean the survival of a clan or a village."

He looked me straight away, for a moment, the fire in his eyes catching mine.

I hesitated, then suddenly thought to recognize his concern. "You're not completely certain I can be trusted. Perhaps that is understandable. I am ..."

Sying Hao interrupted, "Bao Ling. I would trust you with my back, even my life. There are few I can say that of. But from your perspective, this pouch is not just me, or my back. It is you, your family, perhaps your own village, your people and their destiny. Why shouldn't they come first? It is too easy for a man to be honest where there are no tests. Put temptation before him, and ratchet the enticement. Note what happens. Sages of highest character have stumbled under such weight of twisted conscience."

I went to the pouch, lifted it, then opened to look more closely at its contents. Gold, precious stones, ancient jade, and a ransom in ornaments and jewelry. I stared at a particular piece. Green jade. Little more than a pebble, the size of a fingertip. Polished to sheen. Translucent. At first clear, then opalescent as I angled it toward the light. To myself, I whispered, *"One piece of jade such as this, so translucent and green, would secure me for life."* Just as quickly another thought raced through my mind. *"Sying Hao wouldn't know if one small stone like this were missing!"* Indeed, a quick solution to all my problems, and the promise of a life free and independent. I could disappear in the west. No one would ever find me.

I shuddered at what I heard within myself. Am I so weak? How do I quiet that sinister voice within? Is it the same with others? So delicately balanced, a mere feather's touch can push the scale's weight to the other side, tilting one away from righteousness. So delicate, so very delicate. One can never fail to keep one's guard and vigilance at the ready. I must not ever stumble.

I looked to Sying Hao, "How is it possible for peasants to amass such fortune? In my home, I've never seen anything like this?"

"Oh, it's there Bao Ling, just beneath your gaze. Frequently under your nose, your feet, or at the bottom of an abandoned well, perhaps nailed beneath your pedestal in the crap house, but for certain, it's there. Even the poorest and lowest will slice bits off their meager sustenance to cushion against the unknown. Always, to provide for those they love. Each succeeding generation adds to the hoard. It grows simply, almost as though by itself. Usually left untouched, each descending line provides for those who follow. Just knowing it's there means you won't have to touch it. Sooner than you think, some clever families gain their own considerable ballast against uncertainty, famine, or threat of occupation.

"But these particular brigands already knew all about this stuff, and more. They had no interest in occupation. Simple villages were their fields, ripened and readied for harvest. They've been there, done it before and will do it again. A routine so practiced as to become second nature. Their certain key to the villagers' secrets would be relentless brutality. Time always pressing upon them, better the brigands flush out the treasure before their more ravenous superiors arrived. Why settle for the scraps and crumbs? Careful and quick, they slice off gruesome bits of obstinance and determination until all resistance and hope fade useless. Then they reap their grim harvest, confiscating anything of value and easily transported. Afterwards, they leave no witnesses or residue of their deeds. Annihilate all. Those who followed would never know the extent of what passed. Not even their own superiors to whom they would volunteer nothing. 'Some natives resisted. We had no choice but to neutralize them.' That would be their report. Free bounty, no trail of accountability."

I looked to Sying Hao, having myself already witnessed the slaughter insinuated in his words, "Yet you chose to let the bastards live?"

"I am a man of peace and compassion Bao Ling. Before every action, I seek Guanyin's good counsel. That evening in the camp, Guanyin chose not to speak. I listened, but heard only the brigands. I ate as they made light of mutilations. Then drank as they competed and boasted their escalating tales of first violated then reluctantly accommodating maidens, spent, then desecrated and left at the bottom of village wells for others to fish out.

"For them, a great jest. I have little regard for such play, and such banter, whether or not they ring true. Why boast of sins? Could it be Guanyin was equally horrified and speechless? So, I had to think for both myself and the goddess. To that end, I stripped them of their takings. When I left next morning, they were again transformed to warlord slaves, all dreams of salvation and independence gone. Doubtless, once they broke camp and discovered their loss, they would suspect someone among themselves did the dirty deed. I'd no doubt, they would before long be employing those same methods against their once fellows."

My stomach turned at Sying Hao's description. It matched what I'd seen elsewhere, and what had first prompted me to take arms. I looked again at the pouch, brimming with temptation and spearing hard into my soul, touching to my most guarded memories. The horror of it all! Knowing the true lure of temptation, now doubting my own ability to resist. I looked to Sying Hao, "Big brother, perhaps it would be best for you to right the theft, and for me to work with the Southlanders."

He replied, "No Bao Ling. It is clear to me your path leads first to the north and eventually to the east. This may well prove to be your test, and your time. The ultimate fate of the treasure now falls for you to decide. Even better than you, I know you will not fail my trust."

I didn't ask for this! I stared at him and wanted to scream I had reached my limit, and could not be imposed upon to bear more trust or responsibility. But as my wild eyes focused on Sying Hao, I saw for the first time the very same in his gaze. I realized then how great a weight of care and responsibility he had been shouldering this entire time we had been together. Much later, I learned there had been more, much more, which he, from simple courtesy, had kept from my awareness. As I recall that moment, I feel myself to have been a selfish, self centered, and inconsiderate fool.

But such is life. There are no ends of opportunities to learn more about ourselves.

"Bao Ling, first you'll head north from the mountain's base. Then cut eastward. Eventually you'll run into others, then villages, and finally some towns of size. There, you will ask the whereabouts of Crystal Springs Temple. It is well known, and you should have no problem finding your way. Be careful. You'll cross through remote areas, and anything can happen. Remember, the warlords have already dispatched advance troops to scout for threats. You may cross paths with them. A threat, that's exactly what you'll be. A lone man, not bound to the earth or any discernible purpose. A threat indeed! Be discrete, and never forget. Brigands will smell the treasure if you draw too near. Their instincts are keen and well honed.

"Once at the temple, seek out Abbot Shi-Hui Ke. Advise him you are under my dispatch. He will grant you audience and safe harbor. Just so you know, he is a friend and an impeccable warrior, one who has mastered the art of mind over matter. Let no one know your purpose. When you deliver the parcel, put it directly into Shi-Hui Ke's hands, but only when you two are alone. Remember, the temptation from the pouch can turn the most spotless heart sour. This must be a direct transmission from you to the Abbot, trust him to do the rest. Also, since I will be in the Southland for at least three lunar cycles, spend time with the Abbot, if he allows. He is one who has touched the fire of truth. Nothing false can take refuge in him. When the winter moon draws near, return to Southern Mountain and mind things until I too return. Be prepared for all possibilities.

"If things change, I'll find a way to let you know."

Journey North

We parted at daybreak on a rain soaked morning. My trip was the easier, mostly downhill and following the water's descent to the plateau far below. The first two days I encountered no one. My steps paced to the sounds of wind gusting in the trees, the rustle of leaves and the inescapable burbling of racing waters. Brief glimpses of sunlight pushed through the cover and broke the monotony. When resting, I took care to memorize the high country landmarks for my return. Rivers swelled from the unending seasonal rains. Crossings presented challenges, particularly while having to safeguard the precious package.

My third day, on alighting exhausted from a stream, I staggered unexpectedly over tracks from what I figured to be a party of seven. Among them, I counted four pack mules. Wary of their purpose, I vectored their intended route, then cut high and away so I might spy them from above. Eventually, I could hear them in the distance, though they remained invisible under the tree cover. I needed to know more. With the responsibility undertaken, I couldn't risk being ambushed.

Sounds in the wilderness can trick you. Rarely do they reliably indicate location or position. Scent is always the better if you're needing to find someone. Best yet, the evening glow of a campfire, or its long tail of smoke.

I waited patiently till dusk, not risking accidental discovery with unnecessary movement in the approach. Late day shadows had turned their fingers to darkness when I caught odors from the campfire, and the scent of cooking. The subtle glow guided my eyes straight to the heart of their camp. Before night thickened I walked down trail, pretending to stumble directly into their midst. No better way to flush out someone's character or intent. Eyes wide open going in, owning the timing of what follows. My ambush, of sorts.

"Stop there stranger," demanded a voice from far within. Two men emerged frontward with blades drawn and to the ready. Not good. First contact and already a betrayal of mountain etiquette. Strangers were to be decently received and welcomed into a campsite. A custom rarely violated or disregarded. It had to do with rules of survival and hospitality to those in need.

Worse yet, they drew their weapons without cause or provocation. They held jian, the two edged swords oft favored by foot soldiers. Standard warlord issue. They were not of particularly high merit. They appeared to be bronze, hard to tell whether alloyed with copper or tin. One closed upon me, much too close, and pointed tip toward my throat, "State your purpose! Be quick about it!"

"No trouble intended friends. I am a simple woodsman foraging an evening meal, saw your tracks and thought to beg the kindness of your fire to warm myself against night's chill." Hoping to downplay any threat, I asked if I might sit, suggesting perhaps we could barter if they were willing to tender victuals and open a spot by the fire.

"What might you have for us?" asked the hard gravel voice hidden ahead. Unexpectedly, from in the woods to my right, I heard what sounded like muffled whimpering, and then a groan.

"Sounds like your pack animals are wanting your attention." I already knew the whimpering had nothing to do with pack animals.

"What's in your pouch stranger?" asked yet another from behind. He saw my pack tucked beneath the slung bow. But for incidentals, it was now an empty pouch. I had taken the precaution of removing its contents and placing them under careful cover before entering. Should I not survive, Sying Hao would know where to find them from the signs left.

Thinking me too naive to notice, they were already carefully maneuvering, staking positions against me. My instincts scanned all directions for the others I knew to be there. I would have to be quick, clever, and nimble. No margins for error here, or for surprises.

"The good stuff is here friend," and I reached into my pockets to pull out an assortment of herbs, balms, sinew strings, and a collection of arrowheads which I spread in my right hand and held out for their survey. "Take your pick, any three for a meal and a seat by your fire."

The voice behind responded, "I think not 'friend.' We are seven. We are all that stands between you and your ancestors. Again, answer me now! I won't ask a third time. What's in your pouch?"

"Actually friend, I count eight. Your captain to my front concealed in darkness. Your two comrades standing between at angle with jian. Then you to my rear with your Qiang[11] pointed to my spine. Another minds the mules and wares. Two remain otherwise occupied by the fertile meadow."

"That's seven imbecile."

"Oh, my oversight. No imbecile here. There's the muffled but terrified voice of whoever is being held by the two at the meadow."

It gave them something to ponder. Was it just me, or did I have accomplices? How did I know so much about them? I must remember to thank Sying Hao for that.

Just then the one behind touched the razored front edge of his spear to my left throat. Luckily for me, in that same instant, a young maiden came staggering from the bush, bloodied and naked below the waist. The distraction briefly snatched their attention from me.

---

[11] A spear possessing a pointed tip atop a two sided metal blade.

Grim Work

Her barely audible "Help me!" ignited a wave of rage as I flung my arrowheads like razor stars toward the faces of the two to my front.

I dipped rightward, then circled upper body beneath the spear, disappearing from its touch. I stole position and clearance before its holder could adjust and react. Spears can be fine weapons in skilled hands. This man knew only its rudiments, and not how to be quick and efficient should the prey suddenly dart. Turned fully his way, I squared off as my left hand gripped mid shaft, weighting its tip to the ground. My right hand reached forward and lashed for his face. To no avail, he tried to lift his Qiang back to advantage. Weapons are like that, they can sometimes be a distraction. By then, I had already turned my fingers forward into Tiger. Their nail-hard claw like tips raked the delicate membranes of his eyes. He fell back stunned and incapacitated.

I tore the spear from his distracted grip and quick-stepped left foot forward. Its tip traced a circular arc until, like a descending hawk, it touched precisely where his right collar joined to the throat. Turnabout indeed. His panicked eyes showed he knew his predicament. Before he could move, I finished him. How naked stands vulnerability, when one can no longer dominate or intimidate.

My rear now exposed, I pivoted in a rightward arc, dropping my right leg back to where the spearman lay. A space opened before the closing swordsmen. I could see my carefully honed arrowheads had done their work. Gashes and lacerations dripped blood as they trimmed the distance between. Whatever their injuries, they hadn't slowed.

The one on the left threatened first. The tip of my spear met his blade, then snake coiled over. Down and around it went, culminating with an outward flick of the shaft using all my weight and strength. He stared wild eyed as his weapon sailed over his right shoulder into the darkness. I barely had time to backslash when the other drew near. The cut felt to be true, but I had no time to see if I had hit or finished the man. It took all I had to angle right and drop a hard downward knock with the butt end of my weapon against the second swordsman's thrust. His attack momentarily deflected, I parried the staff off the down block and cracked it high against his left skull where the bony birth plates conjoined.

The leader, still lurking in darkness, had by now armed his bow. I heard the touch of arrow against bow and had time just enough to shift his way. My body's turn energized a swing and throw of the spear overhead. Like a whirling scythe, it flew with savage intent on clearing all before it. The move obviously surprised him. He tried to avoid but couldn't. I heard only a glancing blow. Just enough to trim the aim off his arrow causing it to skirt my left shoulder.

Before he could reload, I too positioned into the shadows, my own bow now at the ready. As he steadied for a clean second shot, I quick fired two shafts. Resonating in the dark, two precise thuds, like drumsticks beating on a chest. From where I stood, cloaked in shadow, I could now clearly see his two felled companions. The first swordsman had already bled out. Brain matter from the second dripped eerily to the soil. To my relief, they were done with. Three remained.

"Keep your focus!" ordered the voice within. It startled me. For an instant I hoped Sying Hao had surprised upon all of us. It sounded so real, and so like him.

How about that? Now he had taken residence inside my head!

The two who had designs on the young lady ran deeper into the meadow. For the moment they disappeared, presumably rendezvousing to conspire with the mule tender. I looked to the girl, then stood momentarily in silent listening. Whispers darted about in the distance as my mind tried to glide around movement of water from the meadow for a bearing on the voices. I sniffed the air, gripped the silence, and could almost taste their footprints on soft meadow cover. Then, I sensed their fast approach circling back toward the camp. *"Ah, here they come!"* The scampering of feet told me they had separated and were now converging to lay ambush. I pointed to the girl and hand motioned for her to lay low and cover. She remained frozen, standing horrified and uncertain. Sobbing.

No help there. An ominous symphony of doom emerged as the meadow's sounds combined with the wind and the scurrying of feet over the cadence of maiden's sobs. My mind's eye carefully dimmed the campfire and the surrounds, all turned to void. The whimpering and stream-song faded from my attention. Then it came. On a light thread of air, a barely audible quivering. Unmistakably the sounds of the three breathing tentatively on their approach. Grandfather had always cautioned, "Bao Ling, I can hear your breathing. You are too tense. It gives you away. The enemy will find you, and your reactions will be slowed by the same resistance which makes your breath audible."

I sensed their taking bearing on my person. I stood ready, now intentionally becoming visible to them. A lure calling from the side light of the waning campfire. They split two and one to distract and surprise. But I wasn't about to be surprised! From the subtle intonations of their now more tense and hurried respiration, my mind's eye fixed on their trajectories. I readied my arrows, one set to shoot, two in hand. Three ready in reserve. Fifty paces, thirty … . To be sure, I let go all six shafts, cutting through the brush at mid body. I listened intently. Stillness everywhere.

I closed my eyes and silenced my breathing. I then scanned sound in all directions, focusing my senses to points beyond the periphery. I could hear blood trickling from one who lay silent, and the pleading for water of the other soon to be. The last, a listless remnant soiling the meadow's purity.

I looked to the girl, then away, respecting her privacy. I raced to their mules and rummaged the side bags for blankets and coverings. Finding what I needed, I carefully wrapped the girl in a wool blanket, covering her entirety. With arm around her shoulder I guided her to the fire and set more wood to warm her frozen spirit. She appeared slight and barely to my shoulder, trembling, likely innocent until this fateful day. Yet another wakened abruptly to life's all too senseless horrors.

I set another blanket to the ground and told her to rest. We would need to leave at first light and I would be grateful if she could help with what grim work had yet to be done.

Zhi Mei

At first sign of light on the eastern horizon, I made fire and foraged breakfast of wilds and crayfish.

The mules were loaded with contraband and miscellaneous valuables. No doubt, heists from victims prior.

She awoke. We ate. I told her to keep the blankets. She said they were her family's. We agreed to journey together to the nearest village. There she could decide whether to accompany me onward to Crystal Springs. I assured we needn't part until she had found safe harbor.

"Are you a soldier?"

I felt a need to tell her more, but opted for discretion. "No, just a woodsman looking to spend some time at the temple."

"The blankets were my mother's work, the mules belonged to our family."

I looked to her, "Then, if you wish, I will return you to your home."

Her dark eyes plummeted to the ground, "That will not be possible."

I knew from her hollow stare as she returned my gaze, whatever life she had before now lay behind in ashes.

Almost in apology, I added, "Forgive me, I am truly sorry."

"Me too," she answered.

After some pause and reflection, she eulogized, "We were a happy family, living close with nature's cycles, satisfied in our ways. We wanted for nothing. We took from no one. At sunset and day's end, we would often sing. Some of us would dance. Late in the evening father would tell stories of journeys to the east, monkeys fighting demons, or the trials of the legendary Duke of Zhou. Sometimes friends would visit. We'd have music, or on the best days, opera.

"Then, one morning, they rode out from some sinister nowhere and descended upon us. A day typical in every other respect. Who knew such creatures existed? On approach, they showed no courtesy nor regard for propriety, their designs fast evident. Father already seemed to sense the danger as he first set eyes on them. He quickly signaled to brother who hid me with the family valuables, a pittance really, my safety being their true concern. Brother cut some tubes from stalks then buried me. He instructed I should hold out until I could no longer take air. 'Do not reveal yourself, no matter what happens!' He promised to return when he could."

Her story tailed off in hopeless and confused twists and knots, framed by tears and wailing. I stared helplessly. She dropped to the ground banging her head at my feet, "Please sir, show your mercy. Deliver me to my family. I know they are waiting."

I started to answer my intent to do just that, when I realized from her desperate pleading, she was only asking I dispatch her to the afterlife.

"No little sister, your family wants you here. Even as we share tragedy, they rejoice in your survival. No need to rush things. All lives serve a purpose. Especially yours. They will sit patiently by the celestial shore, watching, and waiting until your rightful time comes to rejoin them."

"But without them, I'm alone, and I'm soiled. All I see is bleak, uncertain and empty, and only more of the same to follow."

"Yes, me too little sister," I looked to her eyes, which lifted for a moment to reveal deep springs of running sorrow beneath her vacuous gaze.

"I am Bao Ling of Ling Village. I will tell you this only once, so please do remember. What happened here, and what they did to you will be forever between us. The things I've seen and done are like stones dropping into a deep abyss, resting forever at the fathomless bottom, riding the back of karma, where no eyes can go, nor ears hear. They will never again rise through me to the light of day."

Her eyes misted as she answered, "I've never heard of Ling Village."

"Yes, it is far to the east in the midlands. It's been some time since I've been home, and I'm heartsick for it. I've been on Southern Mountain these past several seasons, and I've also spent time with the Southlanders."

"And you're a woodsman, and not a soldier?"

"Yes. For now."

That was all the talk she had for then. I loaded the seven bodies onto the mules, and scattered the remains at various points in the wilderness. I trusted nature, and my beast friends of the forest to do the rest. Stripping them clean of possessions, I took care to burn all in the next evening's fire. Their weapons, I destroyed and scattered elsewhere. No need taking chances with armed ghosts of bandits not yet knowing of their demise, plaguing the night.

There would be no traces for snooping eyes. No one would know.

The next morning she was first to wake. The fire was ready and rice boiling. I walked about to scour edibles, found nettle, some quail eggs and cress. Our meal was set.

She recalled how she remained buried alive for what seemed an eternity. Soil and grit had worked its way into her mouth and beneath her eyelids, stretching her concentration to the limits of endurance. Only then did the insects discover her still warm torso, taking full opportunity to explore every nook, crevice and cranny of their find.

By her first reckoning, it was likely only a single day had passed. But her mind quickly turned and she estimated a week. She looked confused. I could see everything had dissolved into twisted fog. She recounted how time had ground to a halt. Moments seemed like minutes, minutes ... hours. She finally reached her limit when she could no long take in air. The weight of soil blocked her breathing to any degree beyond life's bare necessity. She swore of feeling horses, carts, then wagons, passing over her. Unable to hold out a moment longer, she pushed upward breaking through to the surface. She immediately detected the smoke of her family's homestead still hovering in its last lingering earthen touch. Only her heartbeat disturbed the surrounding silence. Locusts, usually everywhere, suddenly become conspicuous for their quiet absence. A short glance to her right revealed the remains of her delimbed and desecrated brother. A supreme hero who had protected her whereabouts beyond all comprehensible measures of human capacity. Father was strung from a post in the distance, serving as target for the intruders' war play. She now realized she had been in the ground only a short while, a few hours at most. Horrified, she ran back to her crypt intending to recover its safety. The villains caught the suddenness of her movement against the background of the endless sorghum. You know how that goes. When on the prowl, be mindful of the whole. Anything which disturbs the field will draw your quick attention.

They were instantly upon her, and from that point, her own ordeal unfolded until fortune smiled and delivered the "woodsman," Bao Ling.

"My name is Zhi Mei," she said, "From the honorable family Mei."

But That's His Name!

"How is it you've chosen to spend so much time on Southern Mountain?" she asked. In our village, we think of it as mysterious, the gateway to the heavens, not a place for mortals. Some tell it guards the great lands to the west and to the far south."

"It would seem destiny dispatched its messenger to me one day. Perhaps karma from my past actions dictated I follow his invitation and lead. Mysterious? No mystery about one thing. I quite like it on the mountain. But my heart remains with my people and my land. When I'm away, I am lessened as a person."

"Yes, this I understand." she said, "Always with my people."

As we prepared to break camp, she asked, "Have you ever encountered the famed mountain spirit?"

"Mountain spirit?" I thought at first to laugh, the question so unexpected. Don't get me wrong, I believed in spirits too. I'd witnessed too many things to take my own skepticism too seriously. But I didn't fear them. No more than I would fear a wolf, or a bear. They too needed to be respected. Acknowledged for what they were, and if possible, left unimpeded. I wondered what precipitated her question, then remembered the gravity of our circumstances. "No, I can't say I ever have. My friend and I have have traveled all sides of the mountain. If something were there to be seen, we would have seen it."

"Your friend?"

"Yes, destiny's messenger, the one who found me. We've traveled a common path for some time. Sying Hao, that's his name, has become like the older brother I never had."

"You said his name was Sying Hao?"

"Yes."

"What does he look like, what kind of person is he?"

"Well, he's about my height, taller than most, well proportioned, and lean. Mature but not elderly, facial hair with chin beard, lined with gray and sometimes a long tailed mustache. He dresses lightly, and travels quickly. He's been here so long, he has clearly become intimate with the mountain. He's acquainted with all its terrain and its secrets. Though custodian to its treasures, he takes nothing but what he needs. He seems to live everywhere about. He's devised a network of hideaways, shelters and cabins always within a day's jaunt from wherever we might find ourselves. He is amiable too, and held in the highest esteem by the Southlanders. Among the wandering monks, mendicants, and mystics, he is deemed a peer. But he is not weak or gullible. Others, of uncertain purpose, would just as soon not make his acquaintance."

"But that's his name!," she said.

"Whose name?" I asked.

"The mountain spirit, the lowlanders call the mountain spirit 'Sying Hao.'"

A concerned Zhi Mei looked closely to me, "You're not a mountain spirit are you?"

I glanced back, smiling at the thought of it, and shook my head.

We continued in silence.

Hooks and Barbs

By third day, we traversed what seemed endless fields of skree. Our tired eyes finally caught sight of the lowlands and smoother passage to our front. The mountain coolness dissipated, and the once constant murmur of running waters faded into the distance behind. We occasionally encountered others: tradesmen, mendicants, wood gatherers, monks, lepers, vendors. And then the suspicious clusters — packs of men bearing arms. Their supercilious gazes studying as if hair were curiously missing from the tops of our heads.

Spying one such pack, I asked Zhi Mei "Who might they be?"

"They're outsiders. Look, see how they're attired. Our people prefer traditional colors, aligning with the changes of the seasons. They're wearing the mud clothing of late winter. They clash with the harmony and spirit of the moment. People here would never be so far off the mark. They come from afar."

"What do you make of them," I asked.

"By how they stare and reckon all they survey, I would not like to be alone with them. They remind me of … of evil people."

"Evil people," I thought *"like mad dogs not knowing their bounds, or respecting the rightful place of others. Always sniffing outside themselves for what might be had. Then weighing the cost and sacrifice to get. Already casting glances our way. Fixating eyes on another morsel."*

She was right of course. I would have to be careful.

Where do such come from? Gather young and naive souls into pliable groups. Corral them where they might get a first taste of power. Throw in a charismatic leader, a few rituals, tests of commitment, perhaps some ideals, a cause, religion or philosophy. Soon enough, they'll take on new identities and purpose, trading in their essential natures — the faces before they were born. They'll be quick to justify their newly refined selfish ends atop their all too pragmatic accommodations to the unknown and uncertain. With safety in numbers and in shared purpose, nothing else matters. All the more sinister if you somehow convince them they act for the greater good.

I suppose it boils down to reality and what you make of it.

In no time, they'll start referring to themselves as brothers, or family. Their leaders become fathers, mothers, patriarchs, or benefactors — and, eventually icons. They justify themselves as the doers. The movers of history, the guarantors of peace and prosperity. Heroes! Call them what you will! What terrible wakes they leave behind. All the worse when they start sporting uniforms and trinkets and create their own tribes or enclaves. By then, there's no way back or out.

According to Sying Hao, Zhuangzi had it right. It takes the highest courage to open into yourself and to swing wide the door for reality to permeate your essential nature. "Stand naked as an infant and get right with Tao!" he taught. "Clear vision is rare. Fear of the fickle moment the common norm!" Per Zhuangzi, greed, fear, uncertainty, worship, patriotism, imperial loyalty, all by their very nature tend toward manipulation. Twisted and shaped, they become barbed hooks for landing the most gullible of fish by the boatful.

Perhaps their unfortunate fate would be tolerable for us, if only they could keep it to themselves. But it's never that way. That's not the nature of their life flow. They come from the land of not enough and push toward the paradise of more is better. They must needs reach ever outward and claw at all others. They take first. Their actions, when successful, stand proof enough for the righteous basis of their cause, all bounds of decency be damned.

Hooks, you see, are set for a reason. To find it, follow the cord back to the guiding hand. It's always there somewhere. You might say it reduces to Yang and Yin. The quest to dominate and control opposing the desire to be left alone. Yang starts the wheel turning. From that first turn, the sublime unity of Dharma polarizes into yes and no, top and bottom, strong and weak, good and bad, joy and pain.

Cycles indubitably ending in turmoil, spiraling endlessly to spawn new worlds of their own.

Until for the weak and the oppressed life simply disappears, leaving only hopelessness and torment. They become like hens in small cages. Bred only to be exploited or consumed. The question begs answer. How to stop the engine of chaos from propelling this ghastly carriage to the waiting abyss?

Of course, I personally struggled with all of this. Often I questioned, "Have I become like them? Just another link in the chain? Have I fallen into the same trap?" If I feared one thing above all, that would be it!

Studying the strangers as we moved cautiously along, I sensed their probing eyes trailing our passing. Just as I felt their hungry stares setting upon Zhi Mei and the four mules.

Usually, within a few steps of my visually acknowledging their presence, perhaps with a nod or a momentary glance into the eyes of the one I deemed leader, I had already worked out their scheme. I saw every available avenue for their anticipated ambush. I had also mapped my response to each eventuality and was confident of success should they make first move. In the final instant of delicate balance, I was determined to be first upon them. I looked to Zhi Mei. She side glanced to me knowingly. A subtle nod struck her bargain to share my fate.

Do Hearts Turn to Stone?

Fortunately, the threat passed. Perhaps they saw something in my eyes.

Clarify threats when they arise. Conclude them successfully in your own head. Ready yourself to play them out. Better than swords, my teachers said. This alone will deter most aggressions.

Can't say whether it's true for everyone. Worked fine for me. Mind can be a powerful ally! Mindful intent that is. Knowing this, Sun Tzu devised elaborate mental exercises. These became cornerstones to his strategic science. Fastidious preparation enhanced one's ability to project intent. Intent in turn motivated chi. Grandfather taught likewise. "Bao Ling. Remember, Chi is the hound; intent, the hare. The one will follow the other. Guide the hare, direct the chi."

Sun Tzu drilled this into his officers. Control the chi within. Manage the chi without. Victory will stand assured. He knew preparation enhanced confidence. Confidence in turn kept at bay the inclination to aggress recklessly. It worked both ways you see. Why battle when you've already won? Why engage when you have no chance.

Why is that you may ask? Confidence unshackles our potentials for compassion, restraint and patience. Loosened, they glide like silent angels racing to service all outcomes. Sying Hao felt strongly about this. "Bloodless victories rekindle hope! Compassion assures karma's unimpeded flow. Much like water continuing unerringly toward equilibrium, our equilibrium. Cutting through mountains of greed and hatred, it runs deep into and through our spirits. Until it seeps through to final clarity and resolution. A judgment of sorts. Aspects of our nature otherwise wasted on fear, avarice, selfishness and exploitation must be let go before they do harm. Can we recognize it if we see it? Do we have a word for it? Yes, we call it Peace!"

Sying Hao made this clear for me. I had never understood the full breadth of compassion. How it bridged all life's issues and concerns. With it, everything became possible including the elusive happiness we all strive for. Be wary. It is not an easy course to find, to set, or to follow.

In my youth, portrayals of Guanyin were everywhere. For humankind, she depicted the essence of compassion. As hardened soldiers came upon her shrine in the woods, they paused to pay respect. What should a child make of that? Murderers and thieves tendering generous offerings to the Bodhisattva of Compassion. Leaving they would spin about with distorted faces like Emperor Yama of the underworld. Once again to dictate the life, death, future and circumstance of whosoever crossed their paths.

In the judgment of my youth, this seemed peculiar. If anywhere at all, Guanyin likely resided within our own spirits. Memorializing her in the form of trinkets, statues, portrayals and shrines took her outside ourselves. Sort of saying, "OK, you're out there. I'm here and separate. I'll go about my miserable business. Wreak havoc, plunder, maim, decimate. When finished, I'll be back to make amends and atone. Here's a few coins for your shrine. I'll tender a prayer for enlightenment and of course for others, then promise to do better tomorrow." Even a child could hear the ring of perversity in this chime. Can not all children? Why not adults too? What happens when childhood ends? Do we grow, twist and split from righteousness? From clear thinking? Do hearts turn to stone?

She and I traded on these matters for several days. For my part, the more to distract Zhi Mei from her loss. Listening to her view on things, and seeing how compassion still guided her judgment told me much about her family and her people. I wondered what would have been. What if I walked the lonely road and wandered one day into her village? Who knows?

By day four, we tired and quieted from our banter. It took enough just to push along. Zhi Mei still carried the burden of her loss. But each day's escalating demands slowly dulled the lingering cuts of tragedy. She proved a stout companion. More than up to the task of overseeing our little caravan and gleaning edibles from homesteads passed. I enjoyed her company, even as we ate in silence.

She had never been to Crystal Springs Temple. It was on the rain side of Toad Mountain. She told of great torrents said to fill the ravines and canyons. Impassable, she said.

Eventually, I caught first glimpse of the clay tile roofed structures. The red barely visible where they nested on a ridge high above the foothills reaching to the head of the Toad. Alone in the high alpine, barely discernable in the clouds. Isolated from the struggles of men and integrated perfectly into the surround. A reminder I knew nothing about Abbot Shi-Hui Ke, and his connection to Sying Hao.

Zhi Mei told of a town at the base on approach. A prominent trade center for farmers and craftsmen of the west. She added discretely, it also served the Shu hill tribes, as if sharing a secret.

It dealt as well with smugglers and caravans moving goods across the mountains from the east. No easy trip. She related a history of painstakingly maintained passages through the heart of the range. For the Han, an imperial trade route. In those better times, the empire had stretched its influence and prestige westward and southward. Those outside the Middle Kingdom titled the patchwork as "The Silk Roads."

Her family's homestead had been several days further north. Remote passes cut through and behind Toad Mountain. Travelers and traders preferred these less arduous routes, though it took much longer. The conglomeration of trails, and passages cutting through the impossible topography had been known within the empire as the Shu Roads. Home to the Shu hill tribes, a network become defunct. Efforts to maintain had been daunting, even for the prosperous Han. The will to continue doing so had simply faded over time.

Taking less arduous routes exposed one to other perils. Among them brigands, barbarians and military deserters. In this land, all choices necessitated calculated risks. Chances taken reflected in degree of return. Nothing came free. Those emerging successfully and relatively unscathed headed south and west. Most skirted her family named village preferring more traditional trade centers. She surmised the seven assailants who pillaged her home came from the east. Portents of trouble brewing had been evident for some time. All grew aware of the escalating westward flow of troops and armaments.

She asked what I knew. I could only answer with a shrug. After Han lost grace with the will of heaven, chaos overran the eastern lands. Initially, there were the two lords. Each claimed rightful continuity from the Han. Then there emerged the kingdom to the south. Remote, but powerful, blessed with resources and wealth. And ruled by a third lord aspiring to the same. Their relentless quests for dominance resulted in complex alliances, constant twisting of loyalties, deceit, treachery, and always, staggering loss. By the end of the first generation, Liu Bei ruled the west. Cao Cao controlled the northeast, and Sun Quan the southeast. Three mighty emperors. Each with a fabulous kingdom already in hand, but needing more. Some righteous in their want, some not.

Until Sying Hao, I only knew their names and the legends of their doings, none of the particulars. They had become ancient history. A faint scribble in recollections among our elders. I made no judgments, explaining to her I still had much to learn. Despite their dominance of the era, all three were gone. In death, they succeeded the Han in their own unintended fashion. In their place, hundreds of warlords roamed the land. Fiefdoms grew from residual crumbs, empowered by clenched fists. Scavengers, taking all they could for themselves. A fine mess indeed!

Part 4

Fortune's Gateway

Two Coins

Water and springs from the Hanshui River irrigated, fed and nurtured the town to our front. An amazing achievement for a community virtually in the middle of nowhere. For that reason, though isolated, it stood well situated to prosper. Its people remained self sufficient in essentials. They flourished by re-supplying endless tides of traders passing through. Zhi Mei said she had family there. By now they would likely know of the tragedy and be wondering over her fate. Perhaps they would have news to offer, and a haven for Zhi Mei. "You can rest before going on," she assured.

We entered at mid-day. Two of us, road worn and leading four tired mules. If circumstance permitted, a clean sleep under dry cover would be a welcome change. On approach, we encountered a road gate with a channeling blockade. Those entering were directed to the forefront of two toll collectors sitting within a gilded portico. In side posts, positioned for trouble, armed guards carefully monitored approaching traffic.

The elder of the two collectors looked me over carefully. An experience wizened fox faced man, he stroked the delicate strands of his thinning chin hairs. His long nails marked him as one of the leisure class. His bent fingers and enlarged knuckles spoke more directly, confirming a history of hard work and trials. I thought of old Iron Hand Gao. The elder's somewhat frayed attire whispered of a one-time academic, or perhaps magistrate. Likely one who had seen better days.

"Do I know you young man? Seems I've seen your face before."

I looked to his eyes, "No sir, this humble drifter would certainly remember having crossed path with one so honorable and distinguished as yourself."

His partner chuckled and turned away at my words. It surprised me. I had not intended ridicule or disrespect.

"Passage is one silver coin."

I set down one imperial token then proceeded. The gate remained closed. I looked to the collector. He clarified, "Per person."

I threw down another, and faced again to the gate. Still no movement. I turned once more to the two, then the fox added, "And one coin for each four legged animal."

Looking at the two I asked, "Six silvers! That's more than I earn from a month chopping wood. Let it be two, and allow this lowly peasant some seeds for an uncertain future. Should I do well, I'll be sure to make good on the four delayed."

He laughed, "A clever tongue young man. I admire that. As to your seeds, I am helpless. You see this worthless bag of flesh beside me. He embodies the very eyes of my lord. As fate would have it, one of my own many nephews. His only responsibility is to ensure I collect what I am obliged to collect, and that I turn the entirety over to my lord-nephew at day's end. Heaven help me should my count not match my overseer's own."

Responding with a modicum of sarcasm, I said, "In that case, we will err on the side of heaven and ensure your continued well being."

I threw down four more coins and turned toward the gate, clearly miffed. The guards, now laughing among themselves, opened the gate, bowing graciously to accent my humiliation. At least the path cleared as I moved forward.

"Young man," the fox called from behind. I turned to see him reaching into his front pocket. He pulled two coins and passed them to me. "From my own purse, two small seeds for your own future. I may be an old fox, but I know a young fox when I see one and am bound by nature to ensure the continuity of our line."

I looked into my palm. They were gold imperials. The watching guards had no clue, likely thinking they were coppers, and intended to salt my humiliation.

The transaction had turned hard about to my favor.

The others, not knowing what had been passed, laughed at the jest on me. To keep them off track, I touched the coins to my head in mocking appreciation and the fox tilted his head forward ever so slightly in acknowledgment.

Upon entering the town, I turned to Zhi Mei, "The town, does it have a name?"

"Yes," smiling lightly toward me. For just an instant, the clouds lifted from her crown, and her natural radiance struggled to push forward. "Fortune's Gateway."

Ah, her first step in return to the living.

I steadied my eyes trying to downplay the irony, then handed the coins to her keeping. "I'd feel better knowing you had some seeds to counter any threat of uncertainty."

She looked at me, expression blank. To an outlander such as she, gold coins were rarely encountered. In a crisis, they might buy a life, safe passage, a way out, or a way in. She pocketed one, then reached back toward me with the other, holding it between the tips of her right thumb and forefinger, with the bottom three fingers unfurled in lotus hand, "Me too."

I held my hand out palm up. Turning her hand over, she dropped it into my palm. I put it carefully away.

It didn't take long to ask among local folk and learn her uncle was a prominent trader in town. They knew him well. Actually, just about everybody in town traded one thing or another. We saw livestock, edibles, beverages, children, gold, jade, art, weapons, currency, and young ladies from the outlying villages — dressed to secure their futures and line the pockets of their sponsors. It reminded me of the now wild east from where I had come.

Might it be their outlying villages had already been raided to nourish the aspiring new masters? I had seen it all before, this marked only the beginning.

The townfolk had no sense of the horrors and sufferings which might soon be laid upon them. These changes can move like a great plague. Sometimes slowly, over the span of generations. Sometimes in the blink of an eye. I feared here, it would likely be the latter.

In my home, matters of life had been relatively constant for as long as anyone could remember. Not distracted by warfare, or the pursuit of power, wealth and influence, my people focused on harmony and peace. They sought the will of heaven, and aligned it with their community. At one with the wind and the water, that's how we thought of it. Feng Shui. It moved within our bones. We embraced nature and all its nuances, including our own roles within. Marveling at the sunlight, as well as the storm. Certainly there were ups, and there were downs. Sometimes the swing of fate went wide, and the deeper downs proved hard to bear. For that, we had compassion, and sharing, and trust that karma's justice though not always understood, would never be false, or indiscriminate.

In my home, the change came suddenly. First outsiders drifted in, seemingly happenstance. Soon after, they were followed by armed bands. We grew accustomed to their presence, and then came the military. At first, companies, then brigades and regiments, finally caravans. In no time, our home was ground to dust beneath the heels of unimaginable numbers. Children were pulled from households to serve, some as armed cadre, some as servants, and some as transient pleasure pets. The elderly, once their resources were depleted, were conveniently done away with, or simply ignored into oblivion.

In still bustling Fortune's Gateway, there existed only the opportunity of the present, blinding all to the sinister beast slithering their way from the east.

Uncle Wei

Uncle Jin Wei obviously ate well. He stood impressively attired in his merchant's embroidered silk gown. Hands nested over a bulbous abdomen, he moved confidently about overseeing transactions, deliveries and arrivals. As we entered his storehouse, I could see his eyesight had weakened with age. He donned a constant squint, and always seemed to be looking down his nose to whatever lay before him. It gave one the impression he was focusing on your every word, but I learned quickly his focus was everywhere. He possessed a remarkable facility, sight be damned, to take in every bit of information his environment had to offer. Unlike the traditionalists, he wore his hair short, and trimmed. At this first meeting, it reminded me of a raccoon, but not one to be discounted or taken lightly.

I stared to Zhi Mei. Her eyes misted as she stepped softly forward. Though facing away and directing the symphony of goods dancing about, Jin Wei stopped and raised both hands palms out. Motionless, like a great bird heartening to a returning breeze.

Perfectly still, as if speaking to the space before him, he called, "Are you a ghost? How can it be? You are here little one? We have all heard of the great tragedy to Mei village, and have searched to no avail for your brother and father. To hell with how can it be! Bless the guardian spirits! Bless the goddess Guanyin for delivering you to us!"

He turned about, eyes delighting upon Zhi Mei, then spying cautiously my way. A trail of tears already traced his rounded chest.

Zhi Mei sped forward into his now outstretched arms, and buried her head into his shoulder.

"Praise Buddha. It really is you little one. For once, I am speechless."

The giant raccoon reached both arms around her in silent embrace. While I stood in the shadows, I sensed his unturned eye staring deep to me, measuring the purpose and reading the heart of his niece's companion.

He called for all in the warehouse to hear, "Shut the doors, we are closed for commerce today. I have urgent matters to attend to. Continue unloading and stocking, and prepare for double duty in the morning." Pointing to one of his runners, he ordered, "Quick, to my home, tell my wife Sao Wei to prepare for two honored guests, soon to follow."

He finally addressed me, "I am your humble servant, Jin Wei, uncle to Zhi Mei, brother to her venerable deceased mother. And you, honorable sir are?"

"I am Bao Ling, of the Ling Village, far to the east beyond where the Hanshui becomes the Yang."

"You have come a very long way. And what commerce brings you here good sir?"

"No commerce, I am a humble wanderer, looking for purpose, contentment and peace," I replied.

Staring to me, he said, "Ah, peace. You have found it here in Fortune's Gateway. But only to the degree you have purpose. As to contentment, time will tell. Do you have any intentions from this moment?"

"My present journey is to Crystal Springs Temple. I plan to stay a bit, then return to Southern Mountain before the weather hardens."

His eyes widened, "Southern Mountain. A difficult place. Wild animals, unforgiving terrain, impossible weather. I hear there's gold, and precious stones are said to be there for the taking by one rightly qualified. Perhaps that motivates your return to adversities most would avoid?"

"I couldn't say, good sir. If those things are there, I haven't seen them. Though admittedly, I have seen some who searched long and hard for them, and left disappointed. For the moment I hunt, work wood, and trade light wares. I wait patiently for peace in the east, and think mostly of Ling Village, and my eventual return home."

I could see abacus beads shifting in his gaze, when he added, "If the call of Crystal Springs Temple can spare you, I would be honored if you join Zhi Mei and my family in brief respite from your journey."

"The honor would be mine kind sir."

"Good, I will leave now and make preparations with my wife Sao Wei. My man will guide you there, after arranging stabling for your beasts. Until then ..."

As he rushed excitedly to leave, he leaned again my way and asked, "On Southern Mountain, I hear there are ghosts. Any truth to it?"

"Most likely, ghosts can be found wherever one looks for them. For my part, I hunt, and travel with my companion and 'elder brother' Sying Hao."

After pausing to consider my response, he reflected, "Sying Hao, you say?"

I almost expected the reaction, remembering what Zhi Mei had told me earlier.

"Yes, Sying Hao I say."

He grunted, nodded, then left.

After tending to our animals, we made way to uncle's home.

Zhi Mei had much to share regarding Uncle Wei. Her mother had passed shortly after her birth. Her father never re-married. It was the three of them. She, her brother and her father, plus seasonal workers who would occasionally share labor, chores, and yields. Uncle Wei loved his sister, and knew for himself the heavy weight of life's sorrow, having lost his first wife and mother of his own children to the lung disease. Zhi Mei said how he would be sure to visit whenever trade carried him to the north. Typically, he arrived with abundant gifts for all, then at day's end would sit in silence with her father, communing over their shared taste of bitter sorrow. Always, next morning, as Wei prepared to leave, he would turn to her father and part with the words, "I envy you brother-in-law. Your life is so much closer to the bone of reality than mine could ever be."

Startled, I replied, "He said that, did he? About life closer to the bone of reality?"

"Yes," she answered, "Is that important?"

"Only in that such crafted expressions reveal much about their speaker's character."

Sao Wei

"You might be right. Father often said there is more to old merchant Wei than first meets the eye. He thought of him as a brother."

"At the warehouse, he mentioned Sao Wei. He eventually re-married?"

"Yes. She had originally been a concubine, and nursemaid to the children. Over time, she proved to have great skill in trade, and a zealous sense for profit."

"A concubine," I puzzled, "In Ling Village there were none, so I'm always curious when I hear of the arrangement. How does the wife come to terms with it? Is there not conflict? It would seem certain to boil over in time. Please excuse my cynicism. Myself, I look to the birds and ducks, simple, loyal, beautiful to behold."

Possibly catching my reference to their monogamy, Zhi Mei glowed and smiled at my response. "Surprisingly, the wife and the concubine got along like sisters. I hearsay there were ruffles at first, but in time, it became clear Auntie Sao's skills and business acumen were a boon to all of the family.

Granted, she lacked the wife's warm and generous heart. Nor did she have the same interest and talent for music and the arts. Her ambition and practical nature, and her careful eye, soon had her standing as uncle's partner and equal in the business. Everyone recognized her contribution to the family's well being. All respected her role accordingly. We would often joke how the smallest nat could not pass her scouring eye unnoticed."

"Doesn't sound like my kind of people," I responded.

"Perhaps" Zhi Mei replied, "I always keep in mind two things father said about Auntie Sao."

"Now you've caught my interest." I looked to her, impatiently waiting for the rest.

"He made it clear that when wife number one was on her deathbed, she turned to uncle and gave her blessing. He must promise to wed Sao, lest his lonely heart use him out."

I wondered, "And how could she see that as heaven's will."

"Father also said, 'When you try to unravel the puzzle of Sao Wei, remember. Inside that woman runs a heart as big as the Yangtze.'"

The home's exterior marked well the status of its occupants. Simple, elegant, clean lines, not overstated, but nonetheless substantial. On entering, we were taken to a cleansing area. We washed the road dust from our bodies and servants took our belongings for cleaning and storage. I never place my bow beyond quick reach, and was careful to keep close the brigands' treasure pouch as well as some blades alongside. That done, it was good to relax in steaming water. For once, no thoughts of concern, at least for these few refreshing moments. New clothes and a phoenix robe were brought for my change. An invitation to dine soon followed.

As I entered the grand room, Old Wei was seated at the head of the table, an empty chair to his right. He signaled I come beside him. Sao Wei sat stoically to his left, and Zhi Mei, adjacent. Wei had grown sons and daughters. They had also entered, filling the balance of spaces.

Jin Wei looked to Zhi Mei, "I must apologize, not all your cousins could accommodate our short notice. I'm sure you remember Lee and Qiao, and their sisters Ting and Mayleen."

Zhi Mei stood to acknowledge them, whereupon they all left their chairs and rushed to her. They touched, embraced and then as quickly glided as one from the room. Amidst chiming calls and responses, I overheard their trying to get a handle on her miraculous re-emergence from death's door. I knew she would be discrete.

Jin looked to me and suggested, "It looks like we'll be delayed a bit. Let's take our own moment to relax. Maybe a smoke, as Sao attends to the dinner and final finishings."

He nodded to his wife, "We'll take a few moments. The children need this time."

She nodded politely, stood and stepped away. I noticed her discerning glance my way as she turned.

As we arose, he raised his arm leading me to the right. I heard the sound of water and after a few steps saw a side-wall opening into a central courtyard.

There were springs feeding a pond, and the sparkling water gleamed with bright colors of cultured carp swimming lazily about. I had heard such fish existed, but their brilliant appearance and colorations far exceeded my imaginings. Birdsong filled the space from all directions. Only then did I take in the careful arrangement of cages, blending so naturally into the surround as to be nearly invisible.

"Please feel free to feed and entertain our fish," Wei said, pointing to a baked clay container with assorted grains and dried insects. "They are quite friendly."

He lit two pipes, sharing one to me. It was a sedative blend, I could feel its effects as I returned to standing after hand feeding the little rainbows.

"It's an herb we have growing in the wild. Some varieties are used for rope, some for fabric, but there are some which make for a very pleasurable smoke, especially at day's end."

I looked to him, "I have seen this, my people call it 'ma' and sometimes use it to flavor their foods. Particularly during evenings when song and dance promise to follow."

"No song and dance for us," he replied, "Just easing life's tensions as we let the cousins have their moment."

We sat in silence, the sound of water eddying through the pond, then gently exiting along the downside rockery over carefully set colored stones. My mind returned briefly to Southern Mountain, and then, through time's tunnel, to Ling Village, and better days.

"So, you and Zhi Mei travel together with her family's mules?"

"Yes."

"Their farm was decimated, burnt to ashes, nothing left alive, nothing of value remaining, all possessions and animals taken. I saw it myself. The same fate fell to others in proximity."

"Yes, I have heard that too." A nightingale began its melody, delicately floating it upon the wind gliding in with the scent of distant trees. I refilled my pipe. Dinner seemed to be taking longer than I anticipated. Curious, I peeked outside over the courtyard gate. I found an adjoining back alley, seemingly a world away. Suddenly, the stately head of Sao Wei bobbed as she hurried by beneath me, caught off guard by my unexpected stare as she returned from some unknown dispatch."

The Will of Heaven

Wei continued, "We searched for Zhi Mei of course, and found nothing. What little remained gave us no hope. We uncovered where she had been hidden. Her brother and father were no fools. Again, nothing! Then we saw what we took to be her footprints. Close by to where my nephew made his noble stand. We found shards of Zhi Mei's clothing. Signs she had stood ground briefly. Of course, we concluded the worse."

"Yes, there could be no other conclusion."

"But Bao Ling, sometimes what happens turns far worse than our darkest imaginings."

I knew what he was getting at. "Yes uncle, sometimes far worse."

Jin Wei stared hard at me, probing past the reflections of life in my eyes, studying corners where more might be gleaned. Coming up empty, his gaze returned to front and he allowed, "Perhaps what is worse than our imaginings should be left to conjecture?"

I answered, "Or forgotten."

The cousins burst suddenly upon us with oldest son Lee inviting. "Come, dinner awaits. We can talk more as we dine."

Dinner of course was as sumptuous as anticipated. It spoke well to Sao Wei's skills of oversight that such a feast might be prepared on short notice for two unanticipated guests. For a time, she stood in a far corner of the room, watching silently as servants laid full the table. Conversation centered on Zhi Mei, and her miraculous reemergence. At Jin Wei's beckoning, we began circling the food and selecting from the generous array of offerings. While I marveled at the trays, my attention remained on Sao Wei. A smile barely graced the front of her normally taciturn countenance. For a moment, I softened toward her. She had used all her skills and devices to make the event "right," with no compromise taken as to the well being of her husband, and his, now her family. It reminded of my days back at Ling Village, standing alone and apart, but ever watching and prepared to act.

In that sense, we were kindred spirits.

Before long, the conversation turned from Zhi Mei's return to what is now known to have occurred in Mei Village. For me, it constituted an old tale. I had seen decimation, senseless desecration, abuse, and abandonment. The burnings, the bodies, the violations, dismemberments, defecations, enslavements, thefts, purgings, and the unending flow of purloined goods from one set of hands to another in an endless chain of exploitation and abuse.

Not unexpectedly, I remained silent, preferring to listen intently.

Wei turned to me, "And you, Bao Ling, what do you make of this?"

I reflected, then turned to Uncle Wei. I don't know why I said this, they came to me in the moment. Words from a deep well. As I spoke, another part of me stood aside and listened intently to what poured from my mouth.

"In the Classic of Changes, Ge represents the condition of fire in the lake. Revolution ... a new order. Today it marks our lives. This influence comes and goes with the passage of time. It leaves no specific or immediate answers. Just questions and befuddlement, and the clinging need to find clues lest it fail to resolve.

"How can fire be in the lake? A condition counter to nature. Why it's no different than trees growing with leaves in the ground, and roots facing the sunlight. A new order? Perhaps, but who can find nurture in this mess. Where is the shade, or comfort, or the song of birds. We can ponder heaven and the celestials, and contemplate their involvement in our affairs, but fire in the lake goes beyond their influence.

"You know, it is we who make it this way. All of us. Why is that? We're here with free will and judgment. We have the ability to see deeply into such matters, but are forever distracted by reflections glistening on the surface, particularly ambition, greed, skewed philosophies, twisted beliefs, fears and emotions. Laozi spoke clearly as to these factors. So too did the Buddha. We honor them and praise their words, yet fail to recognize. Honor too can be a reflection — a distraction. Their words were not placed as artifacts for our fawning and praise. They were directives on how to free ourselves from all reflections. Guides to unlocking our world to its full realization."

Cousin Lee laughed uncomfortably, shaking his head, "You've lost me. I'm a trader's son, and happy with my lot. I have studied the works of Master Kongzi and struggle to uphold the moral life. I am honest and fair in all transactions. Is this your fire in the lake?"

His younger brother Qiao broke in, "Bao Ling needs to speak further. I'm interested in where this takes us."

Looking to them both, I assured, "I mean no disrespect to your honorable endeavors. Father Wei asked my thoughts. Normally, I hold no opinions. At least none I would be comfortable sharing, lest my ignorance push too far frontward and I embarrass myself. However, the least I can do to mark my appreciation for your hospitality is to respond with true respect, sharing what I have gleaned from my experiences."

"Go on Bao Ling," Qiao encouraged, "I am a fish caught in your net."

The girls exchanged glances, acknowledging Qiao's playful impudence.

"It seems at times the will of heaven is not about us, but about change. What we see as moral or righteous conduct, though commendable, no more represents heaven's will than does the plague, or hordes of locusts. The finger of heaven which touches us is felt only in change. What we make of it is up to us. Nothing we do can detract from, or add to heaven's will. The dance of change takes care of itself, and eventually, everything else. It happens within us and without us and when we seek to harness it to our selfish ends, we only seem to get in each other's way."

Cousin Lee responded, "But Bao Ling, concealed in your words is the conclusion we somehow transgress or wrong heaven by doing business and accumulating wealth. Perhaps we are among those you feel are in the way?"

"No, my brother, heaven lies beyond our ability to offend or to wrong. I cannot speak to what you do or do not do. I only know what I know for myself, and that I struggle to move in accordance with heaven's flow. Perhaps with compassion and right action, we will both find ourselves already buoyed in its eternal grip."

A Way Stop for Ghosts

Sister Mayleen added, "You mean like Monkey, when he tried to jump from the Buddha's palm. Monkey catapulted to the four directions, to the winds and outreaches of creation. When he looked again, he was still standing in the eternal hand."

While I had to think on her words, old Wei nodded in proud affirmation. No doubt appreciating what he deemed his daughter's poignant contribution.

"And what of the Han," chimed in sister Ting. "Were they not important to heaven? Did not the Emperor have heavenly status. It's fostering?"

Sao Wei intervened, "Yes. The Han. Hundreds of years of stability, prosperity, art, music, philosophy, trade, growth, influence, education, science, consolidation of our threatened borders, and keeping our enemies at bay. Certainly, there is much to commend in their achievements. How can it be in the end they were not the incarnation of heaven's will. Would you say their miracle was an accident?"

Looking to Sao and Jin I responded, "While I have not mastered the classics, I have had some slight exposure to their messages. Mostly as related by Sying Hao. Sometimes by other masters of his acquaintance when they passed our way. They know much more of these things than I. Hearing your affirmation of the Han, they might ask, 'Where are the Han today?' Hijacked by eunuchs. Imperial succession passing to child nephews. Child nephews assassinated by overseers sworn to protect. Torn from grandeur into three contentious domains. Supplanted by a reign of lawlessness and anarchy. Warlords and once sworn vassals continually stake out what they can if only to ensure their own influence and preservation.

"Perhaps they too believe themselves under heaven's munificent smile as they take what they reckon to be theirs. Does heaven have more than one face? I judge only from my experiences and could be wrong. I believe nothing is certain but for the assurance of change. Empires will eventually fragment, then crumble. Chaos will eventually coalesce, then aggregate. A Han of another name will in due time emerge. Meanwhile, the Ling's and the Mei's suffer. Generations are lost.

"And what becomes of the kings and emperors? In the far West, legends speak of endless columns of ants marching beneath heaven's timeless gaze. Each one, once head of an empire."

Sao Wei turned, her normally intense expression now more directly focused on me. "I am most interested in what you can tell us of events from the east. What do they portend for us?"

I related my life in Ling Village. "We lived in close contact with creation, and with each other. Though isolated, simple people have their measures of art, music, philosophy, skills, stability, influence and trade. Integrated into a tapestry rooted in the continuity of time. Our people had a sense of oneness with everything, every moment leading to another. They sang as they worked, played, or congregated. Silly I know, but true. Fishermen spoke to the fish. Rice grew in fields which felt like extensions of our homes, more so our bodies. Comfortable everywhere, we enjoyed the involvement necessitated by our toils. We knew there would come times for rest and life's simple blessings."

I noticed a tear dropping from Zhi Mei's lowered head. She tactfully wiped with the back of her sleeve glancing again toward me, expecting to hear more.

"As to enemies, generally there were none. In fact, we were of little interest or consequence to outsiders. Excepting perhaps the occasional tax collector milking some warlord's due. Strange as it be to some, you might say our meager existences gave us great joy. Aging and death held no threat. Our elders possessed skills of a lifetime and our esteem. They served as store for our knowledge, engaging their later years sharing with the young what they knew. From them I learned herbs and remedies, as well as internal fundamentals, proper movement, and the properties of physical objects."

Cousin Lee interjected, "Properties of physical objects?"

"Yes. Weapons studies and martial arts."

"Why a need for that in your patch of paradise?"

I shook my head with some uncertainty, "I'm not sure I have good answer to your question. Certainly we had our gods, our ancestors, and our shrines. Most importantly, we valued awareness, and harnessing one's awareness to heaven's will, in effect becoming one with change. We felt this would ensure our liberation from distraction. I trained frequently with elders to that end, and reveled in what they were able to share. True, we studied the fighting arts. Still we abhorred violence, and all which went with it.

"You are familiar with the book of changes I am sure. Our elders consulted it regularly. They weren't so much looking for answers. Living one's life on the basis of an oracle is a bit like surrendering. Worse yet, using it to chase after desires tends toward selfishness. But as a vehicle for insight, and seeing things in all dimensions, it cannot be surpassed.

"You can perhaps imagine their consternation. There came a time when the readings shifted from benign inclinations to portending ominous developments. Our elders were baffled. Uncertain outcomes lay ahead. Were these portents of disease? Of locusts? Floods? Nothing showed with certainty except dramatic change, rolling in like a wave from the north. Our simple minds lacked the breadth of understanding to imagine the scope of horrors to follow. When the evil tide struck, we were powerless to resist its sweep.

"It manifested as a never ending deluge of warlords whose minions scraped the land to raw dust. We became fuel and feed for the insatiable appetites of their battle engines. The elderly were systematically eradicated. Youth were used, violated, and exploited. In no time, Ling Village became a way stop for ghosts. We held tightly to what we remembered of the old, unable to let go of what no longer was. Some, like me, resisted, trusting it would eventually pass. But what passed were the years. The occupiers, whoever they might be in any moment, tagged me as a threat. It was humorous to behold, one savage troop came, then left, replaced by yet another. It was as though the first told the second all about me, if only to ensure I remained isolated and adrift."

Jin Wei looked to me, "So, you became an outlaw?"

"A matter of perspective perhaps, or twisted words. I survived in the wild. Others succumbed. Some remained in the villages and surrounds, scraping what they could. Thankfully, they were careful to leave food and articles of living where I could find them. In the beginning, survival on my own was hard. Isolated, deprived, sleeping cold or wet for months on end would try anyone to their limit. Luckily, just when I felt I could tolerate no more, I sensed a change in how I processed and experienced the continuing challenges. Fact is, I began to enjoy the extremes. Unexpectedly, I drew strength from the endless trials. In time, I learned to accommodate my newly honed habits staying out weeks at a time, or longer. In spite of contrary odds, I found comfort in challenge. What better opportunity to perfect what I had learned in the village regarding herbs and wildstuffs. Forced by necessity to integrate with the land and its subtle bounties. What meager skills I first had in hunting, gathering, and fishing were perfected of necessity."

The Stripes of a Tiger

"By then, wayward bands had overrun the province. First they took the crops, then the livestock, then the young. Finally the children, and whatever meager pickings remained. The population lay gutted, left with nothing but their memories, and perhaps the fact I and a few like myself were still out and about. Rightly or wrongly, some counted our continuing resistance as their only glimmer of hope for the future. Am I an outlaw? One should first tread my footsteps before judging or opining. I have no secrets. I'll tell what I did, you decide for yourself!

"After establishing refuge in the wild, ofttimes I stole secretly into villages, as well as the surrounding towns and encampments. I needed to see for myself. The occupiers now used everyone. Good folks just like us sitting here tonight, fodder for their longings. Could none among them simply say no? Enough! Weren't we all cut from the same fabric? How could a few weapons, an occasional coin, a uniform or an insignia so poison a free mind?

"As I trust you all appreciate, at some point I could no longer remain meek to the relentless onslaught. As fate would have it, occasions arose where I came upon something amiss. A homestead pillaged, a matron abused, livestock stolen. It seemed my karma had already primed me to intervene. The first instance, there were several — I forget how many, they were already setting fire to the pitiful hut as I found them. I could hear the screams and wailing within. No doubt, they thought to make quick end of all of us. But it was not to be. On that day, it was their karma to confront their own ancestors in headless shame.

"Such episodes repeated, at first sporadically. Mostly as I happened serendipitously upon the scene. But it became too much to bear. Deciding to do more, I began to lie in wait, anticipating, scouting opportunities to act, to ambush. Their numbers were many of course. The oppressors ever multiplied. So too did their ambitions, rapacity and sordid proclivities."

While I spoke, Sao Wei nervously reached into the breast fold of her jacket and passed a paper to Uncle Wei. She leaned to whisper what only he could hear, and he glanced to me. I saw a provincial seal on the form. From long experience I knew it to be an offering of reward. Could she indeed be so treacherous? I turned discretely to Zhi Mei. She was blank faced and confused by my look of concern. I glanced for a moment toward my bow, and shafts, which I had taken care to place strategically nearby. She didn't miss it.

Jin Wei motioned for me to continue and gestured for his wife to hold as he listened.

"Efforts against these hordes could leave one questioning the usefulness, or the point of resistance. Neutralize some, there were always more. One army left, another entered. Warlords driven out by the Imperial forces, then befriending them. Then both being driven out by the Western Armies, soon again by the Southern. But wait, here comes the North again. Finding there's nothing left, they leave. Finally, the bandits come and scour for crumbs. The few natives who remain try to re-establish life. It is little more than a gesture, a last reflex of lingering habit.

"Legend has it, the only constant through it all remained one, or perhaps he was more then one. Identified to be the 'Dragon of the Midlands.' In time, this Dragon emerged as nemesis to all but those righted by birth to the province. Convoys disappeared, bands of soldiers were reportedly assassinated. Recovered contraband magically returned on its own to the locals, sometimes deposited conspicuously in the heart of town squares for all to bear witness. I personally didn't see any of these things, but the tales spread everywhere. In no time at all, smiles began to show again on the once oppressed faces. The wronged had a hero and could see the oppressors had sampled their own bitter brew. The table had turned. Now it was they who found themselves unsafe on the roads, or in the darkness, even in the latrines. There were no ends of stories regarding their vulnerabilities."

Cousin Lee questioned, "And you were part of this."

Zhi Mei looked to Lee, then to Sao, uncertain where this thread might lead.

"I never drew arrow or blade to anyone, who had not first drawn on me, or on some other innocent. To the extent of my ability to control, I would walk by or away. Does it surprise they read that as weakness, and considered it an enticement?"

Lee asked, "Are you so skilled no soldier can take you down?"

"Hardly, but in a crisis, I am of one mind, and frequently lucky. Some might say clever or quick, but I think luck plays the greater part. I'm sure you know what I mean. Isn't it the same in your world of business? You see, being of one mind, everything I do is with certainty and with complete abandonment. I always expect death. Sometimes even hope for it, or at least an easier life. Brigands travel in packs, and always have their many minds to contend with. Within their groups, some dominate, some are weak, some ambitious, some with loyalty fading. None expect to die, or want to, or stand ready to. Especially when facing a humble woodsperson like myself holding a wild yew bow, and lightly armed to boot. They saw me like they saw everyone else."

Lee reminded, "Fine, but what does this ultimately have to do with us, in this remote outpost?"

"Don't you see Cousin Lee. Bao Ling tells us it has already started," Zhi Mei broke in.

Qiao added, "But Zhi Mei. A warlord's army can't make it through the mountain passes. There are simply too many narrows, and canyons. Our trading partners struggle to get through with their simple caravans. Many have to turn back. It's all been tried before. The story is ever the same."

They looked to me for insight. I said only, "Fire in the lake. The wave of chaos has embraced and overrun the eastern provinces. The three kingdoms are long depleted. Still we have no clear victor, and no end in sight. Those who remain now look elsewhere to replenish. Like locusts, they will devise ways to circumvent obstacles. Mountain passes, thin trails, and narrow bridges alone will not stop them. Not if they have you in their sights and plans. It's an instinct for them. Persistence! What you are beholding now is just the beginning. Look about, you can already see their vanguards.

"I speak as a witness. That's how it unfolded in the midlands. First a few strangers passing through. Curious about everything. Watching, measuring, counting, assessing. It might seem a curiosity to some, but like skilled tailors, they take your measure and report to superiors bent on tracking all which can be conveyed to their purpose. Should somehow your locale gain the scourge of their attention, the numbers will become evident. First, bands of five to nine, usually armed, and scouting the four directions. They will not be as polite or proper as the tailor-spies who came first. There will be incidents, perhaps of violence, or intimidation. Your allegations of misconduct to their chieftains will of course be disputed. There will be a price if you raise your voice too loudly. Their superior officers, after all, have their own agendas. Like a noxious wind, their numbers will mount and almost before you register shock, they will set upon you in multitudes so formidable your own world vanishes. All you can do is hope to grasp for survival. When the overlords arrive they will pose as princes, kings, emperors, sages, and heroes. Those left among your people will in time bend to accommodate, perhaps sing their praises and honor them as liberators, paragons of virtue to be emulated. What do they know? Not doing so means death, imprisonment, or deprivation. It is part of Yama's cunning trickery. The zenith of his cleverness, our tribute and accolades given his agents while they deliver us to death's door."

The others now sat silently. Regrettably I had turned the celebration of Zhi Mei's resurrection into a forum for my own pain. Perhaps I had been away from people for too long.

Jin Wei, staring at the parchment passed to him by his wife wondered, "How much time is there, really?"

"I believe you know it has already started. The perfume of what you have beckons their attentions here, as well as to the south and west. Whoever occupies first will have the mountains at their back and the advantages of time, natural obstacles, weather, and the seasons as they replenish and regroup. Fortune's Gateway will undoubtedly feel the tread of their hooves."

Qiao looked to me, "And you could see no way to advantage this situation to your end? You seem clever, and clearly have gifts. No less than Sage Fa[12], at the gate, has

---

[12] Fa Miu - "The Fox" who Bao Ling encountered on entering the town. In another book, *Master Li Confronts the Wei*, he appears as a younger man, and is key to the events of the story. Here, he is a much older, lessened, but wizened by his years and past experiences.

spoken well of you, inquiring as to your purpose and asking who might know of you. Maybe a fit can be found, surely you might serve their lacks and accommodate your self. Get a footing, develop plans, find allies. You might stay here. I'd welcome you as a brother."

"Brother Qiao, I must now tell you the most important thing you might ever need to hear."

He asked, "And that is?"

"A tiger who paints his stripes to gold, is no longer a tiger. My destiny is Ling Village. There I will make my mark. I seek nothing more from life."

The Parchment

Jin Wei nodded toward my bow in the corner. "Is there a reason your weapons stand ready, even as you join us for dinner?"

"The reason Uncle is habit. A huntsman always remains close to his tools. On Southern Mountain, and elsewhere in the wilds, there are many hazards. Carelessness invites trouble. I have learned to keep ready, having them always within two steps reach. Please forgive my idiosyncrasies. I mean no disrespect. It's just my nature tends toward caution, and clings to long worn habits."

Seeming to understand, he met my eyes, "Else a tiger would not be a tiger, or perhaps a dragon, not a dragon?"

He stared at the parchment delivered by Sao Wei. Zhi Mei rose from her seat, then timidly walked behind to where he sat. Looking over his shoulder, she also studied the parchment. She looked my way, a hint of sadness in her eyes.

"Five hundred imperial pieces of gold offered for the capture, or head of one Dragon of the Midlands! Look here.

He goes nameless, but is believed to have once lived in Ling Village. At least before turning into a bandit, murderer, robber, assassin, and rapist." Incredulous, he continued reading aloud. "And, he has fornicated with animals in the emperor's stables, and is believed to have had a part in the provincial regent's death. There's no telling how many he's killed. According to this, he appears to have stalled Northern Army liberation efforts in their campaigns to the south. Mind you, against the very Southerners who have also apparently posted their own bounty. Only the west has been spared from the wrath of this demon."

Catching my eyes, Jin continued, "One could be set for many lifetimes if he had the determination and skills to bag this prey. That's your neck of the woods isn't it Bao Ling? Have you ever crossed paths with this Dragon of the Midlands?"

"No sir, can't say I've ever met him, nor had a desire to. Despite that, I can tell you with some measure of confidence he has the regard and support of most everyone in the midlands. Excluding perhaps the transgressors, and their puppets."

"Would you be included among his supporters?"

"Truthfully, I never give him any mind. I know he will do what he does, and that like me and everyone else, there are reasons for his actions."

"According to this, Bao Ling, you are about his age. Like you, he chooses to live afield. Do you suppose it might be someone you know? Can anyone be so deviant? Better question, can any single man be so sublimely skilled as to draw the wrath of an aspiring empire? Actually two empires? What do you make of his being a murderous bandit, or pervert, assassin and rapist. Certainly not traits to profess his having any higher calling?"

"I would trust he could answer for himself as he saw fit. Those asking would be wise to listen. You know, as do I. Truth seldom lies in proclamations. The supposed higher calling of the 'liberators' from the north, you will soon enough have opportunity to witness for yourself. Their advance agents and scouts already mingle among your own townspeople. I know their look and their way and with what I saw today, there can be no mistaking. I tell you from what I remember in the east. When this so called Dragon went about his business, the warlords and their minions kept to the safety of their camps. Their once unchecked overreach to the surrounds stood effectively sealed and contained. Lives were spared and saved. It also bought time for those needing refuge, or escape. Proclamations of evil aside, most people would prefer his simple good will over the lure of those offering gold or influence. You do understood, it's one thing to offer, another thing entirely to pay."

Lee, now also looking over Jin's shoulder noted, "See here! An archer without peer, master of the dragon tail blade, always with weapons at hand. Treat as dangerous, make no attempt to communicate or detain. Notify authorities immediately. Reward contingent on capture or demise."

Zhi Mei interjected, "Remember cousin Lee, ofttimes one hides one's own faults and failings by declaring them the proclivities and perversions of adversaries, then brewing potent stews of slander."

Lee continued, "Look there's more. On other occasions, he single-handedly took on bands of armed troops and cavalrymen, sometimes numbering five or more, and dispatched them readily. Sounds a little like Guan Yu to me. Whoever he is, five hundred pieces of gold might not be enough. Though it would certainly accommodate one through this existence and guarantee endless diversions in the afterlife."

I told Lee, "There are no five hundred pieces of gold. The promise might just as well be the moon. It's simply a ploy to get between him and the many. Without their support he can not continue, or survive. Should one somehow lead them successfully to his lair, and should gold be put into the informant's hands, by same day's end he or she would already be dead. The gold would end back in the coffers where it would remain. It's not something they relinquish readily. Who or what would they be without it?"

Listening intently, Zhi Mei soon connected the emerging pieces and patches into her own quilt of comprehension. A slight trace of a smile brightened her gaze as she looked mischievously about, "Well this I can tell you. Had we relied on Bao Ling's skills as an archer, we would already have gone hungry before this evening."

For a moment, silence, then everyone seemed to relax.

Returning her smile, I added, "Fortunately, Zhi Mei has Uncle's gift for commerce. She was somehow able to materialize each day's fare, bartering among homesteaders we passed. I'm a much better trapper, but it takes time and patience, and we did have to eat. I am grateful for her cleverness."

Sao then looked to me. She of course would not be so easily diverted. "Perhaps we should have Bao Ling meet the magistrate. Any leads into this 'Dragon' fellow would certainly be appreciated. If not rewarded, at least some degree of recognition might accrue."

Jin Wei looked to her, fully catching his wife's calculation, and said nothing. For a moment, the raccoon looked to be an emperor. With a slight tilt of head, communicating with a language of nuanced glance developed between them over a seeming lifetime of mutual endeavor, he signaled her to let the matter go.

Making sure all could see, he tore the parchment several times over, then walked to the far room where he relegated the remnants to the hearth. Returning to the table, he said for all, "We will not trouble Bao Ling further with this dragon business. Nor will we risk distracting his purpose by invoking the magistrate. I don't know how, and I don't need the details. He did what we could not, and brought Zhi Mei back from the beyond. Newly risen like the Phoenix, part of our lives has been restored from the dust. We owe him. From this point, I call him nephew."

Zhi Mei, looking to me in relief, clung to Jin Wei's arm in welcoming the gesture. Sao looked at the two, alone in the moment, when Zhi Mei then turned to embrace her aunt.

Our spirits lightened from that point, and we sat for hours. I listened quietly and with great interest — eavesdropping as the others talked family, business, life, and aspirations. Uncle Wei quietly passed a pipe or two, and for the first time in years, I felt surrounded by friends, and family.

Fighting off my tiredness, I lingered late, wishing the evening to never end.

What Do Birds Know?

Next morning, I awoke to find Jin Wei tending his birds in the courtyard.

He turned to acknowledge "Do you like our feathered friends Bao Ling?"

He had quite a collection. Set about like flowers on display in their generous cages, they complemented the rockery and the meticulous plantings. Bird songs floated atop murmuring waters reaching everywhere within the surround. How this contrasted with the chaotic clamor of early morning trade and commerce spilling in from just outside.

"In my youth, they were part of our daily lives. Always among us, no cages. They lived in our thatched roofs, as well as stables. They visited our tables as we ate, and we often shared. You could hear them in the trees, or in the tall grass. They were everywhere. As you might imagine, birdsong filled our mornings and evenings. Grandfather relished opportunities where he could stop everything and simply take it in. He would pause whatever occupied his concerns to listen intently and with reverence.

"He said their songs drove the changes of seasons. So too did the croaking of the frogs and the chirping of the crickets. Ever curious, I would ask he explain. What did he hear, or take from it which made him believe they influenced the seasons? 'Everything, Bao Ling. It's all in their song. More power than we could ever imagine, or hope to take in. And you don't have to be selfish about it. Just a taste can lift your spirits to lofty heights!'"

"I hope your people didn't eat them." He looked to me with some concern, likely acquainted with the ways of sustenance farmers. And the dictates of survival during thin times.

"Well, we tried our best to live in harmony with the elements and with all life. As you know, life is said to root in fire, earth, air, water, and metal. What springs from those elements sometimes falls beyond our ability to control and to reconcile. We respected all life, including that of our feathered relations. But never forget, they are part of the ebb and flow, the coming and going, the taking and the yielding — as are we."

"Never an easy answer from you Bao Ling!" he barked. Looking now more lovingly and protectively at the birds, "What the hell are you trying to say?"

"Yeah, when times were tough, we ate birds."

"Barbarians!" he declared.

"Here, please humor this barbarian and allow him to help tend your little angels."

Wei nodded, grunted, and passed some seed and implements.

Old Wei noted the young man's quiet skill and grace as he moved from cage to cage. He would murmur to the creatures, and it seemed the sound of his gentle voice drew them closer. When later recalling this to Sao, Jin Wei swore all the birds in the yard suddenly fell silent. "They stepped delicately to the edges of their cages where they could more carefully scrutinize this stranger as he moved about. Recognition? They seemed to know him! No, that would be impossible!"

More likely, cuing in on familiar patterns of movement long forgotten. By then, skeptical old Jin Wei began to register with interest the flow inherent within the young man. He moved about easily, freely, like water, everything integrated, seemingly continuous, taking many forms, as though nothing were in the way. It reminded Wei not of a man standing, or walking, but almost of a bird in flight. Most astonishing of all, according to Wei, when Bao Ling finished he turned to the courtyard and spoke to the feathered angels. "Now, will you sing for me my friends." At those words, a wave of sound filled the yard. Bao Ling sang too, recalling for all of the host present the simple earth songs of his people.

Wei thought and then attested to his wife, "This young man is no barbarian. Nor is he a murderer, thief, or rapist!" On hearing what happened, the usually cautious Sao Wei felt compelled to agree. She had often said, "One can learn a great deal by studying how birds react to others in their presence." She too had acquired the standing habit of escorting her intended business associates into the courtyard, and seeing how the birds would or would not take to them.

Walking with Uncle

After a quiet early meal, Jin Wei invited we take a
morning walk, "We can see what's going on. Perhaps talk in
private. Get better acquainted."

I saw now how Wei's residence stood near the great
circle, heart of everything in Fortune's Gateway. From here
he could keep close eye on its commercial pulse and
whatever else was going on. We exited Wei's quiet enclave
into an explosion of bustle and activity. It took barely a
glance from me, but I could see what I knew to be soldiers
curtained in merchant's clothing. Seven of them, positioned
strategically at market corners. Spies! Taking careful
measure of trade and traffic. Sent here to identify the
players, and the triggers for wealth and persuasion. Further
along, I picked up the movement of supply wagons, larger
than those of simple trade vans. Suspicious, but not quite
foretelling imminent military incursion.

"Bao Ling. Tell me, what brings you to Crystal Springs
Temple?"

"Sying Hao, my elder, has asked I run an errand on his
behalf. He would have preferred going himself, but had

affairs in the Southlands to address. That business will likely keep him there until season's end. Our plan is still to winter together on the mountain."

"Winter on the mountain? Is that even possible?"

"Certainly, if you're a crazed barbarian."

Uncle Wei rolled his eyes. A signal one should not take his proclamations so personally.

"But what sort of errand would require you take on a risky journey as this. Surely he has considered the uncertain times?"

"I am to deliver something to Abbot Shi-Hui Ke."

"What might that be?"

"Truthfully Uncle, it is best you not know."

"What, am I not to be trusted? You don't think old Wei can handle himself?"

"Not at all sir. Sying Hao's business is Sying Hao's business. He asked I deliver a package with instructions to Abbot Shi-Hui Ke. I am bound by my word to Sying Hao to guard it's secrets. Just as I would guard yours, if so instructed."

"Ah, then it would seem you don't know it's contents or purpose. Let me tell you young man. Always know what you are carrying. Acting as someone's gullible go-between invites no end of trouble. When questioned by authorities, you alone are bound responsible for whatever you have in your possession. Saying it belonged to someone else, or you didn't know what it was or that you were only doing a job for someone only makes matters worse."

My look to Wei made it clear I knew what I had. "No gullibility here. I am bound to guard its secrets with my life. By doing so, I protect you, Zhi Mei, and your family."

For once, Wei held his tongue.

After a brief lull, Wei took up a new topic, "I must ask your opinion on something. In probing the tragedy at Mei homestead, we could not help but notice other troubling developments. Surrounding homesites had also been violated and despoiled and we learned of others murdered. The entire countryside adjoining was pillaged, not unlike what you described last night from your past. I remember thinking packs of wild beasts had arbitrarily descended. No rhyme nor reason! It made no sense: brazen and barbaric destruction and death. I've seen wolves to have more conscience than that! Judging by degree of disruption and evidence of movement, the invaders came in numbers. How many we can't determine. We saw no evidence of armies, or masses of troops. Our conclusion: several independent bands acting loosely in concert. But under whose authority? It begs explanation. I am not a military man and these remain mysteries to me with no easy answers. What can you say to this?"

"With due respect Uncle Wei, answers often stare one in the eye. Frequently formed in the very questions themselves. Still, they may not be discernible if your thoughts focus elsewhere. I have seen what you describe, many times over. The explanations are invariably straightforward. Armies on the move thrive on chaos, death and disruption. Not on tending birds or sowing fields. They have an infinite capacity to turn the substantive world we know into ash. Communities empty and become hollow shells. Smiles and once lively eyes become vacant and stricken. Like Yama's steeds, legions of war require constant feeding. Sucking all fortune, resource and life into their bottomless gizzards, they drop ash out their asses as monuments to stupidity. These of course become in time their very shrines.

"I suspect they fanned outward from the mountain passes and positioned their vanguards. Next, they coerced tribute or premiums from surrounding villages for 'protection.' Then they systematically eliminated those who resisted, even while begrudging admiration for their very obstinance and courage.

"Initially, periodic stipends will keep them out of one's way. While their sights settle on less fortunate others, there'll be precious time for you and yours to discretely sneak off. But of course, stipends soon lose their capacity to distract. With each passing week more requisitions come. What had once been adequate now falls far short. Demands escalate, becoming more brazen. There'll be notably less tolerance for explanations and delays, or pleas for reasonableness. Family heirlooms, stored gold, wife's jewelry, valued stores, eventually all go to feed the beast. Is the hunger appeased? The beast sated? Of course not! Livestock and essential foodstuffs become final prey to their endless requisitions. Picked clean, once prosperous villagers are reduced to eating grass and insects and scraping the bark from trees. Hanging by life's meanest threads, they expect the intruders on finding the well run dry to move on, taking their wanton glances elsewhere and away from now depleted coffers.

"Not so quick! Yama guides their hands and swords while their hearts kowtow to greed, ambition, and lust. He whispers, 'More can yet be had. Only for the taking!' Daughters are sold off, sons are conscripted, elders left to rot. The untended land is all which remains. Working the soil with their own hands means nothing to them. Not a productive engagement of their time and martial energies! No upward mobility there. In response, the land sits vacant and untilled, tendering its own judgment on what has passed. Where crops once flourished, dust runs off in the wind looking to escape.

"Given his long view from experience, old patriarch Mei likely understood the sinister read in all this. Doubtless, he resisted from the first, as did his peers. Regrettably, their karma put them square into Yama's gaping jowls, though their principles never wavered."

"Where do you fit into this?" a troubled Wei asked.

"I don't. At the moment I am running an errand. In the time ahead, destiny will return me to address the spoliation of Ling village and Jing province. When, or how, I don't know. I simply believe and, like the dust run off, wait expectantly. Today, I am bound to do a friend's bidding, as he would have done for me."

"Ah, I sense somewhere inside that riddle filled head of yours Bao Ling, there exists a plan. Care to share it?"

"As for plans, there's nothing for me to share. I want nothing from life but my home. Simple and humble though it be. Let the fools with ambition play their grand mahjong, I refuse to partake. I'm not in any game, certainly not theirs. Plans? None. Purpose? Yes. There is a toll to be paid for delivering chaos when other ways were readily available."

"What other ways?" Wei asked.

"Community, compassion, service, humility, caring, fairness, restraint. I could keep going if you wish."

Wei interrupted, "Heaven help us, now you're a monk. You'll be in good company at Crystal Springs Temple. You know, you and Zhi Mei are two birds of a kind. I'll grant you this though. It's her most ingratiating attribute, just annoying as hell. For me, I do business. Each day is a new battle! Chaos is the sea on which I sail. My duty is to survive, and to secure my family. There is little beyond that which draws my attention."

"Where does that leave your birds?"

"Let's not go there. You know what I'm trying to say. Besides, they're family too."

"That's where I struggle Uncle Wei. I see everything as family. For me the stakes are always high. I too know the duty to survive, and to what I consider my family."

Troubling Matters

Taking measured pause for reflection, Wei nodded his understanding, then continued. "If I may impose Bao Ling, I'd like to inquire of some other troubling matters which have come to my attention. You may be able to shed light. They remind of what you said at dinner, and your comments regarding Dragon of the Midlands.

"Not too long ago, small companies of armed men began passing through. They were disciplined, and fierce in demeanor. Not knowing their purpose, the townsfolk gave them wide berth, hoping they would simply move on without making trouble for anyone. We've learned to avoid crossing paths with tigers. We have our own constabulary after all. But their arrival coincided with the changes, at first so subtle, then more blatant. You probably dealt with the toll gates and guards at town's edge. It doesn't make sense. You can't do commerce at arm's length when you pick the pockets of clients as they come through the door. That started more recently, again after they came.

"They first arrived in small bands. Their numbers were few, trivial. Just passing through. So they said, and did. At first it meant nothing, that's how it's always been here, nothing so unusual as to draw our concern. The land beyond is vast and untamed. We trade and facilitate. We've learned to respect privacy, and to do business at arm's length. Questions get in the way. Their leaders arrived soon thereafter. It all seemed so benign. Manageable, if you catch my drift. Now, they are slow to leave, and many are inclined to linger far longer than their commerce or proper welcome dictates. I feel uncertain, wary of these developments. You may ask why do we tolerate this? You know Bao Ling, much profit can be had in changes. For merchants, uncertainty often means opportunity. So long as one is quick, gets a good read on the circumstances, and is able to deliver. But there are always risks. That's my worry! Our own leaders, including myself, sensing threat as well as opportunity, reached out to accommodate and to integrate with these new influences. You do understand? It's how we survive and prosper in this remote outback."

A polite acknowledgment, then a nod, with no untoward reaction.

Wei continued, "New accommodations and alliances arose almost daily. First the formalities, then the ceremonies and the socialization. Their chieftains became frequent guests at the homes of our elders, leaders, and magistrates. Now, some are nominated to be on our courts, while others have begun to appear in our constabulary. For the life of me, I don't see what qualifies them, nor why our leaders don't object to this. Worse still, why don't I object to it?! Am I so gutless? The townspeople murmur constantly. Perhaps being at the bottom of the press gives them a clearer view of what's rolling their way. I just can't say! New dispatches and movements have become almost too regular, with our humble city transitioning into what is becoming a logistics home port. For what? Who knows? Yesterday, I learned of marriages being arranged. Can you believe it? Locking our elite by familial tie, into the yet undeclared intentions of these interlopers.

"The goings on in the east have made it all the more difficult to chart a reasonable course. We've been through these things before, many years ago. When I was a child, a great master[13] called them out for what they were, and made it stick. Now their progeny return. With the breakdown of central government, and the fragmentation of the Han Empire, it's no longer clear who has authority for the region, the province, and now even our humble city. Until this moment, we've always managed to stand on our own. The Han have been dead in place for several generations, even longer, and we are left with only their ghosts. Whatever authority and structure exists today merely echoes what once was, but begs for new masters. Suddenly, new faces, wielding might and flaunting power, emerge in our midst. Before new seasons turn, our businesses are paying tolls and security taxes. Now, with what happened to Mei Village and others like it, we can't help but suspect their thugs are out there ravishing the outlands. Where will they be sticking their noses next?

"I tell you, the spirits of our ancestors take offense to this. I want to share something curious which came to my attention as I recently sought audience with the Minister of Justice. On entering the tribunal I passed through what

---

[13] The heroic stand of Li Fung can be found in our earlier work, *Seed of Dragons*.

must have been a brigade of troops. From where, I don't know. Representing who, I don't know. In charge, absolutely. Those inside were holding what appeared to be several squads, perhaps numbering twenty in total. They faced charges of theft, hooliganism and murder. As I waited patiently, the constable read the list of charges, and I took careful note of the particulars. Apparently, this crew was entrusted by their lord overseer to secure delivery of proceeds from collections and field activities, whatever that meant, encompassing our region. I understand it was a very considerable sum and consisted of coin, gemstones, precious metals, and jade artifacts. One can only imagine how they came by them. The coin I can understand, they've been picking our pockets for some time now. But the gemstones, precious metals and jade? Well, we know that comes from only one place, the hidden folds within the hind pockets of victims.

"I'm speaking with you about this because I can't trust anyone else. Wagging tongues draw unwanted notice. Also because it turns out their path crossed through Southern Mountain. As you well know, whether you admit it or not, a place where ghosts and spirits roam freely about. Two days into the mountain, they set up camp. Everything is perfectly normal. Nothing happens, not a thing is seen. There is no attack or engagement. The package rests securely with their leader who wisely positions himself at camp's center. The bundle is not once removed from his tent, where he reports to have carefully hidden it beneath a boulder as added precaution.

"Next morning, it is gone! No tell tale signs the boulder had been moved! Nothing was disturbed! The perimeter had been guarded vigilantly the entire night. Having no better explanation, the leader accused members of his own band, at first one, then several others, of theft. His squad members turned upon him with skepticism, one firmly speaking for all and voicing their combined protest. He then summarily lost his head, as it so happened to be attached to his wagging tongue. This proved too much for the others to bear. A mutiny unfolded among them, and in no time, swords were drawn, bowels opened and throats slit. After getting an ample taste of their own medicine, and deciding it not to their liking, they had the good sense to stop their nonsense. The headsman ordered they would all return to Fortune's Gateway where they would submit the mystery to be resolved before appropriate authorities. He felt certain the culprit remained in their midst, and said as much. They agreed. So long as they kept together the wrongdoer would be flushed out. The flushing would be left for their superiors to perform as they saw fit."

Mystery Solved?

"The headsman reported all to his lord. He, knowing the delicacy of the matter, as well as the risk to his own head, immediately petitioned the Minister of Justice to get to the heart of the affair. Preferably, if possible, to get to the missing treasure. No stranger to the subtleties of political calculation, the esteemed Minister of Justice found reason enough to worry over his own head. You understand how that goes, I'm sure.

"Well, you can bet I listened as their tale unfolded. The Minister I know to be a clever man, and can attest he has straightened some very twisted trails and tales in the past. He questioned one, then the other, and then the next. Astoundingly, they agreed on everything raising no arguments, protests or disputes on the facts! Nothing was ever found in the possession of their now dead buddies. Nor was anything found in the camp or the surrounds. None disagreed on any of these points! They searched everywhere, everything was exactly as it should have been. There were no intruders. No one else came into or went from the camp. Before they returned to town and before killing themselves off, they negotiated a tentative truce. The leader, accompanied by others selected by the group, searched every parcel, pouch, orifice, and animal, as well as every bit of clothing. Nothing! At the conclusion, the roles reversed and the leader along with with his aides also succumbed to full search. Again. Nothing. So they all swore! They knew for certain, the only explanation was they still had it! Just as they knew for certain it had disappeared!

"Now you understand Bao Ling, rumor has it these are not nice people. Heaven only knows where they got their treasure. For me, the message is clear. Trouble looms too close, and will follow to wherever this trail leads."

"Uncle Wei, sounds to me like the trail leads here, and the trouble is already upon you."

"Just a second young man, let me finish. So the magistrate, after hearing all sides, takes a break from the session to deliberate in solitude. Flabbergasting everyone, he returns in surprisingly short order to announce his conclusion."

"He knew what happened?"

Uncle Wei stopped, turned directly to me, then stared hard as though he knew I already knew.

"Well, what did he determine?" I asked.

"Just two words Bao Ling. The magistrate returned and said there was only one explanation for what had occurred. 'Sying Hao!'"

"Sying Hao?" I gasped, feeling my blood drain to the ground.

"Yes Bao Ling, Sying Hao, who everyone in these parts knows to be the spirit guardian of Southern Mountain. He and his army of ghosts have roamed the mountain for generations, and they are very protective of it. It's not the first time a disappearance like this has happened. Others have gone before, and never returned. Nor were they heard from again. Scouts, squads, companies, once even a brigade attempted to cross through one of the passes. Their mission to 'clear' the mountain of 'squatters.' Take that to mean they were tasked to fleece the prospectors. They returned to their barracks two months later, drained and starved. Some ranted mindlessly how they were forever going in circles, as though the mountain were some kind of maze. Seemingly possessed, they reported. Their comrades laughed and spat on them. Their superiors said nothing beyond executing a few to set proper example. Spirits, Bao Ling. They mock us. But I don't criticize them. They pick and choose their prey carefully. There are just as many woodsmen and foragers such as yourself, who seem to have no problem at all on the old hill.

"Which of course leaves my question, now begging all the more to be asked."

"Yes, Uncle. You wish to know more of my elder brother, Sying Hao."

A look of satisfaction shaded red across Uncle's face. His chin lowered as his eyebrows raised in anticipation.

"Not much can be said." I could see old Wei already rolling his eyes and looking away.

"Maybe it would be best to share a bit of my history with Sying Hao. You saw the parchment yesterday. Whoever this Dragon of the Midlands is or was doesn't matter. We match in age, and general appearance. Anyone reading the description might think it to be me. Like this Dragon, I refused to become yet another slave to warlords and overbearing military commands. I refused to hitch my survival onto the pain of others. In a different world, apart from being on the dealing end, any of these scoundrels could have been me, my family, or my friends. Instead they chose to oppress.

"I wasn't the only one who refused. To the credit of my people, there were many others of like mind. In short order they were targeted and eliminated. Some for being who they were or for what they said. Some, mistaken for this Dragon of the Midlands and choosing, for only heaven knows why, not to deny it. Those in power were taking no chances. Anyone remotely fitting the profile was deemed a threat and terminated. I'm sure you see where this leads. Dragon or not, my days were numbered. It was for that reason I took to the wilderness. But rather than simply survive, I began to resist. We spoke of that last night.

"It was during this time, while in retreat and using the opportunity to hone my skills, a stranger came upon me. He actually caught me unawares, no mean feat! Had he been a foe, I would have been finished! We shared the day, and in no small measure, he proved his remarkable skills. His facility with the bow far exceeded mine. Because I enjoyed his company, we portioned our meager foodstuffs and shared a joyful evening meal under the stars. We became quick friends. He had no links to the warlords, nor to the combatant armies, and told of his home on Southern Mountain and its isolation. Though content with his solitude, he fretted over the state of humankind outside his sanctuary, thus explaining his inclination to occasionally wander about. Checking up on things if you will, hoping to find the never ending stream of violence had begun to subside.

"Of course, it hadn't. Sying Hao is a brilliant scholar, mind you. He chose to walk about and try to get his reasoning around the many threads of greed and ambition driving the chaos. He didn't have to do this. He was searching for answers, for solutions. Wanting to make a difference. On finding me, his quick mind recognized my predicament. By next day, he voiced his concern my days were numbered if I remained. He invited me to journey with him to Southern Mountain. 'Only until the evil wind blows over,' he said.

"But now, it seems I have lost track of time, and Southern Mountain has become like a second home for me. Sying Hao, who started out as a friend born of necessity, became a constant companion, then a confidant, and eventually a brother. But, above all, he gave freely of his knowledge and skills without reservation, and I have gained much. In his arrays of huts, caves, and hideaways, he has collected scrolls and writings on almost anything one might conceive or imagine, and then some. I can tell you he has studied them carefully over his time and knows them well. Everything is tactile to him, at his fingertips. All able to be delivered with a touch, a glance, a turn of the head, or a thought. In our constant days together, he advanced my martial skills to levels I never dreamed of. Honestly, I can't tell you how he did it. Being with him is like being with the temple Buddha, covered with its gold leaf. Touch the Buddha, and part of the gold leaf rubs off on you. That's how it is. Sticky stuff. Something happens between us, and part of him jumps to me then stays. In our travels, he also took every opportunity to broaden my understanding of the medicinal plants, and the healing arts, and I once accompanied him to the Southland. Those remote people think of him almost as a bodhisattva.

"I will share one peculiar thought with you. When I look back to how I first crossed paths with Sying Hao, I felt at the time we met by accident. Knowing Sying Hao as I do now, I don't think he succumbs readily to fate. Nor do I believe his destinations to be happenstance. In retrospect, I would say he sought me out, met me, measured me, then thought I deserved saving."

Jin Wei playfully mocked, "Ah, so the mountain spirit is now your savior?"

"Savior? Not! For me, he is truly big brother. I could stay there forever, and never tire of his words or his lessons or his company. I am but a peasant, happy with the simple things, based on the ways of my people. Sying Hao has shown me possibilities without measure or limit as to how one can realize oneself, and yet not be slave to greed, ambition, power, lust or fear.

"Though he assures I can stay so long as I wish, he and I both know destiny calls my eventual return to Jing Province and to Ling Village. There, I will set the seed of promise straight, where once again it will sprout clean and free from within its native soils."

Jin Wei lightly stroked his chin, then looked to me, "So that's all there is to know? But there is so much more swimming about in the broad spaces between your words."

"How so, Uncle Wei?"

"Well, the name 'Sying Hao.' To us in the north, it identifies a spirit, known to have roamed the mountain for as long as I or anyone can remember. In fact, the hauntings associated with the name came long before my time, and perhaps well before the time of my grandparents. Please, humor this old man for the remainder of our walk, and allow me to share our legend of the man on Southern Mountain."

Wei pulled his pipe from a vest pocket as we agreed to take the long route around the town.

Part 5

A Ghost Legend

War Orphan

As we strolled leisurely along, old Wei recounted the local saga of what he called the ghost from Southern Mountain.

"First, Bao Ling, I'll frame the happenings. I'm told in his youth, Sying Hao lost his entire family in a terrible battle. Consequences of war, as they say. Stupidity, say I!

"An officer from the noble Shu army rescued him, then took him under his protective wing. Guilt over the carnage perhaps? It happens. One cannot shut conscience to such things. His benefactor assumed the roles of guide and protector. The boy learned the martial arts and associated military skills. His mentor trusted these would assure survival should he no longer be there for the child.

"But soon enough, all realized the boy had potential far beyond that. His instincts and cleverness brought him quickly to the attention of the first minister. The minister was a close friend and frequent confidant to the officer. Many believed him to be a great wizard. Some say, an immortal. The boy thus came to have two fatherly influences. Each, in his own way, carefully cultivated and protected the youth as together they all traversed the vicissitudes of the times.

"He grew into a warrior officer of the highest caliber, as well as an esteemed tactician. His knowledge, acumen, and counsel brought him recognition and wide acclaim throughout the land. It surprised no one he drew the attention of the Western Emperor. The first minister might have been part of that. Before attaining full manhood, Sying Hao had become first counselor in the royal court. His influence was great. As you can imagine, all feared his disfavor and courted his grace. Senior officers in the other kingdoms took note. Perhaps they thought to turn his loyalty.

"But power and influence did not suit him well. As always, the greater Empire leaned toward conflict, cycling in and out of it as it had for thousands of years. Long united — must divide, long divided — must unite. You know how it is. Nothing is static. Whatever is, can not endure. That remains the great tragedy of our life experience, but also the basis for our unending hope things can be better.

"As remains the case today, four primary classes drove the empire. First, the farmers. All depended on them for the essentials of life. Then the soldiers and their officers. Those on whose backs fell responsibility to make real the visions and dreams of their Emperor. Or whoever's rule they followed. Next, the intellectuals. Survivors of countless batterings of challenges, debates, arguments, and internecine strife, upon whose judgments the policies of state hinged. Valued only so long as their influence held sway. Lastly, the aristocracy, in theory at least, ruled absolutely by the

Emperor. The supposed divine center around which swirled all constellations governing affairs of the kingdom.

"Oh, perhaps we should include the eunuchs. Not quite a primary class. Rather like venomous entities forever roaming beneath the floorboards of the Emperor's household. Slithering about where no armies or loyal guardians might protect his back or his exposed vitals. Shall I also throw in the concubines and their endless webs of ploys and ambitions? Let's agree to stop here. The list will only grow if we pay it too much mind.

"Sometimes it seems like everyone wants their piece of the play. You see Bao Ling, in some ways, you and that Emperor have much in common. Both of you bobbing in your own seas of uncertainty, sucked in to other people's games. It's just that you're on the shat end of the power spectrum.

"Sying Hao's stature as first counselor gave him no joy. We're told personal woes troubled his mind. The passing of his wizard father and sage teacher for one. Alas ... not an immortal after all! The sudden and mysterious disappearance of his warrior father and mentor for another. On top of those profound losses, evidence lay everywhere that the once great and noble state of Shu had begun disintegrating into itself. He bore direct witness to the lingering essence kicking its death throes. Only a few more gasping breaths while the world surrounding quaked and crumbled in its own unwitting demise. Go figure, will you! There was no purposeful reason nor justification for it all. At least none I can discern. Three powerful empires came and went. Each wanted what the other two had. No outcome, no resolution to anything. Nothing accomplished! All that energy and commitment, wasted! If they had used it to tend crops, we'd all be fat now! If I were judge, I'd say this fall of empires just boils down to consequences, and how they are laid haphazardly onto the backs of the people. Then, at the top of my voice, I would proclaim them all 'Guilty!' for the unforgivable crime of blindness by choice.

"So, it doesn't surprise me. He longed for the day he could be 'finished.' Assured of the Emperor's blessing and 'Well done, counselor!' then released to mind what he deemed most warranted his attentions. By then, he had grown to maturity. The creases of middle age started to settle upon him. Others had preceded him in his post, and others would be eager to follow. But the ceaseless cycles of birth, growth, maturation, decline, suffering, and death promised to continue. No matter who minded the state. Was this what first brought Siddhartha to despair? Was this what the Buddha came to know and somehow resolve under the Bo tree? Years came, years went. If the pain of it all were not so consuming, it would simply have been laughably boring.

"Eventually, affairs of state fell to momentary quiet. Not for want of determination, greed, or ambition. Lulls in fighting can not be avoided, no matter how unwisely we prod forward. Resources simply become depleted. Can you imagine? Everyone starving. Relieved nonetheless by the respite. Because for once they can walk about without being robbed, raped, pillaged or skewered! Seizing that opportunity to take leave from the Emperor, Counselor Sying Hao departed the court on good terms ostensibly to enter the Temple. To his lasting regret, the Emperor reluctantly assented."

A Spotless Mirror

"He found temple life austere, and simple. A marked change from the always accessible pleasures of courtly surround. While cloistered he studied the Tao, and the life of the Buddha. He immersed himself in the classics and spent days in deep meditation, searching for the stillness within. The inner calm would free him from all distractions and doubts concerning the very purpose of his existence, in fact, all existence.

"That would be nice wouldn't it? Now you know why I do business, and choose to raise birds!

"Before too long, it became clear the way of the Temple was not for him. You see Bao Ling, in many ways, this man was spotless. Perhaps he had perfected the ability to see into the core of all things. What can one say? A great talent for sure! I'm a practical man. You have to be to succeed in business. I like to think he found the same intrigues and plays for influence within the temple and among its enlightened ones, as he had within the court.

"It's my belief, these things go with the creature and not the setting. We are what we are, in the court, or in the temple. We like to tie ourselves into knots, then ponder philosophically our plight. Then we look for quick release, relying on crutches like endless meditation and the choreographed art of doing nothing to free us from our predicament. Despite what had been promised as certain, for him the meditations and rigors of temple life distracted from inner peace. Same as had the pleasures and gratifications of the court. Of course, behind it all remained the riddle of his missing adoptive father, a supreme warrior who appeared to have simply vanished from the face of the earth. A riddle which tormented him to no end. Maybe that best explains why his ghost still lingers. I never learned how the riddle resolved.

"With the Abbot's permission, he returned to the world. The Abbot gave his blessing, explaining that 'Each must define his own course. In the Tao, all paths have great potential to yield merit, and sometimes fulfillment. Just stay the course.' Which meant I suppose, finally stumbling upon what your were looking for all along.

"He journeyed far to the south. To no one's astonishment, disease, hunger, the oppressive rages of war re-ignited everywhere. For him, much like rediscovering old acquaintances, but for the worse. You know what I mean! The kind of friends who always seem to find you, but you would prefer not to have around. I suppose these things spoke more directly to him and were visited upon him by karma for a reason. One day, he came upon a headless corpse lying unburied in a body strewn field. This triggered what the Abbot might have described as an awakening. Enveloped by the stench, he eyed the vermin veering from his gaze within the corpse's armored encased cavity. With absolute clarity he connected how his once well reasoned counsel to the Emperor had set into motion a long ripple of events. Events which led directly to this lifeless shell lying at his feet at this spot at this precise moment in time.

"Have you ever noticed just how long the tail of our actions can drag behind us? Is it no wonder we sometimes trip over it? Or stumble from the drag of its weight as we struggle forward?

"He vomited of course. He had done so before, nothing new. Except for this once he expelled the vile poison which had long touched his soul. Cynicism! What he needed was compassion, real compassion! He saw now how cynicism had taken over and become his great burden!

"It felt as though he had lifted from his body. Was he ever a real person? Might this all be nothing but a dream? Couldn't this simply be a 'lesson' from the Tao? Yes, *'I must be dreaming,'* he thought. In the stream of sunlight, he saw his face's image staring back from the breastplate. *'It all makes so much sense now. This man, his fate, the connected web of doings and dealings. I, and the Emperor, and the ebb and flow of state are all one and the same. All independent, yet links forged by fate and strung by destiny onto a common chain binding all. Leading inescapably to this.'*

"As though awakening from a dream, he bent forward to touch what remained of the rotted corpse. But the harsh edge of stench cut deeply into his senses and snapped him right back to reality.

"This was no dream!

"Thinking then to his days at court, he wondered. *'Why couldn't I see the full run of our actions when I was the Emperor's counselor? What good was my learning, my years of training, my dedication to the absolute if in the end, we find ourselves here?'*

"Having respectfully buried the hapless footman, he continued his journey to the western outlands and then to the remote south. After a long period of wandering, and deep retrospection, he arrived at the Southern Mountains where in those ranges he departed our world once again. It was as though the mountain called to him, beckoning a lost friend, or son.

"Here, he was thoroughly alone. This was a whole new knowledge. He needed this if he were to find the self he had left behind. Within the Temple, in the deep silence, there was always the awareness of others in proximity. Forced silence, but never true solitude. Here, solitude reached cosmic in its scope, and like the surrounding emptiness, proved integral to his awareness. A spotless mirror upon which he might see the true form of his own reflection.

"He learned again the lessons of hunger. Traces arisen of what so long ago had plagued his youth. Regretfully, he was too far removed from his ancestral past, and too softened by the court to rely on natural instincts in gleaning nourishment from the wild. For days, he ate nothing.

"It was an eternity. Never had he thought of nothing but food for so long. Nor with such mounting intensity. For every waking minute of every waking hour, he focused on his hunger. And the hunger grew, and as the hunger grew, he focused on it all the more intently. Until time itself crawled to a near stop. Tortuous hours became days, and days months. Or so it seemed. I'm told it was four days before he found food enough to quell the howling of his starving organs. But through the hunger, he had spied eternity!

"Fair trade — don't you think? Just a businessman's perspective.

"He began to adapt. In his early forages, he targeted the accessible. There were the frogs, the snakes, the cattails, the swamp roots, and the berries. But it did not come easy. Temple food seemed extravagant by comparison. He fasted often.

"The first month, he derived nourishment from the crystal waters, and the warm radiant rays of the sun. I hear you can do that! Sit in the sun and be nourished. Same as eating! Never seen it though! To supplement his meager fare, he ate the leftovers of travelers and highwaymen. Without at first realizing the change within, he began to follow the natural cycles. When tired, he rested. When hungry, he foraged for food. All very simple, but bringing to him a deep sense of harmony and integration with his surround. Some say the mountain warms to some, just as it rejects others. Apparently she took a strong fancy to Sying Hao. Don't you wonder about things like that? Why is one fancied, and another not?

"He came to know the plants and the ways of the animals. Remember, he was already an educated and sophisticated man. There is however a difference between what you know in your head, and what you can do in fact. A gap bridged by none other than hard experience. For him, meat and sustenance soon grew to abundance. What once took a whole day to garner, could now be done quickly. Feeling the first pangs of hunger, he would begin his search for food. In no time at all, his stomach would be full.

"There were others like him. Like him that is, in that for reasons of their own, they chose to live in the Southern ranges. There were the outlaws, the deserters, the mystics, the brigands, and the outcasts. Initially, he watched them from afar, and wondered what had brought them to the wilderness. Sometimes, his curiosity would get the best of him. Those times, he would maneuver to vantage points closer to their camps. I'm told he came to be so skilled at this, he could come within hearing range of their voices, and they wouldn't suspect a thing. That was how he kept abreast of the affairs of men.

"Makes you wonder about our troop and the missing treasure, doesn't it?"

Immortal or Ghost

"Some suggest other more complicated reasons for his remaining there. Of that I cannot speak one way or the other. I can say he or his spirit has been there for as long as I can remember. My parents and my grandparents said the very same while they lived. Makes one wonder, doesn't it Bao Ling? Allegedly, he entered those hills during the troubled reign of Liu Shan[14]. My great grandparents would have been children then. You can see the conundrum. Either he is an immortal, or he is a ghost. Can you think of a better explanation?

"One morning, legend has it, he awoke, and inexplicably, he could 'see.' To 'see' went far beyond the normal capacity of sight. For example, on that first morning, he 'saw' a band of soldiers entering the valley across the Saddle of the White Pony. That mountainous pass was one full day's ride away. But he saw with certainty, and with unshakable confidence.

"On other occasions, he 'heard,' he 'smelled,' and he 'felt.' It was as though he had become one with all things, or perhaps just the mountain. When a bird flew overhead, I'm

---

[14] Liu Bei's son and successor.

told he could 'become' the bird. Able to will his consciousness into the creature and instantly look down upon his own physical body from dizzying heights.

"We are told, he tracked those soldiers as they crossed toward the great valley. The very next evening, he found them. Still in the highlands. He visited their camp, sat in their midst as they talked, partook of their food, and shared the warmth of their campfire. Then he left. The soldiers however, but for the missing food, never knew he had been there. A ghost story if ever there was one. They got the message though!

"Does any of this sound familiar to you?

"Who can say if this is true, or what is true? Certainly it didn't come from the soldiers. Beyond joking about the disappearing food, they knew nothing. And the man of the mountain? Well Bao Ling, if I am certain of one thing, he is one who knows how to keep secrets. So, we simple folk cling to our legends. Conjured by some first narrator for sure, then passed along. Until they become part of our very fiber. But young man, you mustn't forget. There's a reason for these stories. They never happen on their own, or for no purpose. As well you know, legends and stories survive to serve our needs. They help and guide us, and perhaps shed needed light into the otherwise unknowable.

"With the likes of this being propagated, it should surprise no one that in time there came to be the legend of the Man from Southern Mountain. In these parts, we derive great pleasure recounting the stories late at night. Usually by the warming fires, always taking full liberty to color them with our own imaginations. When travelers hear strange sounds in the night, or see strange shapes bounding about in the darkness, or when they awaken to find food missing from their sacks, they typically exclaim 'Looks like we had a visit from the ghost of the mountain!' That's how it is.

"To establish his rightful place on the mountain, he became one with the animals and the surround. In the beginning, when he still ate the flesh of animals to survive, he would walk undetected up to his prey. Silently he issued the coup, as though he and the prey were fait accompli, sharing in some intimate parley.

"With infinite patience he studied the animals closely — all the animals — from the bears, to the panthers, to the lowliest insects.

"He had learned what no book could tell, no scholar or intellectual could pass on. The human entity is a composite of thought, substance, emotion, experience and form, cradled and bound within spirit. Self awareness, affirming our life and tie to the worldly surround. As natural a tie as the stem holding a leaf to the tree. The path to knowledge and understanding was not to be found in scrolls. Look not to the halls of power, or others purporting to shape one's destiny. The mountain taught otherwise. Look first within! There were deeper truths to be had. Realities in fact!

"No one knows what became of the man from Southern Mountain. Legends abound and diverge. You know how that goes. Some say he left the mountains to rally the southern villages in campaigns against marauding warlords from the north and east. Others say he founded a temple where he consecrated his newfound knowledge to the Buddha. There are even reports he became one of the Taoist immortals. To this day he is said to haunt the camps of those entering the mountain's sanctuary. It is a known fact that troublemakers avoid the place. For them in particular, it has acquired very bad karma.

"What is certain is that eventually, the now grown to maturity Shu Emperor sent his agents to retrieve the errant counselor and return him to court. At first, a polite refusal was sufficient for the agents to leave without mischief. Of course, before long, the Emperor lost patience. Enemies surrounded him within the palace, and the once powerful Shu empire barely held its borders against encroachers. The continuing refusals offended his imperial sense of dignity. Why without the Shu and their patronage, Sying Hao would have died just another war orphan, along with the other collateral unfortunates. Frustrated, but demanding results, the Emperor sent his 'enforcers' to persuade. And should it be necessary, to capture and drag the unwilling hermit back."

The Dragon

"Capture and drag him back? How do you think that went?

"The games began. You see, Bao Ling, compassionate as he was, Sying Hao had little tolerance for arrogance and selfishness. Nor did he readily acquiesce to the impositions of others. He had become self-aware. Like a butterfly, he had emerged from the confining cocoon of courtly affluence, never to return. Truthfully, he found no further utility in their sport. Perhaps he came upon something bigger, and of more consequence. But that we'll never know with assurance. Lifetimes have already passed. We've seen nothing to suggest an answer.

"Reports filtered back to the Emperor of a man who fought with supernatural fury. Who, on one occasion, had singlehandedly disarmed and disabled fifteen officers of the imperial guard. Not since days of early Shu, when heroic deeds were common, were such feats heard of in the land. The intolerable embarrassment amplified by the poisonous tongues of his counselors only heightened the Emperor's concerns. The weight of it all pricked more deeply his sense of propriety.

"'I'm sure it's true,' he thought, 'Sying Hao's martial skills are already well documented and appreciated. But he is no Guan Gong! I'll just have to send more.'

"What the Emperor and his imperial guard did not know was that during his years in the wilderness, Sying Hao had changed and evolved. Melding the lessons of the mountain into new tapestries of flow and motion made him invincible to those of lesser discipline. His universe shifted to between where they were, permanently stuck, and where they aspired to be, in charge. They could not know or react to what they could not see or understand. Unquestionably, that's where the ghost stories got their real fuel.

"From studying the bear, he learned strength and rooting power. Full commitment in attack. Instantly, he could issue forth with unnerving sounds while mad swipes of his 'paws' easily smashed the strongest suits of armor.

"In the blink of an eye, he could become the panther. Vaulting near and away, slashing out and weakening his opponents before going in for the kill. Fortunately for most, he remained a compassionate man. Just when death stared one in the eye, he as quickly relinquished and disappeared. Leaving you to your own reflection, gifted with the opportunity to contemplate change within. Perhaps take a new direction. A nice touch indeed!

"As the humble grasshopper, when attacked, he could be there or not there. Just when you thought to have him in your grasp, you held nothing but the breeze. The animal variations proved endless. He and they were one. For one opponent he was the eagle, for another, the monkey, and for still another, the mantis. No one could get bearings on his intentions, or his tactics.

"I suspect the goodly creatures admired him from a safe distance. How like them he must have seemed.

"My grandfather, no ordinary man mind you, tried to make sense of these accounts. He recalled his own people. Many were animists, capable of recognizing the spirit life in all natural forms. They felt the source of all worldly power, even that of the mountain, to be the dragon. Dragon rules positive karma. It protects Dharma and the nourishing forces of creation. It governs survival. It drives the natural order. Grandfather concluded the hermit came to understand dragon as the common factor within himself, the animals, the mountain, and his maker. Who or whatever that might be.

"The dragon is master of position. Though words are weak in description, a sage might explain, 'The dragon is always where his power is maximized, and his power is greatest wherever he may be.' Therein lies the mystery and perhaps the riddle. A matter of what's in your head. I suppose it means to never err, but I don't see whether this can be. In my universe, error and misjudgment are the norm. It seems our hermit Sying Hao managed to tap into the dragon's underlying strength. Somehow, he roots inextricably into his environment.

"My grandfather explained how, when finally the dragon sets, there are never openings. When you aggress, it is you who are left open and exposed. An inviolable natural law.

There are no other possibilities. I feel this to be a deep well Bao Ling. One you might choose to explore someday. Ask your friend. I only wish I had the know-how!

"Today, accounts of the hermit's many deeds are bandied about the countryside. What I'm sharing with you are things I've heard memorialized by others, wandering monks, story tellers. Even old soldiers, who will sometimes tell drunken tales of how they managed to survive an encounter with the mountain demon. Believe it or not, opera performers too, have their own take on this. Honestly, I don't know what's what, or what's true. Never having openings, or leaving yourself open, I can't see how thinking you're a dragon changes anything. But that's how the legend has grown, and for your sake, I'm trying to get it right.

"Story has it the hermit on Southern Mountain first learned about dragon as an attitude, from his own teachers. I prefer to think he perhaps met a dragon up there in those clouds, or at least knew where one had hidden away. They say he was always in dragon posture, whether walking through the woods, relieving himself, or even sleeping. There simply were no openings. Ever! The emperor's men could not comprehend this enigma. A secret power? An unknown energy? Possibly a trick? They recognized their helplessness and, without exception, returned to the court in disgrace. They never got him!

"It could have been worse for them. At least they had their spared lives.

"Finally, unable to risk further humiliation and the courtly perceptions of weakness and failure, the Emperor opted to feign tiredness of the pursuit. Cleverly, he diverted everyone's attention from the sad state of internal affairs by returning to yet another round of wars. Having no choice, he made do with alternate though lesser counsel.

"Bao Ling, be sure to mark these words. There's nothing like conflict and carefully exploited patriotism to take a population's mind completely off their hopelessness and suffering. To recover some vestige of self dignity, he proclaimed Sying Hao an esteemed Marquis and made him Duke of Southern Mountain, guardian of the Emperor's interests to the south. Then left it at that. There ... he thought: *'Whether Sying Hao knew it or not, he was still working for me!'*

"They never met again. A sad outcome, as I'm told they truly cared for one another.

"Even the renegade warlords found they were better served propagating their self interests elsewhere. They would leave this man to his realm and give him wide berth. Likewise, I am told the richly endowed Southlands beyond the mountain were ultimately spared. No military expedition could pass through or around the mountain without great risk and exposure. By then, the mountain and the man had become of one mind. No one wished to provoke their ire.

"When the mountain and its surrounds were finally purged of marauders, soldiers, and brigands, others came, hoping to learn from the 'powerful holy man.' Of the many who ambled directionless through the woods of Southern Mountain, legend states a handful were chosen to be students. For the others, the man from Southern Mountain was not to be found, and probably never existed. Except as the ghost named Sying Hao, a once fugitive dream sprung from the troubled mind of a waning and distressed western Emperor.

"'Sying Hao!' That's how we know him here."

Like a Rising Phoenix

After allowing a few moments for the words to register their effect, Uncle Wei continued. He was not one to let a good tale fail to reach its destination.

"As to the chosen, it is said all in time returned to the world of toil and trial. It was the teacher's wish once they touched the heart of Southern Mountain, they should return to the affairs of human kind and serve as guides for others.

"Perhaps they were all bodhisattvas. Who can say how these things work? Remember, I do business, not alchemy. Certainly, judging by legends which sprung from their turns of deed, warriors all. Would you believe Bao Ling, I once heard an interesting tidbit. Turns out Sying Hao greatly admired the sage Zhuangzi. Do you think he followed Zhuangzi's precedent? You see Zhuangzi showed by personal example how one who achieves full awareness can only be truly aware by acting as a beacon for others. In the case of Zhuangzi, no better vessel could be found for his brilliance than living a simple life with his family. He inspired from his door sill, first illuminating his community, then all humankind. Even I, old Wei the merchant, cannot find fault with that.

"Those who returned to the world taught others. They in turn taught more. I have witnessed these things, and have a story for you. You will see for yourself how it unfolded. Once, as a child, I was headed to market with my grandfather. So long ago, but I remember as if it were yesterday. We saw an older fellow walking the same direction. A monk, as I recall. He looked tired and road worn. Grandfather, Buddha bless his compassionate heart, invited the elder to come aboard our market cart. He was beat! No sooner was he aboard, then he fell fast asleep.

"Later that day, some highwaymen surprised us and threatened our lives. Grandfather wisely knew to protect our safety as first priority. He immediately surrendered his coin purse and told the thieves they were free to take the goods in the cart, begging they not harm the old man sleeping inside. I remember hearing the old man stirring from his slumber, wakened by the unexpected noise.

"Our fate uncertain, their leader and an accomplice went to the rear. A third, unmounted, lifted the cover and reached for the wares within. A roar emerged from the figure curled on the straw. It brought to mind a dragon waking from its sea cave. 'This bed is mine, who disturbs me!' he yelled. The three in the rear stumbled back and away. The one lifting the cover tore it completely free then took refuge alongside the road. Those guarding us in front struggled to keep control of their suddenly fear stricken steeds. No right minded animal wants to contend with a riled dragon. Animals can sense these things, I'm certain of it! Same as when the earth shudders! With a voice that could have been that of the Celestial Emperor, the old man, still sprawled in the straw, opened his eyes and squinted rearward toward the chieftain yet seated high upon his mount. 'Whoever crosses my path, without my blessing, will feel the scorching wrath of the fire dragon's tongue.'

"The chieftain warily backed his steed, then cut to his right. I surmise using the technique of breaking angle, but what do I know? His sideman meandered to the left, in effect checking any possibility of escape, or resistance. The now recovering chieftain laughed haughtily, then challenged, 'I see no dragon's tongue old man.'

"Not a fool, the chieftain kept his distance, looking to further assess the risk of the moment. By then the old timer shuffled from within the cart, then lowered himself ever so cautiously down to the ground between the two at the rear. Still hunched at the waist, now positioning his staff vertically as though for support, he humored his old bones by slowly stretching to full standing. I could hear his bones cracking as he straightened. Heavens Bao Ling, it was like watching a tree grow. He didn't look so vulnerable anymore! His monk's robe was disheveled and one sandal remained buried beneath the straw somewhere in the cart. I thought he had lost his wits. For a moment, he turned absentmindedly as though wanting to find his sandal but then, showing annoyance, returned his attention back to the two armed riders mounted alongside.

"He pointed to his meager staff. 'Tongue' he said. Then he tap touched his thumb to his chest, 'Dragon.'

"The chieftain, turned to his accomplice, knowing the only course was to test the moment. 'Let's kill this old bastard first! Then we'll deal with the old man in front. Spare the boy, we can sell him.' My sensitive young ears could hear the words, and terror seized me. Incredulously they watched as the old man ignored them, then turned again to the cart, presumably still determined to find the sandal.

"They had no clue. It was a final courtesy extended to the villains. That's what he told me afterwards! 'Always allow a way out, even to the most vile wrongdoer!' Unable to witness the degradation and fearing for our own lives, grandfather and I lowered our eyes, already weighted with sorrow over what we were sure would follow. The thought crossed my mind. The old geezer'd still be safe if we hadn't thought to pick him up!

"As soon as the monk turned away, the now inflamed chieftain lifted his killing ax and stood high on his mount, centering and balancing his mass for a death toss at the old fellow.

"I saw the move. The child in me reacted. 'Watch out!,' I cried. The old man turned hard about. Was it my warning, frankly I couldn't tell. He took a single step, and like a rising Phoenix ascended high airborne. His staff floated and spun in two hands over his head. The death ax sailed just beneath his upfolded legs, impacting into and dropping the sideman's steed. The old man seemed to linger in the air a moment beyond what the chieftain had calculated for his now broad swinging sword. That bandit was one ferocious fellow, I'll give him that! The staff came down with the old man's full weight, powered by gravity, looking more like a whip or bent rope than an accelerating piece of seasoned wood. It struck so hard upon the chieftain's skull his body crumbled helplessly toward the ground. Dead before the bounce. The beast beneath stumbled at first sideways then too, collapsed downward. Finding itself unmounted and free, it jumped back to its feet to gallop off in terror. The old monk, now dragon, glowered at the others. 'More play children?' Leaderless, and having a taste of their own sour medicine, they turned about in shocked silence. With eyes lowered in acquiescence, they returned our purse and cleared our path.

"Grandfather insisted the monk join us for evening meal once we got to town, and further, that he share our accommodations for the duration of stay. The old man told grandfather, 'You needn't be polite. I'm always a bit grumpy when strangers interrupt my afternoon nap.'

"Grandfather said, 'Not courtesy sir, I am an old man and have often heard tales of dragons and their wondrous deeds. Never in my imaginings did I expect to see one, and to stare in awe as he flew across the span of my shocked gaze banishing evil without compromise or delay.'

"The old man politely consented to join us, but extracted our promise we let him know when his idiosyncrasies began to outweigh the welcome. He was with us for several days. After each day's trading and commerce, I had him all to myself until late evening. Indeed, it was he who related most of what I've told you of the legend regarding Sying Hao.

"Amazingly, he spoke of how more than four generations had passed from when the mountain hermit first transmitted his knowledge to another. If pressed, the old man could name the entire family and line of teachers. Starting from the man on Southern Mountain, he listed them all. He capped it off with proud tales of his own master, one-time Duke of Fragrant Woods — a small fiefdom now monastery in the Westlands along the former Silk Road.

"He was clear on one thing. Unlike the other fighting arts, which varied from teacher to teacher, the style of the animals remained the same. As with the dragon, the animal styles were forms portraying deep rooted energies, which adapted through thought and intent to suit the individual idiosyncrasies of each person. They flowed like water, free to roam within, and capable of radiating outward into the environment. They could be taught and transmitted. The forms or should I say the geometry behind them remained pure and unchangeable, like beacons in a world darkened by ignorance.

"He made sure I grasped two things. First, the dragon embodied compassion, and required integrating one's compassion with the Dharma of the moment. Second, whenever there was a question to be resolved, one only had to find his own Southern Mountain to once again speak to the master. He assured this path would never fail a true tested heart. He smiled to me as he added, 'Though it be a child's.'

"I never quite understood that, but there you have it. Others have different takes on the story, and there are ghost tales galore. I know only what I know, but have the advantage of having seen the old man and heard his account, which I believe to be authentic.

"As you can see Bao Ling, there is more to Sying Hao than meets the eye, as is the case also with you. Ghost or no ghost, it was clearly no accident you two found each other."

A Great Gift

"Bao Ling! What's up? Are you all right?"

Old Wei looked to me as I stood frozen, staring intently into emptiness, trying to catch images pushing from the recesses of my memories. His story triggered something deep within.

"Hey, I meant no offense. Sometimes I get to talking and my big mouth goes off on its own. Before I know it, something slips from my lips and I've offended. Forget what I said about you and Sying Hao! I'm sure he came upon you by accident. Think nothing more of it!"

Ignoring him for the moment, I remained still, racing through banks of memories to a time deep in my childhood. So remote it had all but vanished from any trail of recall. Even as I stood there, I remembered it more as a dream than as something which transpired. Too much had happened since. Was I forgetting things to protect myself from the weight of what I had lost?

Old Wei started to say something else, when I lost patience and abruptly raised my left palm outward, begging he be silent. Something was coming to me at last.

"Hey, I'm just trying to apologize," muttered the disgruntled elder.

I'm sure he noticed the light of a smile emerging as I turned his way.

"You've helped me revive something. Something I had nearly completely forgotten. I wonder why that is? Something at the time so important, yet until this moment all but gone.

"I don't know how it slipped from my memories. The experience had been so profound. Though only a passing circumstance, I can honestly say it likely shaped much of my childhood and guided my attitude in most everything which followed. Perhaps, it bolstered my faith in the possibility other things existed. Like the dragon your grandfather mentioned.

"Can you imagine? Though to us mostly unseen, they are powerful, and true, and always there at the ready. I wonder why that is so."

Now Jin Wei stood frozen, staring expectantly. No doubt waiting for the explanation he hoped would follow.

"And?"

"Your grandfather knew this. He knew tales of dragons and their wondrous deeds, but never presumed the good fortune to one day stumble upon one. Banishing evil without compromise or delay. There, right before his eyes, and yours too. Do you know what a great gift that was?"

"Yes Bao Ling. It's all true. It happened just as I said. But gift, I don't get your meaning. Nothing was gifted. What happened, happened. The bandits controlled the timing, and paid the price. Grandfather simply honored the old monk with what meager sharings we could offer."

"But Uncle Wei, it's happened many times over again. Just as you described it, my own experience merely an echo. As I stand here with you, it's coming back bit by bit, like a whisper from the other side of time, a message to myself preserved in the amber of a buried memory, now resurfacing."

"Now you're confusing me again. Speak straight! Cut the riddles! What are you saying? Tell me, what does it mean?"

"Hope, the gift was one of hope. Just when all seemed lost, and the bandits prepared to have their way with the three of you. What seemed insignificant and vulnerable became sturdy and strong, then manifested with courage and resolve."

"Yes, yes, the monk fooled us all, that I understand. But how is that a gift?"

"It's a gift because the monk had come to teach you a lesson."

"What lesson?"

"To act with conviction when the moment called for it."

"Yes, that's exactly what the old monk did."

"With respect, uncle I'm not talking about the monk."

"Who the hell else was there?"

"The little boy in the cart! You. When you called 'Watch out!' Everything pivoted precisely on that moment. It was you who seemed insignificant and vulnerable but who became sturdy and strong, then manifested with courage, resolve and action. The monk was a warrior bodhisattva. To him, the bandits were insignificant. The gift was the opportunity presented for you to act fearlessly in the moment, when it really mattered. And you did what so few could. I didn't see that in you at first, but now I do, and I must apologize for my oversight. You deserved better from me. We are truly kindred spirits."

My words had flustered Jin Wei. Unexpected recognition from a once stranger. Someone he had already determined had a very high price on his head for reasons he politely chose to disregard. Or perhaps because he saw they were true.

Wei countered, "But I was only a child, why would I be the recipient of this bodhisattva's attention? Can't we just

242

explain it as what happened, happened, and leave it at that?"

"Do with it what you will. He came to show you your potential. Seems to me that's how it works and that's what they do. Though I might be wrong. It's my belief he did so for a reason. What that is, I can't say. I'm only Bao Ling the drifter. I don't know the minds of celestials, or bodhisattvas. Perhaps in the future, I will."

"But what am I supposed to do with it?" Uncle Wei pleaded in frustration.

I admired Wei's earnestness, no false bones here. Laughing in resignation, I could only answer "Nothing."

"Nothing, you say? There is never nothing! Look for the nothing in an egg and you'll go hungry!"

Part 6

One Hundred and Eight

A View of Death

I shrugged and answered, "Who's to say what is nothing, or how to distinguish substance from naught? Or life from death for that matter? Let me tell you of an incident from my childhood which may shed light.

"Once I encountered a master of the iron hand. As I understand, he had been a friend, perhaps a one time associate of my grandfather's. Old Iron Hand Gao, so the people called him. Grandfather explained Old Gao had mastered the secrets of 'iron shirt,' one of the most guarded of the seventy two arts, and had developed inconceivable striking power in his right hand. Perhaps he hoped his friend might be able to impart some wisdom to me. He left me with him for a month.

"We broke things. At first it was simple sticks, then came more formidable targets. It seemed a never ending stream of challenges re-visited each morning as local villagers ensured the storehouse never depleted, each day replenishing the rocks, tiles, bricks and boards. You see, they were invested in Iron Hand Gao. He kept them safe. He had a reputation for generosity with his knowledge and talent, and would teach any person of good character. Per grandfather, bandits and ill-doers veered clear of him, or any place they felt he might show up. They all knew. He didn't tolerate thugs!

"Well, the first several days, he had me standing like a post, watching him as he went through his toughening routines, followed then by his breaking drills. The toughening had to do with iron shirt. It's hard to explain what it is. Imagine something like a spider's web encasing your entire body, but instead of web filament, it's made of spun iron. Now imagine the iron being as thick as your finger is wide, and that it's invisible, though most certainly there. The first time I met him, I couldn't resist reaching to touch his arm as he reminisced of old times with grandfather and momentarily became distracted. I can tell you this. The shock of what I felt, caused me to recoil. He turned to me, saying only, 'Iron shirt, Bao Ling. I knew you were there, and I let you feel it.'

"Well, you can bet I touched him, and grazed him and bumped him every chance I got those first several days. He said little about it, but looked to see my reaction after each contact. What could I say? It felt like hitting a rock wall. Why once an acupuncturist friend came to check on him, then concluded his chi had become deficient in his spleen. He pulled out his packet of needles to make the necessary corrections and adjustments. He couldn't penetrate the surface. Old Gau laughed heartily, exclaiming 'I don't like needles, why should I let them in? Besides, my spleen feels fine to me. Don't you agree I'm the one best qualified to judge?'

"It was his choice to remain poor. He could have milked the powerful, and gamed his remarkable talents. He didn't.

Others may have puzzled over this, to me it seemed right. Beyond the training implements, and the stream of students, he expected nothing more from the surrounding villages and took nothing. The thatched roof of his hut leaked, and just as frequently he slept outside in the elements, which is where he spent most of his time working out and teaching.

"Why, one morning I woke to the sound of a great downpour. I was already cold, damp, and frightened by the howling wind crashing into the timid walls all through the night. I raced about inside looking for old Gao, a child needing the assurance I wasn't suddenly alone, but found nothing until I peeked outside. There I came upon Master Gao asleep in his chair, propped against the corner of the hut, with rain water spilling from the thatch directly onto his head. Literally soaking him top to bottom. I was freezing. I ran over to him. It was just the two of us, and the sun had not yet pushed over the horizon. I found him motionless, stiff, his color a frightening blue violet, same as the morning pre-dawn. I saw no evidence of breathing. If I felt any pulse, it seemed more like I had imagined it. Then it hit me. He was dead! Done in by the exposure! I felt so gravely alone, helpless, not knowing what to do for him, or for myself. Here I was in the middle of nowhere, with a corpse. I knew the villagers would come later, but it would be too late to make a difference."

"What did you do Bao Ling?"

"I did the only thing anyone could do. I ran inside and lit some incense, then returned to Master Gao, taking care to plant the smoking sticks alongside him where no water dripped, then placed a blanket over his body so as to protect his dignity. Not knowing what else to do, I started praying to the gods to look favorably on his spirit, giving a careful litany, to the limited extent I could, of his accomplishments, his reputation, and the good he had brought upon his community. I can tell you, I had never encountered death first hand. Not like this! Regardless, as I prayed, I still couldn't resist the temptation to reach for his cold, steely hand. While I mumbled the prayers, I marveled how his hand and flesh felt the same in rigid death as they had felt in days prior when he was yet vital."

"A tragedy Bao Ling. Especially when set upon one so young. Still, these experiences build character, and teach us to deal with life's many uncertainties."

"Perhaps more than you think, Uncle Wei."

"How So."

"Well, it's true the gravity of the situation weighed heavily upon me. I had only just made Master Gao's acquaintance, but had already grown quite fond of him. Like grandfather, he had no false bones. I began talking to the blanketed old man, already the blanket dripped sopping wet and trailed water to the ground. Now, I was shivering and soaked. Wanting to see his kind face one more time, I reached for the blanket and pulled it back, if only to remember the nobility of his final mask."

"A solemn moment indeed!"

You Were Dead!

"Yes. I told him I wanted to thank him for teaching me, and expressed my regret it had ended like this, too soon. I assured his ghost I would work diligently to perfect all he had shown me."

"Good. Proper respect and courtesy!"

"Then, both his eyes sprung wide and open. Next thing I know I dropped the blanket, knocked over the incense and screamed 'Ghost!' at the top of my lungs. I spun around and took off, intending to put as much distance between me and him as possible.

"Behind me, I heard the rapid approach of thumping footsteps, enveloped in a cloud of loud and raucous laughter. He called, 'Wait child! It's really me! Come back!'

"For an old man, he could run like a rabbit. In seconds he passed me, then turned about, now facing me, but running backwards, still managing to keep pace ahead of my frenzy. Witnessing that impossible feat made me all the more certain he was a ghoul! He put his two hands up beckoning me to stop. Only then could I confirm Master

Gao, appearing entirely normal, though still dripping water from his wet clothing.

"We both stopped and squared, staring at one another. I remained cautious. His laughter, at first boisterous and almost mocking had slowly melded into a kind smile of understanding."

"'Come Bao Ling. It's cold, and we're wet. Let's go inside and talk this through, I'll start a fire, and we'll have a bite to eat.'"

"It wasn't until we warmed by the fire my voice returned. Finally, I looked at him and said, 'But you were dead!.' That only drew another burst of uncontrolled laughter as the man of iron looked almost jolly in the light of the fire enveloped by drifting smoke."

"'No Bao Ling, not dead. I was sleeping, and dreaming.'"

"'But you were stone cold, I saw no breathing and I felt no pulse.'"

"'They were there child, but you could not find them. I can explain if you'd like, but I'm not sure you'd understand. If you promise to listen carefully and to take what I tell you for truth, I'll do that for you.'"

"'Of course, Master!'"

"'As you know, I love outdoors, and revel in the elements. Hot, cold, muddy, wet and dry, all my friends.

No better way to make their acquaintance than to sit with them and accept what they have to offer.

"'Did you know? Your body has great knowledge hidden within, which can only be triggered by trusting it to find its own ties to the world about you. Don't be surprised if what you deem important fails to match what it seeks and finds for itself. It knows better than you! Most people run from these experiences, and cloak themselves in their artificial constructs. I take no issue with them. We all make our choices. In that way, using our free wills, we earn our rewards and deserve our consequences.

"'Last night, after I made sure you were safe inside, I went to my corner perch and studied the heavens as I frequently do. A panorama of infinite mystery, all the more enticing as the evening cooled and the moon went into hiding. In the early morning, the clouds had gathered. I found the same beauty flowing in their dance, knowing before daylight there would be rain. As it likes to do, the rain came cloaked with its veil of mystery, the feeling of wetness, its smell, and the wonderful sounds emitting from all directions as the night world came fully alive.

"'I couldn't pull myself away. So instead, I gloried in the moment, stayed put, and let myself be drawn into its heart. You might think of this as going to sleep. Perhaps it is the same. You must understand, like your grandfather, I have passed through hard and troubled times. For more than a generation, we wandered homeless, aimless and in constant strife, our families cast hard by fate to the four directions. A great loss, and a great tragedy. Words cannot adequately convey the cut of our loss. At first, living in the elements was torture, and many among us did not survive the early years. Gone quickly were the naive young. Soon after, the life-worn elders, but then, even the seemingly strong and robust failed the endless gauntlet. Some simply decided for themselves. I remember thinking, *'Who could blame them for taking the easy road?'* It wasn't until I learned to accept my station and then to befriend it we made our truce. Once I turned that corner, I began to prosper. Not in terms of wealth or material things, but rather in the sense of a delicate harmony and balance, which reached to me, just as I reached to it. I'm sure your grandfather can attest to this.

"'What had once been miserable nights of disturbed sleep became daily explorations, each yielding poignant insights into the mysteries of life and creation. Can you imagine? My dreams became real! This may not mean anything to you now, but our dreams provide sanctuary and the opportunity for profound awareness. Would you believe when I dream, I am still wide awake? That first came about during the hard years, when for our own safety, we had to always sleep with one eye open. So, as I began to doze, I would say to myself, 'I am asleep, but I am still awake' making myself conscious and aware of everything in my vulnerable surrounds. Unexpectedly, that same awareness carried into the dream state. To my delight and surprise, I found myself awake and aware in my dream state, just as I was in my awake state. Child, mark my word! There are entire worlds waiting to be explored. In fact, over time, it was hard to tell the difference between here and there. I simply moved from one room to the other. Except of course, in the dream state, anything seemed possible. That particular universe seemed to dance to my will and my intent. You can be assured, I learned a great many lessons once I made that discovery. I share this with you now, think of it as you will. In time I trust it will make sense.

"'As I became adept in the dream world, the skills I perfected there returned with me to the awake world. It took years, but I concluded the remarkable skills which developed in my dream state, were in fact part of the same consciousness which governed my awake state. Once I had that realization there were no secrets, just continued explorations and the unlimited potentials of awareness set free.

"'So you see Bao Ling, what you perceived as my death was me hovering about in my dream state, immersed in the rippling momentums of dream and reality, where so few have dared to go. Many would prefer their own death to the opportunity of visiting upon infinite mystery. Yet though I was there, I watched as you puzzled and tried to reconcile all which you saw and encountered. Lest I forget to mention, I was touched and humbled by your kind words, all truly spoken in your moment of perceived crisis. From the center of your heart, always the best place to root your feelings.'"

"'But Master, how can you go to that land of death, and come back here to life. Is not dead, dead?'"

"'Ah Bao Ling, there you touch upon the great question. I can tell you only this. It is the truth, and cannot be more clearly stated. I know you will not understand it today, but please, promise to hold the words in your heart and trust a time will come when their meaning will open to you.'"

"'I will do so Master.'"

"'Death is not death as you know it. Life is not life as you know it. When you experience death, you will find it is death, but not the death you expected. When you're in that moment, be sure to ask yourself how you have become dead, yet know it is not the death you expected. That will help steer you back. Life is no different. When you truly experience life, you will find it is life, but not the life you expected. Remember this. Beneath both is a common thread. When you stare at your reflection in the water as you drink from the lake and one day see only the water, and not your reflection, you will know you have found that thread. When that awareness opens, you will know the thread to be a great and formidable root from which all things spring, even the water before you.'"

The Four Freedoms

Jin Wei pondered my words in respectful silence.

"Old Master Gao continued my training with renewed enthusiasm. Something about what occurred that morning had pushed my feeble efforts to the forefront of his focus.

"The following day, he put a large rock in my hand. It looked like a melon, at least to me. Arguably a small one, but still a melon by any impartial assessment. Allowing my opportunity to scrutinize it, he anticipated my question and said, 'Bao Ling, you have one objective this month. It is to split this rock with a strike from your hand. It will not be easy. If you train hard and with commitment, you will succeed. I'll do all I can to help you. If you break it, many doors will open for your exploration. If you fail, those doors will remain closed. Either way, we will part as friends, and you will take with you what you have learned and deserve to know.'"

"Oh boy Bao Ling, all this talking in circles. Can't anyone just say anything straight?" Old Wei pounded his head, mock venting his frustration. Then added, "I mean, breaking rocks? For what purpose?"

"Precisely what I asked old Iron Hand Gao."

"And?"

"Well Master Gao had quite a bit to say on that. He sat me down and explained about limitations, sacrifice, and the relationship between effort, risk and return. I'm sure you know those things well, but as a child, I was yet ripe and innocent. Gao felt that in life, only a handful of freedoms truly existed. Most others were illusions. We had the freedom to be compassionate. We had the freedom to choose action over inertia. We had the freedom not to be paralyzed by fear, and we had the freedom to push beyond our limitations. Then he explained how in many ways, our beings were shaped and governed by our actions and inclinations. Not passively, or accidentally mind you, but as a direct consequence of our choices. We forever made decisions which produced who we turned out to be. Almost like artisans, or sculptors, working jade or agate. With every cut of our blade or grind of our wheel, the stone changed and moved closer to its ultimate character. Would it become perfect, or ruined? The answer inevitably lay in the character, and the skill of the craftsman. Gao said the same applied to me, and to all of us. Each had been blessed with a crude yet perfect slate at birth, and each of us had the freedom to make of it what we choose. That was the ultimate value in breaking rocks with one's hands."

"Breaking a rock the size of a melon? A child? Impossible!" cried old Wei.

"Master Gao explained it all to be a matter of choice, and then putting choice into the work. Interestingly, he stressed how the energies bestowed on us by nature were ample to the task, but because we had already hoodwinked ourselves into entrenching our limitations, there was no way around the work. He assured if I succeeded, I would soon enough see the truth in his words."

"Well, did you break it?"

"The first day proved difficult. Every passing hour would begin with me taking ten strikes at the rock. As I prepared, he would take opportunity to explain the importance of establishing a solid base, and then show me how best to hold the rock so the base might work in concert with my strike from above, and not contrary to it. Then he showed me the eight hand positions. The hammer fist, the elbow, the forearm, the descending palm, the side hand, the punch, the palm strike, and the still hand — and how to harness each of them to the right situation. By the end of the third day, my hand turned blue and swelled. Old Gao took that cue to acquaint me with his concoctions for healing, and his 'hit' medicine, which of course led to my having to learn the formulas, then gathering the herbs to make more. In no time, I learned to recognize them all. Then he taught me how to combine them, and distill their essence into working mixtures."

"Did they work?"

"Yes, each did what it was supposed to. The Die Da Jiu[15] dissipated the swelling and bruises, pretty much overnight.

The liniments toughened my hands, and the improvement on impact was obvious."

"Ah, so before too long, you broke your rock?"

"Truthfully, no. But each day I upped the energy, the intensity of added effort pulling me closer to the edge of reckless abandon with every strike. Old Gao scrutinized the mounting failures, then immediately devised lessons tailored to encourage subtle corrections in my dynamics. For example, one day he said I was hitting with my hand. I stared at him disbelieving. 'Wasn't that the point?' I asked. 'No!' he replied. The hand is attached to the shoulder, which is attached to the body, which is attached to the ground, which is attached to the universal root. Your strike is not rooted. It's like a nat flying aimlessly around in the air.'

"He would have me motioning through hand strikes endlessly, carefully mapping for my awareness how my hips rotated and provided needed circular momentum to the effort. Then of course, hours more of standing like a post.

---

15 Known more colloquially as as "Dit Dat Jow." Literally translates "fall hit wine." There are many formulas, and among them, an assortment of closely held secret recipes. The secrecy of course relating to the perceived tactical advantage of having a more effective compound. Typically, it's applied as a liniment over injuries or bruised bodily parts. Some varieties accelerate toughening of limbs and joints, for example, the hands, when training for breaking and iron palm techniques. Those who use it regularly attest to its efficacy.

Except now he had me mentally moving energy around the circuit defined by my posture, usually in the form of a pebble or token of consciousness, which would race through the circuit until it returned to its starting point. Sometimes, he would slow count ten, and in that time, I was to have run my thought and energy through the circuit sixty times. By the end of the first week, the child in me had disappeared, replaced now by a single minded gnome having only one objective, and the sooner it was out of the way, the better. By then, I had upped my strikes to twenty per hour, but still no luck."

"How did you keep your sanity?"

"Old Gao took care of that."

"More of his special concoctions?" answered Jin Wei, half in jest, half in taunt.

"No. Just by being there for me. Every step of the way. Always encouraging. Always looking for the one adjustment, or the one scion of insight which would push my hand through that stone."

"Do you think he could have broken it?"

"Of course, one strike."

"You know this for sure?"

"Yes. As I struggled, he was constantly pulverizing rocks, the equal or better of my own nemesis. You see Uncle

Wei, more than anything, he was guiding me to the objective by setting his continuous example."

"Hmmmm" was all Jin Wei could say in reply.

"Well, the month of my tutelage under Master Gao was fast drawing to a close. With only a few days left, I began to have doubts. He knew this of course, and to counter my apprehension, he came to me one morning and woke me with the words: 'Bao Ling, today the rock will be yours. Make sure to bring your best game. Go to it as if your very life depended on it. I know already you will never choose failure, but you need to learn that for yourself.'

"He said nothing more, turned about and left. I rose, prepared myself and, though still a child, felt as though I were going up against Yama himself. Until that day, I had been terrified of my daily encounters with that rock. Now, I wanted to see its pieces lying in my wake."

Tests of Character

Jin Wei urged, "Go on Bao Ling, tell me the rest."

"One hundred and eight."

"What? One hundred and eight? You lost me!"

"It took one hundred and eight strikes. Master Gao watched as I did my first ten. Nothing happened. I pushed myself harder, using every granule of energy I had, and took the count to twenty. I could actually feel the rock warming, as though it were gathering my energy then mocking me with it. *'Just another distraction,'* I thought. The rock and I had forged partnership in this endeavor. Its job was to take me to my limit, my job was to push through. By the count of thirty, my hand and arm buzzed. It felt like bees swarming inside my flesh. By sixty strikes, I didn't know how much longer I could continue. The morning sun had spilled onto the breaking station, and I welcomed its friendly glow of warmth. In that brief moment, I understood Master Gao's devotion to nature, and what that connection brought to him in terms of his solitude and awareness. In the surrounding fields I could feel the morning stillness, and from that base the sounds of nature took flight gifting us with the fullness and intimacy of their concert. I turned to old Gao and told him I would continue striking until the rock split. I would not leave until it did."

"Good boy Bao Ling," encouraged Jin Wei, now in the role of cheerleader.

"Old Iron Hand Gao obviously thought so too. I took a moment to further study the rock. He discretely lit his pipe. No doubt he knew I still had a ways to go.

"Sixty-one, sixty-two, sixty-three. Each strike harder than the previous. I didn't know from whence it came. The sensation of energy coursing my bones and body became tactile. I could feel my root in the ground. Every fiber of my being connected that root to the flow of energy within. Which, matched with my mind and the strength of my intent, I transferred from hand to rock at the moment of each strike. Whatever pain, resistance, distraction, and uncertainty plagued my quest dropped off at number eighty. By ninety, I knew I could endure to journey's end. Now, only I, and the rock remained. The perfume of Gao's pipe assured me of his continued interest and close attention to what followed.

"After ninety, with each successive strike I drew back and reached further into the well of chi within. I could actually feel myself doing it. Drained nearly depleted, my right hand shaking uncontrollably against my will, I carefully paced my timing through those final moments. With each failure I readied for the next. My body, mind and spirit somehow recharged, finding renewed center in anticipation of success. As I neared one hundred, I felt sure the rock had heated considerably and recognized it too was not giving up the fight. Somewhere within I convinced myself to expect the rock would split at one hundred and pushed my hardest to that end. Yet again, to no avail!

"A test of character I suppose. I paused to breathe and studied my antagonist one final time, whispering 'Thank you for your valiant effort.' What else could one say? Then I mounted the final onslaught. Eight successive strikes, each harder than I ever imagined possible, my whole body floating high, feeling momentarily airborne, then falling downward, with my arm accelerating from mid sky position, while my torso leaned forward and in, adding to the drop of gravity as I delivered everything I had to the intended point of contact. For sure, I expected the rock to give with each loud crack. It became much more alive to my hand as I felt its final resistance, and still I had to push harder, thinking only I must somehow gather more strength — and not knowing how, I somehow did.

"It was then, a final register of contact, an impact so clean and smooth. I wondered for an instant why I felt nothing — no resistance, no rebound of energy, no pain. The rock had split nearly perfectly in half. I looked at the pieces, for a moment incredulous. Then felt a tinge of disappointment. A bit like too soon losing a friend. I picked the pieces up and studied the new edges and the infinite irregularity defining them. For a moment, I held them back together, perhaps not quite trusting I had done it, fitting them again to convince myself it was indeed the same rock. There could be no further doubt. Then I let the pieces drop apart once more, turning them and studying each broken face as though looking for its pulsing heart, which I almost expected to see in its final throes. I found it was just a rock, nothing more. It was I who transitioned, and my heart which firmly beat the cadence for both. Finally, I turned and walked to Master Gao, to gift the remnants to him."

"'I will keep them for you Bao Ling. So you don't ever forget.'"

"I took a breath and thought to relax, only to find Old Gao reaching into a sack and pulling out another melon like rock, nearly identical to the first. He walked to where I stood, lifted it to my scrutiny, and said 'Now, another one, please.'

"I almost fainted!

"Those were the last words I wanted to hear that day. His look made it clear, He meant business! Reluctance on my part would not be condoned. I set the new rock on the breaking mount, collected my thoughts, trying to remember the feeling and spirit of number one hundred and eight, then struck."

"And what happened Bao Ling?"

"First strike break! Can you imagine my astonishment!

"Gao then took out another, and then another, and each I split or shattered with one hit. Before long he returned with still larger specimens, and then he began lining them up on the ground beside me urging I continue, saying only, 'You must do this Bao Ling, until you are certain the first break was no mere accident.'

"And I did just that. I won't exaggerate. As the morning turned to afternoon, I tired and then struggled to maintain my focus. Some of those latter rocks took more than one hit. Particularly the larger ones, one of which could have been the parent of the first rock. That one I did break with one stroke, it was my last for the day. Master Gao had produced thirty additional challenges, and their scattered fragments lay all about me. At that point, old Gao came to my side. To my considerable relief, he brought no more rocks."

"'I think you've done enough Bao Ling. I, for one, am convinced. You have bridged the divide. You'll not fall back into complacency. Very few can say they've done what you have today.'"

"'But Teacher Gao, what about tomorrow, and the day after. Will I still be able to do it then?'"

"'Yes,'" he assured.

"'But only if I practice constantly, isn't that right?'"

"'No Bao Ling, you have bridged the divide. The skill now lies within you, and it will come to your aid should you beckon. But, I must have your promise.'"

"'Yes master, what would you have me promise?'"

"'Only this child, that whatever you do in life, you do it with the same focus you showed me today. Accepting anything less will mean your defeat!'"

I stopped and turned to Uncle Wei, then added, "I would not have understood his words, had he spoken them to me a few short weeks before. He took me to his world, and made it part of mine."

"Bao Ling, it's an amazing accomplishment, and surely a life changing experience. Don't you think so?"

"You should know Uncle Wei, you had a similar encounter."

"What's that you say?"

"The warrior monk who allowed the moment to totter to near catastrophe — but for the warning call of a young child, who in the moment of utmost trial, acted impeccably."

"I still think you're overstating it Bao Ling. I did what any frightened person would have done."

"You may think that true Uncle Wei, but so few can do it, particularly those who are frightened. Listen, we've shared much today. Earlier, you asked me what you were to do with the lesson from the old monk. I said, 'Nothing,' but now, it has become more clear. May I be so bold as to beg a promise from you."

"Go ahead, I'm listening."

"Only this Uncle Wei. That whatever you encounter in life, you bring to it the same courage and ability to act, as you proved to be your very nature on that fateful day with the monk. Remember what you did, and the true spirit that drove your action when you did it. That's all. Remember what you did, and trust you can do it again. Much may depend on it."

"Yeah, yeah, yeah, now you're sounding like the old monk lecturing me in the late evening, 'Because in all of us, there are inclinations to acquiesce, to surrender, to accommodate, and to forgo. Worse, we court others who stand ready to make our excuses and justifications for us, thereby assuring our inaction or our complicity continues without interruption. As the world comes undone before us, the unscrupulous rise to steal life's fruit from beneath our very noses.'"

"He said that?"

"Those exact words."

"Wow, sounds just like Sying Hao!"

Part 7

Learning To Not Choose Failure

The Marquis Shunping

After mulling my words a bit, Jin Wei turned the thought on its side. "Do you think that's what drives the actions of someone like the notorious Dragon of the Midlands?"

Chastened by the turnabout I said nothing. *"Why can't he just let it go?"* I thought. My frustration must have been obvious, or perhaps the wetness in my eyes signaled the merchant to press no further. Old Wei deemed it wise to hold his tongue.

After no small number of silent measured steps, I thought better of Wei, and knew he meant no harm with his words. "How about we return to my account, with what I'm able to remember?"

Pleased the ice had begun to thaw, Jin Wei enjoined, "The one my monk story reminded you of? Great, I'm all ears."

"There are similarities. For one, I too was with my grandfather. And my story also involves what I then believed to have been a monk, but as I tell it to you now, I'm no longer sure.

"You see, my grandfather had mastered the fighting arts. Family lore tells when, before finding peace in the countryside, he had been a soldier, as had his father, his grandfather, and the line before them. My own father lived the life of a peasant farmer, happy and content to follow the cycles of nature. He too had notable martial skills and took them very seriously. It puzzled me what purpose they served a man like him, who abhorred violence. There's a history there of which I know nothing. It didn't seem to puzzle the neighbors or others in the community though. They saw high purpose in what he represented. Though as a naive child, I did not. He clearly had everyone's respect. Now, long after he's departed, I realize he had been their defender. Guarantor of their safety, and guardian of their ways. He had been a hero among them, no less than Iron Hand Gao. I didn't understand, or even know. That likely accounts for his always placing me under grandfather's charge and tutelage. He wanted me safe. Grandfather saw to it.

"Some say our bloodline had been marked by a particular distinction, perhaps a blessing, perhaps a curse. Inexplicably, my forebears all possess the ability to move calmly and without trepidation when threats present. Very much like what you did in your own account. I saw it in my father and he in his. I daresay it's a trait I've inherited. Though sometimes I'd just as soon not have it. You see, it disposes its holder to unwanted troubles."

"Bao Ling," interjected old Wei, "Never sell your gifts short. They're yours and not mine for a reason. Claim ownership, and appreciate what has been bestowed by life. It knows more about us than we know for ourselves!"

"Of course." I knew the old man was right on this point.

"Well, I'm told grandfather had been a soldier of some prominence. Later in life, as an officer, he rose to considerable distinction on the battlefield. I've also heard talk his own grandfather had been personal adjutant to one of the notorious Tiger Generals. Those were only whispers of course. Peasants like us have little stake to anything more than our names, our heritage, and our present — mostly our present. No one scribes our lineage or doings. It's all word of mouth. Who's to say where what we hear of honest heritage ends, and what we want of fantasy begins."

"One of the Tiger Generals! Which one?"

"I can't say for certain, but I have heard mentioned the name Zhao Yun, or was it perhaps Ma Chou or Huang Zhong. Nothing but rumor and tale, but I like the idea of Zhao Yun."

"Really? Zhao Yun, the Marquis Shunping?!"

I nodded. I knew in fact it had been Zhao Yun. I did not want to be boastful. I also knew much more than I let on to my friend. You see, Zhao Yun dedicated his entire life and lived above all things to serve the cause of Liu Bei and the Shu Han. Despite the tendency of time to erode the memories and deeds of some, long after his death, his high principle and righteous character remained common knowledge throughout the land. They modeled a standard revered by all. Doubtless, for that reason, accounts of his valiant deeds endure.

The story goes his dedication to the cause had precluded him from raising a family or having anything resembling a life of his own. Duty makes harsh demands against one with talents so abundant as his. Seemed as though history couldn't stumble forward without Zhao Yun somehow being stuck smack in the middle of it. Much like the all seeing eye within a great storm. He could be trusted to recognize the moment, act independently, and strike ruthlessly at whatever threatened. Records show he had two sons, Zhao Tong and Zhao Guang. Little is known of the mother, perhaps a concubine. They too served the cause of Shu Han with distinction, up until it entered into its death throes. We know nothing certain regarding the fate of Zhao Tong, but younger brother Zhao Guang reportedly met his end in the northern campaigns against Wei. A hero until the very end. Their blood line would have ended with the two of them, but for one subtle wrinkle.

You see, family lore tells of how Zhao Yun had a trusted adjutant, almost a shadow if you will. Accompanying him through all the campaigns and exploits from which his well deserved reputation took root, a third son. Presumably from a past liaison, or maybe a fleeting indiscretion. The mother did not survive the birth and Zhao Yun, accepting full responsibility, felt great remorse. He regretted the needless loss of her life and attributed it to his own selfishness and inability to belay base needs. He reasoned she would still be alive if he only had the sense and discipline to keep his appetites in check. The incessant wars had taken all of her family, except for her aged parents. She represented for them the very end of their line. At her passing, the remorseful Zhao Yun swore his oath to the distraught parents. He would ensure their lineage would continue and the family name would live on and flourish.

"Your graves will not lay untended," he promised.

The grandparents raised the boy child, at first as their own. When he reached maturity, as agreed, they delivered him to the trust and care of Zhao Yun. The general was as good as his word. He set a peerless example for the youth, who quickly advanced through the ranks until Lord Liu himself suggested he serve as Zhao Yun's adjutant. In time, the child learned from the father's own lips of their true relationship. It remained their secret, and their bond. Zhao Tong and Zhao Guang knew nothing of their brother, except for considering him a peer and valued comrade in battle. The father wanted no complications. Adjutant Cao Ling brought great honor and a notable degree of notoriety to the grandparents. They who had reared him in the village which eventually grew to bear their family name. Ling village, in the midlands!

He remained at his father's side through thick but in later years, more often thin, until the old warrior passed at age sixty one. By then Guan Yu and Zhang Fei were also gone, as were the other Tigers. Zhuge Liang too had only a few years remaining. Though old, worn and crusty, the still crafty wizard took careful note of the matchless and now battle-minted Colonel Cao Ling. The evident link to Zhao Yun did not slip his purview. He knew a very special blood tie when he saw it. Regrettably, his many years of performing miracles had left him nearly depleted. Little remained of his once wondrous talents. Indeed, too little to take on yet another apprentice, or project — though it might be one so gifted as this Cao Ling. Or so it seemed anyway. Perhaps he considered again how the young officer might yet be conjured into one of his celestial schemes. Unfortunately, we'll not know for sure. Whatever he decided on this, Zhuge Liang never whispered a word.

"You know Bao Ling, the title Marquis Shunping came to him posthumously. It represented a rare proclamation by the emperor Liu Shan, whose very life Zhao Yun once saved. The pictographs in the name-title 'Shunping' were carefully chosen to commemorate his exemplary traits. Loyalty, virtue, fearlessness, and his never ending quest for righteous tranquility while forever thwarting the sea of chaos."

I cast a wistful glance to my friend. These things I understood all too well. They were imprinted by my forebears, and preserved in that same blood which now coursed my veins.

The Voice

"In the midlands, we congregated and traded in networks of villages. Naturally, because of this villages grew and prospered. Among the peasants, some found the art of business and commerce more to their liking, and that is where they directed their energies."

"Nothing wrong with that!" exclaimed my friend, knowing full well he fit the same bill.

"Indeed not. They provided a needed service and effective access to goods and implements which might otherwise not have been available. Our clan chose to remain in the outlying ring of villages, preferring closer ties to nature. Farmers all. Need I say, the life has its own virtues, once it takes full root and …"

"Yes, I already know all that!" interrupted Wei, clearly agitated, possibly tying my words to village Mei and the lingering pain of family and friends lost, "Go on with your account!"

"So it was, Village Ling remained our home of choice. Still, the journey into town always promised new

experiences and surprises. Mostly good, sometimes not.
The possibilities never failed to charge our imaginations.
You see, the city represented a different world. What we
saw amazed us, particularly in how town dwellers seemed
to have become so different. Though a child, I could see
they felt the same about us, from their own side of the fence.
To think, we came from the same soil, split from the same
stone. Now, for them, we were bumpkins. Opportunities
perhaps, targets for solicitations maybe, or just there to be
humored and exploited.

"We didn't see ourselves that way. Our lives were
riddled with challenges. Marked with struggles. By
pushing through them, we survived, and our spirits grew
strong. They turned out to be blessings. Our hard acquired
skills were like extra appendages, sure and certain when
needed. Simple in our insights, perhaps. Bumpkins, not.

"We could see they had lost all that. Other talents had
taken their place. It's hard to say what makes people
change. Different time, different place, different person. We
seem so innocent and alike as children. All of us. Then in
just a few short years, innocence and camaraderie are taken
over by agendas. Great divides! Ever wonder where that
comes from, or how it happens? Before you know it, the
world no longer exists for us to serve in harmony and to
protect. We exploit to suit our individual inclinations,
rooting our sense of self in place of it at center.

"Onto that self we mount thrones of perceived
importance. Arrogance perhaps? In due time, our once
neighbors and kin become part of the surrounding

landscape. Game pieces on a board. If only we can somehow persuade them to suit our ends and needs."

"Careful Bao Ling, you're leaving out 'De.'[16] Righteousness, respect, morality, virtue, integrity, compassion and proper behavior. These are the traits which ultimately govern our conduct. They ensure the continuance of life itself, and preclude chaos. Community! Sages like Kongfuzi and Mengzi meticulously spelled it out for our benefit. No one falls outside the governing principles of conduct as, without them, we have no hope for mutual survival."

"True Uncle Wei. You and I understand this, but do others?"

My friend could only answer with a growl-like "mmmmmmm" as though acquiescing to the harsh realty.

"Regardless, the journey to town represented a great adventure for the child in me. Grandfather never hurried. He liked to remind me. 'Bao Ling. It's true that time is of the essence, just as it's true destiny frowns on procrastinators. But one should never hurry unnecessarily. Look at me, your poor old grandfather. As I'm standing here, I can think of all the times I rushed and pushed carelessly through life, causing great waste, even damage in

---

[16] "De" a term relating to one's inherent character. The meaning differs somewhat within the various traditions. Here, Uncle Wei is alluding to the Confucian standard as it relates to virtue and moral character.

my wake. Honestly, I can't say I got to where I am standing right now one heartbeat sooner.'

"He had an admirable sense of humor. Come to think of it, the same proved true of most masters. They knew funny when they saw it. Even when finding it soaked in tragedy, they could not be deterred, or resist the temptation to spin sadness and despondency into a laugh.

"For me, his 'one heartbeat sooner' seemed to challenge more than teach. A riddle he wanted me to unravel, but left for my own devices. Of course, the solution lay in the premise for action. Don't move selfishly! After a few bumps and disasters I figured for myself the appropriate adjustments, and made them. I learned to take life with steady keel, deliberate and focused. Hurry when necessary. Never sacrifice awareness, intent and compassion.

"Thinking back, perhaps it was for that very reason we needed two weeks for trips to market which others might have accomplished in several days. He traded, he talked, made new friends, visited temples and shrines, sought out shamans and loitered with taoists. He told me he was getting a pulse on the surround. He knew everyone, and they seemed to know him. Nothing escaped his awareness. But even he could not always predict what we might encounter, or find. For that reason, the trips always simmered with the promise of magic and mystery. All of which would have passed unnoticed had we rushed. In life, unnoticed is the same thing as 'not there.'

"I remember clearly. One time a ferocious storm blanketed us. Black clouds layered our campsite, followed by rain weighing down upon us from the heavens. He pointed to the distance. For a moment I swore to be seeing frogs dropping to earth, mingled with hail in the torrent. By then, we were under our wagon's apron, doing what-all to keep dry. Grandfather taught me we were surrounded by mysteries, just as we were prone to be victimized by chaos. For him, mysteries held the key. He would say 'Chaos may take us to the very precipice leading to our ruin. But it cannot push us over, unless we do it first to ourselves. Cloak your intent in mystery. Chaos will not be able to read your heart or get its grip on your will, or your fate. Remember, it seeks the obvious, and twists the once known into uncertainty, sowing fear. Therein lies its power, and its frailty. Thus, our hope. Bao Ling, be true, be mysterious. Learn to engage doubt and uncertainty without fear. When confronted with fear, act decisively, and never, ever underestimate the power of restraint.'

"'Are the frogs real grandfather?'

"'Just as real as you and I.'

"'Will they live?'

"'Most of them probably will.'

"'But how can that be?'

"'Though rare, ascending to the heavens is within the collective experience of our frog friends. So too is their return to earth. Somewhere within, a voice has grown. Louder with each generation's repetition of these wonders. It speaks to them clearly what they must do to survive.'

"'And they do?,' I asked incredulously.

"'Yes!' Then he added, 'You too Bao Ling, you're just like the frogs. Many experiences lie deep within you, some originating before the nascent ascendance of your memory. Listen for those voices, and learn to trust them.

"I nodded in obedience and in complete sincerity, but the unease wouldn't quiet. His words flew over my head.

"'I don't understand grandfather. How do I know what is the voice, and not my own imagination deceiving me?'

"He waved his hand out at the storm, which had grown. In the darkness, arcs of lightning leaped from cloud to cloud, and disconcertingly, cloud to ground, sometimes close by. It was then I noticed the frogs, now making their way to the many newly formed puddles of standing water.

"'Look to the clouds Bao Ling. See if you can make them dance! Light them up!'

"I had no idea what he meant, but as I looked, the image of a heavenly dragon lit in my mind's eye. As I imagined it in its majesty, I thought instantly how marvelous it would be if the lightning danced in the sky, just as the dragon had in my mind.

"No sooner had the thought clarified than the ground shuddered with explosions, seemingly coming from all directions. In fear, I reached for grandfather's arm, but it already lay over my shoulders, assuring his vigilance and protection.

"'Bao Ling, look! On the horizon. Can you see it?'

"I certainly did. It filled the sky left to right, starting at each side, consummating in the middle, like two waves colliding, and ending with yet another seemingly cataclysmic explosion of sound and tremor. The dragon I had moments before imagined, had been uncaged and, for the brief span of my own heartbeat, danced before both of us in the heavens. 'Did you see it too grandfather?'

"He remained silent, studying the play between flashing light, and deep shadow, breathing in the wet aroma mingled with the strong bite of lightning's scent[17]. A frog jumped nearby, which he picked up and admired in his open palm before lowering it to where the creature might return again to its familiar ground. Smiling profoundly, he then turned toward me and nodded.

"Yes Bao Ling, your dragon. You let him out. A wonderful creature I must say. Pure, pristine, powerful. That came from the 'voice' Bao Ling. Had it been your imagination, nothing more than a fleeting dream could have emerged. I would not have seen that, since it would not have been real."

---

[17] The scent of ozone - an odor resulting from molecular reactions when lightning strikes nearby.

Wanzhuxiang

"I lay stunned. From the perspective of grandfather's affirmation it seems what just happened, actually happened.

"Only when I came to my senses did I ask, 'Grandfather, do you have a dragon too?'

"He laughed but said nothing. From the tone of his laughter, and the nothing he said, it seemed he knew exactly of what I spoke."

I had to stop at that point. The details became confused, like flakes fluttering in a distant dream. I took a moment to muse in silence reaching for the lingering fragments of memory.

"So that's your story? I'm not sure I see the connection with my own?" asked Wei, clearly puzzled.

"No, just the beginning. I beg your patience, I want to get it right."

"Of course! We have time. I'd prefer to hear it all."

"Before long, the setting sun again pushed through it's radiant splendor. We rested, carefully taking ample time to dry ourselves, and to check our goods. To our great relief, everything survived. We chose to rest there and enjoyed the spectacle of starry night. Next morning, we picked up where we left off, still two days out from the trade center.

"Not long after mid-day, I spied a roadside shrine in the distance, built in traditional style. It stood alone and defiant, surrounded by expanses of grain. Their not quite ripened tips traced waves as they danced in the breeze. A child's curiosity awakened within me. By way of pointing the shrine out to grandfather, I let him know my curiosity must needs be sated. He had elected to walk this final leg. Though up in his years, he wanted to spare our tired old mule the extra labor. I had been up and down, on and off the wagon, depending on my mood. My frustrated little legs sometimes could not keep with the old man's pace. He hobbled from ancient wounds, but still managed a long and confident stride. Sure, he was old. I'm not sure how old, but he was definitely old enough for everyone we ever met to refer to him with the honorific 'Old Ling.' In spite of that, he had the stamina of men much younger. On top of it all, he remained a peerless martial artist as I can personally attest.

"Don't get me wrong, he was a man like anyone else. He had the pains and limitations typical of others his age. Life left him with a pronounced limp on his right side. When he woke to pee in the middle of the night, I would watch in silence as he sat unmoving on the wagon's edge. His old bones demanded their due before allowing he was free to confidently stand and move about. When he removed his topshirt, you could see marks and scars covering his body.

Long-ago arrows had glanced or penetrated, and blades had passed but failed to strike fully their mark. I had once been curious about the stories behind each of them. Typically, he remained silent. Until one day, perhaps vexed by my incessant asking, he turned a pained gaze toward me. 'Pay them no mind Bao Ling. Whoever struck first at me did not survive the wasted effort. You are safe for now. In time you too will encounter their kind. Just remember, your grandfather said you will do just fine when that happens.'

"I nodded quiet acceptance of his words, being certain to remind myself our idyllic existence held no such threats. Of course, his wizened prediction proved to be true. More true than I dare to say. And yes, I did do fine, just as he had predicted.

"To do him full justice, I will tell you now, he was a man who understood the teeth of compassion. What others consider compassion is little more than a contrived demonstration of what they in fact lack. He would never strike first against an adversary. Why I can hear his voice as I speak now, 'There can be no first strike Bao Ling. Stay your hand. Only then can peace have a chance. Many will work to convince you otherwise, or to have you thinking their initiation of violence represents the only rational path to peace, success, or prosperity. They lie! Remember that! And somewhere buried in their lie is their investment in the outcome. It may seem inconceivable to your young mind. For some, chaos, destruction and suffering represent great opportunities. The promise of riches. Don't ever go there. Trust me, I'll be watching. For those folks, and how they've twisted their minds, it may be hard to comprehend, but peace represents what comes to us most naturally. It's what should be first sought after. Sure, I'll bet they knew it once. But the awareness got in the way of their ambitions and had to be excised from their thinking. Only years of acquiescence to chaos and the associated ills and deprivations can cause us to lose sight of underlying reality. It's then we learn to satisfice, and to cater to our immediate needs, particularly survival. We become something new, different and apart from our very natures, forgetting peace avails all options while chaos enslaves. Life's fundamental inclination is toward peace, just as water always runs to the sea. It may not happen today, or tomorrow, but it will get there. Otherwise, we are finished. Zhuangzi said the same of 'De,' as he hoped to encourage the art of virtue among those with power and influence. I don't doubt him. He's better than all of us put together. Without peace there is no freedom, and without freedom, no reason to live. Be strong Bao Ling, never lose track of yourself. Let evil take its best shot, then banish it without wavering. Never go over that precipice when you can still turn about and square off on the enemy.'

"When he finally departed this world, a profound sense of loss and detachment descended upon me. It has remained with me since. I admit it. I miss my innocence! I felt fortunate to have spent a great deal of time in his tutelage. In fact, once he was gone others referred to me as his wanzhuxiang[18]. As though I had been attached to his side for the time it took ten thousand incense sticks to burn. Honestly, it could have been. It seemed to be years. During that time we never idled or wasted a moment. His being as old as he was made it all the more remarkable to behold his

---

[18] Incense shadow

skills while we worked. Actually, I like to think we played. Together. No longer strong, or fast, he compensated with craft and ingenuity. He liked to think of himself as a shifty old monkey. Not unlike the famous Monkey King, whom, he hastened to add had been his friend before destiny split their paths. Ever curious, I would ask, 'What happened to him? Will you ever see him again?' 'No matter,' he would say. 'If someone is truly your friend, part of their spirit will always be with you.' Then with a slight glaze over his eyes, he would look wistfully off to the western horizon as though the wind might carry his message to a long parted mate. Sometimes I thought he was just cleverly pulling my leg.

"Now, as I think back, I question if he felt to be racing time itself. Getting all into me he could, before the door slammed shut. Who's to say? Looking back, I can only wonder. He acted with great purpose, as if everything depended on what he did in this moment, and clearly, what he did with me had been part of it. Today, I recall the quality and the vitality. How everything we undertook could not have been done better. Therein lay the great message. To be truly alive requires not wealth as much as full commitment to the moment, and to the purpose and quality of your actions."

Yellow Tinted Eyes

"Ah, you see Bao Ling. You too had a bodhisattva. We were equally blessed. But I protest. We have digressed. What about the roadside shrine?"

"Well, as we closed upon it, we saw no signs of life or activity. You know how it is. On the long journey from village to town, one's not likely to encounter others. Lots of empty space. In the middle of emptiness, we came upon this shrine."

"It sounds eerie to me. The way you say it. In the middle of emptiness. How many others might have passed it never noticing? As a practical person, I wonder how it got there, and why? For what purpose? Go on, I want to hear more."

"I saw how grandfather noted my curiosity. His keen eye took measure of the cooling shade within the compound. Glancing upward he allowed it would be sensible we take cover from the now blistering sun. 'There won't be a better place to cool, relax and grab a bite.'

"Not unexpectedly, on passing through the ornate portico, we found we were the only ones there. Cautious by instinct, grandfather held still. Centered in the walkway, he looked as though collecting his thoughts. I knew better. Perhaps something in the shadows caught his attention. Without moving, he took account of everything, listening and surveying. I could see nothing, not at first anyway. Ahead, a larger than life statue of Guan Gong occupied the focal point within. The legendary crimson beard majestically framed his reddened face. He stood to ready, adorned in full battle regalia. Off slightly to his side, his arm at the ready and his right hand gripping the hilt of the downturned but ever fearsome Green Dragon Blade.

"Stunned by the nobility emitting from the creation, I stood wondering if such a person could ever truly have existed. The construction represented the pinnacle of what local artisans had to offer. Stone finely cut and polished. Mortar cleanly applied. Finishings of colored agates and petrified woods. All brilliantly set off by delicately placed elements of decorative wood trimmings, orchestrated to complete the illusion of Guan Gong standing before us in fact.

"Despite grandfather's encouragement, I hesitated before going closer in. I scanned the interior, not large or expansive but a beautifully adorned setting for the jewel before me. I noticed Lord Guan's left hand facing slightly outward. The forefinger and middle digit raised upward as the others curled inward below. 'Why does he hold his left hand like that grandfather? Is he saying something to us?'

"'Perhaps Bao Ling. His left hand is placed as a warning and an assurance. He is warding off evil and chaos. It's for that reason he stands here protecting the approach to town. The folks here trust his spirit will look well upon them, and keep them free of marauders and other insidious purveyors of wickedness.'

"'Look grandfather, over there!' In the shadows angled behind Guan's left side, I spotted another figure. Crouched and immobile, looking a bit like a toad on a rock. 'He has a companion, someone watching his back.' The second figure appeared generously draped in a loose fitting tunic, partially cloaked in saffron. Cloth or stone, at first I couldn't tell. I drew nearer, the cloak covered what appeared to be a resting but alert creature, carved in multiple darkened shades of stone. It held a weapon of its own. A sturdy wooden bo, or perhaps iron made to look like wood. He cradled it in his arms, just below his downturned head. My gaze locked onto the receding brow almost simian in its cast, at least from my angle of view.

"Initially, I thought it to represent a guardian monk. Set by its creator to the rear of Guan Gong, a humble counterpoint. One magnifying the greatness of the other. Considering carefully for a moment, I couldn't resist yelling out excitedly, 'Grandfather, is it the Monkey King? Is that who's watching Lord Guan's back?'

"At first, grandfather seemed not to have seen anything. Maintaining absolute stillness, by his posture and rooting I knew he suspected the presence of someone highly skilled. Somewhere in the enclave possibly a threat, intentions yet to be determined. Then, like a panther he moved alongside me, and staked his own clear line of view. I could read his excitement as he suddenly hurried forward calling back to me, 'Bao Ling, run to the wagon. Bring some water and some jiou[19]. Hurry lad!' He had already reached for his own water skin, and I thought I saw him sprinkling it all over the statue in some sort of respectful homage or ritual. Sensing the import, I thought to pull out some incense before returning.

"I grabbed for the water and the wine, stuffed the incense in my waistcloth, then hurried back. As I angled around Master Guan, what I saw stopped me dead in my tracks.

"To my front, grandfather appeared to have been dropped to one knee. What I thought had been the statue of the Monkey King, had now ascended to full standing with the bo held menacingly in guard position. The fearsome figure stared down at grandfather. Just as I peered from beside Lord Guan the creature's yellow tinted eyes raised to take in and assess my presence. Raw beaming awareness. I shuddered within. Their fire traveled through my own eyes and coiled the spine, gripping tightly as it scorched earthward. I felt as it returned through tributaries unseen to its rightful owner, delivering all he needed to know. In my wildest imaginings I never saw grandfather downed or humbled by any man. This vision came from outside my imaginings.

"I first thought to create a distraction, hoping to buy time for grandfather to recover and act. No sooner did I have the thought than the creature lifted its head a second time

---

[19] Wine.

toward me, almost seeming to read my mind. It smiled, as though sensing and approving the merit of my intention. I could swear I heard his thoughts, 'Go ahead little one, show us what you're made of!'

"And I intended to do just that, but before I could act upon my notion, the man-creature eased it's guard. He set down the bo then stared hard and long at grandfather, becoming again statuesque in his stillness. Can anyone stand so truly still as a post? Perhaps I had taken only a few slowly drawn breaths, but it seemed like the sun moved from one side of the sky to the other as I watched expectantly. Then, a smile cracked across the marble face of the stranger. To this day, I have never seen a smile so broad and so true. The stranger's joy stretched the corners of his mouth almost to the mid of his ears.

"He bounded forward and with arms outstretched. Plucking grandfather from the ground he called out, 'Get off your knee old man. It's me, your friend. Not some tight ass worthless predator trying to impose upon you.'"

Old friends meet again

Child Meets Stranger

"He pulled grandfather into his enormous chest. The two warriors embraced as brothers too long parted. I stared … dumbfounded."

"Bao Ling. Were they in fact brothers?" asked old Wei.

"No, not brothers. Friends! Bonded not by blood, but by common experience. You know we can't choose who might become our brothers or sisters. But friends we do choose, and ever so carefully. One can go a long way with good friends. Not always so with siblings.

"Being a young child, all of this left me puzzled and confused. He called grandfather by his name 'He Ling.' How could he possibly know his name? Grandfather only said, 'It's been nearly thirty years.'

"'True my friend. Thirty years, seventeen days, we parted at dawn. Today, I barely recognized you. And I never forget a face. I see life has marked you well. Mocking offense, grandfather answered he might be old, but he still had a few tricks left. This drew laughter from the apparition, 'Of course you do He Ling. If anyone understood the moment, and the need for readiness, it would be you.'

"I stirred a bit to draw their attention. Grandfather broke gaze from his friend and motioned quickly for me to come near with the water and the wine. He also saw the incense and without missing a beat, lit some to celebrate and signify gratitude for the moment.

"The stranger nodded toward Guan Gong. Grandfather understood immediately, moving quickly to the statue where he ignited the balance of incense stalks.

"Then grandfather returned to his friend nearly breathless from excitement. He took the clay urn from my hands, wet the cloth and feverishly wiped dust from the apparition's face. Only then did I notice the weight of grime, soil and discoloration covering the stranger. His tunic and outer garments were weathered, sun-baked, and shredding. Seemed to me he hadn't bathed for months. I imagined had we not stumbled upon him he might have turned to dust himself. Given his manifestation at that moment."

"'More water Bao Ling, hurry,' grandfather called.

"When I returned, I saw he had given the stranger a hearty cup of wine, which the stranger clearly savored.

"By then, his face and limbs had been rinsed and he lost much of his stony edge. Granted, he still looked something other than purely human with his overgrown hair, demon eyes and arched brow.

"Trying to break the ice, he smiled stiffly toward me. 'Nice boy, thank you for the water. And the wine.'

"In that moment I remained adrift, not understanding anything. A statue had come to life. It now crouched before me as a hermit monk, or gnome. Who could say what? A great energy emanated from his center. I remembered enough from my internal studies to know this energy as singular. Standing there, I felt to be in the heart of a great storm. Much like the night before, clouds and dust swirling about me in a grand cyclone. Could they have been connected? Might grandfather have conjured him as I had the dragon? Of course looking about with my true eyes, I saw nothing had changed. Smoke lightly ascended from the incense sticks. Birds still sang in the adjoining trees. The fields of grain still swayed casually along the periphery.

"But I felt what I felt. I knew it was there, as too did grandfather. So too did his mysterious friend, from whom it all emitted.

"Once the formalities relaxed, grandfather did eventually introduce me properly to his friend and one-time war companion. I learned he was Colonel Sun. He and grandfather had met as the battles along the Shu Roads were in their final throes before exhausting themselves. Some conflicts just lose steam. That's what happened with Shu. Invaders tried pushing through those passes for hundreds of years. Ever heartened one last thrust would somehow succeed where all others had failed miserably before. All counted on the West becoming theirs, as it had been for Liu Bei.

"No one ever truly succeeded. The price inevitably proved beyond ability to measure, forecast, bear and survive. Those same cloud shrouded roads had become the domain of the great strategist and sage, Zhuge Liang. Though long gone, his combination of wizardry, spells, deception, faux trails, and constantly evolving paths left a puzzle which no outsider could solve. On entering, aspiring conquerers found a bewildering maze of roads and passages queued to bleed them dry. They circled endlessly about while their futures turned to dust. Unless of course they were properly guided. Stories abound of mountain people captured and enslaved for that single purpose. Steer us through the treacherous passes. Cooperate and you'll live. Get us to the other side. We'll set you free. That was the bargain. Life for treachery. Grandfather spoke with great admiration for the mountain people always mindful to add not one is known to have broken the trust.

"Those enslaved were not held for long. Mountain people removed from their habitat didn't go far. Some walked from bridges into space. Some willed themselves to die and did. Others simply sat down and never moved again. Even heartless torture failed to force their submission. This confounded the butchers, all the more bewildered as they witnessed unprecedented resistance to their most devious and perverse measures. It had always worked before! This time, a pointless exercise. The natives seemed impervious to whatever might be conjured. Solving the Shu tribes and undoing their will would be no easier than navigating the Shu terrain. Grandfather often told how these mountain people had their own ways. They were a happy people. They only wished to be left alone."

Wei interjected, "Nothing sings out to predators more than the desire to be left alone. You know that, don't you? You'll encounter them soon enough, should you make it to Crystal Springs."

From the Void

"Looking more carefully at Colonel Sun and grandfather, I couldn't reconcile the age difference between them. Especially if Colonel Sun was in fact the senior as purported. Though still robust, grandfather was indeed elderly. An old man at the end of his time. Sun, once cleaned up and polished a bit appeared to be in life's prime. A magnificent physical specimen, though dressed in rags. Still, nothing prepared me for what was yet to follow."

"What can top that?" Wei asked in obvious anticipation.

"Grandfather went about the usual formalities, 'What brings you to our province? How long have you been waiting here?'

"To which the stranger answered, 'I came looking for you He Ling. I barely missed you last time you came to town. The traders knew you well, and said you had been trading for several days, then headed south and west to spend some time at the temple. They also said the boy was with you. I asked if anyone could direct me to Ling village. They all had their opinions. Well, no two of them could give me the same directions, or for that matter agree on whether

Ling Village still existed. I struggled with whether to head south and trust fate to find you, or to simply wait until your next return. They told me you came once every season, so I figured I'd winter here and catch you next time you passed by.'"

"Wait a second, Bao Ling!" Wei interjected, "How did he know about you?"

"What do you mean?"

Wei explained, "You just told me the Colonel said, '… the boy was with you.' In merchant talk, that means you were part of the reason he came!"

"How do you figure that?"

"Bao Ling, in my line of work, such things are obvious. Just as like when you sense the wind before you loose an arrow!"

"Truthfully uncle, I had never thought of it that way."

Uncle Wei made clear with his hard stare, on this point he would not be denied. "Go on with your account nephew, let's see where it takes us."

"Well, knowing where Colonel Sun wintered, grandfather nodded as though understanding. Needing more explanation, I interrupted, 'You stayed at the inn for three months?'

"'No, I came to the shrine. The folks in town told me of the shrine dedicated to Lord Guan and I thought I'd come here and pay my respects. I also knew He Ling would find me here when he returned.'

"To which grandfather countered, 'Have I become so predictable?'

"'No old friend. I simply knew you would not pass without paying due respect to Master Guan. So here I waited.'

"Grandfather replied, half humoring my stare, making it clear to the stranger it was I who wanted to stop and, but for that, we might have passed.

"Sun clearly thought to know better, though he held his tongue and nodded to me in appreciation.

"Grandfather then added, 'Ah, I must be getting old. I sensed a presence on entering, but saw nothing. Bao Ling found you.'

"Sun turned to me approvingly, 'Tell me young man, what did you see?'

"'Well sir, I saw Master Guan. As I studied him closely, I started to cross his front. I couldn't take my eyes from him. But then, his Green Dragon Blade drew my attention as did his left hand. Only then did I see something in the shadows behind. A statue of the Monkey King, crouched and at the ready.'

"I noticed how the stranger winced when I used the expression Monkey King, then thought it best to hold my tongue and not confuse the man before me with the legendary hero of underdogs.

"'A statue? You thought I was a statue?'

"'I'm not sure what I saw.' Colonel Sun's stare told me he expected truth, and would not tolerate deception, even if done in politeness. 'Well, truthfully Sir, to my eyes, you did appear to be a statue. Perhaps I could trouble you to teach me how to avoid such errors in the future.'

"'In fact young man, I had been napping. I knew eventually He Ling would come around, and I have infinite patience. Since nothing else called for my attention, I took the opportunity to nap on this spot. It's true, I am a deep sleeper, but statue I am not. You wanted to see the Monkey King, and that's what you saw. Beneath your imagining I rested. Don't feel bad Bao Ling, I take no offense. Judging by the surrounds I suspect others had the very same thought.'

"Only then did I notice the remains of incense sticks, hundreds, maybe more, in concentric circles around where he had been crouched.

"Cautiously, I asked, 'You were napping? How long?'

"'Since the last time you came to town.'

"'Late autumn? You've been here since late autumn? Napping all winter?'

"'Yeah, that sounds about right,' he scanned the surround, 'Looks like spring has arrived, so that would be all winter I suppose.' Then he pondered for a brief moment, adding, 'Perhaps napping misstates what I was doing. You see Bao Ling, my ways may differ somewhat from your own. When I close my eyes and nap, my mind journeys to a deep well of emptiness. Time does not follow me into that empty chamber, nor does hunger, or distraction. For me, it is very restful. It's a little bit like returning to the home of my own youth.'

"Not wanting to show discourtesy, or to signal skepticism, I stared to grandfather for help. He only nodded in understanding. Clearly he knew more of this than I could hope to fathom. I looked back to Colonel Sun, continuing, 'But while you're there, aren't you at risk from the weather, the cold, thieves, outlaws?'

"He held his hand up as though to stop me, then answered, 'No! Such things do not concern me.'

"Undaunted, I continued, 'But you had become a statue, I saw it, you were stone, rigid, unmoving. Insects crawled about on your face. I return from getting water, and the statue is gone, apparently replaced by a ...' I almost said monkey again. No doubt he glimpsed what had crossed my mind as his eyebrows raised anticipating the unintended slight, 'strange, powerful, and mysterious man. How did that happen, what magic did I miss?'

"Sun smiled at my recovery.

"Only then did grandfather speak. 'It was I Bao Ling. I recognized the Colonel immediately, and knew he had expected us the instant I saw him. I sent you for water and wine, then went to the Colonel myself to sprinkle water on him and to rinse the dust from his eyes, hoping to gently wake him. In that moment, he returned to us from the void, just as you returned with the water and wine.'"

A Fickle Will

"The two men looked at each other. Quietly, grandfather reached for the flask of wine, poured a fresh cup, and passed it to the Colonel. First he sipped, then drained the cup entirely. Nodding in appreciation, he issued a satisfied and sated, 'hmmmmmmm … too long.'

"Grandfather only then poured for himself. When both in time had downed their fill, grandfather passed the drained flask and urged, 'Bao Ling, go to the wagon and fetch some rice and pickled roots. Some dried perch too. The Colonel must be famished. Oh, and cook up some eggs, and water for tea.'

"I wanted to stay and listen, but knew to obey. Especially as it pertained to our honored friend. I too wished to see to his needs. I knew from his demeanor he would be my friend as he was grandfather's. Of that, I had no doubt. He should be as comfortable as we might make him. Still my child's curiosity sprung to life. Would it be too impolite to set up nearby as they spoke? Then while I worked, I could overhear everything, and perhaps learn more.

"'I thought you had returned to your retreat on Southern Mountain. Honestly, I never expected to see you again. Unlike you, I must keep eye on my time remaining. Brother Sun, I have no words to express my joy in coming upon you today. But I fear our moment may be shorter than my hope.'

"'Yes, Brother Ling. For a traveler like myself, life's greatest joy boils down to one essential element. Friendship. Without that, I would have nothing. And you have been a fine friend.'

"Then they spoke of the Jin Emperor. How Jin supplanted Wei in the same manner Wei supplanted Han. Both muttered 'karma' under their breaths as they recounted. Grandfather played historian, carefully taking Colonel Sun through all which transpired in the east and south since their parting. Then they focused on kingdom Wu and the once benevolent, then turned tyrant Sun Quan. The noble leader eventually lost the esteem of his people and in the end forfeited his southern empire to the Jin. 'Yet another great tragedy,' both mumbled.

"Grandfather continued, 'I'll give them this, and this only. For a brief moment, Jin united the land. In the still lingering smoke and flames, a new empire could be seen struggling to take shape and emerge. But the moment passed, as the will of heaven remained fickle. They had no choice but to thread their destiny's difficult course through the tumultuous period of the eight princes. Then the devastating civil wars which followed, culminating in the sixteen kingdoms. Finally, the influx of the barbarians who came first as mercenaries, then as allies, and ultimately as usurpers.'

"I listened intently as grandfather related to Colonel Sun. 'I learned of the Jin census. Done at the time of the short lived consolidation. They determined the size of the population and the number of households to be less than one-fourth what they had been at the time of the last Han census. Just think, but for all the nonsense, forty million more people would still be alive today.'

"Shocked, I blurted out, 'All those people were killed in the conflicts between the three kingdoms?'

"Both turned to me. I wondered if I had spoken out of place. Colonel Sun answered, 'No Bao Ling. They died from famine, disease, wanton destruction, abandonment and chaos. The Lord of War takes only the combatants. The combatants take everything else. It has always been my reckoning final responsibility rests with each person who makes the choice to participate. Every one of us can opt to refuse and find something more useful to undertake. The real enemy is chaos and its signature can be found nowhere better than in its heartless degrees of collateral damage, pillage and exploitation. All speak incessantly of these things. I can hear their murmurs of 'tsk, tsk' to affirm their disapproval. Rare indeed are those willing to sacrifice to change what is.' He turned and looked for a long moment at Guan Gong.

"Then they spoke with sadness of the fall of Kingdom Shu Han. And then how our family sought to remove themselves from yet another seemingly endless downward spiral. The survivors among us found refuge in province Jing. It was there in the pristine midlands where village

Ling gradually took hold, far and remote from everything noxious. Too small to covet, to find or to touch. That was the hope.

"Colonel Sun asked grandfather, 'Will it continue to be so?'

"Grandfather's stare answered for both, stirring in my soul concerns for the future. Our future.

"More than a generation previous, violence had threatened again from the north. Grandfather decided to head there rather than wait for the troubles to reach Jing. A younger man then, he sacrificed much, but never regretted the decision. No stranger to conflict, he quickly re-established his battle credentials. His deeds afield aroused the curiosity and then the respect of Colonel Sun. Finding quick partnership, their combined troops wreaked havoc on the internecine combatants. Relying on the Shu Roads, and the Shu people with whom Sun had intimate acquaintance, the surrounding highlands became cover for their retreats and renewal. Eventually the combination proved a formidable wall securing Jing from any spilldown of the interminable plague from the north. When the chaos quelled, they parted ways. Grandfather, already gone for two decades, thought only of returning home. The home he had hoped to and indeed, did save and protect. Now sworn brothers, he pleaded for Sun to return with him. But both knew, Sun could only return to his western sanctuary on Southern Mountain where in his words, 'I go back to my cell.' Whatever that meant.

"I gleaned much from their discourse, most of which I couldn't understand. Grandfather, who now appeared far older than Sun, constantly referred to Sun as the elder. Sun, to my surprise, readily accepted this courtesy without correcting.

"At first, I found it impolite. Proper manners would have required a gentle correction, or friendly admonishment. To my eyes it was He Ling who was clearly the elder, and deserved the honorific.

"Frankly, I couldn't reconcile why it did not happen.

"Then, grandfather asked Sun if he had worked through his great sadness — yet another riddle.

"Their prolonged silence made it clear he had not. Sun explained that he would be all right in time. He simply had to believe that in the end, humankind would not succumb as had others before. It was that thought alone which would sustain him.

"Grandfather questioned why he had left his retreat, politely avoiding the reference to 'cell.' Sun answered, 'I make it a point to keep an eye on things. As you know Brother Ling, I am compelled to act. When the situation demands my attention, I stand at the ready.'

"Grandfather only nodded, 'Of course. Without you, the losses would have been far greater.'

"'Who can say? Chaos seems always to prevail. Travel to the north, or the east, or the south, and people yet suffer, seemingly interminably. I should have done better for them!'"

I looked to Jin Wei, hoping for his insight. "And there you have it. What do you make of it, Uncle?"

Old Wei shook his head, unable to make anything of it. He smiled and nodded assuringly, "Another Dragon for sure! What could all of this possibly mean? How do we figure in any of it? It's clear that we do, but how? And why?"

We finished our walk in silence.

Part 8

A Somber Gathering

Gone Without a Trace

We returned to Wei's home mid-afternoon. As we drew near, brothers Lee and Qiao anxiously approached. "Father, more trouble from the south!"

"What now?" old Wei snapped.

I looked at the three, but my peripheral vision picked up quick movements in the town circle. Scanning carefully, I saw the bodies earlier milling idly about had become heated and agitated. In the distance I could see uniformed squads taking strategic positions against suspected but clearly unwary targets. Orders from on high, no doubt.

Brother Lee answered for both, "A band of soldiers, numbering seven, has apparently disappeared. Part of a larger group moving westward. Their job: reconnoiter Southern Mountain, identify gateways to the south, and find passes through to the west."

Wei considered, then retorted, "So what! Soldiers always disappear. That's because they desert! You know the game, they roll through towns, hijack commerce, plague traders, plunder the weak. We've seen how lowliest soldiers can stash enough away to chance breaking off on their own. Catch a little luck. Sprinkle with some audacity. They can disappear and start anew tomorrow. Happens all the time. They probably headed west. No one finds them there."

Lee answered, "True, but this time, the explanation is not so simple. These were seasoned veterans and trusted cadre. Proven warriors of unquestioned allegiance. Their loyalty was further bound to promises of reward once they returned and proved the mission's success. They were under direct order from the Provincial Commander. Instructed to identify viable corridors for troop movement, deployments anticipated to soon follow. This has apparently thrown everything into disarray. Tight schedules have unraveled. The troops which had been discreetly passing through, have massed and are now backing up. Once barely noticed, now seemingly everywhere. The numbers confound logic. Who could have known there would be so many? Some are now sleeping in the streets. If we don't watch our step, we risk getting our heads removed. The magnitude of the crisis escapes no one in town. Tension mounts everywhere. Nobody wants these hungry do-nothings hanging around to make trouble. The missing squad had orders to report back to the Western Garrison but never showed. The garrison commander sent scouts to pick up their trail to no avail. His messenger arrived today with the news. The commotion as this spreads is obvious. There's no telling what bedlam will follow."

Wei asked, "What was their last confirmed sighting?"

"They were headed south, toward Southern Mountain. Facts conflict, but some homesteaders along the southern route report being robbed by a party of 7 or 8 less than 10 days ago. Typical but for one thing. Some witnesses recall there was a young woman with them. That only adds to the confusion."

Both brothers looked to me, almost expecting I shed some light.

Wei stroked his Chin, "Gone without a trace you say?" He glanced my way, "Perhaps another case for our wise magistrate. I already know what he will tell us. The mountain is home to Sying Hao. He jealously guards what is his. A girl sighted with them. What do you make of that nephew? And how do seven seasoned warriors simply disappear?"

I knew well what this was about. It meant trouble. My answer to old Wei told nothing. "I'm not the one to unravel this disappearance. Like you, I suspect they had plans leading them elsewhere. Whatever the case, they did what they did. Seasoned veterans know the risks of their game. I assume the girl has not been identified? Presumably she is missing with them? Doubtless some innocent child stolen from the safety of her loved ones. Something to ease the cold nights of their journey. Perhaps her parents, her family, or her village have a hand in this. Mine certainly would. I wouldn't blame them either. Protecting one's own is a sacred duty. I don't mourn for them, but I worry for the girl."

I asked, almost sarcastically, "What have the military leaders had to say about justice for homesteaders, or return of possessions, or finding missing daughters?"

Wei's blank expression gave his answer. These type of questions gain no traction when trouble brews.

He took me by the arm and politely led to the entry. "Come Bao Ling, we will prepare for dinner. I must say this. Sying Hao or no Sying Hao, taking out seven warriors and leaving no trace is the stuff that drives legends. Such events portend more trouble to follow."

We Swim in It

The ever stern Sao Wei outdid herself this second evening. She prepared a noble feast. Entering the dining area, I set my bow and implements nearby and turned to admire the setting. Reds and golds lit the table. Lanterns cast their delicate glow about the room. All there before my eyes, but nearly a dream. I'd never seen the likes of it. The exquisite artistry drew my smile. These several days it had been on retreat. Motionless, I absorbed all I could catch in the moment. Sao remained off to the side. My delight must have drawn her eye. She acknowledged my appreciation with the slightest nod of her head, completing the cycle of courtesy.

Zhi Mei sat with her cousins, Uncle at the table's head with wife Sao, and I alongside the brothers.

Uncle revisited the two mysteries as we commenced. "A military dispatch robbed, but no one can name or describe the thief or thieves. No one disputes any facts. The goods were there, then gone. Nobody came or went. All likely suspects were accounted for. Then, quick on its tail. A second and equally perplexing matter. A trusted crew of seasoned veterans unaccountably vanishes without a trace?"

Wei conjectured, "Two great mysteries in so short a span of time. Almost as though someone wished to send a message. A warning perhaps. I don't have answers. Nevertheless my instincts are sure of one thing. In some way, these events are bound together!"

His eyes touched upon mine, testing for reaction.

Younger brother Qiao Wei excitedly broke in. "Tensions have escalated throughout the city. Everyone's reacting to what's become obvious. There can no longer be doubt or debate. What we first believed to be refugees migrating from the east have turned out to be organized vanguards. Precursors of larger armed movements likely to follow. Until now they've had little to say or do, and have avoided attention. After today's news, they are visible everywhere. All the more conspicuous standing about doing nothing. Toying nervously with hilts of swords hidden beneath their tunics."

Wei's concern flashed evident. "What thoughts have you Bao Ling?"

My eyes met those of each person at the table, then I answered. "I have opinions Uncle, too often wrong. Wrong in that I tend to understate the reality. I am not nearly so persuasive as my brother Sying Hao in lighting the truth for others. Regardless, you have asked, and I must answer. I will tell you some of what I know and believe. You can trust I will speak true.

"Carnage and conflict in the east have spanned generations. There have been no clear victors. Nor benefits. The warlords, usurpers, and emperor aspirants rake back and forth, right and left, up and down. The entire landscape groans beneath the bite of their bit. I know of no place, village, town or province between the eastern slopes and the great eastern sea to have been spared. The broad cuts of their folly have fragmented families and decimated entire populations. All torn asunder with no life purpose but dodge the ill tempered whims of chaos. Where does it lead? Anyone's guess! Meanwhile, famine and pestilence become norms. Scholars during Han's golden years were high minded moralists. They had the luxury of comfort. Now, their progeny preach the harsh ethic of exploitation and survival. Once high minded moralists now grow rich and fat devising strategies for their benefactors. Best favored are those skilled at the crafts of death and deception. Talents which float one quickly to the top.

"In those torn lands, aside from shadow markets, commerce is non existent. If you carry something to market, someone will see and fleece you coming and going. Officials will blame highwaymen, but you know who they are. You know, but you can't say. So you learn to play along. No one is ever sought, caught or charged. Worse yet, nothing satisfies, nothing sates. And still more come. As I'm sure you suspect, armies unleashed demand infinite resources. Nothing less can overcome the will and fortitude of determined opponents. So they say! A terrible downward spiral. All sides stuck in the same boat, lost at sea. No way out or off, except to fight each other. All drifting toward oblivion.

"I'm told how the empire prospered under Han rule. Its radiance blessed many with opportunity, growth and abundance. For generations this held true. It had come to be expected. Then, in short order all reduced to nothing. How could that be? Did no one see it coming? What accounts for the change? Who would favor insanity over purpose? Those who led? Those who blindly took up their cause?

"It's my belief someone or something out there has hands on the rudder. But who or what? Until we know that, we stumble helplessly toward doom. For me, if there be one mission in life, it's to find the answer. I will personally pry those fingers from the till.

"Regardless of high minded motives, when all is told, armies serve the agendas of chaos, sacrifice, and deprivation. They take much from many. What they take vanishes as though it never existed. Then they call for more. Few allow themselves to appreciate this for what it is, and to sound out, 'Enough!' Things therefore become what they do. Order reverses. Anyone with any say, who might otherwise make a difference, too soon sees the practical wisdom of skimming their ten percent. What had grown and prospered under Han rule is now as though it had never been.

"Once, long ago, I had been detained by a troop from the south. Their commander came to entice me and others among us to their side. He promised security, purpose, adventure. Better yet, we'd have food, and earn a stipend. 'You'll be set!,' he assured, 'Much better off than out there.' I suppose he meant I could be one of the ten percenters. I told the good colonel his promises did not seduce me. He answered times would get harder. I would not, could not, survive on my own.

"I reminded, in case it slipped his mind, of the devastation one saw everywhere. The absence of functional rule, the paucity of food, rampant disease — stressing the pointlessness of it all. To what end should I join him? To save only myself?"

"'Your point?' he asked.

"'Not surviving doesn't seem the worst outcome, all things considered.'

"He looked to me and continued, 'You have a head on your shoulders. You can go far in times like these. Where your cleverness fails is in not appreciating where you're standing right now. Peasants, monks, scholars and aristocrats. All in turn believe somewhere outside ourselves exists a heaven. Their imaginations populate it with kindly spirits. Celestial benefactors who have the good ear of a cosmic emperor. There is also said to be a hell, with wailing ghosts and demons, bound to the whims of their lord Yama. All nonsense young man. Hell is right here in our midst. I assure you it's true. We swim in it! Just as I assure you there are no celestial guardians interested in your plight, or petitions. If anything, they are amused and entertained by what goes on! Your only choice is whether hell's grindstone rolls you over, or you act decisively and secure a position which pulls you from its tread. I urge you take this opportunity. Hitch yourself to the trajectory upward. While you can.'

"He then swore he was my friend. My only friend! Strange as it seemed, I believed him."

Qiao Wei exclaimed, "Wow, he said that? How did you respond?"

"I told him the only wheel which concerned me was that of Dharma, and the only test of righteousness, karma. I respected his thoughts, and his generosity in sharing his own take on reality. I then apologized, for at the moment I had become distracted. He questioned my meaning. I responded that in what little time I likely had remaining, I had hoped to become a more compassionate man. From my unsophisticated perspective, it seemed the premise of his enticement led elsewhere."

Crabs in the Pot

"The colonel took one last thrust. 'Emperors, dukes, scholars, generals, counselors, magistrates, governors, physicians; monks and priests too have assumed this path to their benefit! Don't be stubborn little brother. You'll miss the call of opportunity, and your best chance for survival!'

"I thanked him for his concern, his candor, particularly his offer of friendship. I told him I didn't know generals from dukes or monks. Nor did I know why they did the things they did when they did them. I did have some small awareness of the fates of emperors and emperor aspirants. As I did with the rise and fall of armies, and the endless cycling of dukes, counselors and magistrates. With due respect to what he said, none of them held any tighter grip on reality than did I.

"Begging to correct, I told him he erred calling my world 'hell.' 'Shit!' would be more like it. Perhaps his was hell, but not mine! My world was suffering and victimized by deprivation. There was a difference. I stood with the victims, he with the overlords and the oppressors. In my world, what I did mattered. In his, it would not. He had become just another cog in the great machine. I told him hell was like that, from what I could see of it. It made me think of a crab basket I saw long ago in a distant marketplace. Vendors set it out, uncovered, unprotected, for everyone to see and inspect its contents. You would think the crabs would seize opportunity and make their escape. Nothing held them there in the first place. Arguably, they had the wherewithal to control their destinies. Just as he promised the same to me. In fact, those at the bottom were trying to pull themselves upward, just as the crabs at the next level struggled to pull themselves to the level above. This mindless self preserving groping repeated all the way to the top of the heap. Effectively they became locked. All as one. Until finally they were lifted, still clinging, and dropped into the pot. They let go then. To feed 'Who?' Could he answer that? Where in the end did the benefits fall? Certainly not to the crabs! Intending no disrespect, I asked if his offer to free me was not steering me directly into the pot. If I had the good sense of a true crab, I would ask he toss me into the sea and forget he ever knew me, as I would soon forget him."

Young brother Qiao pleaded, "What happened then?"

"I stood before him overcome by a weight of sadness. Everything in my world had reduced to this. Here I was debating the devil's advocate over the nature of reality, when my world had already evaporated. Who kidded who? The colonel looked to me. He had nothing more to say. A veil of resignation, did I detect a tinge of compassion crossing his brow? He smiled, then signaled to his adjutant and ordered, 'Release this one, send him out the western gate, alone. Point him toward the wilderness, and let him be.'"

"So that's what led you here?" asked Qiao Wei.

"It led to my survival. For that, I thank him. He threw me to sea. I will remember to return the favor should our paths ever cross again. As we speak today, an army of men with thoughts same as his intends to descend here looking for new pickings. I fear for your province and the surrounding villages, and for your town and your family. I fear for the western plains, and for the remote centers lining the old silk road. I fear for the Southlanders and for the high mountainous princedoms to the south and west. Understand one thing, and this I fear most. Once this starts, there is no foreseeable end. No one has learned yet how to stop the juggernaut.

"What you've seen today foreshadows what will follow, but only in its first degree. Crossing the mountains was no easy undertaking, nor a decision made lightly. The east lay decimated. Heading west through the treacherous Shu ranges no longer stood to be the worst of options. Anything promised better than where they were and what they had. The old goat had been milked, then bled dry. So now they must head for new spoils. Brace yourselves! Sure as I sit here, they're coming."

"But we're insignificant," countered older brother Lee, "We threaten no one. We trade, we barter, we facilitate. Why do you feel we have a problem?"

"Does it even matter where they go? Over time, it ends the same. Here! And there, too! You see, the problem is them, and seated deep within their natures. They will do what they do. A tiger will be a tiger, and a horse a horse.

Today, strangers surface in your midst cloaked as dignitaries. Some bear elaborate gifts and promises of riches and opportunity. Nothing comes free! Promise what they will, the weight must fall somewhere. Maybe at first, over there, far away. Later, it will draw near, and in the end envelop you. Always think on that! Ask yourself, 'What harm will be born from my actions today?' Is there any doubt some of your own leaders court favor with these influence peddlers? They look to cement their own futures and fortunes anticipating the great change giving no regard to what has happened before and elsewhere. In a year's time, tens of thousands will have marched through your province. Where will that leave you? I tell you, it won't stop with that. When you think it can grow no worse, more will sift through the passes. Battlefields will carpet where rice once flourished, then spread like wild contagion into the towns. Your town! Your people. The elders, the children, the next generation, all mere grist to their ends."

"Bao Ling, we'll never let that happen!"

"No one ever does Brother Qiao. People aren't fools. Nor are they inherently cowards. It's just that after the fact, finding one's will to resist becomes so daunting. The practical course is always to accommodate. It always has been. The intolerable situation becomes just another of life's endless shortcomings, and the effort to change things, disproportionately burdensome. You'd be amazed at the ends people will go to in adapting to hell once it's visited upon them. So, as my friend the Colonel proposed, rather than resist, one should cross over to the other more radiant side of hell where with luck, one might still glimpse the sun."

Old Wei interrupted. Ignoring the risk of being impolite, he called out "Enough Bao Ling. You prophetize our doom. So noted! Surely, there is a way through this tangled web."

Times of Joyful Regularity

Sao, at first looking to having nothing to offer, spoke up. "If Bao Ling is correct, we have a sliver of time. An opportunity to act and do what we must. Trouble promises to be quick upon us, but we still have allies and contacts to the south and west. In the past, we've traded in the Southlands. They too know our word is true. Those who plan to target our humble community will not find it easy. Many among them will be forfeit in the mountain passages. The Shu people will see to that. They have been fierce defenders of their domain, and have clearly benefited from the lingering wizardry and spells of long gone Zhuge Liang. Some of them will make it through of course. But not enough to take us outright, at least not at first. Conceivably, others will trek around the mountain barriers and enter from the north and then eventually from the south and east, assuming they meet no resistance. They'll be exposed. For them, it will take considerably longer than bargained for. But it promises to happen. There will be time and opportunity for others to rise and resist if their courage proves ample. History shows only one, Liu Bei, to have succeeded in crossing the range and emerging whole in the west. Why only one? Because his nobility and compassion turned the hearts of the Shu resistance. His peerless band of warriors found a new home beyond the mountainous wall. In gratitude, he freed the Shu, and kept others out. He may be long gone, but his legacy continues.

"My reckoning is whoever comes first will steer around us to the western plains and the inner empire. A vast land filled with empty spaces, and many dangers. They'll need us and our cooperation at first. They'll want guides, support and logistics. We already know something they don't. They'll find pickings there to be thin. They will look again our way. No longer as staging host or ally, but as something to be exploited or to supplant. Should we commit to early action, patriots who remain here will find many soft targets against the overly extended vanguards. Harbor no false optimism! The outcome can not be predicted. Even as we have initial success, our losses will mount should they continue coming. Expect in time the momentum will swing to their favor. Any resistance here will ultimately falter and buckle. We're very strong, but small. We'll still have enough resources to stabilize a robust retreat. It is after all, our home, our land. Not theirs! We know it well, and how to use it. As to whether we can turn them about, much will hinge on what unfolds elsewhere on other fronts. That is something beyond our control.

"We can only hope there are more of like mind. The invaders may have designs on the south and the west, but not when resistance sets teeth on their tails. Regardless, it's clear the westernmost battle lines will take their shapes right here. Whoever acts first will be advantaged. Whoever delays will be vulnerable, especially if picked bare while they vacillate. We must commence discretely to move our wealth and resources. We should consider relocation to the south, perhaps the Southland, or if necessary, taking our luck, good or bad, to the mountain. There at least, we'll have a chance, and with others, can mount resistance of our own.

"Better to depart the world with dignity, and show one's best effort where it matters most."

I tried, but couldn't manage to stifle a smile. This time, it was I who nodded to Sao, acknowledging the weight and wisdom of her words. Who would have known her to be such a clever general? Truthfully, I expected her to have a different take on these affairs — perhaps more cautious, or more conservative. Actually I expected she would concoct a plan on how to exploit the chaos as new opportunity. "Showing one's best effort where it matters most!" How could anyone say it better? Despite her cool and sometimes offish facade, I found myself warming to her.

Little more needed be said. We ate, and as we sat quietly afterwards, deep melancholy descended upon the group. I knew the feeling. Still fresh in their hearts were times of joyful regularity. A place where life's dreams were courses to be laid, or sailed, and with risks left to the whims of nature. Risks ... an inconvenient aspect of reality, understood, factored in, and dealt with united as family and according to carefully laid plans and preparations. This turn of events promised deep cutting change. One which would shift the trajectory for each of their lives, as it had for my own and Zhi Mei's.

At one point, Uncle Wei, clearly troubled, looked to his wife, hoping for an answer to yet another concern. "Sister, what will become of our feathered friends?"

A servant entered and announced to Uncle Wei someone was at the gate. Wei went to determine who the unexpected visitor might be, and returned a few moments later with "Old Fox," the toll collector whose acquaintance I made earlier on entering town.

"Ah, Young Fox. I see you too have made the good acquaintance of merchant Wei." The old fox smiled as he tendered the traditional martial arts salute showing respect to one recognized as skilled.

I returned the courtesy, as Uncle Wei formalized our introduction. "Bao Ling, I see you have already made the acquaintance of my old friend Fa Miu. Fa Miu and I have crossed paths many times over the years, often as partners and allies. He has become family, I think of him as elder brother. Brother Fa, it is the same with Bao Ling. I think of him as nephew. He alone returned Zhi Mei to the living."

Old Fa nodded in understanding, then playfully added, "Please nephew Bao, think of me as 'Old Fox' as I have already branded you 'Young Fox.' It will be our little game, signifying our appreciation for one another." Looking to Zhi Mei, he acknowledged and greeted, "And you young lady, I am twice blessed making your acquaintance anew."

Zhi Mei smiled deferentially, not knowing what to make of his presence.

Sao signaled the servants to bring more food and gestured Fa Miu to a seat at the table's head.

"Tonight I must decline sister Sao. There are many goings on about town. Fresh guard has been posted on the perimeter, and the Provincial Minister has requested my counsel. I'm afraid it will be a long evening. He looked to old Wei. I came to have words with Jin Wei, if you can forgive my intrusion."

A Skulk of Foxes

Wei looked about then signaled for Fa Miu to sit. "A flask of wine for the Old Fox. Let's lighten his heavy tongue and relax his concerns before he enters session." A troubled glance from Fa Miu to Wei made it clear he wished to speak in privacy. Wei dismissed, "Fa Miu, we have no secrets at this table. Except perhaps Bao Ling, but he assures me it's for our own good. Please honorable brother, speak your mind freely."

Fa Miu nodded, then began, "For some reason, Young Fox and the maiden drew the attention of my upstart colleague at the collection station. He took it upon himself to inform the garrison chief of their passage with four mules. For reasons not entirely clear, the garrison chief took great interest in their showing up when they did. Then, of course, the big news hit. Their arrival seems to have the taint of poor timing. You know how it is when authorities look too hard. They start seeing things they shouldn't."

"Brother Fa, that's ridiculous. Zhi Mei is my niece. The mules were her dowry. This had all been set up some time ago, before the tragic and unexpected passing of her family and the criminal destruction of their homestead. They've taken to the road to survive. Returning now to Mei Village would be insanity, only risking further exposure to marauders still roaming about. You correct me if I'm wrong. They haven't been identified yet, have they? No one's been apprehended. We've heard of no suspects. Can you tell me with confidence they're being pursued?"

I looked to Old Fox and nodded affirmation of Wei's account. Zhi Mei smiled across the table, taking on the supportive role of a betrothed.

Wei continued, "You might remind the garrison chief we'd all be better served if he focused on the real problems."

Fa Miu laughingly dismissed, "Help me please brother Wei." Then looking at me and Zhi Mei, "I am surrounded by a skulk of foxes. Yes. Keep to that story if you wish. It's a good sell. But you don't sneak one by old Fa Miu that easily. The garrison chief is no man's dupe. Nor is he slack in his duties. When he catches a true scent, there is no stopping him!"

Jin Wei raised his eyebrows. There would be no argument or deception between the two old friends. Fa Miu saw immediately to the heart of the ruse, and that would be that!

Fa continued, "I will tell you now. The two will not be safe here for long. Trust me on this one thing. It is only a matter of time before someone associates them with the disappearance of the seven, or worse. They will be targeted for closed door questioning, and you know what that entails."

Whether they understood or not, I knew full well the ways of persuasion. Having been dragged down that road more than once, I saw it did not bode well. The still frail Zhi Mei would not likely survive another humiliation.

Wei sat pensively, running all possibilities through his head. Fa Miu then turned to me, "You will need to move on little fox, while there is time."

I nodded and looked to Zhi Mei, "We will set out for the temple before sunrise. Prepare your things, I will ready the animals. Make your farewells this evening. We will not be passing through on our return."

Tears welled in the eyes of cousins Mayleen and Ting.

Zhi Mei looked to me, knowing she was losing her family a second time, and now found herself unwillingly appended to me. I truly wished it weren't so, as I contemplated my own abysmal prospects. My life held no allure for her, nor should it. All I could hope for was to leave her somewhere safe. It could no longer be here. I was saddened to see her tear rimmed eyes, as she looked to Uncle Wei, clearly hoping he would reject my suggestion outright. But there was only silence, until Wei looked to me and affirmed, "In this difficult moment, you have chosen the right course. Heaven help us all! Who knows where it will end?"

Perhaps to avoid adding to the weight of the moment, Fa Miu begged his farewell and made off to his session with the magistrate. Exiting, he glanced at my bow and the hand fashioned shafts, then turned toward me. "Specimens of the highest caliber Bao Ling. I implore you. Use them only to suppress evil, and never to oppress. Oh, and please do give my respects to the esteemed Abbot." A slight smile graced his lips as he turned to leave.

Risks for all were increasing by the hour. I turned to Uncle to question the reliability of Fa Miu. Wei answered simply, "He has never failed our family, nor our friends. You needn't concern yourself."

I then spoke with Wei about Crystal Springs Temple. There might be risk in our continuing there, and I worried we could be bottlenecked on the slopes if targeted for arrest. Worse still would be the consequences to us, particularly Zhi Mei, if the recovered trove were found in my possession. "Uncle Wei, tell me one thing. Do you know if Abbot Shi-Hui Ke can be trusted?"

Wei looked to me, "Is there so much at risk in this delivery you undertake for Sying Hao?"

I nodded once and affirmed.

Wei related how the name Shi-Hui Ke had been associated with Crystal Springs long before Crystal Springs grew into its current prominence. It served as monastery and village-sanctuary for the wandering mystics and displaced mountain folk. "There are stories he has become an immortal, so his appearance may not be what you expect. We are told he too was once a great warrior. Like you, he favored the bow, until the day came when his fate went awry. He had been captured by war bands from the east and treated abominably. He did eventually return to prominence, but remained forever scarred by his ordeal.

"In youth, he served the Western Shu with distinction, until his mentors and trusted companions passed, one after the other. His long suffering people were again reduced to destitution. Shaped by these experiences, he achieved his full awareness in the heat of a great battle. Tiring of the pointless killing, he cast his lot for all there to witness, by simply sitting and trusting his destiny to compassion. Those closest about took first notice. Then, whatever it was, it reached outward like a calming breeze. The violence raging about him quieted. Weapons lowered and the subdued combatants simply stared at the glow of awareness radiating from his core. The accounts vary, but are consistent in attesting the wave coursed in all directions until blanketing the entire battlefield in seeming goodwill. The commanders were not happy. Opposing armies stood milling about, and combatants began talking with one another, sharing stories of their homes and families, and how circumstance backslid them into this hopeless predicament. Others too began to sit, and the enchantment spread. The commanders puzzled over the sorcery, which in their eyes could only be explained by the disease of cowardice. They rode their steeds into the crowded field, and were ignored by all. So much for battle that day. By nightfall many arose, abandoned their arms, and simply walked off, heading into the mountain wilderness. To this day, those in the east like to say we westerners don't have the stomach for battle.

"Shi-Hui Ke returned to his lord and asked to be discharged from further service. His first inclination of course was simply to walk off with the others. But he had been treated kindly, and he knew to pay last respects. His lord, though shocked at this dereliction, clung to Shi-Hui Ke's past loyalties and victories, and spared his life. The field commanders urged otherwise, stating the need to set an example for others. Before exiling him, the lord extracted his promise to protect the eastern gateway from all invaders. He confided the Western Shu would soon be no more. 'Our time has ended, you are wise to leave. Others will want to pick our bones clean. I only ask you keep them out, and let those here become what they will.' Shi-Hui Ke assented. He would accept his new orders to return to his home in the Shu Mountains and to seal the gateway.

"Doubtless, with these new developments spies have already been planted within his domain. Expect your every move will be scrutinized. They will suspect even you at first. As to Shi-Hui Ke, he is a sage beyond reproach. Trust him before all others."

We readied our gear and possessions in the early morning. Wei and his wife, along with the cousins all lined to bid farewell and pay respects. What emotions had been heavy the night before, had become unbearable this morning. Each family member gave Zhi Mei a small treasure as a hedge against the unknown. The usually stone faced Sao Wei melted with tears into Zhi Mei's final embrace.

I asked Uncle Wei's counsel on one point, "Do you think our leaving is marked and burdened by four mules? Might we not be better served leaving two with you, and taking only two?" Already I was thinking of traveling light, trusting to my years of experience moving about alone.

Though I had come to appreciate Zhi Mei's companionship, I knew it required added vigilance, and worried it would split my focus.

Wei was firm, "It's best they go with you. Their presence proves your story of Zhi Mei's dowry, they bear Mei family markings. Fa Miu will doubtless have worked the 'melody' to your advantage with his superiors. Any deviations at this time will only draw undue notice. Stay the course."

With that, we took our leave.

Just before I turned away from our hosts, Jin Wei called to me, "Bao Ling, one last thing. Don't take it upon yourself to become another one of those mountain ghost legends."

I miss that good and honorable man. Even now.

As we rode off, I too wondered what would become of our feathered friends.

Part 9

Companions

Roads In the Clouds

Whatever Fa Miu said to account for our presence, it worked. We drew little further attention as we mixed with traders and passed through town center. We exited northward. The gatekeepers logged our leaving and reminded of the toll due on return. An uneventful day wound down as we turned toward the highlands to begin our slow ascent to Crystal Springs. The surrounding traffic thinned.

What had earlier been road, now narrowed to a footworn trail. It seemed ancient, echoing countless footsteps trod in the past. Channels scored through rocks and boulders, marking the determination of those who survived the daunting journey from the east. Passing trains of traders were replaced by hunters and foragers. Then occasional monks, some coming, some going. For several days after, we pushed hard. I knew how fickle the authorities might be, and how quickly we might again be in their sights. The more distance between us and them, the better. Gradually, we saw fewer others on the trail. On the seventh day, we saw none. We reckoned one last full day of travel ahead. We parlayed and agreed to set camp earlier than usual.

Without saying as much, we needed to rest, if only for the sake of the animals. Or so we told ourselves.

In an adjoining clearing, we had full view of the temple to the east. It stood regal, mounted high like a ruby capped crown atop a neighboring peak. The outline of Fortune's Gateway sat far below us and to the south, barely visible. The drylands in the distant west glowed yellow orange beneath the late day sun.

From this vantage, one could see distant Southern Mountain as first of many great mountains in the ranges to the south and leading west. It declared its presence majestically on the far horizon. I felt to be staring at a well regarded friend, comfortable for its presence. Just seeing its majesty brightened my spirits. I knew a day would come when I would stare to the southern horizon and see only space. The thought weighed upon me.

One might venture further south and west. In those remote expanses lay great mountains known only from legends left by mystics and a handful of dauntless traders who made the trip and managed against all odds and trials to return. Accounts of those ranges, their size and scope, defied description. They appeared to lead nowhere, at least nowhere a mortal could travel and readily survive. Such realms are said best left to the frolics of the immortals. I do not disagree.

Southern Mountain too had it's perils. Harsh winters gave no quarter to the uninitiated. Sying Hao said it best. "The mountain gives generously and is a gracious host to many. But it won't tolerate fools." He spoke truth! One learned to expect a steep price demanded for each oversight, each miscalculation, each lapse of caution. But justly deserved. Those who couldn't self-correct or adjust to its expectations soon stumbled blindly upon their end. When spring thawed, bodies and carcases bubbled up from the melt. They looked at first like mushrooms flowering in an endless expanse, their spirits sealed by folly to forever trek its vastness.

Passes through the Qinling mountains were to the north. The temple ruled over a forgotten and nameless branch. At least I knew of no name. A pronounced finger which cut southward to the Hanzhong basin, where the Han River eventually flowed to the Yangtze, and then to the midlands.

From ancient times these fickle links connected east to west. Rulers chasing dreams of wealth to be had, sculpted tracks and trails that literally appeared to be anchored in the clouds. The extremes were profound. Breath stealing drop-offs into fathomless space threatened a mere shoulder width from where one found solid footing. Certainly not a place for timid animals, should one be so foolish as to ride mounted. With use over time, the family of passages became known as the Shu Roads. Named for the range, and the people who lived there for so long as anyone knew.

In attitude, Southern Mountain differed. Vast, with endless twisting and turning of its valleys and ravines. Walking there, one would never fear falling into the unknown. The fear would be of being consumed by the unknown. Parts of it remained forever under ice and cover of snow, and other parts invited the challenge of the adventurous. In its ancient woods, trees seemed to speak, and animals seldom seen in lowlands abounded and moved with the conviction of their own freedom. Most had never encountered man, and had no fear of him.

The Shu Roads coursed through the Qinling. Because of their long history of use, then disuse, then rediscovery, then abandonment, many branches sprouted over time. Some scouts and traders prospered by simply knowing some of their twists and turns, and being able to guarantee safe passage through parts of the punishing maze. Others, less scrupulous, would guide traders in and then abandon them to the alpine furies. Left to wander aimlessly until depleted and drained of any further will to go on. Once the mountains had finished their somber work, their goods in trade would be carefully harvested. For some, a fine living. Not so for the others.

It is said the roads grew from the trodding of endless feet and hooves. Over eons, the network eventually consolidated into five major east-west arterials. Named the Chen Granary Road (passing the city of Chencang), the Two River Road (Praised Waters and Sloping Waters), the Camel Gorge or Raging River Road, the Meridian Gorge Road and the Warehouse Valley Road. There were myriad other major branches to the north and south, all eventually connecting to population clusters which otherwise would have been forgotten.

To the most experienced guides, there were numerous cross routes between the arterials. Knowing them constituted power in those hills. Washouts, drop offs and collapses occurred always and often. Not knowing of or having alternatives meant certain death. One could easily get boxed in, and never get out. For those not in the know, these fabled passages to anticipated riches more often delivered one to the vultures and the brigands.

Yet still they called and beckoned to those who, but for this single faint prospect, had no hope.

Long Silenced Voices

I reckoned we happened upon the southern leg of the western network. Somewhere in the lowland channels of Warehouse Valley Road with its northern terminus between Mei Village in the north and Fortune's Gateway to the south. Zhi Mei did not disagree.

In my youth, I had traded and traveled into the mountains. The experience gave some familiarity with the eastern routes. Usually with grandfather, I learned from him what I could, but it seemed never enough. I did know to think of them only as an option of last resort. One could easily misjudge, and end up bewildered. Trekking excruciating spirals and circles until all hope and time ran out. I remember how we would joke about having to carry our horses and carts up and down the mountainous walls. Only it wasn't a joke in the end. The ladders to the sky, and the plank roads over wet bottoms promised an attrition of one third of whatever you had, starting with your own body weight. It represented a harsh toll against whoever, and whatever attempted to pass into and through. Once in, you were on your own. Forget about trusting in numbers, or being surrounded by an army of comrades. Every person ultimately fended for himself. All knew the pact going in. If you fell, no one would pick you up, for no one could carry you out. Nor could they drag you further in and expect you to survive. More than one lamenting friend was left singing the heartsick songs of his home, as his fellows drifted slowly away.

The long silenced voices still sounded in my dreams, some of which passed fleetingly before me as I watched Zhi Mei scurrying about, foraging our simple feast. As a youth, I couldn't see how everything we experience and go through in life is like our own Shu Roads. Every decision, take, or turn has with it a consequence. For guides we have loving parents, elders, sages, and mentors. All of whom must in time be shed. Not willingly mind you! Life dictates this be the way. Perhaps like others, I took the most important things for granted, and relegated them to my fancies of the moment. Now I know better.

Consider everything carefully! Every touch from a loved one, every laugh with a comrade, every moment of contact with life's flow, even the times of unrelenting harshness and solitude. Every moment of every day is a gift. To allow ambition, desire, ignorance or fear to cloak this simple fact is a fate worse than being abandoned on the Shu Roads, where at least you might sing songs of lament with eyes finally opened wide as your end approaches.

Zhi Mei showed great interest in my accounts of the roads. As the evening ambled forward, we warmed before the fire and I stretched the narrative to include some of my many talks with Sying Hao. She riveted her attention on anything I might share from the "ghost" of Southern Mountain.

I also remember how earlier on that day, Zhi Mei's gifts and talents began to shine outward. She sang as we ascended the heights. This continued throughout the afternoon and even into the evening. Over the hours, I heard a never ending stream of folk songs commemorating peasant life, fullness in simplicity, undoing the arrogance of the powerful, the feats of heroes, love, loss and remorse. I asked her how she could remember so many tunes. Surprisingly she answered she had nothing to remember. She voiced whatever was in her heart and tied it to the moment.

I stood amazed, my breath lost for an instant. She registered my surprise and laughed, "What?" I told her she made her songs sound like accidents. How is it a rube like me could see the great wit and discipline which gave them all such firm foundation? Her head tilted down, and her eyes lifted respectfully upward, "My father and brother were both poets of high caliber. That is the true tragedy of these ill and incoming winds. Their words regularly lifted the spirits, and brought awareness and new understanding to many of their close acquaintances, as well as to the community at large.

"Though I was not the second son he had once hoped for, father never showed regret nor held back back from my training and education. He and brother carefully nurtured and tutored me in the classics, being sure to involve me in their own work and creations. Members of the community enjoyed my songs too. As I grew in skill, they welcomed my humble and unworthy performances, never knowing what they heard were my own creations. Father and brother always stood to the rear, stone faced and unmoving, silent until we returned home. No sooner had we put fire in the hearth and warmed, when they turned to me and acknowledged my meager efforts. They said I had taken their humble seeds and delivered them fully grown into profound truths. Accessible to all who could truly fathom my message of compassion. They told me they were proud of me! Of course, they exaggerated! They knew how important they were to me, and would never risk hurting my feelings with their honest criticism. For me though, there could have been no greater gift."

I looked to her and said only, "What a wonderful father. What a wonderful brother."

I should have kept my mouth shut. Zhi Mei again fell prey to the sombre cloud of loss and tremored with pain, her body jerking violently as though to cry, but no tears issuing forth, the well having already drained dry its source.

Darkest of Nights

The stars embraced my melancholy. I separated, giving Zhi Mei her peace and privacy.

Before long however, her voice returned. A melody lifted like nightingale song, to warm the cold empty night.

darkest of nights
silence in the trees
troop of seven,
spirits ill at ease

young maiden in tow
thoughts flitter like angry bees
young men wish to plow and sow
over the poet maiden's pleas

what more can be done
what more can be lost
two lift the parcel soon to be undone
legs crossed, legs crossed, legs crossed

some come, some go
some go, more come

eyes closed, hope drains
calls for help, bang the drum, over the maiden's pains

a new one enters anon
whispered calls for help are set upon
all hopes soon fade, fate looks on
a maiden dreams of dreams now gone

a quick move, arrowheads flash
three fall, the headsman makes a dash
four down three come to surround
the mountain spirit slays them all, barely a sound

today the good spirit acknowledges
the once maiden's discipline and wit
mere echos from a happy past
but in this thought a truth will sit

in Southern Mountain spirits walk the night
befriend them when they cross your light
lest with wit, discipline, and heart's foundation true
they will make a ghost too of you.

As evening's silence dropped upon us, I went to warm by the fire. Zhi Mei passed a flask of herbal tea, signaling welcome to my approach.

Her eyes lifted, reflecting the fire's glow, "Tell me something about the ghost prince, Sying Hao."

"Ah, you enjoy ghost stories?"

Her smile eased my concern over having caused her pain.

"I must caution you, Sying Hao is a person, just like you, and me. Just highly refined, and very finely tuned. Like a vintage instrument. He may be a sage. I am too ignorant to judge, and will forego that reckoning to others. I acknowledge him as friend, brother, and teacher. Before benefiting from his careful mentoring, I had gone adrift. My every moment focused on caution and survival. Enemies were everywhere. Friends and relations had become suspect. At first, I aimed only to survive, and then to preserve our way of life. But then I felt my own self slipping away, sometimes I still do.

"Integrated into life's tapestry, harmonizing with all. Those attributes made us: my people, your people, special. The idea of integration and community defined our natures. Sadly, these elemental hopes and aspirations went to naught when I became more like an animal. A savage beast roving the wild, stalking every opportunity to redress our fate against those who would deprive."

"Is that so bad?" she asked.

"Who's to say what's bad. I only knew I had changed, and prowled about like a lunatic, driven by rage. 'Twas only I did that to myself. My people were kind and compassionate, and met strangers with songs and welcoming smiles. Then, in less than an eye's blink, marauding hordes engulfed our province, grinding that kindness and compassion into disdain and hatred. You see, to brigands and men who live by arms, kindness and compassion are weaknesses and flaws in one's essential nature. Their criers will lecture on how civilization benefits, grows, and prospers from their ambitions, and their relentless drive and determination to actualize their visions. All we have to do to participate is grow some backbone. Nurture and cultivate inborn desire, get ambitious, affiliate with influence and power. Then target the weak and vulnerable. The better we are are it, the better our prospects."

"And that's wrong?" she studied carefully for my response.

"Death, destruction, chaos, exploitation, savagery, molestation, dismemberment, disease, greed, selfishness, waste. Those are wrong. Great masters have taught us there is Buddha nature in everything. The reason they did is clear. We must respect, we must show compassion, and we must exercise restraint. In doing so, we affirm what we already know is there, and become the better for it!

"So, there I was, trapped in darkness and anger, seeing no future, and targeted for extinction. I had become part of their very game, my life purpose reduced to baiting them, and cutting them down. The very same things they did to everyone else. And those I cut down could have been my very kin, having no recourse but to survive by becoming what they at first despised most.

"By doing the War Star's dance, my Buddha nature was turning away as though to abandon me. I didn't know it on first meeting Sying Hao. Looking back I see more clearly. I already stood at Yama's doorstep, waiting for his beckoning to cross. Either someone would have finished me off, or I would have killed myself rather than continue the grim game. I would not willingly become them. Sying Hao threw a lifeline. He gave me protection, and sanctuary. There, under his watchful eye, I still search constantly."

"Search? For what?" she asked.

"For my humanity, perhaps. If I lose it, and others like me lose it, there is no hope for Ling Village, or for Mei Village, or for the province, or any province, or for the Empire. I might be wrong, but part of me feels the bastards are counting on it. Sying Hao is long awakened to these things. In that sense, just hearing what he had to say opened pathways to understanding I could no longer find within myself."

A Forged Petition

We had been talking about the Shu Roads. I related how Sying Hao often cited the Shu Roads in his never ending homage to Zhuge Liang. He argued Zhuge Liang alone understood their complexity, their thoroughfares and their many branches. He possessed uncanny mastery of the bewildering tapestry, seemingly from first encounter. This preserved vital escape passages west for Liu Bei's battle torn armies, worn and ragged from endless campaigns in the east. Perceiving them one step from extinction when expelled from Jing, Marshall Cao's staff had written them out of the grand battle plan.

Until the final engagement at Red Cliffs, Liu's forces had vanished without trace and were regarded to have abandoned their cause. Like everyone else, Cao Cao and his generals miscalculated the influence of Zhuge Liang. It wouldn't be his first orchestrated vanishing act. So too did they misjudge the tenacity of the three sworn brothers. It would take more than a generation to rectify that error. By then, Liu Bei and his forces would coalesce in the west and reform. A third kingdom then entered into the reckoning.

Here's what Liu Bei did. Relying on the guidance of trusted first counselor Zhuge Liang, Liu evacuated the core of his army, then granted release for conscripts to return to their homes in the central plains. He could not feed them, and he would not misuse them. To those in the east, the conscripts were deemed to have deserted Liu Bei's once formidable force. This further solidified impressions of his end.

Of course, the conscripts never returned to their homes. Like everyone else, they knew had they done so, their choices would have been to turn coat and join with the enemy, or face execution. Neither meant survival. Instead, they took to the outlands and wilderness, biding time until the will of heaven clarified options and prospects. This came when Liu Bei finally headed west. They followed his lead and rejoined. Only now as wilderness hardened trustees, no longer mere conscripts.

Liu Bei, once deemed impotent and out of the game, established the Western kingdom of Shu. An empire where before, there had been nothing. Sying Hao would shake his head laughing in consternation over this. He explained how Liu Bei was unassailable in the west and had only to mind his own business. Simply let human nature take its course elsewhere.

By that, he meant on his good days Liu Bei was a paragon of leadership and equity. Under the guiding hand and solid counsel of Zhuge Liang, it would have been nearly impossible for Liu, or anyone else for that matter, to fail. That is, if the object of one's desire were only to have a prosperous and secure kingdom, radiating fairness and equity to all. Liu Bei came very close.

A fairy tale of course. We mustn't forget. Paragons of virtue like Liu Bei still grapple with their faults, fetishes, irrepressible inclinations, and distractions. Liu had already sworn in blood to avenge the death of his distant Han nephew, the once imperial heir to the throne. In those days, blood oaths stood inviolate. Raised a commoner, Liu was said to be the final direct blood tie to the great imperial clan. While he had no practical attachment to its onetime splendor, he made it his life's purpose to restore Han from the residue of its ashes. Ashes now manifest in the form of warlords ravishing the land.

Oh, and of course he coveted the fertile valleys of the midlands. He also saw potential for new empire in the east, and for that matter, the south. And we can't overlook he fell hopelessly infatuated to the charms of Ladies Gan, Sun, and Wu. So you can see, perhaps understand. He, though a paragon of virtue among men, remained first and above all a man. And as would any man, he struggled with and sometimes failed in the exercise of restraint and simple common sense.

That's right, he couldn't leave well enough alone. Sying Hao would sometimes question, "Bao Ling, what's your take on this?" He wasn't so much hoping for my answer or my opinion. He was befuddled by the senselessness of it all and hoped my alternate perspective might somehow clarify. Over my silence, he would inevitably continue, "Zhuge Liang represented the crowning height of mankind's potential for perfection. He spoke with the stars, the winds, the earth and the waters. When angered, he could summon fire to vanquish enemies, when surrounded, he would hide in the very shadows of his foes, then emerge like the dragon he was. He well understood the impact his influence could have on the affairs of men. It had been for that very reason, he early on abandoned the worlds of ambitious lords.

"Instead, he chose to live with the eternal ones high in the cloud lined snow tipped mountains of the far southwest. A retreat deemed sacred and inviolate by those in the subcontinent as well as the nomads populating the breath stealing plateaus flanking their east[20]. For years, kings, princes, generals, warlords, even monks and eunuchs searched for him in the icy unknown. All returned unsuccessful. You see, Zhuge Liang knew their nonsense too well. He steered clear of them all."

But Liu Bei, here was a bird of different feather. We've already acknowledged how his singular character stood him to the forefront of his peers. It may have been that special distinction which wormed its way through Zhuge Liang's great walls of reticence and reserve. What specifically set Liu apart from the others? No one can say with certainty. Sying Hao wracked his brain over the very question. Magnetism perhaps? Eternal lodestones, indiscernible to the likes of us but irresistible each to the other?

We already know how things turned out. Just look around. One wonders, if one such as Zhuge Liang cannot

---

[20] In time that land would become Tibet, the gateway to the unknowable; but in those early days, it was still knowable, to those so inclined.

see a course through to its righteous end, then what hope is there for any of us? If not him, then who? We do know Zhuge Liang remained Liu's loyal minister until Liu passed, his affairs yet unsettled. Though royal ambitions remained unfulfilled, the wizard never assumed the mantle of imperial power.

But forgive me, I digress.

Sying Hao tells how when Liu first found Zhuge's high mountain retreat, he had accomplished more than all the others simply by getting there alive. Before him, no one had been so determined, so bold and willing to bear such prolonged exposure to the elements. Liu left his guard behind and went forward alone, in humility, to the humble snow blanketed hut. When questioned by the manservant, he answered he came to seek the counsel of Zhuge Liang. The manservant responded, "The master will be gone several days, you are welcome to make camp and await his return." Liu Bei did accordingly. The days passed and nature's frigid breath, driven by otherworldly winds soon put the troop below at considerable risk from extreme exposure. After fourteen days, with supplies running low, Liu Bei again went to the cabin to speak with the servant. He questioned whether there might be concern over his master. If so, Liu Bei volunteered his resources to probe the frozen wilderness to effect rescue. The servant only responded it would not be necessary, Zhuge Liang already knew someone was waiting.

So. There stood his answer.

Liu Bei instantly understood the intent behind the servant's words. He would have to leave, or die with his troop. He thought he might be losing his mind. He, a prince of considerable influence, competing for the fate and survival of an empire, reduced to begging services from a man he had never met. All based on the recommendations of wandering hermit Sima Hui and Xu Shu, a once trusted counselor who had turned to serve Cao Cao, the very Yang to Liu's Yin.

Liu Bei felt the loss of Xu Shu viscerally. As first counselor, Xu had proven a brilliant tactician serving Liu's early campaigns. While Xu loved and was loyal to Liu Bei, Cao Cao conjured a path to turn him.

Xu had an elderly mother, still within Cao's domain. Cao knew to leverage the obvious advantage. He would exploit filial piety to turn Xu Shu to his ends. Seeing the opportunity, Cao struck with determination, detaining Xu's elderly mother and simply holding her with no proclamation.

The mother, if she weren't a woman, would have been a regarded sage in her own right. She had a well earned reputation for seeing into history, its twists, turns and quirks. Truthfully, she would have been a fine strategist to any deserving lord. But again, she was a woman. So, short of marrying a lord or general, her voice could only be heard from the shadows.

She recognized Cao's game implicitly, and revolted against its purpose. She called him out on his deceit, embarrassing him in front of dignitaries. Cao almost killed her in retaliation, but was counseled otherwise. Her death by Cao's order would only make Xu more formidable in Liu Bei's service. Looking for other cracks in this impenetrable wall, Cao's spies soon learned to mimic the mother's calligraphy. They forged her petition that she was ill and wished last opportunity before certain demise to see her son.

A tale carefully spun and played. Seeing the communication, Xu knew full well its purpose. The mother would be delivered to the son once Xu swore allegiance to Cao. Xu knew, without his support, this captivity would be the end of his aged and frail mother. He presented his conundrum to Liu Bei, and with Liu's grace and blessing, received discharge from Liu's service to go to her side. Now if that doesn't say something about Liu, what does? Before leaving, Xu issued his last, but most noteworthy counsel. "Master Liu, you will certainly miss me but there remain others of perhaps superior merit. For the moment, your forces are strong and well positioned. Take quick opportunity to find someone to replace my counsel."

Filial Piety

Liu could only smile and shake his head at the suggestion. "When you leave my friend, it will be as if the chi had drained from my body, and flowed to my enemies. I know of no one who can replace you. I see no quick remedies to this dilemma."

Xu objected, "No, Lord Liu, solutions must be sought. In the remote west reside two other disciples of Sima Hui. Either can serve your purpose with integrity, skill and ingenuity. First is Zhuge Liang, the 'hidden dragon.' Nearly his equal is Pang Tong, the 'young phoenix.' Win the allegiance of one or both, and your future is secure."

Xu didn't know it, but Liu Bei had already conferred with wandering hermit Sima Hui. He beseeched Liu seek out and secure the services of both. Particularly Zhuge Liang, whom Sima Hui described as a colleague and fellow wanderer being without peer or equal in all the land.

It was true of course.

The honorable Xu Shu presented to Cao Cao, and Cao Cao in turn delivered the elderly mother into her son's safekeeping. Men of ambition do what they must to procure their goals. A deal is a deal, and a promise made must be kept. Of course, great sages also warn we should take care in what lengths we go to gain our objectives. In this instance, both men would have done well to ponder the warnings. Sometimes the end is not all we thought to have bargained for going in. Here, the sword surely cut in unanticipated ways. Certainly in the early instance, toward Xu Shu.

Surprised at encountering her son, the old woman questioned, "How can it be you are here my son, in the camp of Cao Cao?" He explained about having received her petition pleading he come to her aid. Shocked, she immediately berated her son. In stark disbelief, she pronounced his "brilliance and common sense blinded by the trickery of a fiend." Distraught, she questioned how he failed to distinguish truth from ruse? How could he forsake his destined role as counselor to Liu Bei, last hope of the Han? For once, Xu Shu had no answers. He did what he did for love and filial piety, that's all. In his ethic, this relegated all other concerns to being secondary. Had not the master Kongzi made the principle clear in his teachings? Though he suspected trickery going in, his mother's rage made it all too painfully obvious. He had been played hard by Cao Cao. He saw now the repercussions might reach far beyond his selfish concerns over filial piety.

First evidence of this was his mother. She, no longer wanting to fog his judgment, immediately committed suicide. It changed nothing of course. Xu Shu had already sworn fealty to secure her release from Cao Cao. She had been delivered as promised. As a man of honor, he was bound by the oath. As to the worth of his counsel to the new lord? Well, to set a trap, one must use the finest bait. Lord Cao got excellent counsel. Exploiting it he consolidated the north.

But according to Sying Hao, there came a day when Xu's freely tendered brilliance postured to float away like chi from a dying vessel. This happened when he affirmed the wisdom of Cao Cao's linking the vessels of his navy in preparation for the final siege at Red Cliffs. Lord Cao lavishly praised the subtle genius of that recommendation. Cao's gift for strategy and tactics could not be disputed. But even Cao the strategist could not unwind the complexity of the trap's full play from its set. History records how that carefully placed parcel of seeming brilliance balanced Xu Shu's ledger. For his sake, we hope he entered the next life freed from his mother's lingering ire.

A Practical Man

Having failed in efforts to meet Zhuge Liang, Liu Bei returned[21] to his eastern sanctuary. From there, he scoured the land for someone the caliber of Xu Shu. Of those he found, not one met the standard. The situation had become critical.

His acquaintances considered Liu a great and true leader. In the field he stood firm with the front. In retreat, he held the rear. What more could one ask? Perhaps he became this way ascending from a humble background. Early on, he fabricated sandals, fans, and other simple implements of convenience which he sold at market. Despite these modest beginnings, he was generally held to be distant blood uncle to the Emperor Xian. For what it's worth, I believe it true. Liu Bei said it. He bore the family name. The Emperor called him uncle. Liu, as a man of indisputable honor would not have wasted his life on something he did not believe. I don't think he would have made it all up. Do you?

As with everything political, Cao's historians disputed the point, floating counter threads wherever possible. "He

---

[21] This transpired before he first journeyed to Shu.

has never cast eyes upon the Imperial Seal" is what they said. That convinced some, but not me.

When first rebuffed by Zhuge Liang, Liu's accomplishments were already quite extraordinary. He had come from nowhere yet stood as a force to be reckoned by all who aspired to rule. From what we know of him, he wished the best for his people. Almost without exception, territory under his control developed and flourished. That is, until lost to others less scrupulous. As a leader, Liu never had the benefit of resources as did those in the north. Nor did he possess the blessings of a rich and abundant homeland as did those in the south. Often on the run, he and his followers were finely tempered by a diet of insects, thirst, and empty stomachs. Impelled to rot under remote suns, they repeatedly did the unexpected, turning emptiness and previously ignored scrub into fertile rice lands. Starting with nothing, they harnessed the flow of rivers, created infrastructure and engaged commerce. From there, they bridged mountain gateways and crossed deserts. Commendably, they preserved native cultures and forgotten wisdoms. What was there not to like?

He had a gift. But like all, he had a weakness. I call that weakness, "Not enough."

The hardest thing for many to achieve, is enough. When is enough, enough? Master Laozi understood this self struggle to its core, and spelled it out for all of time in his eighty one statements. He tells us the great leader simply lets go, and enters only when invited.

Being a simple man, Liu Bei lacked the sophistication of conceptual titans like Xu Shu, Zhuge Liang and Pang Tong. But neither could they become Liu. He had been cast by history and fate to be a great and munificent leader, capable of nurturing boundless empire. But only if wisely guided, and restrained by proper counsel.

As a practical man, Liu Bei understood this well enough. More than anyone, he saw and recognized his own flaws and weaknesses. He above all, knew he would topple without ballast always nearby. A trusted someone, whose strong hand could rein in his unbridled inclinations. I don't judge Liu Bei, or his failings. I decry their effect and the unintended consequences. As to his inclinations, he's no different than any man. Much of who we are is determined by what we have allowed ourselves to become. Strip the tattered robes from the mystic or the sage. Take him from his cave or retreat. Dress him like a prince. Surround him with generals and sycophants in some faux divine court. Witness what happens. Why in time, you or I might feel the same as they. As though the world needed our good insights and meddling hands in all of its affairs.

But the question of ballast, and Liu Bei's acknowledgment of the need. That may have been the lure which eventually hooked Zhuge Liang.

Few concede this, but it's fact! For sages, boredom weighs as the greatest affliction. I suspect Zhuge Liang had already achieved supreme self awareness. He may very well have surpassed the great sages of earlier times, perhaps even Laozi, in his comprehension and practical understanding of underlying reality. Unlike old Lao, Zhuge Liang was a dragon with real teeth. He would never be the one to give it up and say, "You guys have got it all wrong. Hey, here's an indecipherable road map. Study it for a few hundred years. Figure out what it means, and maybe you'll get it right. See ya later."

Zhi Mei proved quick. She immediately caught the irreverent reference to Laozi stealing his exit from the empire then started giggling. She remembered aloud how the sage had become unsettled by declines in morals and righteous order. Like Zhuge Liang, he decided to become a hermit. By then, he traveled unnoticed and unknown. The population, distracted by want, had long lost site of his brilliance. To many he may have passed as a simple beggar or herdsman. He prepared to take his leave through the western gate intending to disappear into the wilderness beyond. Luckily, he was recognized by the guard Yinxi. Only Yinxi remained to speak on behalf of those blinded-by-suffering multitudes left behind. He pleaded the sage not abandon them. Could he not leave some guidance and seeds of hope for the future?

Some like to think compassion compelled the sage to act. Recognizing the sterling character of the guard Yinxi, Laozi, as an enlightened man, knew compassion decreed action when the need spoke. Acting on Yinxi's plea, he paused and rested several days. He used the time to compile the Tao Te Ching, at first intending only to guide and center the young guard. However, seeing Yinxi's excitement on first viewing it, he reluctantly agreed to the young man's request he might share it with others. "Certainly, the sage said. Do with it what you will. You might say you wrote it yourself. I like the thought of it. Then again, you might decide to make more practical use of the pages." Master Lao then disappeared into legend.

Zhi Mei liked how my portrayal turned the legend on its side, while still holding to its essential elements. Master Lao's classic seemed to defy understanding, though the briefest glance at its surface left no doubt of the truth contained within. For a poet like her, my clever (her words) turnabout deserved to be acknowledged by a hearty laugh. So, we laughed aloud, then quieted. I could see her face outlined by the fire's glow, and delighted in her warm smile. She was beautiful.

Not surprisingly, these things encouraged I continue.

They Whisper My Name

You understand, for one like Zhuge Liang, meditating on a snowy hillside only goes so far. Enlightened or not, emptiness is emptiness. I may be mistaken, but my feeling is it's not all we hear it promised to be. I prefer to think Zhuge Liang, like Zhuangzi, would have delighted in the ordinary. Certainly more than he delighted in his self imposed exile. He would have fit well in Ling Village, or perhaps Mei Village where he might have reveled in its poetry and song.

Unfortunately, destiny compelled his feet to tread elsewhere. He wandered long and far, ending finally where he hid. Then one day Liu Bei rose like a lodestone tugging the wizard's insatiable curiosity back to the affairs of men. He at least had the good sense to ignore Liu's initial advances. I like that. It draws a clear line of expectations to be met and sifts out the insincere.

Liu Bei would not give up so easily. Knowing his predicament, the following summer he trekked again to the high country. He remained determined to find the elusive wizard. Zhuge, ever mindful of needy enlightenment seekers, playfully orchestrated a never ending shell game of concealment. Decoys, deceptions, moving invisibly from lair to lair, some days even he forgot where he was. Perhaps that explains his great surprise when waking one morning, he found Liu Bei prostrated outside his door.

That never happened before!

The early summer light backlit the mountain flowers, painting the fields blue and yellow. Its glow tinted Zhuge's face as the master scanned about. Only a handful of trusted companions accompanied the general. He saw no army evident in reserve. The attendants kept a respectful distance, camped separately and waiting quietly.

"What, no troops to back you?"

For the first time in his life, Liu Bei shuddered. The man before him spoke with the authority of the mountain. Even the ground registered the echo of his will. Liu Bei felt the wave roll beneath his own root. He had no doubts the man standing before him could be none other than the long sought Zhuge Liang.

"No master, I feared when last here, my troops may have corrupted your sanctuary. The less who know your whereabouts, the better."

"You can say that again. You should have told them to bury their shit in the snow!" the master replied, scrutinizing Liu Bei for any overt signs of fault or weakness.

Zhuge Liang you understand, could read people. He understood well the language of the body. It is also said he sensed the colors and the energies surrounding, knowing which identified high character, and which were cursed. For once, having been caught unawares, he needed a clear understanding of what had just transpired and its significance. What did it portend?

"You came to drag me down with you I suppose? Good luck with that!"

"No sir, I came to seek your counsel. Please, a few moments of your time. You can send me off if I trouble you, and I will honor your request."

Knowing most would never risk the high mountain hazards to find him, in this case done twice, Zhuge studied Liu Bei. For an instant, he saw only colors and energies reflecting opportunity. He wondered to himself, *"Opportunity for what?"* Even for masters like Zhuge Liang, life withheld some answers while tempting with mysteries and obscure riddles of its own.

They sat beneath the ascending sun, warming as the morning progressed. At mid-day, they walked about and gathered berries, and in the early afternoon, rested by the pebble creek. Marmots joined them, chirping their thanks as Zhuge rolled berries their way. Perhaps Zhuge told stories of encountering the celestials or their avatars as he trekked about the mountain passes or crossed glaciers into new worlds. During his early years, it is said Zhuge Liang had made the hazardous journey over the western ranges, venturing into lands far to the south. Reportedly, it was there he mastered his understanding of the stars, and their connections to the life centers of the body. This ultimately played part in his own passing, still many years in the future.

Others have held he communed among the avatars, particularly one Babaji, whose Yoga and lessons are said to have further opened Zhuge Liang's eyes to awareness and deep understanding. Apart from Zhuge Liang, no one could reliably say what form these myriad apparitions took. I like to think his time in the high country and then in the subcontinent more than offset the echoes of silence, stillness and deep reflection in nurturing his sagedom.

On this occasion however, guiding angels chirped in the guise of marmot choirs. A background chorus to Liu Bei as he detailed his history from peasant, to sandal maker, to warlord, then revolutionary ... finally, general and now exile.

By mid afternoon Zhuge raised his left hand, gesturing Liu Bei to end his recitation.

"I've got it," he explained, "Most of these things I had already heard on the wind, or in echoes from the camps of others seeking me out. Are you going to ask me if I can make you emperor? Might I help you restore the Han? Is that why you're here?"

"That was the case last time," Liu admitted. "Now I'm not certain of anything. Funny thing is, I miss making sandals and fabricating shades. I miss the streets, and engaging the heart of the community. My path has distanced me from my happiness. For what reason? A few drops of blood shared with an imperial line ingloriously hastening to its own deserved demise. Why do people whisper my name in hopes I will somehow rectify the past back to life? What will become of them all if I try? What will become of them all if I don't? What will become of me? Where is righteousness here? I am like a blind man! How did we all get into this mess? Why is it on my plate to chew?"

Zhuge looked to Liu Bei, acknowledging the ethic underlying his struggle for certainty. He responded, "You know, if you stubbed your toe when getting up this morning, all of those other concerns would instantly disappear." Liu Bei thought on it, then laughed at the suggestion. "Doubtless true. But in short order, likely still hopping around on one foot, I'd fall back to my customary ritual of worries, troubles and anxieties, adding lost balance and a throbbing toe to the list."

"You know, it's possible to carefully chart the stars, the elements, the energies, the winds and the unseen influences. One can map out potentials, likelihoods and outcomes. Nothing is certain of course, but lords and kings have coveted such portents from the dawn of time." Zhuge looked to Liu, raising his eyebrows to question whether that had been Liu's intent.

"No. I don't wish for a map of my destiny. What becomes of me will be of my own doing, and deserved. I'm not looking for an easy ride, or for heaven's will. Let the others have that. Just between you and me, their constant need to hitch their cart to something bigger is only fear. Portents will not serve them well if they don't first have the gumption to face the divine wind on their own."

Liu Bei finds wisdom

I Need a First Counselor

Zhuge nodded. "Then why are you here?"

"I need a first counselor. I've lost the brilliant Xu Shu to Cao's trickery. I fear no man or beast coming at my front, but without Xu's insights, I feel my back stands ever exposed. You see, I am well aware of my limitations, and am a practical but simple man by nature. On the battlefield I have few equals, and as a ruler, I am reserved, unselfish, and evenhanded. But in these times, it is not enough. I marvel at the complexity I sense in the minds of some others. Grasping it and understanding it eludes me. Because it is absent in myself and in my sworn brothers, we are now gone adrift."

Zhuge's look to Liu perhaps hinted at admiration. "This I can say with confidence. Mark my words. There is more to you than meets one's first glance. I would wager Cao Cao or Dong Zhuo or Sun Jian would simply have written you off, thinking you and your forces to be little more than a troubling gnat. Such ambitious and sometimes arrogant men would certainly undervalue your simplicity. Very much as you overvalue their complexity. You fail to grasp your true weight on the battlefield and in the play of things.

All this is well evidenced by the love and loyalty you have garnered from those who serve you. Likewise from those you have conquered and won over. Those are the very talents which in the past have turned the destiny of nations and peoples.

"I am mindful of events, and I am aware of your campaigns. You are typically outnumbered, out armed, out supplied, and often are without option but to take the field at forced disadvantage. Though you have experienced loss and tasted failure, you have in fact on occasion defied the odds, and succeeded where no one else could have. Not even those whose complexity you so admire. Your successes boggle the preconceptions of your counterparts. As you already know, Cao Cao is a brilliant strategist, and so too are the generals serving Sun in the south. To them, you represent uncertainty. They look at you and just can't get a handle on why you succeed when you do. You have repeated the impossible with paltry resources. They can't show ever having achieved that. They wonder what you might become if the issue of resources ever resolves.

"Cao Cao, perhaps to discount his mounting concern, convinced himself your successes were rooted in the inspiration and advice you received from counselor Xu Shu. To quell the concern, he hijacked your man. I tell you this for certain. Xu Shu will not forget his mother, nor will he abandon his love of Liu Bei. Cao Cao will taste regret for his trickery."

Liu Bei of course sat mesmerized. He asked Zhuge if he had ever encountered Cao Cao. The sage only grunted, then after some time added, "He is brilliant, and fearless.

Generals everywhere closely study his tactics and strategies and marvel at their scope, breadth, and cleverness. He composes music, writes poetry, and can at times be a brilliant ruler. He respects honor, and holds true to all his commitments, but only if he has voluntarily extended them. He looks upon his loyal staff to be the equivalent of extended family, excels at the martial arts, returns kindnesses, and is supremely confident in his abilities."

Liu sat long and speechless, finally uttering, "Then I am finished. He is clearly my superior."

Zhuge Liang laughed loudly, "Not so fast. He can be merciless and indiscriminately cruel. Worse of all, that ambition of his, like a leech forever sucking away at his spirit. The poor man can never be satisfied with anything. He forever looks to the horizon and wonders why the rainbow's tail isn't his. Can anyone tolerate such self centeredness? Are there no limits to selfishness and arrogance?"

Liu Bei pondered the words, "I too am cursed with the drive of ambition. Do you also mock me?"

Zhuge Liang stared back pensively, "You and Cao Cao are day and night. There is a distinction at the root. It is true, your ambition compares to his in scope. The distinction? It differs in its orientation. Cao Cao's ambition puts Cao Cao at the center. Liu Bei's ambition puts everything else at the center."

"I don't understand."

"Neither do I. That, Prince Liu is why things will inevitably be heating up between you and Cao Cao. There simply isn't enough room under the sun for both of you."

Zhuge Liang spent the balance of the afternoon explaining to Liu how the distinctions in character between Liu Bei and Cao Cao would lead them to endless conflict, sacrifice and waste. The southern kingdom will eventually get dragged into it, leaving no single empire strong enough in itself to unite the three. He spoke of likely intrigues and treachery as sides and alliances formed then dissolved and balances of power spiraled precariously askew into an uncertain future. He predicted the three princes Liu Bei, Cao Cao, and Sun Quan would spend their lives entangled in these machinations, whose final outcome was known only to the stars. Liu understood what he heard to mean the sage Zhuge Liang could not bear to reveal the endgame as mapped in the heavens. Perhaps he feared it would point to no end but chaos and suffering for all.

Their meeting concluded with Liu posing the question he came to ask. Would the land would be better off if he simply gave up the game? Zhuge only shook his head and said, "You are the conscience of destiny. Do you know of another who can fill your shoes?"

Liu thanked the master for his time. Zhuge Liang responded in like courtesy, then added he hoped Liu would not trouble him any further with the machinations of blind ambitious fools. For good measure, on their parting he took care to stipulate he did not count Liu among them.

Or Die Trying!

Liu departed the mountain a changed man. The master referred to him as the "conscience of destiny." The words reverberated as be began the long descent wondering what they meant in the play of three kingdoms soon to be at war.

Two things for certain. He could not go it alone. Not even the steady companionship of his sworn brothers, Guan Yu and Zhang Fei could make him whole. He knew without Zhuge Liang by his side, all would be lost. He wondered if the wizard also knew. He would have to find a way to make this work, but he had no clue.

The seasons changed and the following winter proved harsh. For Liu Bei, it was yet another run of trials. After his role in suppressing the eunuch inspired Yellow Turban revolt, Liu managed to carve a delicate balance between himself and Cao Cao in the north. Other warlords battled amongst themselves in the south.

Then, events accelerated. Cao managed to rescue the Emperor Xian from captivity. Advantaged for the moment with adolescent Emperor in hand and under his thumb, Cao anointed himself chief of state. He then launched a series of brilliant campaigns in the north ultimately aggregating his holdings into what becomes the northern empire, or Wei.

The family Sun did likewise in the south and east. Patriarch Sun Jian had the remarkable good fortune of stumbling upon the imperial seal. The Emperor's Seal carried great prestige. This legendary jade artifact had come to signify Heaven's Mandate in the imperial succession. It had gone inexplicably missing just as the Han declined. Were they connected? We're told the legitimacy of anyone claiming rule stood to be sanctioned by heaven, but only if they could prove possession of the seal. Turns out it had been in the possession of a one time court servant. Having somehow stolen it, then witnessing the terrible aftermath, the once loyal servant could no longer bear the weight of conscience and committed suicide. In the end, it lay simply sitting on the ground, framed in the ashes of a battle's aftermath.

Despite the boon, Sun Jian's streak of luck was short lived. He died unexpectedly by ambush. The seal passed to his eldest son, Sun Ce, who traded it to Yuan Shu. Yet another imperial pretender, Yuan Shu promised reinforcements in exchange for the seal. For Sun Ce, a good bargain. With additional troops numbering several thousand, he soon proved more than his father's equal. In a few short years, with a string of impressive military victories behind him, he seemed ordained and poised to found an empire in the south with himself as head.

Not to be! He too tangled with sour fate by executing the hostile Taoist priest magician Gan Ji[22]. Never did he anticipate just how far the wrath of a vengeful spirit might reach. Sorcery or not, with the unanticipated death of Sun Ce, leadership in the south passed to his younger brother Sun Quan. It didn't take long for the young man's brilliance and charisma to draw the attention, and concern of Cao Cao. Cao of course, missed nothing, and had by then gotten possession of the seal.

As these events unfurled, the machinations in the north continued. Everyone seemingly betrayed everyone else. Liu Bei looked only to somehow pull through, endlessly navigating, hoping to time and leverage advantage from the shifting currents. His fate bobbed like a cork on stormy seas. More than once, he tasted bitter betrayal first hand. To survive, he descended into obscurity, then somehow devised ways to rise renewed. The Emperor hostage is said to have issued an order in his own blood. He begged rescue from Cao Cao. Liu Bei, on seeing the order, committed to the cause. Regrettably, in its failure, he became forever the counterweight to Cao's unbridled drive for more power. He remained in that uncoveted role for the balance of his years.

The emboldened Cao Cao now directs his attention to what he sees to be his prime impediment. With massive onslaught, he puts Liu Bei and his forces on the run. They are saved only by hard retreat to Jing Province where Liu Biao grants entry in exchange for military support. Here Liu Bei finds sanctuary. Liu Biao, a powerful player, and a distant relative to Liu Bei, neither holds nor wants any

---

22 Referred to as "Yu Ji" in the *Romance of the Three Kingdoms*.

claims to empire. He remains neutral, and wishes only to preserve the sanctity of his beloved domain.

That didn't temper the ambitions of Cao Cao, nor the designs of Sun Jian. Both coveted the resources of Liu Biao's Jing province, a rice bowl large enough to sustain an emerging empire. As we've already seen, Sun Jian's ambitions ultimately cost him his life and before long Cao Cao moved on Jing from the north. Hoping to preclude disadvantage and to avenge their father, the sons of Sun Jian, Sun Ce and Sun Quan did likewise from the south.

The once ardently defended kingdom of Jing suddenly fell vulnerable with the illness and untimely passing of Liu Biao. Had he remained vital, he and Liu Bei, each formidable in his own right, might well have withstood the double onslaught. It proved most unfortunate when Liu Biao's instructions on passing were betrayed by his wife in favor of the weak second son. The new ruler lost Jing's south to the Suns. That left him no choice but to secure some residual position of influence through formal alliance with Cao in the north.

It became the fate of the once thriving and blessed Jing Province to be the never-ending battleground. Forces raked from north to south and back again over the decades and then generations following.

From his beleaguered post in Jing, Liu Bei witnessed the unfolding of his worse fears. The remarkable turn of events made real the impressions shared by Zhuge Liang when they last met. All now rang as prophecy. He knew then he would once again have to return to the mountain and somehow win the heart of the wizard.

Or die trying!

He Could Push No Further

The third time, Liu Bei ascended alone. His comrades remained below, groping for survival in the midst of forced evacuation from Jing province. They waited, stalling for time while backed against the western ranges with inadequate resources to cross the uncertain Shu. Complicated by the widow's deceit, and the back dealing second son, their self sacrifice and valiant efforts failed to ensure survival for Liu Biao's once prosperous and neutral realm. The lost cause fell hard upon them. Liu Bei entrusted the safety and oversight of the remaining cadre to Guan Yu and Zhang Fei. They were to hold and wait. Somehow, just manage to survive! He would return before spring, heaven willing. If not, they should conclude he had failed, then act upon their standing orders to disband. In that event, he would wait for his brothers in the hereafter.

Zhuge Liang had already made it explicitly clear. He wished to be left alone. Liu would not willingly violate that directive. He simply had no where else to turn. Only this single gambit remained to be played before all fell to naught.

Going it alone, Liu's ill-timed ascent into the highlands proved brutal. Once there, he found still nascent winter establishing its frigid rule with a steely cold hand. Not long into the upper reaches, Liu's valiant steed succumbed to the cold. Hoping to make the distant cliffs and perhaps find cave or cover, Liu continued on foot, pushing into the blinding wind. Icy crystals hammered into the frozen crevices of his exposed flesh. His breathing struggled against the thinning air. From past experience, he knew he had far yet to go. Though early in his quest, he already found his stride shortening and his strength seeping into the ground.

His will undaunted, the distant outcrops drew no closer. Time suspended, he had stopped counting the days. It served no purpose now. On this particular day, he pushed with all he had left to continue forward as fingers of darkness descended like ripples over the snowy slopes. *Death awaits,* he thought.

He called them his snow visions. Who can say what, or why they were. Hallucinations? Now rampant and unleashed, playing their incessant and pitiless game. In them, he held to the thinning hope answers to all his concerns would soon be revealed. He let drop his supplies, retaining only his weapons and some flint, dreaming to at least attempt a fire once harbored from the elements. He could retrieve the supplies when strength returned. They weren't going anywhere. Darkness fell.

By night's mid, he could push no further. He stood, silently watching snowflakes the size of imperial silvers flooding the airy dimensions around him. They waffled up and about, as though dancing weightlessly on tongues of wind. Though dark, whiteness lit scenes everywhere. He smiled, appreciating the simple beauty, all set perfectly in this remote font of solitude. This stirred yet another snow vision within. He imagined himself as a non-thought in the mind of an immense Buddha. Little more than a distracting indulgence rippling across the enlightened supra consciousness of infinity. Yet even as a mere and illusory distraction, he had the capacity to find delight in simple beauty and solitude.

Enlightenment?

For a moment he considered. One could find worse ways to leave this life.

Now, all he felt was exhaustion. In the snowy field to his front, two boulders stood out. Like expectant companions patiently waiting. Liu had only enough strength to crawl between them, digging a small space at their feet to drop beneath the bone chilling wind. He closed his eyes and marveled at the touch of flakes as they flooded over him. Some coated his hair, others dropped delicately into his opened, now gasping for air, mouth and melted upon his waiting tongue. In moments his body became tinted to the hues of frost.

He thought of fish he had seen in the marketplace, barely alive, gasping. He was comfortable, very cold, but comfortable. "Did the fish feel like this?" His thoughts jumped about like mad rabbits dodging the lynx. Images of home: the Yellow Turbans, his oath brothers Guan Yu and Zhang Fei, Lady Gan, his friends now gone — carnage, fellowship, betrayal, and undeserved loyalty. He could explain none of it, nor understand its purpose. It all seemed so silly from the perspective and simplicity of this overriding moment.

Liu closed his eyes and took a deep, prolonged breath. A laugh bubbled slowly from within, acknowledging his predicament. Fitting, he thought, and perhaps deserved. But so much left undone.

He was truly a selfless man, wanting to do what mattered most. End the chaos! As lights of his vision dimmed on the real world, he knew the end of chaos, at least for him, stood finally in sight.

The last thoughts he recalled were ...

> *In all things, one must have a clear mind*
> *The Way. Who can find it?*
> *Who can deliver it straight and well?*[23]

---

[23] Our homage to Master Gichen Funakoshi, founder of Shotokan.
To search for the old is to understand the new.
The old, the new
This is a matter of time.
In all things man must have a clear mind.
The Way:
Who will pass it on straight and well?
(Poem by Master Funakoshi)

Lingering in the Bardo

"You are no end of annoyance. Here we are at the end of the earth. Surrounded by clouds and blistering winds where no one, I repeat, no one looking to create empires would ever want to be. Not for a moment. In case you've forgotten. That's precisely the reason I'm here in the first place, and not there!

"And even if they did, why would anyone brave it alone. Entire battalions have perished on these slopes, and only because the wind shifted for little more time than it would have taken to pour a service of tea. The foolishness of it all. Idiots have taken charge. It's bad enough the once Han Empire collapsed beneath their hand. Now they do their stinky pinky dance of death, tromping on everyone and everything with no concern for the consequences. Does anyone truly care for 'them,' the innocents, the 'old hundred names[24],' or the 'Tao?'"

---

[24] Lao Bai Xing - "Old Hundred Names." An expression meaning the common people, whose surnames almost always could be found among the most commonly reoccurring names.

Liu's spirit body floated about the room. Uncertain at first, not remembering who he was, or his purpose. The words surrounding sounded to be garble. He heard them well enough, but his mind had cleared of the non-essential as he readied for the state of transition referred to as "Bardo" by past sages. He knew of these things of course. For a warrior like himself, death always lingered nearby. It only made sense to study up on it. What unfolded now matched well with what he had learned. Already he had forgotten himself, and for him, what had once been words now reduced to mere rudimentary sounds. No different than dogs barking, or birds chirping. He felt no pain, that too had lost it's edge and its purpose. Perhaps what the ancients said would prove true, only his karma would remain.

Of course Zhuge Liang also knew this stuff, and what was going on inside Liu. What didn't he know?

He also knew that his words, vexing as they might seem, were carefully chosen to bring the spirit of Liu Bei back to his now warming body. In effect, he had cast his spell, better yet, his lure. It remained for the warlord's spirit to turn back or to continue into full Bardo. Zhuge Liang could not control the outcome, only the setting, and the baited trap.

After some time, morning's light ascended in the east. Within the snow cabin, the fire glowed, pushing its reddish warmth toward all inside, while the world's chill reached in from the snowy wilderness.

Liu's eyes slowly opened. His spirit remained uncertain, not recognizing the ordinary, and tred lightly into this new unknown. Zhuge Liang walked from the fire, bent low to study his eyes, then slapped him hard across the face.

The several mountain people in the room winced at the severity of the strike, but trusted Zhuge Liang to always do what was right and necessary.

Liu Bei, still of uncertain spirit, sat up and looked about, studying everything in the surround. For a few moments, he felt like an infant, seeing everything for the first time. Zhuge Liang stepped intentionally into his field of view, turned to him and asked only, "Why?"

The word was like a push, knocking Liu Bei from his no longer icy cocoon, back into the world of awareness. The demand for "Why?" seemed to tug at his memories, just an instant ago gone, now re-emerging. When he hit reality's wall, his spirit finally turned fully away from the Bardo. Liu Bei, the warlord prince, had returned.

"You know, some would have your tongue for speaking to me like that?"

Not one to miss a jibe, Zhuge responded, "Perhaps, but you would still hear its scolding. Don't think you don't have it coming!"

Liu, again feeling the weight of his ordeal, dropped back onto his bed of furs, if only to let the fire's heat soak into his uncovered pores. "How did you find me?"

Zhuge answered, "In this unspoiled landscape, imbeciles and blemishes can be spotted from afar. Most of the time we ignore them. But you, how could such arrogance be ignored. Alone, here, to what self-driven end? Like a dog with three tails. Who could miss it?"

Liu thought, then slowly cracked a smile, "Would you accept that my hook landed a big fish?"

"Perhaps," Zhuge responded, "But you weren't thinking that wise ass stuff last night."

He went on. "I'm sure, like the many others, you succumbed to the fixation I am somehow the solution to all your problems, and decided to confront me alone. To prove your earnestness? Yes, you planned to beg me to return as your counselor. In your own fantasies you concluded everything now hinged on my willingness to serve your ambitions, your drives and your needs. How many times have I heard that? It gets boring you know!

"Have my tongue! Hardly! I speak what's on my mind. Those who wish to silence me are not for want of trying. I've been around a long time. I'm still here, they're not! You came alone to convince me of your earnestness and humility, but also to assure I would not be forced into servitude. Good boy! Of course, just another foolish stunt. I've seen them all! Shame on you! Could you not come up with something better? Doubtless, things didn't go as you planned, that happens a lot around here. There you were, iced to the bone, but not before you had ample time and opportunity to weigh the impact of your escapades on the lives and futures of others. Tell me, what did you gain?"

"Well, I suppose there was a lesson to be learned."

"And might it be a lesson you could share with others. Some who might be curious?" Zhuge asked intently.

"Well, just as I entered the peaceful state and the fullness of ending, everything I had ever done reduced to one thought, 'silly' … can you imagine that? Everything ever done at my instigation spun into a funnel, dropping out from its bottom, transformed to 'silly.'

"Silly shit. A clever use of imagery!"

"Then there was the mantra."

Zhuge Liang looked hard to him, "The mantra?"

"Yes, the final whisper, as all became still."

> *In all things, one must have a clear mind*
> *The Way. Who can find it?*
> *Who can deliver it straight and well?*

He Kowtowed Three Times

Zhuge Liang allowed Liu Bei to rest. It would be some time before his strength fully returned. With luck, in several days he'd be moving about. Liu Bei may have called it a mantra, but Zhuge Liang recognized it immediately to be a message directed to him through Liu Bei. By fate? Destiny? Who knows for sure? When he shared these things to me, Sying Hao reckoned it to be a riddle posed by Dharma — a call for involvement. I liked the thought of it.

The implications were clear. Only one could find it. Only one could deliver it straight and well. The sage wondered and feared the effort, however noble, or righteous, might prove just as misguided in its end. He knew the one who could, but he shuddered at the prospect.

And thus were they bonded!

Some time passed. As expected, Liu's strength did eventually return. He almost felt like his old self, though new questions lingered from his near death. Particularly as to what would be his role in life from this point. His thoughts soon turned to his sworn brothers Guan Yu and Zhang Fei, who remained behind, and in charge. Both were unmatched warriors. Marshall Guan, fearless and capable beyond measure. On more than one occasion, he had ridden alone through enemy gauntlets to behead generals. Feats which made him the icon of legends.

And Zhang Fei, when all appeared lost in Jing Province, Liu was forced to retreat with only a shell of his cadre. Zhang Fei and his meager band of twenty secured the retreat into the lower Shu. Zhang Fei burned the bridges at border's edge, then waited along the far shores, promising he would welcome any who wished to raft across and fight him to the death. He stood taunting for an entire day, and not one person of Cao Cao's legions crossed. The following day he rode his fearsome steed both ways along the river banks so all could see he yet stood to the ready against all comers. He promised to wait until spring for their courage to thaw and ripen. Not one crossed. Why tempt certain death? The time purchased by his valor secured Liu's rear and assured what remained of his forces would survive.

Liu Bei grew heartsick for his companions.

The day eventually came, as both knew it must. Liu looked to Zhuge Liang and said, "I'll return to my destiny, wherever it leads. Thank you for saving me. My brothers Guan and Zhang will soon have grief beyond their measure if I'm not there to complete them. Rest assured, I will trouble you no further."

He went to the door and looked about. Snow had drifted to the height of his body, and but for the air holes through the ceiling, there would have been no fire or life inside. He pushed outside where icy fingers, driven by winds accelerating downslope slapped him sideways. He knew the journey would be perilous.

Zhuge Liang and his mountain friends helped him prepare, cautioning on the need to take shelter quickly when winds changed, and to conserve food and resources until finally exiting the snow cover on the down side. It might take a week or more of determined trekking. They explained about cracks and crevasses, instructing he would be best served staying to the ridges, but while there, to always look for signs as to whether the ice and snow could be trusted. It was not unusual for entire hillsides to suddenly come loose and drop beneath the footing of the unsuspecting.

Liu Bei asked if he could "hire" some of the mountain people for the trip, promising Zhuge Liang they would be treated well, rewarded, and permitted to return when the seasons turned.

Zhuge only answered, "They want nothing to do with what is down there. They respect that you came here alone, and that you have chosen to return from where you came. They are not invested in your or anyone else's game. Please honor that."

Liu nodded, smiled, "Of course," then signaled his gratitude and respect to the highlanders still milling about the hearth. They acknowledged by walking a bowl of stew to Liu. The warlord joined them at the fire, ate, and drank, then laughed and sang with them, though he understood little of what they said. Before retiring, he prepared his gear for leaving at morning's first light.

There were no words of parting. On leaving, Liu Bei first kowtowed three times to Zhuge Liang, and then likewise to each of the mountain people. The mountain folk knew of Liu's stature among the lowlanders, and were greatly touched by his gesture.

The down trip turned bleak from the first. By the end of that same day, Liu experienced what mountain folk refer to as the wind from hell. On first feeling it, Liu thought it might rightly be called the wind to hell. As he took out his skin flask to drink, he forgot Zhuge Liang's adamant caution he always keep it secured to his person. Liu Bei stood stunned as the skin lifted and floated skyward to the east, disappearing somewhere in the crack between the horizon and the cloud cover beyond, upon which it seemed to skip. Pushing harder and forward, within minutes he found himself immersed in clouds, cocooned in white, now not able to see his feet. The blistering cold already began to cake his skin. "Time to secure shelter!" With his hands and the simple tools gifted by the mountain people, he dug furiously into a bank, remembering their instructions and Zhuge's admonitions regarding time being of the essence.

Though it started well, Liu, perhaps limited by the thin air, or perhaps not having truly regained his full strength, unexpectedly began to tire. The cold sapped his energy and in moments, he began panting, then losing his concentration and finding himself stopping to recover his senses when he should have been pushing harder. The troubles compounded when his frozen hands could no longer grip the tools. He helplessly stared as they dropped to the icy surface and slipped away on their own as though abandoning his plight. He realized his fate may have finally been sealed. Unexpectedly, another set of hands emerged from the gale, grabbing Liu and pushing him aside. The figure stepped to the front then dug furiously and, in less time than tea might have been brewed, a shelter was hollowed in the bank, with walls and seats for two to sit close by, sharing body heat while frozen hell danced outside.

The stranger, who wore slitted bone over his eyes, returned and dragged Liu into the cave, positioning him securely inside, then sat tight alongside.

He removed his hood and eye protection, then turned to Liu, "I've said it once, and I'll say it again. You are no end of annoyance!"

Liu looked to Zhuge Liang abjectly. What could he say that would have mattered?

Zhuge well knew the deep pain and solitude of Liu's somber state. He had been there many times himself. Though he sat quietly alongside Liu, he still felt the lure of stars and winds playing with the gravity of oceans. And in the distance, the tilt of eagle's wings and the barks of dogs mingled with the words of men. These things he truly missed but feared, lest he be drawn in, never again to escape. Silently Zhuge pondered the quirks of fate as he sat beside the now thawing Liu.

"It falls to me to escort you down," he said to Liu.

"No, please. Stay only a bit, until the weather breaks. I'll trouble you no further. Return to your celestial retreat!"

"I'm afraid that will not be possible. Expect no break in this weather. We'll starve if we wait. Welcome to winter's poisoned touch. It's only the beginning. What you see today, a light brush of it's hand at most. Once the great winds change, as it's now clear they have, the surface becomes playground to the dead. No mortals can survive the unfathomable cold. By spring, the snowfields will be spotted once again with the fallen trunks of those like yourself who saw fit to venture into uncertainty. As to the playful spirits in their celestial retreat, I will certainly miss their dancing and endless frolics."

Liu looked to Zhuge, puzzled, not knowing what to say.

"Rest and warm. We will have to travel together, summoning all our strength and perseverance. Should we split, or should tragedy strike, don't linger. Remember to head downward, always downward. In two, perhaps three days, we will pass below the bite of the great winds. It will still be hard, but the quieter air will renew us, and there we can take rest."

Liu looked again, "Then you can leave me and return."

But it was not to be. Zhuge Liang knew this trip led only one way, and there could be no return until this new season ran its full cycle. Regardless, it would not concern him. Now, it was out of his hands. He knew his compassion for Liu, and his encouragement of Liu's remarkable path of righteousness would chain him to the affairs of men for the balance of his days.

And so it was. Zhuge Liang remained with Liu Bei until Liu entered upon his own celestial journey. Brothers by then, they parted with Liu entrusting the western kingdom to Zhuge's stewardship, particularly as regards his son and successor Liu Shan, still only a boy. It is told Zhuge had Liu's instructions to remove the boy, if he proved to lack competence.

But Zhuge Liang, sage in the flesh, never wavered in loyalty to his friend, or to his friend's goals of restoring the empire. Their story yet remains. Hidden in the drift of stars and winds turned by the gravity of oceans, spun with the tilt of eagle's wings, and echoed in the barks of dogs sounding with the cries of soldiers. Dharma!

Zhuge Liang

The Light of Truth

Astonished, Zhi Mei could only ask, "How is it you know all this? I mean, it's like you were there, and you could see, feel and think what they said and did. Perhaps you were making it all up to amuse me. Or creating a portrayal of how you imagined things were? Much like I do with my songs and poems."

Then again she smiled, as though with realization. "You have another gift Bao Ling, perhaps greater than your archery. You sense the many threads which hold tight together the fabric of a great tale. My father would have told you it's a rare gift. A talent for deep insight into details which forever elude the attention of others."

I looked to her, at once flustered and humbled, and not knowing how to take her kind words. "It's Sying Hao. His knowledge and experience are vast. As I've already admitted, he's the best I know of with the bow. Still his mastery over the bow pales in comparison to his near total recall of history and events. It's as if he had lived them all.

"What I share with you comes mostly from his lips. The quality of the telling is his. Though I may take occasional liberties, I merely echo his words while dressing his impressions in their best light. During our travels through the hills, ofttimes in the late evenings, or warming over the campfire, he would simply start talking. Usually beginning with a question, or posing a mystery, then using that seed to spin a marvelous tale of life and its many reaches.

"In part, I suspect he did this for my benefit. As though reaching into a great personal well and pulling from it clean water, then offering it for me to see, taste and experience for myself. 'Clean water, dirty water, Bao Ling, if a man can see the two side by side, he will always find the clean. For some, it may take longer, but they will eventually. My little stories preserve the threads and fragments of truth, so well hidden within this dark age. I can only whisper while historians at court and elsewhere fabricate gilded tapestries spun from the wants and wishes of those they serve. I may be a recluse, but I am not a poor man. I place my stock in truth, and my belief it will shed light wherever it leads. In time, these token tales and fragments may well become your maps as they have been for me. Hopefully they will one day loose and guide your thoughts away from uncertainty and chaos, and head you toward life and freedom.'

"I can only repeat what he shared. But, I must tell you, when Sying Hao speaks of these things, the trees and the earth listen. As you said, it's as though he were there, privy to everything, and you are there with him. You feel you know what they were wearing, where they stood, what they thought and did … even what they ate, their personal habits, their strengths, their frailties. Sometimes it's overwhelming.

"He made clear it wasn't Liu Bei who set the wheel of turmoil into motion. The Han had their day, and it was over. The remnants of their reign were corrupted, unreliable, weak, filled with plotting and overreaching. It was the will of heaven they should fall to ruin. But the chaos and suffering, and the decimation, carnage and butchery, how did that come to be? Well, on that particular point, Sying Hao argued Liu Bei and Zhuge Liang were of common mind and will. They abhorred chaos and its consequences, and felt their partnership alone and above all others, preserved hope for return to natural order and eventual stability."

"But wasn't all of that long, long ago? Does it matter to us?"

"Yes, one or two hundred years, even longer I suppose. And yet today the same wheel still continues to turn."

"What happened next, when the two finally returned to Liu's camp?" she asked.

"Well, as mentioned earlier, Liu had barely managed to escape from Jing with his loyal cadre. While he sought out Zhuge Liang, those behind found temporary respite, and paused to regroup keeping the mountains to their rear. Cao's pursuing forces stalled, having to deal with renewed attacks from the south where the Suns gave his legions no respite or quarter.

"Keen to the opportunity, Guan Yu and Zhang Fei only then decided to attempt what no strategist in his right mind would have recommended. Their orders aside, they knew remaining where they were through spring would mean their end. The land had been picked clean. Worse, Cao was already deploying additional forces from the north anticipating to quickly finish them off, then reinforcing the southern front against the Suns.

"The forbidding Shu Roads were now their only remaining option. Push west and risk death, or stay put and die for certain. When death stands certain, the impossible will beckon convincingly. They chose the impossible. They would cross unguided through the Shu, knowing others their equal but not their better had failed miserably in the past. It speaks to the combined wills of Guan Yu and Zhang Fei. If alive today, either of them would tell you, neither could have done it without the urging of the other. Together, they urged, pushed, cajoled, tugged, kicked, and carried their troops to ultimate refuge in the sanctuary of those hills.

"With instincts which defied belief and all history of past failures, Guan Yu and Zhang Fei found passages, roads, and cuts, where others saw none. They had accomplished what all before them could not, carving their own independent path through the Shu. Cao's troops, who attempted to follow and harass their rear, ended up hopelessly lost. The journey worked its own magic on the no longer despairing cadre. The hardships, insurmountable as they had been to others before, only served to forge their now renewed determination. Though in the end much fewer in number, they were fierce, battle hardened, tested, and determined. No enemy stood eager to follow or track them, knowing the risks they had endured and survived.

Three Brothers Become Four

"The only alternative for those hell bent on grinding Liu's forces to dust? Send an army to the far north. Bypass the mountains. Overwhelm the flank and the rear. Marshall Cao considered this tactic, but deemed it unwise and fraught with risk. There were other enemies up there. Barbarous outlying tribes best left undisturbed and ignored, at least for the moment. Why add to one's headaches? Besides, avoiding the treacherous highlands by circling north would only leave his rear precariously exposed to threats from the south. The Sun clan and their emboldened forces were not running from anyone. You can see how quickly complications mount in these matters. With lines so extended, the intended prey can turn table on the now weary and over stretched pursuer.

"Cao came to recognize one indisputable reality. Under the capable leadership and example of Guan Yu and Zhang Fe, Liu's meager forces remained secure. Safe in their isolation. For once, good fortune showered upon these worn and all but defeated warriors. They longed for sanctuary, and had now found it. They took full advantage of their remote station to rest and recover. Then they re-armed, retrained, and re-energized their ragged force. That was the status when Liu returned with Zhuge Liang in spring.

"Only after descending the western range did Liu Bei learn what had transpired. At first furious the two trustees had disobeyed his direct orders, he could not resist marveling at the achievement. Without saying as much, he wished he had been part of it. His own feat had been no less in their eyes.

"Strangely, the troops seemed to enjoy what had become of their predicament. It seemed they had emerged into a new world, one full of possibility. In the late evenings, campsites lit with bonfires while they idled in warm fraternity under diamond skies. They had never known stars to shine so brightly. It lifted their spirits. Sometimes small bands of comrades wandered off into the mysterious darkness where they marveled at how the heavenly lights gave bluish tint to their bemused countenances. Some had never felt so much at home.

"Liu could only smile when he heard the camp chatter among them, their morale now firm, boasting on the deeds of Guan Yu and Zhang Fei. Each seemed to have his own personal take on their gallantry. Typically it recalled having reached the moment of abject despair. Strength gone, dropping exhausted alongside the trail, expecting only to be abandoned. Then plucked up and carried on the back of one of the two mighty generals. All agreed. Renewed by such splendid example, their combined will to continue returned.

"When Liu showed up with Zhuge Liang, Guan Yu and Zhang Fei were at first jealous and guarded. Long content with three, they were not bargaining for or anticipating a fourth brother. Zhuge Liang knew he would have to earn their trust. Time permitting, he would do just that. But first came security of the rear. He bombarded the two with questions concerning their passage through the maze of mountain passes. Then he carefully sifted their recollections and perused their records to discern how they had managed to accomplish what so many had failed to do in the past.

"Guan Yu and Zhang Fei weren't accustomed to such close questioning. Might we say interrogation? Privately, they brought their bruised feelings to Liu. There's no telling where it might have led. But finally Zhuge Liang petitioned for a meeting with the three where he hoped to offer some thoughts and suggestions. In Liu's presence, he thanked both Guan Yu and Zhang Fei for their carefully executed notes and battle drawings. And for their keen memories and willingness to work through his incessant questions regarding what lesser men would have deemed the most picayune details.

"Wisely, he added he had never seen such close attention paid to field study and mapping by two generals in the midst of a flight for survival. Looking to Liu, and he meant this in all sincerity, he said no other generals could have accomplished this successful retreat. Not in the face of overwhelming forces snapping ferociously at their rears. The accomplishment stood epic and singular. All the more notable considering the constant and ever changing maze of trails and roads to the front. He could not fathom waking each day to face an arena of supreme confusion. Surely, they were his betters.

"For once, albeit briefly, Guan Yu and Zhang Fei stood speechless. They had come to demand Zhuge Liang's ouster. Now their tongues sat frozen. Then Zhuge, realizing the strategic potential, invited them to join his planned expedition. He would undertake a close inspection and exploration of the Shu Roads in their entirety. He argued to Liu Bei the value in mastering their seemingly infinite complexities, particularly the innumerable and fickle off shoots and cross paths. The two noble warriors balked at first. Glad to have survived their first crossing, they had no inclination to unnecessarily court misfortune a second time. Guan barked, 'Fate doesn't tolerate fools. Nor does it allow second chances to those lacking the sense to stay put once out!'

"Zhuge Liang teased their reticence. Perhaps not yet knowing how close to death that may have put him. But these warrior souls were not ever going to be humbled by the sarcastic gibes of a scholar. Particularly one seemingly intent on meeting his own end in the high passes. Guan spoke for both, adding he didn't feel much could be gained beyond what they already knew. But in warfare, nothing should ever be left to chance. Zhang Fei grunted his agreement, carefully adding, 'And perhaps the wilds will tell us more as to just how far we can rely on this man's counsel, and fortitude.'

"Forgoing the draw on resources of a full fledged expedition, Liu wisely agreed, but only if they went as a threesome. Two of the three questioned whether they would ever return. The third braced with delight, eager for yet another great mystery calling to be unraveled.

"The two war brothers were soon enough amazed at Zhuge's stamina and determination. Liu had seen it first hand and knew. He gave no hint to his brothers, preferring to avail them the opportunity to discover for themselves. In time, between themselves, Guan Yu and Zhang Fei grudgingly voiced respect and admiration. Not only for Zhuge's surprising endurance, but also his fearlessness in confronting unanticipated challenges.

"Zhang Fei proudly boasted to Liu of one particular incident. They had been surprised and nearly over run by marauders as they camped near a mountain gateway. As you know, narrow gateway passages can be controlled by gallant warriors with proven mettle and courage. But only if they are in place and properly armed. That was not the case here. The three had been sound asleep in their camp. Zhuge Liang was first to his feet, running hard to the front, reaching for whatever weapon stood near. In the darkness, he inadvertently seized Guan's dragon-sting sword. Which, Zhang Fei quickly added, had never been unsheathed by anyone but Guan Yu. Long ago, forged from the densest metal excised from a meteor's heart. The weapon, until then, had only been wielded effectively by the mighty Guan. No one but mighty Guan could have swung it without collapsing beneath its weight.

"Zhang Fei then quipped how Zhuge stood shirtless and nearly naked, absent all protective armor. Shielded only by undergarments, he single handedly held a marauding force of nearly two companies at bay. This heroism purchased time for Guan and Zhang to don their gear. Soon enough, they advanced in counter to decimate the horde. Zhang Fei joked how but for the fact Zhuge Liang did not have Guan's magnificent red beard, the attackers might well have mistaken the wizard for the warrior. Guan later made sure to add he would never have engaged an enemy wearing only night garments. But apart from that reservation, also set his seal on Zhuge Liang's proven valor.

"They would witness it many times again, while the three lived."

Here, Beneath Our Feet

"After the skirmish, they returned to their camp. Guan Yu and Zhang Fei glowed with new found respect and admiration for Zhuge. Playfully poking him with elbows, they admonished, 'Next time, be sure to wake your brothers before dashing to death. No telling what we would have found had the racket not stirred us. Not even a shout to your fellows? Shame on you! We might have missed the fun. What fool runs alone to his end?

"Zhuge smiled knowingly and said, 'Certainly, not this fool. Besides, who knows what added mischief you two might have evoked if I hadn't gotten there first to temper your otherwise noble intentions.'

"Hearing Zhuge use their gibing 'fool' in referring to himself, the two warriors immediately clarified. They were speaking rhetorically and in friendship, not in disrespect.

"The wizard only smiled and nodded. His two lions had been tamed. For once, the three shared a cup of Guan's secret power wine. A recipe said to consist partly of fungi, fermented in rice wine along with other rumored unmentionables. 'Gan Bei' echoed loudly in the hills that evening. The moon seemed to dance overhead to the choir of three voiced in harmony as one.

"They returned to the hills many times the next year, always probing deeper. Eventually winding north, then south, methodically detailing each finding and discovery. Per Zhuge Liang's recommendation, Liu Bei mounted a broad campaign to organize a functioning state in the west. To all appearances, he made quick progress. So reported his spies to an increasingly alarmed Lord Cao.

"The three companions ended their mission only after a puzzling turn involving Zhuge Liang. The end of the eleventh month approached. He had for reasons unclear selected a perch on highest ground. Mind you, not until after trying and rejecting many other like perches. He then entered a deep meditation, facing to the east.

"Zhang Fei recalled how he and Guan bided time practicing martial arts and strategies in clearings nearby. For three days, they paid the motionless Zhuge no mind. Interrupting would be impolite. But then, there arose a sense of gnarly concern. Guan had already begun to joke, but now with some hint of forboding. Zhuge looked to have expired. Zhang Fei scowled, clearly not appreciating the inference. Then he laughed and playfully posited. How would they ever explain the loss of yet another counselor to Lord Liu? Finally, nearing the end of day three and to their great relief, Zhuge Liang twitched. That caught their undivided attention. A bug perhaps? Nothing followed as the sun traced across the heavens. Their hopes began to fade until late in the day. To the great surprise and delight of both, Zhuge Liang unexpectedly rose to his feet. He walked nonchalantly to his two friends and announced, 'I have considered all possibilities. We are secure.'

"Not knowing what had transpired, the two titans stared blankly at one other until Guan turned to Zhuge Liang and asked, 'OOooooKaaayyyye, that means we're done?'

"'Yes, with some final touches and proper placements, no one will ever get to us through the Shu Roads.'

"He then told how even in his meditations, he had eavesdropped on their martial play. He noted his profound admiration as witness to their remarkable display. He asked if Guan would be so kind as to instruct on the masterly use of the dragon-sting Blade. Careful to avoid offense, he also begged Zhang Fei's tips on working the staff.

"Not wanting to displease their newly ordained brother, both eagerly assented.

"Dinner that evening turned to be more eventful than usual. A famished Zhuge Liang couldn't seem to get his full. Guan and Zhang, each boasting of the great skills he alone could impart to their friend, soon were quarreling over whose input promised to be more relevant. In short order, they were arguing. Their tempers seemed to flare. Both butted chests, then thrashed at one another, inevitably finding themselves entangled and falling to the ground. There, neither would let the other up. They began wrestling, morphing from arm locks to choke holds until finally rolling wildly about and ending in the campfire. That of course cooled their tempers, if not their bodies. The evening's stew pot turned to its side where scavengers quickly made off with the balance of their intended feast. 'No matter,' said the wizard. 'Guan, you have any more of that power wine?'

"In due time, the three returned to Liu Bei. In council, Zhuge shared his intricately devised system of controls and check points. These he supplemented with stunningly engineered fortifications augmented by strategies of harassment directed to the east. All made possible by their hard gained knowledge of the mountain pathways.

"Zhang Fei pointed out. 'Even the mountain people acknowledged what we already knew for ourselves — the wizard had somehow unraveled their endless riddles. Their carefully gleaned secrets for safe passage had been harnessed.'

"To which Zhuge Liang added, 'We will make them our allies. We will protect and nurture their culture and their ways. This in exchange for their commitment to secure our backs. There will be no secrets between us as regards the Shu Roads. We will make them privy to all we have learned, as it secures us and them from the eastern hordes. That will be their incentive and reward. Freedom and independence in exchange for vigilance.'

"Liu Bei took all this in without a word.

"Zhuge assured their current forces were more than adequate to secure the mountain gateways. His strategy of sealing tightly proved to be as effective as promised. In the years following, all enemies who targeted Liu Bei through the Shu Roads were mercilessly decimated by the marauding Guan Yu and Zhang Fei. The two lords of war considered each campaign a joyful lark in the high country. An opportunity to spend time with their many new friends among the mountain tribes. All of whom they came to love and trust.

"Zhuge Liang vouched to Liu his freshly minted maze in the hills assured the realm's survival. They would have the needed time and opportunity for his newly rooted but fledgling kingdom to grow into maturity."

Zhi Mei interrupted, "Then they prospered?"

"Yes, they prospered. Bolstered by the wisdom of Zhuge Liang, and the fearless prowess of Guan Yu and Zhang Fei, supplemented by the ageless fury of Zhao Yun and the remaining tigers, Liu Bei proved a better ruler than any had imagined. His domain flourished. Safe and secure, with prosperity accruing to all. It is said the lowliest peasants were free of want.

"The remote west, where the eastern lords had driven Liu Bei to presumed extinction now grew independently wealthy and powerful. Borders expanded, waterways were harnessed. The once impossible southern ranges proved to be a springboard for commerce to the far south and west. Deserts were crossed regularly by traders and explorers under Liu's watchful eye and encouragement. In less time than a generation grew to new maturity, the Western Empire of Shu solidified to nearly rival the Han at their peak."

Zhi Mei brightened, "Then it went well for them, their sacrifices were rewarded. Are they still out there, where is the great Kingdom of Shu? We can go there ..."

Bao Ling's disappointed look to Zhi Mei brought a quick stop to her musings.

"It is here, beneath our feet."

Epilogue - The Itch

Zhi Mei nodded silently, her silence a testament to what had been lost.

Bao Ling continued, "You know. There's an itch plaguing humankind. Robed in subtlety, it hides from our view. So faint, one barely notices. Standing amongst other things, you would never know it was there. For example, if we were hungry or thirsty, our minds would be centered on finding food or drink. The itch would step discretely to the background and bide patiently. Same if we were chasing after a goal, or rushing, or otherwise distracted or engaged.

"But, a mind at rest becomes Yama's play field. Just waiting for the fire star[25] to sow its seeds. The mantra of long united — must divide, long divided — must unite begins to beat its time and cadence. Rousing that gnawing itch. Awakening its propensity for overreach and misadventure. Once aroused, nothing less will quell its hunger.

---

[25] "Huo Xing" - The planet Mars. Also referred to as the War Star.

"The Shu kingdom grew in stature. So too did the armies of King Liu. Talented warriors came from all regions to see if this reported paradise on earth were true. Young hearts pined for discovery, opportunity and adventure. Liu, along with his counselors and war tested brethren, diligently scoured for new talent.

"Meanwhile, in the east, Cao Cao consolidated his many victories into the formidable Wei Empire. In countering ballast, the southern lords Sun became the Wu. Absent daunting topographical barriers between them, Wei and Wu had only each other to gawk at and to covet. Their pointless excursions to finish or contain Liu Bei proved costly and disastrous. Each felt better served directing its ire and ambitions toward the other.

"But that damned itch. Liu, having achieved more than any might once have predicted, or had reason to expect, still had not restored the Han. He could not relieve his mind of one troubling fact: Cao Cao occupied the traditional capitol, and through the hostage Emperor Xian, controlled the gateway to heaven's validation. Further, he noted Sun Quan's growing wealth and prestige in the south. A land seemingly blessed with infinite resources. If that weren't enough, Liu still aspired to return to Jing province. He intended to bring into his fold what had once been Liu Biao's. Sun Quan felt the same. He often mused how the price of Jing had already been met with the deaths of his father and brother. He had every intent to collect on the blood investment.

"Those undercurrents aside, in the moment, it was Cao Cao and Sun Quan who stared across the thin separating buffer. Like two game cocks eager for sport to begin, each coveted what the other held. Neither would become the other's vassal. A formula for war if ever one existed. For Liu, the option to opt out remained viable. Except for that dastardly itch.

"Its whispers manifested first in the form of seemingly casual concerns voiced to Zhuge Liang. 'What if Sun Quan defeats Cao? The combined war machines and resources would dwarf those of our west. Are we well served biding our time? Worse yet, what if Cao took the south, or suppose they allied?'

"You get the idea. Liu Bei was beginning to lose sleep. Compounding this was the influx of brides, concubines, and weddings of convenience. These lined like acupuncture needles on the King's every limb. Each triggering its own meridian and rolling Liu's Kan and Li to their inevitable boiling point. He was a grand king, loved, highly regarded, and invincible — so long as he exercised restraint. Was it expecting too much? Eunuchs inevitably found welcome in his court. Zhuge Liang counseled and then warned. Talented though they might seem, loyalties among eunuchs inevitably played to favor themselves and not their lords or their people. 'Remember what happened to Han,' he reminded.

"And of course, Liu craved the beauties. Supreme above all, the lady Sun. Only daughter of Sun Jian and sister to Sun Quan. If men's dreams and visions could be seen walking about they would take the form of Lady Sun. It was said Cao Cao had once made her acquaintance, and afterward had never again been able to love another woman.

Now if that's not a recipe for chaos, what is? Old Yama can be a clever fellow."

Zhi Mei noted, "So, as you lay these pieces on our board of study, much appears open to risk and uncertainty. I have heard some of these tales. But not with the same detail and background which you've been able to share. I am worried for Liu Bei, and sad for Zhuge Liang. The brothers Guan, and Zhang, and Marshall Zhao Yun too, they were made for chaos, and to serve a righteous lord. But Liu, I can see his struggle. Like the crane, he has snatched victory from the jaws of defeat. But it isn't enough. Actually it is. But he doesn't have the capacity to know or appreciate the relevance of his position. Nor to hear the concern of his counselor Zhuge Liang. For me, or the poet in me, Zhuge deserves better. Does he ever return to his mountain retreat?"

"No, tragically not. He hitched his destiny to another's dreams, but had no way to rein them in."

Zhi Mei looked to Bao Ling, "Why couldn't they simply be happy?"

Now it was her turn to regret her words. Looking to Bao Ling she saw he too could not be happy. The itch, it was there too, within him. The same as with Liu Bei, and just as beyond his ability to control. She wondered if he had made the connection for himself. She saw how it would eventually drive him away and far to the east where he would strive, perhaps in vain, to re-kindle the ghostly ashes of his past.

Bao Ling sat silently, looked to Zhi Mei, then said "I don't know. I can only speak for myself and not for them. Happiness seems so far behind me. Sometimes it's hard for me to remember what it's supposed to be. Or if it ever really existed. I cling to the thought of it because something inside tells me its part of who I am. Or who I'm supposed to be. But then again, even that falls into question.

"I believe Liu sensed he was a pawn of destiny, and came to see his time in the west as fate's reward for his having fulfilled the first part of destiny's bargain. But I don't think for a moment he considered his work finished. His time in the west promised recovery, and eventually manpower, wealth, and resources with which to continue his quest. Ultimately, that's what he did. Like all men, he had his weaknesses. But his keen eye remained true to his first goal, and to the oath he swore to his brothers in the Peach Garden[26].
  I do not fault him.

---

[26] The Peach Garden Oath - Three young men meet in fate, and find themselves of common heart. They agree to bind their destinies to hopes for a just and prosperous land. Liu Bei, Guan Yu and Zhang Fei swear to be as brothers in united purpose. Avenge the Han, restore the nation, bring peace, exercise compassion to the helpless and needy. Liu Bei as eldest, becomes leader. Guan Yu his second. Though not born on the same day, by their oath they commit themselves unto death, memorialized in their expressed hope to die on the same day, in the same month and year. They call upon the immortals to seal their pact, and to strike dead whosoever fails its purpose or betrays their sworn fraternity. The actual oath can be found in Chapter One of *Romance of the Three Kingdoms* by the 14th century playwright

"For me, I would have exercised restraint. And cared better for those whose lives wound round and within the Western Empire. Those who might be impacted by my folly. To his credit, when his adventures recommenced, he did not rape and impoverish the west. Though ultimately, they did suffer immensely from the chaos and conflict his choices rendered, including the regrettable fall of Shu. As to Zhuge Liang, yes, he deserved better than to be mired in the affairs of mortals. But chaos is what chaos does.

"It's true, don't you think? Just as we — sages, and saints too, have no choice but to dance once the tune commences."

Their stories yet remain. Hidden in the drift of stars and winds turned by the gravity of oceans, spun with the tilt of eagle's wings, and echoed in the barks of dogs sounding with the cries of soldiers. To this very moment, promising to seed our futures with sacrifice — and with that, unwavering hope for the better!

To be continued …

Luo Guanzhong.

Acknowledgments

Creating a work such as this can be a daunting task. First, the work itself, the endless array of details, the countless re-writes, the editing, the touch ups and fine tuning. Then the layout, now necessitated twice, once for hard copy, once for E-Book. While these processes roll along, life beckons, and insists on our attention. Crises arise, illnesses come and go, surgeries, pandemics, plagues, political upheavals, pipes leak, pets get sick and so on to no seeming end. Should I also add the constant stream of pointless texts invading my phone, the advertisements flooding my postal box, the tidal waves of memes shooting across my brow.

No different than you, I too get sucked into distractions. Luckily, I have one effective counter, without which nothing would ever arrive at the point of final fruition … having a dedicated editor.

That role has again been voluntarily and unsparingly filled by my friend and fellow explorer of life's mysteries, Bryan Smith. Bryan is a retired professor of mathematics and computer science (Professor Emeritus, University of Puget Sound), who on learning I was a writer, offered his expert services to edit and opine on anything I planned to publish. Mind you, life's distractions challenge him no less than you or I, so the generosity of his offer speaks clearly to the kindness evident in all Bryan's life undertakings.

Way back when he first offered, I hesitated. I had been down the path before, and often as not, it proved to be an exercise in diversion, if not outright distraction.

But I must say, from the very first, Professor Bryan attacked (I mean that in a positive sense) whatever I tendered with a ruthless, yet fair-minded passion targeting excellence, clarity, polish, and pertinence. In this particular instance, I freely admit for all who will hear. The work has been bettered because of him. Dare I say, even better than had I gone it alone. Thank you Bryan. You have made a profound contribution. To spare you any taint of guilt, I must acknowledge the mistakes and oversights are all mine. Except the misspellings, those we'll have to share.

Renee Knarreborg once again conjured the artwork you find within. The quality and unique originality speaks for itself. Behind the scenes, I've come to suspect Renee may well be a mind reader. When not tending to regional power and utility issues, or running audits, she somehow finds the time to take in my story lines and convoluted character sketches to come up with the final images which grace these pages. As I witness her images and scenes emerging from the void, I almost feel she has stolen into my subconscious and made real what I could only imagine. As you see, she keeps it simple, often pencil or ink on paper, running through many iterations and exchanges until the images and depictions align, adding an intuitive third dimension to the unfolding tales.

Finally, I am also indebted to the many masters and teachers who have befriended me over the years and who took great care sharing their sagely insights and remarkable skills with this stumbling pilgrim. Most have already passed on, so their work falls to me. To spare any sense of embarrassment, guilt or regret to those remaining, I apologize in advance. None of this is your fault or doing.

About the Author

Billy Ironcrane is the writing and music performing pseudonym for Bill Mc Cabe, a lifelong explorer of life's experiences and unending surprises. Raised in inner city Philadelphia during the 1950's and 60's, he partook in the revolutionary currents of change, protest, activism, and idealism which characterized the era. While a teen, he spent summers on the Jersey coast hawking newspapers, tossing burgers and exploring places like Atlantic City where he encountered flea circuses, Gene Krupa hanging between sets at the Steel Pier, petrified mermaids and the fabulously wealthy promenading the boardwalk at night flashing mink stoles, diamonds, tuxes and studded canes. Atlantic City dubbed itself, "The World's Playground." All the stuff of dreams as he returned to some flop house where he slept for ten bucks a week, sharing occasional space with Polish immigrants working the summer trade, and the ever present army of cats.

He departed the inner city still in his teens, and pushed blindly into the unknown never to return, sensing to be static and do nothing would be terminal, as in fact it proved to be for many of his mates. In the decades following, he pursued new awarenesses, swam exotic currents, wandered remote tropical forests, became a soldier, ambled southwest deserts at night, slept through thunderstorms alongside petrified forests, trekked the Rockies, mastered the martial arts, jogged with blacktail deer in hills surrounding Monterey, explored Zen, motorcycled the California coast, scaled Pfeiffer Rock, freelanced, traversed the Cascades, slept beneath ancient redwoods in remote Los Padres, raised a family, bridged the corporate jungle, then hung a shingle and lived on wits and ingenuity until the muse of the 60's again tapped his shoulder, ordering, "Time to shift gears, Billy."

Other works in the same genre by Billy Ironcrane

Returning to Center
(A Collection of Stories, Vignettes and Thoughts)

Seed of Dragons
(Surviving an Empire Undone)

Characters and Incidentals

Bao Ling - "The Dragon of the Midlands." Protagonist around whom many of our stories revolve. Master archer, outlaw, peasant, farmer, healer, wanderer, revolutionary, and in the end, a father. In some ways, he is everyman … trying to make sense of the unknowable and the uncertain, while preserving his connection to the simple life of his forbears, and to the ways of the land he loves.

Cao Cao - (155 - 15 March 220 CE). King of and then posthumously declared Emperor of Wei. Ambitious and talented general who sought to harness the Will of Heaven and establish a new empire, intending to succeed the failed Han. A talented leader, warrior, strategist, and scholar, as well as a renowned poet. Remarkably loyal to his friends and allies, he was equally regarded as ruthless, cruel and merciless in securing his objectives. History tells us he succeeded to a considerable degree, and his empire is remembered as the "Cao Wei" not to be confused with lesser successors, also named Wei. It lasted less than half a century, a mere blip in the roll of dynasties. His doings unfolded long before the events of our stories, but were factors nonetheless. What remained after his demise rapidly descended into chaos. Suffering beset the land for generations. The "Wei"

alluded to in these accounts are a mere shadow of the
original "Cao Wei." No more than a specter of what once
was, but still vying for control of the land, scrounging every
which where to replenish resources depleted by successive
generations of war machines foolishly unleashed. Therein
lies the significance and relevance of once forgotten places
like Ling village, and the Shu mountain passes.

Cao Ling - Bao Ling's ancestral tie to the legendary hero
Zhao Yun.

Colonel Sun (Sun Wu Kong) - Honored officer and
counselor in the service of Liu Bei. Close comrade to Zhuge
Liang, and colleague to Guan Yu. Mentor and fatherly
influence to Sying Hao. Possibly an immortal, possibly a
descendant of a different species. Forever shrouded in
mystery due in no small part to his guarded and reticent
demeanor, barely offsetting his forboding and ever solemn
presence. His life and deeds linger as monuments preserved
in legend and enshrined as myth. Directly, or indirectly, his
influence and spirit can be felt throughout our tales, and
ripple through the ages. Over the course of many accounts
and recollections, we will speak of him at considerable
length.

Dragon Bow - The incomparable bow of Sun Wu Kong.
Recognized by those who knew of it to represent perfection
of the bowyer's craft. Believed by witnesses of its power to
be divine in origin. While simple in appearance, close
inspection showed it to be complex in every detail, designed
so its very core resonated with and drew strength from the
character of its holder. One unworthy could scarcely draw
the cord, let alone use it. Supreme in its authority, it came to

be known in legend as the "Hundred Li Bow." In the hands of one with righteous character, and the requisite degree of skill, there seemed no end to its tactical reach. Through Sying Hao, it found its way into the hands of Bao Ling, who, like Colonel Sun and Sying Hao, casually referred to it as "One-Li." Perhaps they preferred not to draw undue attention to its limitless potential.

Fa Miu - "Old Fox." He is a character appearing in several of our tales. A practical, gifted, and worldly wise gentleman, he often appears at first to be slave to whatever system or scheme he serves, yet somehow always manages to function independently with his hands subtly on the helm. Truth be told, his true nature is excellence, and his aim inevitably directed toward the common good. We first meet him in *Seed of Dragons*, where he is a shadow principal shaping events, a true and fearless though unsung hero. Here, we find him at the other end of life, as the elder of two toll collectors encountered by Bao Ling on entering Fortune's Gateway. At first glance, a fox faced, world-wise and very clever old man, seemingly relegated to obscurity, bemoaning his fate, but adept at working within its limitations. He makes a quick and lasting impression on the young archer. Likewise, toll collector Fa Miu takes special interest in Bao Ling and his lady companion Zhi Mei.

Fortune's Gateway - A major trade center on the western end of the Shu mountain ranges, backed by the great western wilderness, an endless expanse, and what remained of the defunct Silk Road which had long before proven so beneficial to the Han Dynasty. Despite the collapse of Han, and afterward, the collapse of the Shu Han (the western empire headed by Liu Bei), Fortune's Gateway proved very much to be deserving of its name. There, one found a lineage of traders who prospered by treating all parties as equals, so long as they had something to transact, and needed something in return. Foremost among those parties were the Shu people of the mountains, long oppressed, and forever contending with invaders from the east. Being practical, many in Fortune's Gateway recognized the continuing benefit of their association with the Shu. So long as the mountain tribes fended off those in the east, Fortune's Gateway remained for all practical purposes, autonomous. They had flourished under Liu Bei, and at the time of our first story, still remained insulated from upheavals in the east, thanks to the resistance of the Shu mountain tribes.

Guan Yu - (160-220 CE). Also referred to as Guan Gong (Lord Guan), or simply Guan. Sworn brother to Liu Bei and Zhang Fei (bound three as one by their Peach Garden Oath). Virtually peerless among human warriors. Revered as a staunch patron of righteousness. Protector of the oppressed, guardian of the weak and vulnerable. In the lineage of our accounts, he becomes companion and peer to Sun Wu Kong (Colonel Sun). He is the only human ever considered by Sun Wu Kong to be his martial equal. In his prime, with no more than his Green Dragon Blade in hand, Guan Yu could by himself, stand down an entire enemy army.

He Ling - Paternal Grandfather to Bao Ling. Of considerable influence in shaping his character and developing his unique talents. Though little is said of him here, in time he will be shown connected to a history of mysterious influences which only become apparent to Bao Ling as his own journey into uncertainty and challenge begins.

Iron Hand Gao - Friend of He Ling. Martial and life tutor to the child Bao Ling. He is mentioned only in a passing reference. Though their time together had been short due to harsh necessity, the impact of his character on Bao Ling had been profound. Once one knew a man like Iron Hand Gao, he would fear no other.

Jin Dynasty - (265-420 CE). War of the Eight Princes. The period leading up to and enveloping our stories.

Knights of Wei - The supreme warriors of the Wei Empire. Bred by hard trial and constant challenge, then endowed with the full support of the state and transformed by the highest and most sophisticated metaphysical arts and sciences into the most formidable killing machines ever devised. Their feats and accomplishments became legendary and were heralded throughout the land. They were even likewise grudgingly recognized by their enemies. The imperial court took great care to orchestrate a formal code of chivalry and morality surrounding these killing machines, citing them as the high standard to which all good citizens should aspire. Their enemies of course, knew far better. The Knights of Wei were no less than the unleashed hounds of Yama, as capable of unforgivable atrocities as any man turned demon. The five in our story are the pick of the crop, the most feared in the land.

Liang San - Town head (mayor) of Fortune's Gateway when Li Fung issues his challenge to the Knights of Wei. A rarity for the time, selected by the people he governed, and not appointed by the royal court or regional authority. His constant love, hate relationship with Fa Miu, his right hand man is evident throughout our account. He holds loyalty to only three things. Fortune's Gateway, himself, and, depending on his mood, Fa Miu.

Li Fung - "Master Li" of the Mountain People. Village elder. Martial master. He figures prominently in the personal development of Shi-Hui Ke, both as child, and as man. The first story speaks much of him, and for now, we'll say no more.

Liu Bei - (unknown 161 – 10 June 223 CE). The incomparable man of righteousness. A common man, though distant relation to the Han emperor. A sandal maker who rose to prominence as a formidable military commander — driven by his unsparing dedication to restoration of the Han Dynasty. Retreating to save what remained of his forces, he founded the Shu Han empire in the remote west, and prospered beyond all expectations — his achievements the stuff of dreams and legends. Until his demise, he remained a key principal during the period of the Three Kingdoms. He felt the Shu tribes to be a most noble and honorable people, believing that so long as they remained viable, there would be no direct path for Cao Cao and Wei to attack from the east. To that end, he ensured the Shu remained independent, and always, a respected ally. He nurtured, encouraged, and taught them how to fend for themselves.

Long Hsieh - Wei minister who agrees to the challenge tendered by Li Fung, setting up the match between Li Fung, and the feared Knights of Wei. As representative of the empire, he had been sent to secure the loyalty of Fortune's Gateway to the imperial eastern court, and thus sever the western logistical lines supporting the resistance of the Shu tribes. The story unfolds as he seeks to weave his spell with promises of unprecedented riches to the gathered townsfolk.

Shi-Hui Ke - One of the Shu Mountain people. Abbot of Crystal Springs temple, a mysterious preserve and one of several fortresses meticulously conceived by Zhuge Liang to secure the Shu Roads from invasion. Created to protect, as per Liu Bei's directive, the culture and heritage of the mountain people. Although a monk and man of peace, Shi-Hui Ke remains an ardent patriot, and has found purpose in his role as defender of his people and their ways. In his youth, he had attained renown as a singularly gifted martial artist, particularly in archery, before losing his left arm midway from the shoulder resulting from unlucky encounter with a sadistic band of Wei mercenaries. They cut off his left thumb, assuring he could wield no bow. Gangrene set in and the arm could not be saved. In some ways, the unfortunate loss of his arm proved a blessing … in time, the once consummate archer, now monk, found within his higher states of awareness, the secret of the "thought arrow." Bao Ling had already seen Abbot Hui's remarkable skill, projecting nothing but concentrated thought to strike and deter a stalking tiger. The full account is presented elsewhere. He also appears to have gained privy to the alchemy of longevity, or so concludes Bao Ling, but that is a different story.

Shu-Ting tribe - The displaced mountain people residing in the environs surrounding Crystal Springs. A collection of Shu tribespersons, looking to reform and restore their culture. This branch of the Shu had a long history of dealings with those in Fortune's Gateway, and over time, the two groups became respectfully interdependent.

Sun Ce - (175-200 AD). Eldest son of Sun Jian and older brother to Sun Quan. A naturally talented leader, brilliant tactician and gifted martial artist. Assumed oversight of his father's warlord domain while still in his teens, and quickly established himself as a leader around whose charisma and penchant for success, others of great talent could willingly attach. He won loyalties readily with his demeanor, his fairness, and his inclination to encourage others to rise to wherever their gifts and skills might carry them. Before his untimely end, he had carved a significant warlord state in southeastern China, which ultimately became the state of Wu. He had one son … still a child at the time of his death. Rather than complicating the fate of his infant son, he passed control of the state to his talented and capable younger brother Sun Quan, in whom his trust proved well placed.

Sun Jian - Warlord and progenitor of what would become the powerful state of Wu. Father to Sun Ce and Sun Quan.

Sun Quan - (182-252 AD). Ruled as King of Wu 222-229 AD, then as Emperor Da of Wu 229-252 AD, a combined total of 30 years; initially a great leader, warrior and patriot, intent on the survival of his nation against the overwhelmingly powerful forces of Wei under the leadership of Cao Cao. Enters into controversial alliance with Liu Bei which ultimately proves decisive in the momentous Battle of Red Cliffs. Subsequently, their on again, off again alliances over the course of years darken their relationship and set the stage for seemingly endless challenges crossing their life paths. In his later years, much of what defined his youthful greatness becomes lost and swirled in the constant distractions of power, insecurity, confusion and ultimately mistrust.

Sying Hao - Mentor to Bao Ling. A onetime war orphan who became apprentice and adopted son to Sun Wu Kong. Friend of the Southlanders, archer supreme, master of the transformations, able to project consciousness, and to move about without detection, scholar of the classics, a bow craftsman of singular caliber. Sometimes called "Fenghua Yan" (weathered rock), or "The Man from Southern Mountain."

The Five Tiger Generals - The five generals who served Liu Bei with uncompromising loyalty throughout his reign. Many times, their valor and exemplary leadership proved decisive against what others deemed insurmountable odds. By Lord Liu's designation they were:

Guan Yu, General of the Front;
Zhang Fei, General of the Right;
Huang Zhong, General of the Rear;
Ma Chao, General of the Left; and
Zhao Yun, General of the Center.

History honors them as "The Five Tiger Generals."

Yama - "King Yama." A devil of sorts, or perhaps what we might think of as the incarnation of death. Presides over hell and is accountable for the life, death and transmigration of human souls. Keeps true the final ledger and ensures his fearsome legions bring the newly departed to their end judgment. Relishes chaos and induces strife. Truly enjoys his job, particularly the part where he gets to torment those deserving. Once, when confronted by the Creator for his evil doings, he defended himself most eloquently, arguing to the Creator, "Hey … isn't this my job? Did you make me for any other purpose? Can you think of anyone who can do it better than me? Forgive me sire, but I fail to see where there is a problem." His logic and integrity, thus convinced the Creator. He justly earned his release and was freed to go about his business unimpeded.

Zhang Fei - (unknown - died 221 CE). Sworn brother to Guan Yu and Liu Bei. Also a singular warrior, one whom Guan Yu deemed his peer and often boasted of. Known for his uncontrollable temper, it proved to be his ultimate undoing, said to have been assassinated by his own men, but not until fulfilling a life of epic feats and undeniable heroism.

Zhao Yun - One of the illustrious five generals serving Liu Bei throughout his lifetime, and beyond. Zhao Yun passed in 229 CE. His day of birth is unknown but most believe him 60 years old at the time of his death. He dedicated his entire life and lived above all things to serve the cause of Liu Bei and the Shu Han.

Many remembrances of his deeds echo Romance of the Three Kingdoms in honoring his supreme martial skill, unbounded courage, penetrating intellect, as well as the loyalty and admiration of those who served with and under him. To the present, his high principles and righteous character remain common knowledge throughout the land, modeling a standard revered by all.

Even today, in Henan Province he may sometimes appear as entrance deity, along with his comrade Ma Chao, together protecting Taoist temples from the influence of evil spirits.

Zhi Mei - A farm girl whose family (father and brother) were killed by Wei marauders. She had been kidnapped and abused until stumbled upon and rescued by Bao Ling, then of necessity became his traveling companion to Crystal Springs. She comes from a family of skilled poets, and though a common farm girl, has consummate skill in rhyme and song. In time, her words become the voice of the resistance, and her accounts and stories record the noble deeds of its heroes, particularly, the Dragon of the Midlands.

Zhuge Liang (181 - 234 CE) - Sometimes referred to as "Kongming" the Sleeping Dragon, attesting to the extent of his essential nature, once unleashed. A wizard, scholar, musician and hero whose influence and guiding hand threads either directly or indirectly throughout our accounts, and perhaps beyond that. Despite those of record, in our recitations, the dates of his life are indeterminate. He has achieved longevity; though, not having fully mastered its alchemy, he is not a true immortal. As a Merlin like sage who has perfected awareness, he stands singular, and among humans and other creatures, is spoken of in the same breath and with the same reverence as only the likes of Jiang Ziya and Sun Wu Kong.